THE THREAT OF MADNESS

THE LOST PROPHECY

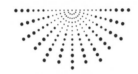

D.K. HOLMBERG

ASH PUBLISHING

MAP

PROLOGUE

The tavern room was getting dark, the pale light of the waning dusk tossing shadows onto everything it touched, and the moist air of the evening was warm and heavy with the whispers of a coming rain. Through the shadows of the room, a small fire could be seen against a far wall, its flickering flames adding to the shadows. The flames twisted and leaped, the shadows cast seeming to take on life and move slowly around the room before circling back and beginning anew.

Brohmin watched the shadowy movements from his table in the corner, his face the blank expression of a man grown hard from long travels and many journeys. His eyes jumped and darted with the jerky movements of the burning fire, his senses heightened for movement within the smoke and darkness, and his body tensed for it. Nothing ever came.

At another table not far from Brohmin sat four men drinking mugs of ale, each man deep into their glass by this time with the loosened tongues the drink gave. He sat and listened. Men like this knew rumors, and those were what Brohmin needed.

The first hour of watching the men carry on had been amusing to him, but as the men had steadily grown more raucous, he had turned away and begun watching the flames. The earlier stories the men had shared among themselves were what he had focused on, his amusement feigned to more easily watch and listen to what was said.

One of the waitresses approached his table. "Do you need anything?" Brown eyes bunched up along her tall forehead begged him to say no while the crossed arms under her breasts almost dared him to ask her for anything.

"Only more water," he said.

"Water, not ale?"

He shook his head and she scowled at him as he turned back to the moving flames. Brohmin scanned the room as he listened.

Two men with sword belts looped about their waists ate quickly and without talk. The quality of their steel and the shine to their boots screamed to his eyes of an organized army, and he suspected that they were among the troops sent north out of the city to maintain peace on the Old Rehne Road. Stories told that the sheer number of people moving south on the road was causing local problems, and he wondered how many armored men had moved north already and how many more would have to go.

At another table sat an older couple and their young children, a boy and girl, huddled over a meal that he guessed was given to them through the kindness of the owner. They didn't look as if they could buy Bastiinian sand let alone the large dinner that was placed before them. He suspected that the owner, a stout man with a large gut and a face now permanently reddened by excessive drinking, had given away many such meals in acts of kindness. With the increased number of southward travelers, such generosity could not last much longer or the owner would soon be facing empty pockets as well.

As he turned to observe the rest of the common room, most had the dirty look of travel and sadness in their faces. He had seen that face on many of the people he had passed on the road, sadness and the look of dejection at leaving one's lifelong home. Each person's eyes also carried the look of fear; the near mad fear that one feels when fighting and facing an invisible and unknown foe. None knew what they faced. Brohmin considered that a blessing. Few knew they were lucky they still lived.

After the waitress returned with his water, she stopped at one of the lanterns hanging on the wall to the left of his table, her arms reached up stretching for the almost-out-of-reach wick, and Brohmin looked down at the floor as she strained. He could see the muscular definition in her calves beneath her long skirt as she raised herself up onto her toes, and his eyes caught on the dark outline of something around her inner ankles.

As she lowered herself back to her heels, her skirt covered what he might have seen.

He quickly sat upright, pushing his chair away from the table, the shape marked on her flesh now burned into his mind.

His eyes darted up to her face as she turned around, catching her glare, and he flicked his eyes back down to her feet before looking into her eyes again.

She froze, realization sweeping across her face before she gathered her composure and hurried off, looking back long enough for him to catch the frantic gleam to her brown eyes.

As he tried to rise and chase her, the air seemed heavier around him.

He struggled against the sudden weight to the air, before closing his eyes and felt a familiar tug at his mind before the weight lifted from him.

Brohmin turned in the direction that she had gone, but saw nothing.

Had he any doubt, what happened after he'd seen the marking verified his suspicions.

He sat again. The waitress wasn't going anywhere for now, and he still needed to listen for more gossip before deciding what he would do. The front door swung open and then shut quickly. Several more men streamed in, grabbing tables and hollering for ale. Town locals by the look of them.

A second waitress, younger and rounder than the first, came out to whistles and shouts from the men. Her hips swayed as she walked as she approached the men carry mugs of ale.

Brohmin shook his head as he turned away, his gaze again falling on the soldiers while he thought of the other waitress and what he

needed to do. He should leave her, but if what he saw had been real...
Brohmin knew he couldn't.

Shouting caught his attention and he turned.

"I don't know why anyone would be heading north these days!"

Brohmin's ears perked up, and he turned his head slightly to the
side to hear better but not be seen listening.

"Why's that, Ricken?" he heard another man ask in response.

"From what I's seen," the man Ricken began, his speech heavily
slurred and his mug waving about in front of him as he spoke in a
slow drawn out tone, "men be coming down from the hills without
their families. Sons disappearin', daughters the same way, and wives
either missin' or so scared they already left their men and are waitin'
for 'em in the south. Something's going on up there, and I wouldn't
want to have to go up and find out firsthand, if you know what
I mean."

One of the smaller men, his face drawn thin and tight with age and
hunger, nodded. "If we don't know what is going on, and we don't
know how to stop it, what's to keep it from coming further south?"

"We send Davin and his brother to block the road!" someone
shouted, arm outstretched and finger pointing to a huge man across
from him who engulfed the stool he sat on.

The tables erupted in laughter, a couple of men clapping hands to
the back of the man who pointed at Davin, but the thin man who had
spoken earlier shook his head quickly, and his eyes could be seen
jumping from man to man.

"I'm serious. What happens if whatever it is moves south? I don't
want to move my family because some northerners can't control a
pack of wolves or whatever." The thin man's eyes glanced over at
Ricken.

"I never heard it was wolves or nothin'," came the voice of one of
the men at the end of the table, his head balding and the long nose
jutting out from his face demanding attention. "I heard it was a village
of cannibals who live high up in the mountains and can't catch food
no more."

Brohmin's mouth turned in a wry smile when he heard the explanation, a new one to his ears.

"Then we just send them Davin, and he'll feed them for a year! Either way, we're set!" the joker piped in, the table filling once again with the sound of most men's laughter, Davin's own face grinning broadly.

"You know what I hear?" Ricken began somberly. "I hear that it is some strange creature from the unknown lands to the east, flying overhead and snatching up people for food." He nodded his head grimly as he spoke.

"I heard that the rocks came alive and started moving, mad at all the people climbing all over them," came another.

"I thought they said it was the gods throwing angry fire from the sky!" another said.

"No, no, no," started still another voice. "It was the gods coming from their homes in the earth, angry that the miners had awakened them and were stealing their wealth, so they rose up and attacked them."

Brohmin sat and listened as the differing explanations came in a constant stream, oftentimes the same man having several different explanations for what was going on, and smiled as the rumors became more bizarre. He had heard most of them before today, travelers along the road were more than willing to share their gossip and their fears, but some were new. He suspected that the new ones were not so much rumors that were filtering south as they were stories that some of the men had come up with on their own.

Finally, the tirade of stories tapered off, the laughter from some of the more exotic stories dying with it, and the group sat quietly for a moment before one of the men who had not offered a story spoke up quietly.

"I heard none of those stories, 'cept the talk of the children missing and the wives leavin' scared," he began, his speech slow with a strange accent to it that was every so often accentuated by the drink. "I hear that when it comes, you can't see a thing. It just comes. And sometimes, you can see shadows if the light is just right, shadows that make you feel sick as it moves around you as if it was dancin' on you. Sometimes, you can feel something there, but you can't see nothin.'" He looked around at the other men who were silent now, no trace of the smiles and laughter that had been there before. Drinks were forgotten for the time being.

"One thing that I heard most often from people," he continued, his eyes darkly intense, a sad look on his worn and wrinkled face, "was about this smell. Some say the stench alone has killed men. Others say it makes you so sick that you can't see anything, and you pass out. That's when you disappear. Still, others told me they always smelled the odor after someone had disappeared. Like nothing in the world, they say about it." He took a drink as he finished, his eyes watering over slightly as if he remembered something horrible, and no one spoke.

Brohmin looked at the man, seeing his short, graying hair disheveled about his head, a brown cloak thrown carelessly over shoulders that slumped with the weight of pain and sadness. He had the look of dirt to him, the kind of dirtiness that only the road can do to a man. He'd said too much that was accurate not to have experienced it.

The men fell silent for a moment, the road-wearied man turning to his drink.

"I'll tell you what else is strange, besides them goings on in the north, is the king's new advisor. Rainstaff... Reillem... Raime... or whatever his name is," Ricken said.

Brohmin tensed at the comment. It couldn't be coincidence, could it?

Not coincidence, not when it came to that man.

He cast another glance at the men before rising and hurrying up the stairs that led to his room on the second floor. As he topped the staircase and turned the corner to go down the hallway, his focus was drawn to a slight movement along the wall further down the long hall.

He moved quickly, not quite a run, but never taking his eyes off the spot where he thought he had seen the movement.

As he neared the location, he concentrated on the differences in darkness between the doors along the hall and the rest of the wall. Finally, he saw what he knew he would.

Instead of the shadow deepening where the door recessed from the wall, he saw something that almost looked right, but he knew was not. He reached his arm into the doorway and grabbed.

Suddenly standing before him was the waitress from earlier in the night, still wearing the brown skirt and the dirty shirt that she had been wearing last he saw her. He dragged her down to the end of the hall to his room's doorway and quickly pulled a key from his pocket, shoving it into the keyhole and hearing an audible click as the lock tumbled out of place. He opened the door and roughly shoved her inside.

He closed the door and locked it again. He could see her eyes widen in fear as he put the key back into his pocket. "You are," he started before catching himself, "excuse me, *were* a Mage." He said the statement simply, no sign of fear at having mishandled one of the Magi were he correct, and saw the fear in her eyes change to surprise.

"How did you... how could you know?" she asked as she sank onto the bed at the far side of the room.

"You don't carry yourself like a waitress," he replied as he crossed the small room to where she now sat. "And there were other things," he muttered as he grabbed one of the already lit candles in the room and lit the remaining ones. He then turned to her and casually pulled up her skirt, exposing the length of her calves.

She gasped as she tried to pull away from him, but a firm arm across her legs and a rough squeeze to her exposed calf froze her.

"I will not harm you," he assured her, but noting the scared look still in her eyes, said, "nor violate you."

He could see that she began to relax, and his eyes looked at the marking he'd seen on her ankle earlier. He noticed now for the first time that she had an identical marking on the other ankle as well. Burned into her skin, both looked to be three jagged teeth biting at her foot, but he turned the shape over in his mind and took it for what it was meant to be. Any question about what had happened faded when he saw the brands. He released her skirt, and it slowly fell back to the floor.

"You are weakened?" he asked, more of a statement than a question, and she nodded. "You were in Rondalin?" Another nod. "You are, or were, the Great Teacher of the city?" Another nod, so brief and full of embarrassment that he almost didn't catch it. He sat thoughtfully for a moment, his eyes taking in her aged face, dignified in its wrinkles, and shook his head slowly. "The new advisor?" he asked, this time the answer not a foregone conclusion. Could Raime actually have shown himself in Rondalin?

She looked at him, her expression now full of wonder, and her mouth struggled as she searched for the right words. "Who are you?" she finally asked, his question left unanswered, but the look on her face all the answer he needed.

"I have gone by many names," he said as he looked around his room, "but you can call me Brohmin," he finished. A glimmer of near recognition flashed in her eyes and was gone again. "I go north in the morning. You may come if you choose. I can offer some shelter. Perhaps some healing." He doubted she wanted to return to the Mage city of Vasha. Powerless and tossed out of Rondalin as she had been, a return would mean certain humiliation.

She nodded slowly, and he grabbed her ankle again, each hand cupped around the width of it, and it felt somehow both hot and cold at the same time. He closed his eyes as he traced the lines of the marking, his fingers feeling along the unnatural groove in her skin. He felt the soft tug at his mind and mumbled something inaudible under his breath for a time as he followed the design with his hand, then finally took his hands away.

She shivered as he released his grip, her mouth slowly opening before she shut it again with the unspoken question hanging in the air.

"We should see if we can do more about that at a later time, but for now, we need sleep." She nodded, and he left the unspoken question unanswered. He rose and unlocked the door, opening it for her before saying, "I leave with the first light. If you should come, you will meet me here before then."

~

A knock at his door awoke him in the morning, and through the window, he could see the faint lines of the morning sun peeking over the horizon. He had slept longer than he'd intended, but at his age, he didn't care so much anymore.

The woman standing at the door only vaguely resembled the woman from the night before. Where last night there had been a dirty skirt and face there was now a well-dressed woman before him. A light blue riding dress fit snuggly over her proportioned frame, and he discreetly admired the tightness of it over her bosom. She blushed slightly, and he realized that he'd not been all that discreet.

"I will come with you," she said with eyes forcing his gaze upward. "And you can call me Salindra." She had a small bag slung over her shoulder and a plain, brown cloak in her other hand. As she turned, he caught sight of a thinly bladed knife tucked inside her belt.

He followed her out of the inn and to the stables behind the large building. They waited silently while the stable hands saddled their horses. He quickly tied his pack to the back of his horse, along with some other wares that he had purchased from the kitchen the night before, and climbed into the saddle. Moments later, he led them away from the inn and headed north.

Time passed slowly, the sun's position gradually rising higher into the sky until it reached its peak. They had come upon the forest, and the great trees' limbs arched high above the well-trodden path, an occasional stone from the old road turned up to reveal the past. They traveled under cover of the trees for a long time in silence, the only sounds from deep within the forest. Every now and again, they caught a glimpse of the sun through an opening in the trees unfiltered by the leaves. It was then that they could see how the day progressed, each opening revealing the sun moving higher.

As they came around a turn, they caught sight of the two soldiers from the night before resting along the path. A giant red leaf tree had been felled and lay across the path.

He looked at the tree that blocked the road, noting that the base of the trunk ended in a gully not far from the path. The branches were spread out in the opposite direction, hundreds of feet into the forest. They would be forced to go around the end of the branches. The gully would provide too much of a challenge for the horses.

"We'll stop here for now, and then travel around the top of the branches." He pointed, and she nodded.

"Something about your name has puzzled me," she said after a long pause. "Do you know who else shares the name Brohmin?" He slowly nodded his head, and she smiled. "I suspected as much. Curious." Another pause and then, "Brohmin Ulruuy, the last great failure of my people."

He smiled at that, almost to himself, and said, "I do not know if you should say he was your *last* failure."

"There aren't many who claim knowledge of the Magi history."

"I know... some," he replied.

They ate the rest of the meal in silence, then stood at the same time and brushed themselves off. Brohmin turned to the two soldiers who were now repacking their horses and said, "We'll go off around the top end of the tree. You're welcome to accompany us."

The soldiers glanced at each other before one nodded.

They reached the top of the mighty tree and turned their horses back toward the road when one of the soldiers suddenly sat upright in his saddle.

"Does anyone smell that?"

Brohmin's eyes widened quickly as the soldiers wrinkled their noses in disgust. He scanned the forest but didn't see what he feared.

"Aye," grunted the other soldier. "And it's getting stronger." The man suddenly leaned over in his saddle and vomited.

As he did, Brohmin caught sight of two dark shapes sliding along the fallen tree.

"Go north through the forest. Catch the road, and we'll meet you!" he commanded.

The men looked at him questioningly, hands moving to swords.

"Don't be fools! Move!"

The soldiers paused, uncertain, then released their swords and spurred their horses on.

Salindra looked at Brohmin, with a question in her eyes. He nodded to the shapes, two strange figures that were now pulling away from the tree and moving closer to them, surprised to find them this far south. Salindra turned her head and stared.

"Can you?" he asked, but she shook her head, her eyes flickering to her ankles.

The figures moved further from the trees, and the horses backing up in fear.

Brohmin closed his eyes, words quietly spoken under his breath. A slight bead of sweat touched his forehead, and he welcomed the sensation in his mind. He didn't know how much longer he would have the power it granted but was thankful every time he felt it.

"What are they?" Salindra asked.

Brohmin didn't open his eyes, murmuring to himself. Suddenly, a tree branch fell. Then another. And another. The branches kept falling over the figures, eventually covering them. The branches had fallen into a sort of cage around the creatures.

Smoke rose above the tops of the branches as they caught fire, and horrific screams came from within the tree-branch cage. He allowed himself a moment to relax.

Movement caught his attention, and Brohmin pulled a knife out from within his cloak and threw it, catching another of the strange creatures through the throat with his knife. Dark grayish skin was now stained with its blood.

"Those are..."

He nodded grimly, and finished for her, "Groeliin."

Her eyes turned in a question at the name.

CHAPTER ONE

J akob Nialsen watched as Novan squinted out into the distance
through the shimmering veil of heat rising off the dry rock. He
saw nothing, but Novan seemed able to peer farther than he
could manage. "What do you see?"

"Denraen," the tall historian spoke, though it was mostly to
himself.

"Denraen soldiers?" Jakob asked.

Novan turned to him. "Yes," he answered with a thin-lipped smile.
"And I see at least one Mage." His long face took on an unfamiliar
expression, more sour than not, as he squinted through the eyeglass.

Jakob whistled softly to himself. The Denraen weren't rare—they
were the guardians, warriors who protected the Magi and roamed the
land keeping peace—but the Mage was. "We haven't seen a Mage here
in years," he told the historian. He was never certain how much
Novan knew of Chrysia. The man had been in the city a little over a
year, plundering the library and quizzing the priests. How much had
he learned in that time?

"I know," Novan answered, looking through his glass again. "They
rarely leave their city these days. There was a time when the Magi
chose to be a part of the world, but..."

When he didn't finish, Jakob pressed him. "Where do you think they travel?"

Novan chuckled before staring once more into the small valley. "There's only one destination on this road. The better question is *why*."

Jakob stared. "What are you thinking?"

"Nearly one hundred Denraen. This is more than a simple squad. Whatever reason they travel, this is *something*." He scrubbed a hand across his shorn head. A nervous look passed quickly across his eyes. "We had best find the captain."

"For what?"

A gruff voice came from behind them, and Jakob and Novan both turned to look.

The captain walked stiffly up to them before looking out over the valley. His long hair was pulled back in the style of the commanding officers, and he carried his helm under his arm, always mindful of the saber strapped to his side. When he looked over to Novan with tired eyes, he ignored Jakob.

"What do you see, historian?" he asked, shifting the helm to his other arm.

Novan's mouth tightened again before he answered. "I see the reason I suggested this journey, Captain. The rumors are true."

"Rumors. I don't put stock in rumors."

"What of the Denraen marching toward us?"

The Ur captain grunted, squinting down into the valley. "Are you certain? How do you know it is not raiders, or worse, Gom Aaldia?" His voice turned into a sneer with the last. After decades of fighting between the nations of Thealon and Gom Aaldia, few among the Ur felt anything other than hatred for Gom Aaldia. From the heat of the captain's words, he felt a special disdain. It surprised Jakob, as the tentative peace that had held between the nations had lasted nearly a decade.

Novan chuckled, and the captain snapped his gaze back to the historian. "Not raiders. Too organized." He paused, looking over to the captain with a slightly incredulous look. "And do you think Richard would send so few men so brazenly across the border and into Thealon?"

The captain shook his head rigidly. His shoulders remained tight, tense. "You're right. Yet Denraen? My scouts tell me there are nearly eighty men camped there. That's too many for the Denraen."

"There are at least one hundred Denraen," Novan answered, handing the captain his viewing glass. "And a Mage," he finished. "The numbers are significant."

The captain took the viewing glass from Novan, and after a long look down into the valley, he handed it back to him, nodding. "That is what our scout described," he said. "Though he should have recognized Denraen soldiers. Not raiders. Not Gom Aaldia." He turned and walked away without saying anything more to Novan.

Novan watched him leave before turning and looking back down into the valley. "Why are you here, Mage?" he asked to himself. "Why now?" The historian's soft voice barely carried to Jakob.

"What are you worried about?" Jakob hoped Novan didn't mind him interrupting his thoughts. In the time he'd spent serving Novan, he was never certain.

The historian didn't look up. "Long ago, the Magi themselves served as priests to the Urmahne. They have slowly pulled away from that role, and now priests like your father guide the Urmahne."

The Urmahne taught peace as a way to serve the gods, claiming that only through peace would the gods return. As the Magi were said to be the only ones able to speak to the gods, Jakob still didn't understand why they had abandoned their role, leaving men like his father to serve as priests. Had Jakob the necessary faith, he was to have followed his father into the priesthood, but how could he serve gods that would allow such suffering to befall his family?

"Do you think the Magi speak to the gods as they claim?"

Novan shook his head, then stood suddenly. "That is what they would tell you. We should return to camp. I'm sure the captain prepares for our departure. We must ready to meet the Denraen."

The historian turned and led them away from the bluff's edge, striding back to their camp. It was a well-organized camp, though hastily set. They had ridden out from the city after a scout had discovered evidence of a large camp of soldiers. Too many raider attacks upon the surrounding villages had warranted more investigation, but they had found no sign of raiders.

And now Novan found the Denraen. It wouldn't please the captain. The man had been annoyed that Novan had wanted to come, but pressure from the ruling council and the priests quickly swayed him. Jakob wasn't sure which had influenced him more. The Ur served the Urmahne first but protected all of Thealon as well.

They quickly reached the camp, and once back among the Ur soldiers, Novan waved Jakob away with a quick instruction to gather their horses. Jakob hurried away, and as he neared their mounts, he heard his name called out by the only other person he knew in camp.

Braden had been like another brother to him since they were young boys and was a new member of the Ur. He had always been quick with the sword—quick to learn, quick to attack, and quick on the defense. More like his brother Scottan than himself, Braden and Jakob had been unlikely friends, though both raised within the palace walls. Braden had learned from Scottan what Jakob had failed to master, and before the madness took Scottan, he had helped secure Braden a position in the Ur.

"What is *that?*" Braden asked, pointing to the sword at Jakob's side.

He looked down and laughed. He knew he wore it awkwardly. "When Novan told me what we were going to do, I went looking for Scottan's," he answered, "but couldn't find it. This was under my father's bed, and I borrowed it."

Braden wiped his brow, brushing his wavy hair away from his eyes. "Why would a priest need a sword?"

Jakob hadn't thought of that. Why would his father need a sword? "I don't know." Images of strange Urmahne ceremonies jumped to his mind, but he dismissed them, knowing it unlikely.

"You'll need to get better using it if you're to wear it," Braden said.

Jakob was barely average with the sword. Scottan had been the one with the ability; he had risen quickly among the Ur until the madness struck. Yet his strength and skill still weren't enough. Now he rested with the healers like the others afflicted with the madness, unable to feed himself, strength and muscle wasting away, and nothing left of his mind.

Jakob looked up at his friend and saw a hint of strain under his pale blue eyes. He knew how hard Braden worked for his position, having seen what Scottan had gone through to rise in the ranks, and he understood what it meant for Braden to be out on his first patrol. Rarely was one his age allowed more than city patrol. Yet it was taking a toll on him.

"Novan says there are Denraen in the valley," Jakob said, hoping to give Braden some good news. He knew how his brother had felt about the Denraen, a sense of awe and intrigue mixed with the hope that someday, he would be chosen to join their ranks. It was a rare event, supposedly coming only at a time when the Denraen numbers were low, and few were chosen. Most men were born to the Denraen.

"Is he sure?" Braden asked.

"I never question Novan." The historian was rarely wrong and remembered everything he saw or read. It was an amazing skill and the reason the priests allowed him such unfettered access. It was the reason they were even allowed out to ride with the Ur. "He says there's a Mage with them."

"A Mage?" Braden laughed. "There hasn't been a Mage in the last five years! Why would one come now? Especially when Thealon is in the midst of so many raider attacks?"

The Magi were averse to violence, refusing even to take up arms to protect themselves. That was the role of the Denraen. They taught that it was the only way toward the peace of the Urmahne, the only way to truly know the gods.

His father had explained the gods expected more from the Magi than they expected from other men. For a Mage to travel through lands under attack raised questions Jakob had not considered.

But Novan must have.

It explained why the historian had wondered at the reason for the Mage, along with the Denraen. What did Novan know? Working alongside the historian had been challenging at times. When he'd refused his position as an acolyte, the first step to becoming a priest, his father had arranged for him to assist Novan during the historian's time in the city. Jakob hadn't expected it to last as long as it had. Chrysia, his home city, had known a few historians of the guild to visit—the proximity to the capital of Thealon and the Tower of the Gods gave it historical importance—but none had ever stayed more than a few months.

Novan had been in the city for nearly a year, time Jakob had been asked to simply observe and assist, nothing more. It gave him the chance to delay decisions about his future, though he suspected his father hoped the time would eventually bring him back around to serving the Urmahne.

I will not join the priesthood, he told himself for the hundredth time. His father was disappointed when Scottan had joined the Ur, but the Ur still served the priesthood and the Urmahne. He maintained hope that Jakob would one day join him in the church.

"Novan is convinced," he answered, finally shaking the line of thinking from his head. "I've learned not to doubt him."

They were interrupted by another of the Ur running up to Braden. The man was tall, though not as tall as Jakob, and had the hardened look of experience. "Captain prepares to depart."

Braden nodded and saluted before the man ran off and then moved in close. "I don't like it that you're here. It's not safe. You should return to the city." He left unsaid that he, too, thought Jakob should return to the church. In that, Braden shared his father's position.

"I'll be fine," he said, patting his sword. "Besides, Novan feels we must observe, and I'm with Novan." *For now,* he didn't say.

But what else would he do?

～

The historian sat hunched atop his mount, staring at a small notebook in his hand and squinting. His dark gray eyes were unreadable, and Jakob wondered what Novan was thinking. He always wondered.

They rode toward the bluff, toward the slow switchback leading to the valley floor. The captain led them, and nearly fifty Ur rode ahead of him and Novan. Jakob didn't mind but suspected the historian did; he preferred to be in the midst of the action. Better able to observe, he would say.

"Why do you think the Mage would come?" he asked Novan again. "With the raider attacks increasing and the Ur spread thin." The last was merely supposition. Novan hadn't indicated there was a problem with the Ur.

The historian looked up from his book and smiled. "Indeed," he answered, pausing and watching as the column of Ur began to disappear down the road. "Why would he come? I have a theory, but we will have to wait to find out."

Novan turned back to the small book in his hands. The road meandered down the side of the bluff, forcing them to move slowly. The valley was the last true boundary between Thealon and the plains of Gom Aaldia; beyond the valley the Ur would not travel, though borders did not sway the priests. The Ur served as protectors of the Urmahne faith, and of the priests, but lately, they had become little more than the guards of the entire nation of Thealon. With the tower situated in the capital, Thealon had long been the stronghold of the Urmahne religion, even when the Magi had led the church.

"They say a river once flowed here," Jakob commented, staring over toward the valley. His father had told him that when he was a child, and he was not sure he believed it.

"Once," Novan agreed. "One of the three great rivers. It was known as the Shaen. It was a wide river, powerful, running from the northern mountains through the great forest and on to the sea."

"Where did it go?" How could a river disappear?

"The lands change," Novan answered. "If you look, you will see evidence everywhere. The Shaen is but one."

Jakob shook his head, unsure how the land could change that much. "When did it dry up?"

"Records would say the Shaen last flowed over a thousand years ago." He returned to his book after answering.

Jakob looked over to the valley and marveled at the sight. Once, it had been full of water? Now it was little more than a boundary between nations with an uneasy peace. He looked one last time before the road turned away from the valley.

As he did, he heard something up ahead, shouting, screaming.

He moved to stand in the stirrups, hoping for a better view, and sat back as quickly as he had stood when he saw signs of attack.

Novan glanced at him. "What did you see?" It was a question Novan often asked as he tried to train Jakob to be a better observer, to record what he saw in his mind so that he could later write it down.

The Ur in front of them had heard the same and unsheathed their swords. One man had a bow, with an arrow was nocked, and turned side to side looking for their attackers.

"Archers above," he told Novan, thinking of what he had only glimpsed briefly. What else had he seen? He had seen it fleetingly, fear driving him back into the saddle. "There's a small clearing below. I saw soldiers there."

"How many?" Novan asked. "How were they dressed?"

Jakob leaned forward, starting to stand again, but Novan restrained him. One of the soldiers in front of them suddenly went down, an arrow lodged in his neck in a spray of blood.

Jakob pulled back in horror. Novan yanked him from the saddle, and they ducked down under the horses. There was a grim smile upon Novan's face as they moved for better cover.

"How many?" Novan asked again. His voice was strangely serene.

Jakob tried to clear the sounds of the battle from his head but could not. He heard screaming and shouts far too close for his comfort. How could he remember anything with what was going on around them?

"Visualize what you saw, Jakob."

Closing his eyes, he tried to envision what he saw. "I don't know, maybe thirty. Dressed in brown and black."

"Good," Novan said. "The brown and black signifies raiders, not the Denraen. And there were nearly forty by my count. Your observations continue to improve."

Jakob looked at him, surprise and irritation coursing through him. Even now, Novan pushed him.

The historian led him forward, crouching beneath the nervous horses before moving to hug the dusty rock wall and creep along the craggy trees growing there. It was not much cover. They passed several more Ur with arrows through them, though none who Jakob recognized, and for that he was thankful. There was a coppery stink of blood about everything. The remaining soldiers had already moved forward, leaving them isolated.

Novan pulled at his sleeve. "You have a sword?"

Jakob nodded. He had forgotten about the sword until Novan had reminded him. He pulled it free, the old leather wrappings along the hilt dry and cracking. The blade, too, was covered in leather wrappings, and he recognized his folly. It was a ceremonial sword, he realized with surprise. It would do them no good.

Novan looked at it, and a tight smirk curled his thin lips. Jakob wondered what the man thought about him now. How was he to know he had grabbed a ceremonial sword? He held it out just the same, hoping it would offer some protection.

Novan led them down the slope. Jakob never questioned why they didn't return to safety, though he should have. He thought of what his father—or his brother—would have told him had they known how foolish he was.

As they moved from trees to rock cluster, the sound of battle rang in front of them. He heard screaming and shouting and the clang of metal on metal.

Braden was down there.

Novan slipped on the rocks, and a spray of dust and gravel went sliding down the path.

Jakob grabbed him. As he did, a man jumped down in front of him holding a gleaming sword at the ready. He was dressed in all black, breaches and shirt the color of a moonless night. There was a new tattoo on his sword arm with dried blood and a welt raised around it.

The man growled when he saw them, swinging his sword at Jakob.

Instinct took over, and he ducked, barely missing the sharp edge as it whistled through the air near where he had been. The man grunted and swung again. Jakob scrambled backward, pushing Novan as he did. He raised the leather-wrapped sword before him, and the man laughed.

Jakob's arm quivered as he held the sword in front of him.

This is it, he realized, squeezing the hilt of the sword. Was this what his mother had felt when she was about to die?

The thought passed him fleetingly. He rarely thought of his mother anymore. She'd been gone for nearly three years, and his father's refusal to speak of her had worn off on him. But now, as he sensed his own death, he thought of her again as memories flashed through his mind with bright clarity.

The man swung his sword down, and Jakob managed to move his sword to block it. As their swords met, the raider's sword shattered. A shock shot up Jakob's arm and into his skull, and he shook his head, trying to clear it.

The man looked at the stump of his sword before shouting and rushing at Jakob.

Jakob kicked at the man but managed only to kick his own sword.

It bounced up, and the only part of the blade not wrapped in thin leather—the exposed tip—caught the raider in the stomach. He fell forward and impaled himself upon it in a spray of warmth, landing nearly atop Jakob. He thrashed, kicking his legs, before twitching and falling still.

Jakob watched the man's death throes with a morbid sense of fascination. A wave of nausea set upon him as he smelled the coppery scent of the man's blood, the stink of dirt and sweat that lay upon him, and something else, something worse, underlying it all. Blood pooled from the wound, before running in a thick stream down the rock valley toward him.

He struggled as he suppressed the urge to vomit and scooted himself to the side, away from the blood.

A hand gripped his shoulder, and Jakob jerked around, dislodging the sword from the raider as he did. Novan kneeled near him, his thin fingers resting on Jakob's shoulder. A look of concern lined his face, and a bead of sweat dripped down his temple.

"Are you hurt?" Novan asked.

Jakob checked himself over. He didn't *think* he'd been hit. Both his hand and the leather-wrapped blade were now maroon stained. Nausea threatened to overwhelm him again, and he swallowed to settle the bile rising in his throat, licking his lips with a too dry tongue, shivering. Loose strands of his brown hair hung in front of his face, forcing him to shake them away. "I don't think so."

"An ambush," Novan said, shaking his head.

"The Ur?" Jakob asked of their soldiers, wondering if they survived.

Novan nodded down the slope where a strangely dressed soldier approached. Clad in solid gray, heavy mail overtop it, the man's hair was shorn short like Novan's. Unlike the historian, a long sword was held easily in his hand, and a dented shield slung on his other forearm. His face was streaked with dirt and blood and pulled tight in concentration. He saw them and stalked up the slope toward them.

Jakob looked over to Novan. "Is that—" The man neared before he could finish.

"Denraen," Novan finished, nodding.

The soldier stood over them. "Historian?" Novan nodded. "Are you injured?"

Novan looked over at Jakob again, rechecking that he was unharmed, before shaking his head. The historian stood slowly and dusted himself off. Jakob did the same, though moved more slowly. He wiped the stained leather blade on the dead raider before sheathing it, wondering if he defiled the dead by doing so. With the thought, he shivered again.

The Denraen looked at him carefully before turning to the raider, flipping him over, and looking at the man. He inspected the injury carefully and then turned his attention to the man's tattooed arms as Novan joined him. "This is—"

"It is," Novan answered curtly, looking back to Jakob briefly before returning his attention to the dead raider. "The others?"

"No markings," he answered. "Raiders only."

Novan grunted. "This is unexpected."

"What's unexpected?"

The question came from another man, squat and heavily muscled. He carried an air of authority about him. He was dressed the same as the other Denraen, though carried no shield and his sword was sheathed. The Ur captain followed him. He wore a strange look on his bloodstained face that Jakob could not read, and walked stiffly behind the large Denraen.

Novan nodded to the dead raider, and the Denraen moved to

kneel next to the man briefly before standing. "I must speak to the general."

"Endric is among you?" Novan asked.

The large Denraen eyed Novan a moment before nodding. "He sends his greetings, historian."

Novan laughed. It was barely more than a cough and did not carry. "I am sure he does. I would like to see him."

The large Denraen nodded. "We escort Magi to the city. They're to meet the Council. He can meet you after."

"Magi? How many?"

"Two."

"Who has come?"

The Denraen smiled. "I suppose it does no harm telling you as you'll learn soon enough. Elder Haerlin and an apprentice, an interesting Mage named Roelle."

Without giving Novan a chance to react, the large Denraen signaled to the other, and both men turned and strode down the road.

The Ur captain turned back to the body. "Damn raiders. Killed ten of my men. If not for the Denraen, we'd all be dead."

"More than raiders," Novan muttered. Jakob wondered if Novan meant for it to be heard.

The Ur captain frowned at Novan. "More than raiders? What do you know, historian? What is the importance of this man?"

Novan closed his eyes and shook his head, speaking low and to himself. Jakob still managed to hear. "Magi and now this. Endric, what else do you know?"

Jakob and the captain shared a glance, but Novan turned from them both and offered no answers.

CHAPTER TWO

Roelle hurried alongside Elder Haerlin through the large stone building in the city of Chrysia, still trembling from the attack. The remainder of the trip into the city had been unremarkable, but she still struggled with seeing battle—a real battle—for the first time. All the time that she'd spent learning to use the sword, practicing with the Denraen, and she still hadn't been able to do anything to help. But then, as a Mage, she was not allowed to help.

She still couldn't believe they'd encountered the Deshmahne during their journey to the city. Her uncle had mentioned the rumors of movement from the dark priests, the very name of the religion a mockery of everything the Urmahne stood for. During their journey to Chrysia, she'd heard the Denraen speak about how the Deshmahne had pressed the attack from the south, slowly moving toward Thealon, but seeing it firsthand was different from hearing rumors. Then again, that was the reason for their travels—they were meant to find a way to stem the growing tide of the warrior priests and secure peace—but she hadn't expected to witness it. That they had dared to attack in Thealon... She still struggled with what that meant.

Her mind raced as they walked, led by the Denraen. Roelle doubted they needed protection now, though even outside the city, she had thought herself safe in spite of the warnings her uncle had given her when she'd asked to come along.

It was one thing to know about such violence, and another to see it. The Elders preached that peace was essential. It was one of the first lessons the Magi learned. The nameless gods granted the Magi strength and abilities so that they could maintain peace in their absence. They were gifted with their abilities so that others would not have to suffer.

If that peace failed, they risked angering the gods. Though it had been many years since any had claimed to have seen the gods, none of the Magi denied their existence, just as none of the Magi denied the need for peace. And what the Magi demanded, the priests of the Urmahne religion carried forward.

Or had. For the first time in decades, the Magi had chosen to intervene. Roelle still didn't understand all of what they were here to do, but as she glanced over at Haerlin, the Mage Elder, noting his intense expression, she had the distinct sense that he hadn't been pleased to leave Vasha. When he'd realized that she intended to continue her studies with the sword—something the Council had barely allowed while in the city—it had only increased his displeasure. And then the attack... she thought that was the final insult to him, almost enough to send him racing back to the city.

"You don't have to observe this," Haerlin said. "You can run off and practice with the soldiers if that's your preference."

Roelle suppressed a smile as she glanced at the Denraen shadowing them. Few of the Elders approved of the apprentice Magi working with the soldiers. It had been a game at first, one that had come as a distraction from their daily lessons, and one that only she and her oldest friend Selton had tried. Over time more and more joined them.

"Uncle asked me to observe." Perhaps it was best to remind him of Alriyn and her connection to him. It was better to do that now than to wait and let him get increasingly frustrated with her. She hoped Haerlin didn't discover that Alriyn had so much as sent her to observe, but allowed her to come, and then only after much begging.

It had been worth it to leave the city. "You haven't said much about the Deshmahne attack."

Haerlin squeezed his hands together and let out a long sigh. He'd been unharmed, but she hadn't actually considered the effects of the attack on him. She suspected that he, as someone gifted with prophecy, regretted the fact that he hadn't anticipated it.

"We should not have seen them this far north. The dark priests have been confined to the southlands."

"I thought that was the reason we were coming here. Choosing the delegates so that we could reestablish the peace."

"We choose the delegates to begin exerting our influence once more," Haerlin said. "They will be better received than Magi advisors. *That* is why we are here." He continued for a few paces before glancing over at her. "I'm sure the Second Eldest told you how most of the south has been lost to the Deshmahne. We can't allow the north to fall as well. If we do, then peace fails. The Council cannot allow that to happen."

Her uncle *had* told her about the Deshmahne but hadn't explained much about what she should expect. Had he known what they would find when they left the city? He'd disappeared for a while, and she suspected that he'd left the city himself, though couldn't prove it. Alriyn could be strange that way, disappearing for long stretches of time, and always buried in his studies.

Roelle thought back to the attack. When the attack came, she hadn't been certain how she would react. Practice was one thing, but implementation of those learned techniques during an attack... That was something else entirely.

When the raiders and the Deshmahne attacked, she had been unable to move from her horse. It wasn't so much that she was frozen in place, but that she struggled with the brutality of the attack, the bloodshed. She had been trained her whole life to work toward peace. That was the central tenet of the Magi teaching.

She wasn't sure if she would have been able to do anything anyway. Seeing the Deshmahne soldier fight, seeing how quickly he moved, she wasn't sure if she would have been able to slow that attack.

Haerlin stopped at the wide double door and glanced back at the two Denraen soldiers accompanying them. One of them was Pendin, General Endric's second-in-command. He was a scarred man, one with a stern continence, and he was nearly as skilled as Endric when it came to fighting. She had seen firsthand how he had brought down three raiders and then worked with Endric to stop the two Deshmahne as well. There had been a third dark priest, but he'd died strangely, and she hadn't learned how.

Haerlin sighed one more time. "This is a mistake." He said the words softly, and almost to himself.

"Elder?"

Haerlin squeezed his eyes closed before opening them again. "Perhaps we should have listened to your uncle."

"What did my uncle say?"

"The Second Eldest was not a fan of choosing these delegates. He didn't think that it went far enough."

"What did Alriyn want to do instead?"

Haerlin sighed again. "If nothing else, he thinks the Council should force our way back into the roles we once had, the one we still do in a few places."

"Advisors?"

Haerlin nodded. "Rondalin still has a Magi advisor. Thealon as well. If we can influence the south, perhaps there would be no need to follow the warrior priests."

Roelle heard a note of fear in Haerlin's voice. "Have you seen something?"

He squeezed his eyes shut as if trying to push back a painful memory. "A dangerous vision. One that your uncle thinks means an ancient prophecy has been triggered. The Eldest does not share this belief."

It was the first Roelle had heard of this. "A prophecy?"

"I've said too much. I think the attack has affected me more than I realize."

"But if Alriyn thought—"

"Your uncle is wrong in this. What he believes is something that has not been done in over two hundred years. Something that the

Council has failed to achieve during our previous attempts." He pushed the door open and stood for a moment, looking at Roelle before drawing his back upright. "Forget what I've told you. Let's see if there's anything Chrysia can do to change the growing unrest."

As they started into the room, Roelle couldn't shake what he'd told her, or what it might mean. Alriyn was a renowned scholar, and if there was something he feared, then why wouldn't the Council act on it?

And why did Haerlin seem so unsettled?

~

Jakob knocked firmly on his father's door. There was no answer. His father often didn't answer if he was engrossed in his work, so he opened it and stepped inside, finding the office empty.

The room was small and simply decorated. There was a desk stained with ink and stacked with parchment, several travel chests, and a prayer pad. Incense hung heavy in the air, the after effect of the noon prayer, and on one of the desks, he saw a small, carved wooden bowl filled with ash. A carving of a trefoil leaf hung on one wall. Other than that, there were no other decorations. Simple, like his father.

Jakob hadn't been to his father's rooms much recently. His time with Novan kept him preoccupied, but there was more to it than that. Losing his mother had left him with difficult memories and a foundering faith in the Urmahne and the gods. Scottan succumbing to the madness had turned that into anger. Anger was an emotion his father did not understand.

Jakob put the sword he had borrowed back where he had found it under the bed. He'd washed the leather as best he could, getting most of the stains off, but he suspected he would have to replace the leather wrappings another time. For now, he would make sure his father had it back if it was needed. His father could be strange about things like that if something went missing for too long.

As he pushed the sword back under the bed, his arm and head began to throb again. Since the attack, his head had bothered him the most, but his arm still felt strange. He tried to shake the sensation off, but felt a wave of nausea and dizziness course through him and had to blink a few times slowly before the feeling finally passed.

As he stood to leave, slowly so as not to become dizzy again, the door opened.

His father entered, dressed simply in a brown wool cloak, his wrinkled face exposed and a black ink stain on his cheek above his thick beard. He, like all the priests, wore few ornaments, only a few items of jewelry, markers of the priesthood. Jakob had never taken the time to learn what they all meant.

"Son," he said, smiling. His voice was soft, as usual. "It's early in the day for you to visit."

"I came yesterday as well," he admitted. "Novan had me accompany him on a ride out of the city. We went with the Ur." A look of concern quickly crossed his father's face. Jakob wondered briefly whether it was the mention of Novan or the Ur.

"You were with the Ur?" his father asked, running a hand through his black-peppered hair. Jakob nodded. "The attack?"

Jakob was surprised his father would have learned of the attack. "I was there."

"You saw the Magi?"

That explained his father's interest. He shook his head. He hadn't seen the Magi, only what Novan had described. Neither of them had seen the other Mage the Denraen said had come. On the return to the city, the Magi had remained out of sight. "Denraen, though."

"I'm glad you're safe," he said, stepping toward the desk and setting down a stack of papers.

"Barely. It was raiders," Jakob began. "Though something more, I think," he continued, remembering the tattooed man he had been forced to kill.

"What did you see?" his father asked, using words that strangely mirrored Novan's typical question.

Jakob shrugged. "Not sure what it means, but we were attacked by a tattooed man. Novan seemed to know and was worried by it."

His father frowned and closed his eyes slowly, muttering a quick prayer. "They shouldn't be here, yet," he said softly, mostly to himself. Looking to Jakob, he asked, "You were here yesterday?"

"Novan warned me to bring a sword if I had one, so I came here looking for Scottan's," Jakob said in a rush. "I couldn't find it but found one under your bed and grabbed it." He looked at his father apologetically. "It wasn't until later I learned it was a ceremonial sword."

His father shook his head slowly. "Ceremonial? Why would an Urmahne priest have a sword?"

Jakob shrugged. "I thought there might be some ceremony or service you performed."

His father laughed. It was a hearty sound and the first time Jakob had heard him laugh in a long time. "Perhaps that, as much as anything, tells me how little you're meant for the priesthood," his father said ruefully. "The Urmahne value peace above all else. There is no ceremony like you speak about."

"Then why do you have it? Where's Scottan's sword?"

His father sniffed loudly, scratching his nose, before answering. "Scottan's sword rests at the santrium. The healers hope to use it to aid his recovery." The tone of his voice said that he did not think it likely. "As to the one you found, that is our great-father's sword."

His father kneeled to reach under the bed and pulled the sword carefully out from beneath it. His eyes narrowed as he saw the hint of red staining the hilt. "He was a soldier, I suspect, though I know little about him. The story of this sword has been mostly lost. There was a time when I wondered about him." He glanced up at Jakob. "Much of what remains cannot be more than exaggeration. Though the sword is more than a simple soldier's blade."

His father stood, stretching his back as he did, raising himself to his full height. He was a tall man, taller than most men, and seemed to tower over Jakob. They shared the same chestnut hair and deep blue eyes. "It's been handed father to son through the years, down many generations, to me. I've had no use for it."

He looked toward the door and stared for a long moment. Jakob knew what the gesture meant; he had seen it many times. His father thought of Scottan again and worried. Or he thought of Jakob's mother, remembering. Jakob wondered if today it was more. What sort of disappointment was he to his father?

Looking down at the sword in his hands, his father said, "It was to go to Scottan," as if reading Jakob's thoughts. "He would have had the most use, I suppose. Now..."

"What now?" Jakob asked.

"Now?" He exhaled slowly, as if a decision reached, and turned. Lifting his head to look Jakob in the eyes, he spoke. His blue eyes were soft, and Jakob felt the love of his father radiate from them. "Now it should go to you."

Jakob shook his head. He had no use for it, not like Scottan did. "It's for Scottan," he said, afraid to put words to his thoughts.

His father smiled at him fondly. His eyes glistened with restrained tears. "It's for you, now," he said gently, offering Jakob the sword.

Jakob took it carefully by the leather-wrapped hilt. He knew the wrappings worked all the way up the blade and wondered briefly what the blade looked like. Probably worn and tarnished with age.

"You must honor our family," his father said. "The sword is said to honor the gods. So, too, should you."

His father knew Jakob's struggles, and he wondered if his father shared in them. How could he not? "I'll try." Knowing the sword was his great-father's somehow made if feel heavier as if the weight of their history weighed upon him. "But how can I when I've disappointed you, Father?"

A smile came to his father's lips. "Never." He set his soft hand upon Jakob's shoulder before squeezing. "You must question before you can find the answers you need."

"I am afraid there are no answers to my questions."

His father frowned before pulling him in for a quick embrace. It had been a long time since his father had shown him affection. "I was there, once," he admitted.

Jakob looked at him, surprised.

"There are always answers. They just may not be to the questions you thought you were asking." Letting Jakob go, he stepped back. "Now I want you to be safe with Novan. Learn what he can teach but discover your own questions. It's only then the answers will come."

Jakob nodded, feeling closer to his father than he had in nearly a year. Since Scottan fell to the madness.

"May the gods watch and comfort you," his father spoke, dismissing him.

"And you," he answered, knowing not to push his father by saying anything more.

His father turned toward his desk and sat, grabbing a sheet of parchment.

Jakob left, glancing at his father once more as he did. Novan had asked him to see what he knew yet he could not bring himself to do so. Clutching the same sword he came with, he left his father and his office.

Braden stopped him on his way back to the library to find Novan. The library stood in the middle of a large courtyard in the center of the city, the massive stone structure rising high over the city, almost as if it had been intended to be the center of the city itself. When Braden found him, he still clutched the sword and felt uncomfortable with it, an imposter.

His friend stood in the Ur practice yard and waved him over. Braden's angular face was covered in sweat, and his black hair streamed in the wind. He eyed the sword briefly.

Jakob flushed. "I guess it wasn't a ceremonial sword. My father said it's a family sword."

"Was it Scottan's?" he asked.

"It would have been. Now... now I guess it's mine."

"You should learn to use it," Braden suggested.

"Scottan always tried to teach me. I never had much talent."

"So have I." His friend hesitated, and seemed reluctant to say what he asked next. "How is he?"

Jakob shrugged. Scottan had been locked in the city santrium now for the last year. Jakob used to visit often, but as his brother's condition worsened, he found less and less time to do so, though he often heard updates from his father. Braden had been close to Scottan, as well, seeing him as an older brother and one who had helped turn Braden into the soldier he is now.

"The same. Perhaps a little worse. Stable for now, I guess." Jakob flicked his gaze to the library. Novan would be waiting for him. "There are others there worse than him."

"And more lost every week. It seems like half our patrols involve someone whose mind has started to go."

The madness seemed to spread, becoming more prevalent with each month. Once, it had befallen only a handful a year. Never curable, it destroyed those it took, claiming their minds while their bodies remained. Lately, it took several a month. Jakob wished it could have been different for Scottan. It had been hard enough on their family losing his mother, but when Scottan had fallen to the madness, his father had become a different man.

Braden cleared his throat. "The Turning Festival is soon. We need to find clothes to impress the Mancley sisters." Braden grinned, a charm to his smile that couldn't be faked reflected in his eyes.

Jakob laughed. "You mean you want to impress Jessila Mancley." Braden had pined over Jessila for months while she preferred teasing him; he understood why Braden persisted—Jessila was beautiful.

"Fine, but her sister's nice too!"

Jakob laughed again, shaking his head. Marli was much like her sister, and just as difficult for him to talk to. "I don't think there's much hope for me there. I don't have the same way with women as you."

"You could try. You're too much like your father. Serious."

"And he always said I took after my mother." Braden laughed, and they fell into a comfortable silence.

"I'm glad you weren't hurt in the attack," Braden said after a time.

Jakob took a deep breath. "I thought we were trapped." His voice was distant as he relived the events from the day before. "We'd moved too quickly down the road. They caught us at the narrows, and only a few could battle at a time. Those in front were lost." He swallowed. "If not for the Denraen..."

A sound across the yard caught their attention. Jakob saw several dozen of the guard crossing the practice yard as if just leaving the barracks. "What is it?"

Braden looked over nervously before hurrying to return his practice sword to the rack. "Attacks are getting more frequent. Looks like I have to go, but I'll find you later," he promised as he ran off, catching the other guardsmen and joining them. The promise of the Turning Festival was left unsaid.

Jakob watched as the men welcomed Braden among them, and he remembered it had been the same with Scottan. He wondered if he would ever know a feeling such as that. With Novan, he had purpose, but he never felt welcomed, and never felt a part of anything.

With a sigh, he continued on his way to the library.

CHAPTER THREE

Jakob stared at his sword in the darkened library. The leather scabbard was well worn, faded writing etched along its length, and only a few words decipherable. Other markings were there, too, and Jakob could nearly make out figures now lost to time.

A simple blade guard ran off a hand's width from the edge of the blade. It was of a polished steel, plain-looking when compared to some he had seen, and curved very slightly toward the tip of the sword. Each side ended in a three-pronged split of the guard, the three metal pieces twisting and almost taking on a shape of their own as they curled up at the ends.

Jakob wrapped his fingers around the leather-covered hilt. For a moment, the sword seemed to hum. The hilt was long enough that his right hand securely gripped near the guard still left room for half of his other hand. He suspected the wrappings gave a surer grip in battle. There was some carving to the hilt he could feel under the wrappings, but he dared not remove them.

A heavy brass pommel rounded off the hilt. Opposing sides of it were slightly flattened. The weight of the pommel balanced the weight of the blade, and lettering circled the flat edges of the pommel on each side—tiny letters he could barely see, let alone read.

A single figure was also worked carefully into each flattened edge of the pommel, a different form to each side. Both were foreign to his eyes.

He pulled it carefully from the scabbard. The stains on the leather wrappings unsettled him, and he worked quickly to remove them, both to rid him of the memory of what he had done and to see the blade underneath. The edges of the blade had been well kept, and he ran his thumb lightly across one side, wincing as it drew blood. It was very sharp. There was not a mar to either edge, almost as if it had never been used. The faint lamplight reflected brightly from the blade, its well-polished surface nearly mirror-like in how it reflected the light. More lettering was inscribed along the blade itself that Jakob couldn't read, the language foreign to him.

Jakob was about to sheathe it when something compelled him to turn it over. Rather than the same gleaming metal, what he saw on the other side was darker, almost black. Light was not reflected on this side, rather it seemed almost as if it absorbed the light. There was lettering down the center of this side of the blade, as well, equally unreadable.

Jakob stared at the sword as he began to understand what his father had said. This truly was more than a simple soldier's sword. Why else would it be handed down through generations? It was much different from the dull steel blades he'd seen of the Ur.

How had his family come to it?

"It should have a name."

Startled, Jakob turned quickly to see Novan moving through the stacks toward him. He sheathed the sword with an embarrassed flush coming to his cheeks. "I don't know it. It's been in the family." He paused, staring at the sword. "It was to have been Scottan's."

Novan's eyes narrowed. "It's yours now, and rightfully," he said quietly but firmly. "And it should have a name."

Jakob shook his head, an answer to both statements. "Only mine because the madness claimed Scottan," he said.

Novan clucked at him. "Perhaps, or perhaps it was always meant for you."

"The gods mean for me to have this?" He waved the sword before him before lowering it and sighing. "I don't think there is such a plan for me."

Novan smiled at him with a hint of sadness. "There are powers other than the gods, Jakob. Perhaps something greater, deeper." Novan paused and looked around. "The ancients believed that different lives, their energies, were woven together like strands forming rope, their threads making up a larger pattern. It was this that granted power." Jakob eyed him strangely, and Novan laughed. "I said the ancients believed it, not I. But it matters little. The sword is yours now, and it should have a name. May I see it?"

When Jakob handed the sword to him, Novan quickly examined the hilt and the scabbard before unsheathing and eyeing the bright blade. There was a strange expression on his face as he eyed the sword. Jakob worried what the historian was thinking. Turning it over, he whistled softly, as if to himself, before looking back to Jakob and arching an eyebrow.

"Your family has kept this sword?" he asked.

"So my father has said."

Novan nodded. "So he said," he repeated, speaking mostly to himself. "Nialsen... Yes, it would make sense." He hesitated as if debating whether to say more. "All well-forged blades eventually earn a name, and this was certainly a well-forged blade. It is known as Neamiin." The word lilted and twisted from the historian's tongue, almost familiar as if he had said it many times before.

"How do you know?" Did the historian know his family's story? Had he learned that in the time he'd spent perusing the stacks of books?

Novan smiled. "Nothing as mystical as I imagine your mind might be thinking. Your sword tells me." Novan traced the letters along the blade's surface. Seeing Jakob's puzzled expression, he continued. "The writing on the blade. The language itself is dead, though some still study it and know its uses, but they are few." His eyes locked onto the sword as he spoke before looking up at Jakob. "Neamiin. It is a word from an old language with many meanings. This is surprising. It seems I will have to teach it to you."

The historian handed the sword back to Jakob who took it carefully. He said the name to himself, struggling to get his mouth and tongue to say it properly. There was an inflection to the word Jakob found incredibly foreign. "Have you learned why the Magi have come?"

Novan shook his head. "No, but their visit raises several concerns."

"Why?"

Novan sat and twisted a dark ring on his left hand. "The raider you killed was Deshmahne, Jakob. Do you know what they are?"

A sudden memory hit him with a clarity that was almost like he was there. He saw the tattoo marking the man in black as he attacked and the dark smile that parted his lips. Deshmahne.

"The warrior priests. What does that mean that they are in Thealon?" He knew little enough of the warrior priests—few did—but what he did know was that he was lucky to have lived. How could he have killed a Deshmahne?

"They should not have attacked the Ur, but it means the Deshmahne are on the move. Thealon is no longer safe. If they have their way, their religion will infiltrate even Thealon."

"But Thealon is Urmahne!" Jakob said. Though he no longer trusted the gods, the priests had held Thealon so long, it was foreign to think that any other religion could infiltrate its people.

"Is it?" Novan asked. "And what of Liispal and Coamdon? Once they were all Urmahne, and now they all favor the Deshmahne. Only one hundred years ago, the Deshmahne were nothing but a quiet sect, barely known, yet their power has grown quickly. The south converted first, either by force or by choice, and now Gom Aaldia appears to fall. It was never going to be long before they set their sights on Thealon. It seems that now they have."

Novan looked at him again, an unreadable expression to his face. He turned from Jakob, rifling through one of his many stacks, before turning back and handing him a small, leather-bound book. "Read through this," he instructed.

"What is it?" The prospect of more reading made his tone more forlorn than he had intended.

Novan pulled himself upright, stretching to his full height. "It will help you decipher your sword, Jakob. And perhaps more." He gave

Jakob a knowing look before nodding, a decision made. "You can learn something of the ancient language from it. Not much, but a start."

Jakob took the book carefully. It was older than many he had seen, and the cover was embossed with the trefoil leaf in the top right corner. Jakob flipped through the pages, noting the tiny script cramming the pages, realizing quickly that this would be a more challenging read than other books Novan had assigned.

"Treat it well," Novan instructed. "Few have been allowed to see it."

"Why?"

Novan bent at the waist, bringing his long face closer to Jakob. There was a solemn expression etched into his features, one that was near permanently there. "The language holds a certain power. Nothing magical," he said, waving away the unasked question, "but real, nonetheless. The Magi do not learn to read it until they are fully trained, and only then, few other than the Council know it well. Its power comes from knowledge, and the ability to learn from the past."

Novan said nothing more, turning instead to his own reading, leaving Jakob staring at the book. With nothing left to do, he flipped it open and started to read.

～

Jakob was startled awake by a sound in the library. He knew he'd been dreaming but could remember little of it. His dreams had been strange of late, and this was no different...

There was a woman, tall and pale and mysterious, and she called to him. She struggled in a strange wall-less room. Golden eyes settled on him, and he felt a vibration echo through him, pulling at his still-throbbing head. Jakob struggled to pull his eyes away from her gaze and found a part of him tear as he did. The vibration slowly abated, and he shivered, fear coursing through him.

Yet it was not these things he found strange. Rather, it was the memory of a smell, one of roses and lavender with a hint of rain, a smell that was tainted in his dreams by an underlying odor, a foul rotting stench. He woke up scratching his nose to clear it.

Who dreams of smells?

Something had startled him awake, yet as he peered across the library, he saw nothing. Footsteps echoed across the stone floor, and when he turned toward the sound, he saw the top of Novan's peppered head appear on the other side of the stacks of read and unread books, little changed from the day before. Only the historian truly understood his system. Jakob wondered what Novan had been doing during the day, knowing he sought an audience with the Magi.

"I must have fallen asleep," he admitted sheepishly. "I'll finish the shelving you asked of me."

"I didn't doubt that you would," Novan said as he approached the table. His soft voice carried through the library. He looked down at the book in front of Jakob and reached his long, slender hand down to finger the page Jakob had been reading. "An interesting place to stop," he noted.

Jakob started reading out of curiosity, wondering what place Novan referenced. He understood only a little of it. "It... is difficult."

Novan nodded his head slightly. "From everything I've learned, it was a difficult time. What have you learned?"

Jakob could come up with very little. "War, I think. The language was difficult to understand."

"The language becomes familiar the more you read." He patted Jakob's shoulder. "Your father did well in teaching you to read. Few men have patience to decipher this." It was rare praise. Novan motioned to the text. "It was the last great war. Most have now forgotten." He scratched at the side of his head and fingered one of his long ears. "The why of it is a puzzle and has always been puzzling. Some called it the War of Confusion."

"I'm not sure I follow."

Novan looked at him, his eyes hinting at gold today and piercing. "Most wars have an event which precludes hostilities, but none have been found to explain this war. The historians who first recorded it could not explain the reasons behind it." His gaze fell to the pages again. "Yet each nation found cause to attack another."

"War of Confusion. How did it end?"

"How do all wars end?" Novan asked. "Destruction. Death. The earliest Urmahne struggled against this, and if not for their guidance, the repercussions would have been greater." His eyes took on a faraway look, almost as if he remembered it. "Still, there was much loss. Too much for a war without reason."

He stopped for a while, and Jakob thought it all the answer he would offer. Finally, though, he continued. "This book explains much." Novan motioned over the thin leather book. "Yet leaves much out. The Magi, thinking to help, chose an ambassador, a man, one they named Uniter, a peacemaker for the people. He was said to be the embodiment of the Urmahne, and it was upon him to restore the peace."

"Did he?" The book suddenly became more interesting.

Novan laughed. In the library, Novan rarely smiled and almost never laughed. Books were serious business to him. "Truly, the answer to your question depends on your outlook."

"How?" he asked.

"The Uniter tried his hand at a diplomatic solution but found few receptive. He was forced to find another path to peace." Novan scrubbed a hand across his head before continuing. "Those he could not reason with, he killed, until he found others who were more reasonable." The slight quirk of his mouth returned. "It was a different diplomacy than the Magi expected."

Jakob stared at the book. Did it describe all of that? "Did it work?"

Novan regarded him strangely while twisting a dark metal ring on his finger. "It did. The Magi couldn't stomach the price. Violence to end violence. They felt it violated the Urmahne promise made to the people." He stopped then and stood, gathering his robes about him carefully and scratching at his face and touching his ear again.

"Has there been a Uniter since?"

Novan considered before answering. "The ambassador of that time was not the first, but there have been none since."

Jakob sat silently, considering what he had learned, and slowly forming his question. "Is that why the Magi have come to Thealon?"

Novan arched his eyebrows before tapping his nose thoughtfully. "There is much violence in the world now, as you have seen. If the Deshmahne press north..." He shook his head. "And other tidings, worse than Deshmahne." Novan did not elaborate. "Perhaps they have decided to exert their influence upon the world once again. As I said before, there was a time when the Magi were a part of the world, when they were as numerous as the Teachers." He smiled as if thinking of the scholars amused him. Many had studied at the great University in Vasha. "But most nations have reduced their guidance over time."

"You don't know?"

"I have not been granted an audience. I am afraid the Mage Elder is none too fond of me."

"Why?" Jakob asked.

"There is some unpleasant history between us."

Jakob's eyes widened in surprise. What history would Novan share with the Magi that would make them upset at the historian? "What now?"

Novan inhaled slowly and looked down at his hand. "There is something I must take care of."

"The Magi?"

Novan shook his head. "No. More important that the Magi."

Jakob frowned at him, wondering what could be more important than the Magi, but Novan said nothing.

The grassy yard outside the barracks was bright from the late afternoon sun, today merely warm and not the steamy heat of passing summer. There was a scent of fall roses to the air though Jakob had been unable to find them. Other scents, earthy and wet, mingled with the floral scent, creating a not unpleasant aroma.

It had been several days since he had seen Braden in the practice yard, and he'd hoped to find him. With everything Novan had him doing, he felt isolated and hoped to have a moment with his friend.

Instead of Braden, he found an older man, his white hair closely shorn, moving quickly through catahs swinging a practice sword fluidly. He wore a tattered shirt, more stains than not across it, and loose-fitting breeches that did not hide the fact that, though the man may have years behind him, he still had much strength in him. Nearing, Jakob watched and knew the man was good. He moved in a dance and one that would be deadly for his opponent.

Scottan had once explained what he did when he practiced alone, though Jakob had never understood. "Let your mind go blank, an empty sky, no thoughts or distractions. Let the movements consume you, let the catahs lead the way. It will flow then."

Jakob had laughed. "The catahs will never flow for me."

Scottan had smiled. "It is because you fight them. Your mind is too full. All you have to do is let go."

He had never seen this man before and wondered if he was someone in the Ur. There were many retired Ur that lived in the city. Could he be Denraen? Jakob shook the thought away. The man was too old to be of the Denraen.

The man looked over at him then, pausing in mid-swing, his body hunched in an attack crouch. Clear blue eyes fixed on him, looking him over, examining him. Jakob looked away, unsure what else to do.

"Are you here to watch, or to practice?" the man asked, his voice rough.

Jakob forced himself to look up and meet the man's gaze. It softened, but only slightly. Shrugging, he walked over to the rack of practice swords and hefted one, feeling an ache in his arm again with the movement. It still burned from when he had grabbed his greatfather's sword. Wincing briefly, he willed himself to ignore it.

Turning to face the man, he finally answered. "Practice."

Now that he had a sword, he had better be able to use it.

CHAPTER FOUR

Jakob looked up at the old man, his breathing labored and body doubled over. He had not seen Novan for nearly a week, though this was not unusual. Jakob still performed his expected duties. Mornings and early afternoon were spent shelving and pushing through the thin book on the ancient language Novan had given him. He understood little more than before he had started and had learned nothing about the naming of his sword.

Each day for the past two weeks, he had made time to come to the yard, and each day, he found the old man practicing alone. Each day, he had asked Jakob if he was there to watch or to practice. Each day, Jakob had shrugged and grabbed a practice sword, deciding to learn how to use a sword now that he owned one.

He knew he did not push the man—he never broke a sweat—yet the man seemed content to work with him, never saying more than brief instructions, never offering his name and never asking Jakob's. The old man was amazing with the sword but patient, as well, giving brief demonstrations of catahs and guiding Jakob through them before they sparred. His sides ached from their practice, and he wondered if he might have a cracked rib or two.

He straightened slowly and looked over at the old man. It was warm today, the result of the fluctuating Chrysia autumn, and the man didn't wear a shirt. A large scar crossed the entirety of his chest, destroying one nipple, which had grown angry red with the workout. There were other scars, as well, too many to count, so that he seemed covered with scar and sinewy muscle. A dark tattoo crossed his chest, working alongside the brutal scar, an intricate design to it that Jakob could not decipher.

The man still didn't breathe hard. Jakob's own breaths were heavy and loud, and he was wet with the heat of his exercise.

"Better today," the old man offered, his voice rough and an accent to his words that Jakob had been unable to place. The words were uncommon praise.

He shook his head, frustrated that he didn't improve, and knowing his movements were still too forced and rough. His head throbbed as it had every day after the workout, a slow beating he felt deep within his head, almost pulsing. It was nearly distracting.

Jakob had learned many catahs from the old man and actually knew how to defend most of them, putting names to forms he once thought useless. The old man had shown him otherwise. Putting the knowledge into practice was difficult for him.

The old man quirked a half-smile. "Each day, you come. Do you have other duties?" he asked, steely blue eyes staring at him.

Jakob wiped the sweat from his brow and rubbed his temple. The throbbing was starting to recede. "Some," he answered truthfully.

The old man nodded and grunted. It was all the response he would give. "Some. Tomorrow you are with me."

Jakob smiled, appreciating the comment and knowing that he would have come to the yard anyway. Having the old man's permission to work with him made him feel welcome in a way that he had longed for, but rarely known.

The old man pulled his shirt over his head and strolled away from the yard, his gait a catlike grace.

Jakob hesitated, considering going to the barracks; he hadn't seen Braden in a while, and the festival was coming soon, but he wouldn't bother him while he worked with the Ur.

He could return to the library, but with the daylight remaining, he didn't *really* want to be indoors. Besides, he should delay a visit no longer.

Jakob had been putting off visiting his brother as the memory of the last visit still woke him at night occasionally. Scottan, once so strong and invincible, reduced to a shadow of what he had been. The madness had completely taken him, and Jakob did not recognize what was left.

He quickly passed through the palace gate, past several small patches of now fading flowers, and saw the colored leaves of the surrounding shrubbery signaling that the Turning was near. He sighed quietly as he noticed, knowing that winter would soon follow and with it would come the snow that must be shoveled from the paths. He was certain Novan would have him clear around the library.

Outside the gate, the city was busy.

He weaved his way around pull carts, the occasional horse, and the throngs of people making their way through the city. His pace was quick knowing his time was short, and he found himself jumping several times to avoid hitting someone. Moving away from the palace grounds, away from the huge fenced-in lawn, the smells of the city overtook the flowers of the gardens. He smelled breads baking before he even passed the bakery, the sweetness of the candy shop that was equally inviting, and roasting meat that wafted out of open-doored inns. He kept up his pace, ignoring the scents. The sounds of people talking were all about him, from small groups of people clustered outside shops, to the sounds of children yelling as they ran through the streets playing. He hurriedly avoided the occasional merchant wagon creaking through the streets, never stopping to wonder what the goods were or whether they were entering or leaving the city. The clang of hammer on metal rang loudly from a blacksmith or silversmith somewhere nearby, but he never saw the shop.

Gradually, the streetscape changed, and the people thinned as the road took on a different feel. An occasional dead rat dirtied the road, and garbage was scattered in alleys. The streets were lined with filth, mud, and sewage, and other foulness that filled his nostrils. The eastern Srithan section of Chrysia, once vibrant, had been dirty and rundown as long as Jakob had lived in the city.

The sounds here were different, too, and his step quickened as he passed a brothel. He imagined footsteps behind him, but turning quickly revealed only small children playing in the dirty alleys. He quickened his pace, trying to ignore the uneasiness that threatened to intrude on his thoughts. Unfamiliar echoes came again, behind him, and his heart lurched faster than his footsteps. Another glance back, and again there was no one. He could no longer ignore the feelings he had and found himself nearly running. The strange sounds continued, almost chasing him, and he ran with fear creeping through him.

The road twisted as it worked its way down a hill. He hurried along it, watching the sun fall lower in the afternoon sky, turning the horizon into an orange and pink canvas. In the distance, he finally saw the small square santrium. The echoes of footsteps chasing him had faded as he left Srithan, but he hadn't slowed until he was nearly breathless. Nearing the santrium, he could still see how the once clean, white stones were streaked with stains. Little announced it as the santrium, a house of healing for men and women sick with the madness, other than the thick bars crossing the windows.

He reached the small walkway, weeds and grasses working their way through the stone, and made his way up to the narrow wooden doors. They were once a vibrant blue, but the paint had long since faded and now peeled, exposing the pale pindlewood beneath. Long ago, the building had been well maintained, but it had been many years since the santrium had seen such care.

The door still opened easily, and as he walked into the small entry hall, the low-hanging ceiling always made him hunch. The wooden floor creaked under his feet, and he paused, letting his eyes adjust to the thin light inside. His heart was only now slowing. There was a strange odor in the air, stool and urine he guessed, and it grew stronger as he stood adjusting.

"Who do you seek?" a nasal voice asked behind him.

He turned to find a plump man, long graying hair slicked back and a thick beard to match. His heavy brown burlap robe identified him as one of the Urmahne healers, and Jakob let out his breath. "Scottan Nialsen, sir."

The man nodded and started off without saying another word. He led Jakob down the short entry hall and back through the building, turning several times as they passed a number of rooms. Jakob had been to the santrium many times but didn't think he could have found the room on his own. He had once wondered who the inside of the building confused more, the tenants or the visitors.

Finally, the man stopped him in front of a door that opened as they neared. A short man, dressed in a brown robe that matched his guide's, came out, his brow wet and his face tight. Seeing Jakob, he offered a thin smile.

"Is he..." Jakob was unable to finish the question. He looked at the healer and turned to his guide, realizing that the man had already started away.

The healer shook his head and ran a thick hand through greasy hair. "No better, I am afraid. I do not think he is any worse, either."

Jakob shifted himself so that he could see through the small window in the door, thick bars of black iron filtering his view. Scottan lay motionless on the narrow bed, no sheets covering him and his body unclothed. He'd been told that none in the santrium were allowed anything they could use to hurt themselves. Scottan's once-muscular body was wasting, a starving man.

He turned to look at the healer. "What does he do?" His voice was hoarse. His eyes welled with tears, filled with sadness for his brother he couldn't help. It was like this each time he visited and part of the reason he visited so infrequently.

The healer shook his head again slightly. The movement gave life to the man's extra chins, and they jiggled with life his eyes did not convey. "He does not eat, and he barely sleeps. When he does, he talks, using words he creates. He seems to see others in his room and speaks to them. Sometimes, we understand, mostly we do not."

Jakob shivered. Scottan had been like this for over a year. It had started slowly, first visions others didn't share, then the babbling and the strange words. Progressing quickly, his captain had sought help after finding him talking to himself one morning, speaking words none could understand. His father had helped find him a place in the santrium; his connections with the church getting the care Scottan needed. Little had helped.

"Does he still scream out?" The screams had started later after he had given up talking to himself. It was the way of the madness.

A shrug from the healer, his thick shoulders barely rising. "Sometimes," he answered, unconcerned.

"Will he ever..." Jakob already knew the answer.

"None have ever improved, but the gods may choose to spare him," the fat healer spoke, his deep voice almost soothing if not for the message it conveyed. "I cannot predict."

"May I go in?" He hadn't been able to sit next to Scottan at his last visit. His brother had been too agitated then, and they were trying to get him to keep down a mixture of herbs to calm him.

A nod and the healer opened the door. Jakob slipped in and stepped over to where Scottan lay on the low bed. His brother's golden hair, so much like their mother's, was long and disheveled, and it had been many days since he'd been shaved. He knelt beside the bed, trying to avoid the many stains on the wooden floor, and reached for Scottan's hand.

"Scottan," he spoke softly. "Scottan, it's Jakob."

His brother didn't move, but he opened his eyes and stared at the low ceiling.

How to talk to him? He was never sure how to treat Scottan, always choosing to talk as if he understood.

"The Denraen have come with Magi." Jakob stopped, not knowing what else to say. "And it's nearly the Turning."

Scottan screamed. It was ear-splitting, and the suddenness of it made Jakob drop his brother's hand. He stopped as abruptly as he had started, and Jakob quickly grabbed his hand and patted, trying to soothe him. Scottan began mumbling, and his breaths came quick and ragged. Jakob couldn't understand what he said, and he wondered if this was what the fat healer meant by created words. The scream caused Jakob's head to throb again, slow pounding at the back of his skull. Focusing on his brother, he ignored it.

Jakob knelt there for long moments, patting his brother's hand, trying to calm him, while Scottan mumbled the unintelligible words. Jakob raised his free hand to massage his temple. It didn't help his head, and it ached deeper, almost buzzing with pain. He decided to leave before he needed the healers' help as well.

Standing, he dusted himself off and leaned down to kiss his brother on the forehead. Scottan stopped mumbling and closed his eyes. Jakob sighed and turned toward the door. As he did, Scottan caught his arm with a grip reminiscent of his old strength.

"Jakob!" He sat up suddenly, and his eyes opened wide. "*Detu finri et neamiin!*" The words hung in the air, almost a meaning to them, before Scottan relaxed his grip, sinking back to the bed, and his eyes closed once more.

Jakob smoothed his brother's hair. Scottan had known him. There was that much, at least. A knock on the door before it opened startled him from his thoughts, and he turned to see the fat healer opening the door.

"We must let him rest now."

Jakob looked back once more at his brother who lay sleeping, his breathing now regular. Turning away, he followed the fat healer as he led him away from the room and back out of the santrium. The healer left him at the door without a word.

He stepped from the once-blue doors into the fading light of the afternoon. Pausing only once to look back as he crested the hill, he prayed silently to the nameless gods for his brother as he had many times in the past. It was the only time he now prayed. Maybe his lack of faith was the reason the gods hadn't healed Scottan.

Starting back again, he hurried through the city to the palace grounds. He felt a general unease as he moved through Srithan and was relieved when he neared the palace gate.

A sudden shout caused him to tense.

As he turned, Braden jogged toward him, his muscular form highlighted by his tight-fitting breeches and tunic, yelling his name. "Where were you coming from?"

Jakob sighed, breathing deeply to slow his heart. He nodded down the street, toward the eastern part of the city. "The santrium. Scottan. Novan has kept me in the dark regarding the Magi. I haven't seen you, either. Is the guard busy?"

"More than usual. Raids have increased."

"Have you been on patrol?"

"Some. And the Denraen train with us. I'm allowed to work with them. No one knows when they will hold the Choosing." He paused, a slow grin coming to his face. "I'll be ready for tomorrow, though. The Ur gave me time away."

Jakob groaned, thinking of what he'd have to do to keep Braden in check during the festival. "I haven't found new clothes for it."

"Me, neither, but it doesn't matter! Don't be surprised when I'm at your door early."

Tired or not, Braden would be at his door at nearly first light; his friend didn't take festivals lightly. Braden looked up at the sky, seeming to note the fading sun. "I need to hurry. Make sure you're ready for the Mancleys!"

Braden hurried away from him and toward Srithan, and Jakob wondered how much longer their friendship would sustain. Braden continued to rise within the Ur, and Jakob... he didn't know what he would end up doing. He served Novan for now, but how much longer would that last?

CHAPTER FIVE

The night was cool, and a light breeze pulled at his cloak, his hair, at everything. The weather was quite different from yesterday, and it seemed autumn was finally arriving. Jakob shivered and pulled his cloak more tightly around him. Next to him, Braden seemed not to notice. His brightly colored festival clothes went uncovered, the reds, greens, and oranges muted in the waning light. Braden was not the only one dressed brightly, people all along the busy streets wore their own decorative clothes, some more elaborate than others. Jakob let his remain hidden beneath his cloak, sacrificing a festive appearance for warmth.

"Come, Jakob, I can smell it," Braden urged, hurrying his steps.

Jakob sniffed and followed after, trying not to lose his friend. There were many smells in the air tonight. The Turning Festival brought the scent of savory meats steaming in the night air mixed with the sweet smell of choco and humay and fresh bread. The candies were traditional for the festival, and all who made such things sold them along the streets, each with different shapes and textures, but all tasted sweet. A haze of smoke surrounded nearly everything as the night was bright from a hundred cook fires and lanterns. Another scent caught his nose, faint, but more pungent, and he wondered briefly what it was, but forgot about it as he hurried to keep up with Braden.

Tinkling bells and conversation surrounded them as they walked, a flurry of noise that made conversation with Braden nearly impossible. All around them were other sounds, as well, storymen telling tales new and old, their voices rising and falling with the excitement of each scene, and musicians playing filuit and harp and guitran.

They worked their way through the busy street, avoiding people crowded around the minstrels, jugglers, and dancers, and tried to stay clear of the hawkers selling the meats and candy. The smells were tempting, but the cost was high. In the distance, the noise grew louder, if possible, as they neared the square. It was the heart of the festival and where Braden led him each year.

A man moving toward them caught his attention. Dressed differently from all others in the crowd, he wore a deep black cloak with the hood pulled over his head. Eyes could almost be imagined underneath the hood, catching the light from dozens of fires and gleaming with the reflection. As Jakob stared, those eyes seemed to catch him and held him, the gaze iron-hard.

He shivered and clutched his cloak more tightly around him again but still felt the rise of goose pimples on his arms. His mouth went dry, and he tried to move his tongue to wet his suddenly parched lips, but could not.

The sounds around him faded, and the smoky haze thickened. His head suddenly throbbed with a strange slow pulsation, deep drumming echoing through his mind. Jakob felt pulled to the man by his gaze and tried to look away but found that he could not. He shivered again and wondered if this man was a Mage.

Fear welled up within him, unbidden, and with it was a deep hopelessness. He had never known such emptiness, and it was overwhelming. The sense of worthlessness, a feeling of uselessness, overcame him, and he nearly staggered. Darkness began to surround him, black darker than night crowding in from his periphery, and something pulled at him, a compulsion pulling him toward the hooded man. The night faded so that all he saw was the flickering light of the man's eyes, and Jakob went forward, pulled as if on a rope.

"Jakob!"

He heard his name distantly, and a hand caught his sleeve, turning him around. He shook his head, and the heaviness slowly lifted. Braden smiled at him, laughing.

"Are you leaving me?" Braden asked, a wide grin spreading across his face.

Jakob laughed dryly, trying to match his friend's smile. He glanced back, but the man was gone. A shiver passed through him as he thought about him. The emptiness he'd felt was slowly filling, and he forced happier thoughts back into his mind; it was the Turning Festival. It was a night to celebrate, to eat and dance with friends and strangers, to celebrate the harvest and the bounty the gods provided.

Turning back to Braden, preparing to ask his friend if he had felt the surge of strange emotions, too, he realized another person stood with them. "Jessila," he acknowledged, smiling at her.

"Jakob." Her thick black hair fell in waves down her shoulders, and her face seemed a pale white in the night. Lips were full and wine red as she smiled, looking back to Braden. A bright yellow and red dress fell to her ankles, accentuating her figure. She smelled of lilacs, and Jakob saw several dried leaves arranged in her hair.

"I was asking Jessila where her sister was while you were trying to wander off," Braden told him, nudging him in the ribs.

"She's somewhere," Jessila answered demurely. Her soft voice was barely audible, and Braden had leaned close to listen. Jessila seemed not to mind. "I saw you and Jakob, and with all the people, I worried I wouldn't find you again. How about a dance?"

Braden looked over at him. "May we?"

"First, you worry I'm leaving you, and now, you're leaving me!" The hollow feeling was nothing but a memory now, the happiness of the sounds and smells of the festival overtaking him. The beats and musical sounds around him swept him up, lifting his mood once again.

Braden laughed and grabbed Jessila's hand. "My lady," he started, bowing slightly. The gesture brought color to her cheeks and she smiled. "Would you care to dance with me?" She nodded quickly, and they started off. "I'll find you in the square. Near the Cindernut Tavern," he called over his shoulder before hurrying off with Jessila.

Jakob watched them disappear, smiling at his friend and his fortune before starting forward on his own. He wound his way through the crowd after losing sight of Braden, occasionally pausing to listen to the minstrels and enjoy the songs. He moved slowly forward with the flow of the people before stopping to listen to a storyman.

"A tale from east of the valley!" the storyman bellowed, his voice carrying. "Jarren Gildeun was barely twenty summers old when he made his first journey!"

"No one has ever been east of the valley," a voice called from the crowd. The man laughed as he said it, and others joined him, but it didn't deter the storyman.

"Jarren Gildeun was barely twenty when he made his first journey," the storyman repeated. "A journey unlike any other he had made, longer and more arduous!"

Jakob slid forward, curious to hear. He always enjoyed stories of Jarren Gildeun, real or not. He was the hero of many stories, and Jakob had once tried to read as many as possible. There had been a time when he couldn't get enough of those stories. When he was younger, he had even wanted to *be* Jarren, though Scottan had been more like the man. Well... maybe a part of him still wanted that.

"Barely twenty, but already he had done much," the storyman continued, catching Jakob's attention again. "He had journeyed across the south, through the Blasted Land and its plains of sand, and back. He had traveled the oceans and climbed the mountains, seeking and finding the hidden city."

Jakob smiled as stories from his youth came back, the tales of Jarren's feats. His favorite had always been the time Jarren had gone to Vasha and they had made him a Mage.

He stood on his toes, straining to see the storyman but could barely make him out. He was a short man, and though standing atop a crate, barely rose higher than most who listened. His hands were constantly moving as he talked, and his voice hushed as he spoke, only to rise again suddenly.

"The valley is not crossed easily, and Jarren knew it would be his greatest journey yet. He hired a ship, thinking to sail south and east, his travels to the Paglait Islands teaching him the perils of those waters so that he felt comfortable sailing them alone."

Jakob remembered the tale of Jarren and the Paglait pygmies, and wondered if the storyman would tell more of it. Jarren was said to be the last man to have seen the Paglait people, and he hadn't heard that story in a long time.

"East of Salvat he sailed, landing twice and twice finding nothing but marsh and swamp. Each time he set off into the marshland, hoping to find dry land, but days of travel revealed only more of the same. He sailed further east, past the marshlands, praying all the time to the gods to grant him swift wind and safe journey. Those prayers were answered, yet others were not."

The storyman took a moment to push his tall hat down onto his head before he composed himself and went on. "Beyond, he found sheer rock rising high above the water, mountain peaks touching the clouds, and he knew he must sail further. Sail further he did, sailing along the mountainous shores, unable to find mooring and unwilling to turn back."

The storyman paused, and all who listened fell silent. Jakob wondered if the naysayer still listened or if he had wandered off to another part of the festival.

"He sailed ever north, knowing in his heart of hearts that the mountains must end. He sailed and sailed, day after day, the wind and his spirits never failing. The water turned bitter cold, and he sailed onward, knowing in his heart of hearts the mountains must end. The water turned to ice, and he sailed onward, knowing in his heart of hearts the mountains must end. Finally, he could sail no further, the arctic north nearly catching him, yet still the mountains rose high into the clouds.

"He turned back, his heart heavy, but his spirit unbroken. He reached Salvat a starved man, his body wasted as he had not eaten in weeks. He had tried the water and failed. Still determined, he decided now that he would go north, through the mountains and east around the valley."

Jakob tensed as he listened, nervous for Jarren as always, but there was much of the story left. He looked toward the square, wondering how long to give Braden before interrupting his evening with Jessila, and decided they should have more time. Turning back to the storyman, his eyes caught on a figure standing in a nearby alley. There was something familiar about the shape, and he reluctantly moved away from the story to see who it was.

Nearing the alley, he recognized the old man from the practice yard. He wore a plain brown tunic and dark breeches, not dressed for the festival at all. Jakob would have been surprised to see him dressed for the festival, anyway, surprised he changed his clothing at all. The man had beaten him easily this afternoon, though he felt it had gone better and had shown him several different catahs. Jakob still did not know his name but no longer cared. The man didn't seem to mind his presence and actually seemed to enjoy teaching him.

Smiling, he started to call out a greeting to the man but stopped as another figure entered the alley mouth. Thin and tall, the person moved quickly toward the old man.

"A strange place to request a meeting," the old man said.

"I'm pleased you received the message."

The old man seemed to frown. "Even if I wouldn't have, the Conclave asked me to meet."

"You are needed," a musical voice said, barely audible forcing Jakob to strain to hear. His head throbbed with the effort. "Much is at stake."

The old man nodded, a scar atop his white-haired head gleaming in the lamp-lit night. He said nothing.

"You must go north," the person said, hooded head bobbing as they spoke. He couldn't tell if it was a man or woman.

Jakob knew he shouldn't listen and turned back to the storyman. He could still hear his voice, telling now about Jarren Gildeun's own travel north, but something made him turn back and listen to the old man and his mysterious companion.

"I've been in the north many times," the old man answered.

Jakob moved behind a nearby choco stand, ignoring the inviting stares of the hawker begging him to try her sweets. He could smell the strong sweet aroma of the choco, though it mixed with another scent, one that reminded him of spring. It was almost the smell of flowers in bloom. Frowning, he pushed forward, and the smell of choco faded, though the other did not. Others around him were ignoring the people in the alley mouth, steering clear. He slid ahead a little, still straining to hear.

"In the far north, there is a town called Avaneam. You must go there."

The old man nodded again, considering. "I know most of the northern towns," he began. "I do not know Avaneam. Its name—"

"Means what you think," the other answered quickly. "It is a sacred place, one that must be entered carefully."

The old man smiled, though the expression did not reach the rest of his face. His eyes were a hard stare even from Jakob's distance. "How will I find it?"

"It is in the mountains, along the Elasiin path, not far from the Great Valley. You follow the path until it is no more. It will not be easy."

"I have heard the rumors."

The other shook his head slightly. "Not the raiders. This is something worse."

"I have heard the rumors," the man repeated.

"Of course you have. I should know not to doubt you." The other paused. "There is something you must deliver," the other said and handed the old man an object. Jakob decided it was a woman's voice, but she sounded nothing like anyone he'd ever heard. The object she handed over was covered in a thin sheet, hiding what looked a little like a small chest. "Protect this until it is delivered. Much would be lost with it. This is what he seeks, but he will not be able to open it."

The man took the package and nodded. "He's here?"

"He has ventured far from the south."

The old man chuckled. "He's not from the south."

"No. Once he was... It doesn't matter. It has been many years since that mattered. The priests have watched this for long enough. Now... now the others must keep it safe."

"Not open it?"

"Perhaps they will make that choice," she said.

The man didn't press the question. "Do you really think him that close?"

"I've learned not to underestimate him. If he captures me..."

"I understand." The old man glanced up and down the street, and Jakob shrank back. "Why can't you—"

"This cannot travel the way that I must travel, and there is a certain safety in your men."

The old man nodded, looking down at the package. "I'm uncertain I am the best for this task. I have other responsibilities—"

"Maintain whatever appearances you must. I can't overstate the importance of this."

The old man laughed softly. "You don't need to state it at all."

"You know, then, what this means?"

"I suspect."

"Then know I do not ask lightly."

"I know that as well. You wouldn't risk yourself coming here otherwise." The man sighed and closed his eyes briefly. "If this must be my burden, so be it," he said as he opened his eyes. There was steel to his face now.

"There is another."

The man frowned before he nodded, tilting his head expectantly.

"You have already begun to discover."

"Discover what?"

There came a soft laugh. "A key, one I thought broken. Perhaps... perhaps we are not so lost as I thought."

There was something about the voice that was familiar, though Jakob couldn't quite place it. Where had he heard it?

The old man frowned. "What is it?"

Jakob got jostled back and missed what was said next.

"You will understand in time. For now, this is enough."

The old man turned, and his gaze started to drift toward him. "How?" he started.

Jakob didn't wait to hear the answer. He hurried off, back toward the storyman and beyond, barely pausing to listen and not daring to look back. He thought about the travels of Jarren Gildeun in the north and now the old man, wondering who this other was and when the old man would leave, a feeling of disappointment hitting him. He would lose his new sword master.

Finally, he dared a look back but couldn't see either shape in the alley. He'd thought the old man once of the Ur but now questioned that. The conversation made him wonder if the man had ever been in the guard or if he was simply a man for hire.

He shrugged the thought off as he neared the square, figuring to ask the man about it the next time he worked with him—if there was a next time. Would the old man be gone the next time he went looking for him in the yard? He hadn't stayed around listening long enough to know how soon the other needed him to leave. He hoped to have a few more sessions with him.

The square was even more crowded than the other streets had been as if most of the city tried to squeeze into the city center. The sounds of the musicians and storymen were louder here than on the side streets and the crowds around them were even larger. The minstrels tended to be better and the storymen more compelling at the square. The bakers and meat carts pushed so close together here that they were nearly on top of one another, and the smells melded together so that nothing had its own scent. The fires were brighter here, and tall lanterns hung high over the street, lighting everything with their dancing flames. A larger fire burned brightly in the square center, the Festival Fire. Its flames leaped high above the crowds, and its warmth filled the square. Around the fire were the dancers, each dancing around bands of musicians. He wondered if Braden and Jessila were still dancing.

Slowly, he weaved his way around the square, shoving his way through as he tried to find the tavern. The Cindernut Tavern, the name itself a taunt to Jakob from when he'd once been harassed by the son of a city councilor, Braden often chose it as a place for them to meet. As he worked his way through the crowd, he could see the tavern's huge sign several buildings ahead. An image of an oversized cindernut, cracked to reveal the meat within, announced the tavern in a way the fading lettering around it did not.

Reaching the tavern, he found Braden standing outside, a mug in his hand. Jakob laughed to himself, not surprised that his friend had already started with the ale, and hurried over to him. "Where's Jessila? Did your dancing scare her off?"

Braden nodded over the crowd. "She went for her sister," he said with a wink.

Jakob groaned and shook his head. He often had to entertain sisters or friends of the ladies Braden danced with. Braden had pushed Marli Mancley on him a number of times lately, and he always felt cotton-mouthed around her.

"You gave us a long time. Did you forget how to find the tavern?" A taunting glimmer danced in his eyes.

Jakob looked up at the sign, grimacing, before shaking his head. "There was a storyman—"

Braden barked a knowing laugh. "The Festival Fire." Braden nodded, indicating the huge flames leaping at the heart of the square. "That's where we're to meet them. Jessila said that she wasn't finished with me!"

It was Jakob's turn to laugh as they began to work their way toward the fire. Jessila and Marli Mancley found them in the crowd and paused only long enough to pull them toward the fire. Seeing Marli, he wondered if he could use his aching head as an excuse to stop dancing. Braden looked back at him, shaking his head as if knowing his thoughts, and Jakob knew he had a long night before him.

CHAPTER SIX

"How was the festival?" Novan asked, thumbing through a thick book across the table from Jakob. It was a volume he had flipped through himself but had not really read, something else on the War of Confusion.

Jakob yawned. He had not been sleeping well. Every time he fell asleep, strange dreams met him. Last night, he'd dreamed of the man from the Turning Festival and the strange hollow sensation he had felt. In the dream, the man had seen him staring and reached for him. Jakob had resisted, afraid even in his dreams, and was pushed away by someone else. He hadn't seen the person, but whoever it was smelled of roses in bloom and had a voice like the woman he'd overheard speaking at the festival. After he had been pushed, he landed on a grassy hillside where golden eyes stared at him in the darkness, and he could feel a strangely reassuring presence nearby. Jakob had jerked awake after that and had been unable to sleep afterward.

The dreams had been coming more often, each night stranger. He worried what it meant. Scottan had visions before the madness took him. After that, his brother had never been the same. Was the same thing happening to him or were these just dreams?

He pushed the thoughts away, yawning again. "It was a typical

Turning Festival," he answered, and rubbed his eyes. He had danced a bit with Marli last night, enough to placate Braden, before excusing himself to wander the square. Braden had been preoccupied and had not resisted much.

"You're tired."

"I didn't sleep well."

Novan cocked his head at the comment and arched an eyebrow. "What did you see?"

Even the mundane required a report, he thought with a sigh. Novan considered it part of his training. So he began, telling him of leaving the library for the city gates, the meeting Braden, and wandering past the sweet carts. Jakob could recall the sweet smells easily and smiled at the memory of a choco treat he'd purchased later in the evening.

He debated whether to tell him about the strange man but finally decided Novan would want to know. "There was something strange next. A man came toward me, dressed all in black, with his hood pulled forward," he started. Remaining hooded during the festival was uncommon, but not typically something to comment on. "Something about how he looked at me, the feeling I had with it..." He shivered as he remembered.

"Tell me what you remember," Novan encouraged.

"I remember little," Jakob answered honestly. Novan frowned, but he continued. "I feel as if my mind was clouded. His gaze was intense. Heavy." Novan arched an eyebrow at the last. "I felt fear, hopelessness, and then it was gone." He looked up to Novan, shrugging. "I know you've taught me better, but it's all I can recall. I'm sorry."

Novan exhaled slowly in a deep sigh, spreading his hands out before him. "You have done fine, better than many who catch that man's gaze, in fact." Novan paused for a long moment, and Jakob looked at the historian's thin face, wondering if he would continue. "He is the High Priest of Deshmahne. Few realize he visited last night. You did well in sensing him."

There was a slight strain in his voice as he spoke, an edge to it that Jakob had never heard from the historian. Concern? "Why? Is it true they have abilities like the Magi?" Few heard of the Deshmahne without hearing about the power of their priests.

"Not like the Magi," Novan answered. "Different, though powerful in other ways. They are not born with their powers like the Magi. They are learned, and in some cases, borrowed."

Jakob waited for Novan to elaborate, but he did not. Something the old man had said came back to him. "What do you mean that I did well to sense him?"

"Some are sensitive to them," he said, then quickly added, "I cannot explain why," anticipating Jakob's question. "I suspect you were somehow sensitized by your father. The priests of Urmahne have learned to sense a Deshmahne priest. It is how I learned the High Priest had come to the city."

"Where did he come from?" Jakob asked. At least he need not worry about reporting to his father. The Urmahne knew.

Novan arched his eyebrow. "That's the real question," he said. "Little is known about the High Priest other than rumor. The Deshmahne were once thought a cult, something to be dismissed. Little more than barbarians blaspheming the Urmahne. Yet they gained influence. With influence came credibility and something more." He sat in silence, collecting his thoughts. "Doubt. What if following the teachings of the Urmahne isn't the path to the gods? Could the Deshmahne speak the truth? These questions went unanswered."

"How did the Deshmahne gain influence?" Jakob had read little of the Deshmahne, and the one time he had asked his father, he had been sent away.

"Many a king now listen to the Deshmahne," Novan said. "There was a time when they listened to the Magi, but that is no longer. The Deshmahne claim power from the gods. There are some who would call this a virtue." Novan paused. "Claims of power would have been enough, but the High Priest has demonstrated it to these men. They listen when he speaks."

"Did the High Priest come here to convert Chrysia?" Jakob asked.

Novan shook his head. "That's not something he would need to be present for. I fear this is something else, something worse. He's searching for something."

Jakob frowned, thinking of what he'd overheard. Could that be what the woman had been speaking about to the old man?

~

Looking out over the practice yard, the grass now dry and brown and bare in places where men had trampled out its life, Jakob worried. Was he too early for the old man, or was he late? He'd found the old man in the practice yard at the same time each day, but the overheard conversation from last night left him with questions.

Jakob had begun to look forward to his time in the yard and the lessons. Now he wondered if he had seen the last of his instructor.

He walked over to the covered rack of wooden swords and grabbed one, hefting its weight and ignoring the ache in his arm and his head. The sensation was familiar now, ever since the attack upon the Ur, but other than a mild discomfort, it didn't seem to affect him or slow him. Moving to a now-familiar place on the lawn, he crouched into his starting stance before swinging the sword through the catahs he knew, methodically moving from one to the next, always thinking of their defense as the old man had taught him.

He smiled to himself as he moved, knowing that he was more fluid now than he had been and remembering how jerky and cumbersome the movements had first seemed. He could tell an improvement, if only slight, and was pleased because it had only been a few weeks. It was something he knew Braden would understand; strangely, he had not yet told Braden of his time spent in the practice yard.

Moving through the catahs again, he changed them this time, trying to anticipate a defense and counter it before swinging in an imaginary attack again. He felt a drop of sweat work its way down his brow as his breaths began to grow heavier. His head began to ache, buzzing almost, as he worked. His sword work may have improved slightly, but his conditioning left much to be desired.

Finally, he stopped and looked around the yard and realized that it was still empty. He decided that the old man wasn't going to come today and walked back to the rack when he heard the old man's voice from behind him.

"Giving up on me, boy?" the old man asked, his voice rough and the accent still untraceable.

Jakob spun quickly, surprised, confident that no one had been in the yard only moments before. The old man stood casually before him, his dirtied shirt slung over his shoulder, baring his scarred and tattooed chest. The pale scars looked grislier in the overcast light, and Jakob looked up quickly so as not to stare. The old man seemed unperturbed.

"I wasn't sure if you were coming," he answered.

The old man looked at him strangely for a long moment before answering. "You're early." It was all he said, but Jakob felt as if there was a question left unasked.

He looked back toward the library, unsure how to answer, as the old man slid past him to grab a wooden sword. "Today is three-one," the man explained, moving into their usual places and tossing his dirty shirt to the ground.

Jakob moved to stand next to him, readying his stance and watched as the old man demonstrated the movements of the catah. Knowing that he would next be expected to replicate them, Jakob tried to concentrate in spite of the tired buzzing in his head.

The old man finished the movement, and Jakob followed, working cautiously through the unfamiliar stances, swinging his sword deliberately as he struggled to remember what he had seen. Each day, it was the same, but each day, he forced himself to remember the new movements as he was shown more.

"Good," the old man offered. "Now the defense."

Jakob was expected to offer the attack, moving through the catah as the old man demonstrated how to fend off the advance. The second time through the catah was always easier, and he began to feel how the sword was meant to move—the flow to the movement, in spite of meeting the resistance the old man offered. Finishing the catah, the defense was always shown twice, giving him the opportunity to again work on his attack, and he moved quickly through the motions one more time, his wooden sword moving faster now and the smack of wood on wood more rapid.

As he finished, Jakob moved into the defense. He always struggled with the defense, finding that the old man could move too quickly for him, and he was always trying to hurry to catch the next swing of the wooden blade, but feeling as if he was just a hair too slow. It was how he acquired his bruises each day.

Jakob stepped into the ready stance and waited for the old man to follow. The old man readied himself and began his attack quickly, his own sword a blur as he worked through the movements that Jakob had only just learned. Jakob struggled with his focus. He needed to follow the movements to know how to counter, but he fumbled as the sound of footsteps running toward them caught his attention.

He felt a hard sting as the old man's wooden sword caught his left arm, and he dropped his sword. Ignoring it, he looked to see who had come even as he heard the old man tell him, "You must never lose your focus." His voice was stern, not menacing. "You can shift your focus, but never lose it."

Jakob nodded, mumbling an apology, before looking again to see who had run up. A young soldier, his face stained with fine blond stubble, stood panting. The boy wasn't someone he knew.

"General," the boy gasped, his voice high and breathy, "I was sent for you. You're needed."

The old man nodded and returned his sword to the rack, patting Jakob lightly on his injured arm.

Jakob looked down at his dropped sword before the boy's words sank in.

General?

The Ur didn't have anyone ranking above captain in Chrysia. The general was in the capital of Thealon.

That only left the Denraen.

A memory came to him then, a memory of the Denraen and their arrival. They had said something about the general to Novan.

He groaned as he muttered, "General?"

The old man's scars and his sword skill suddenly took on a

different light. The old man smiled at him as he walked back over his way.

Jakob forced himself to meet the man's gaze. "I've been wasting your time," he said. "I'm sorry." Though he knew he should, he still didn't feel remorse; the old man had taught him much.

The general laughed, the first time Jakob had heard the sound from him. "Time is never wasted teaching those who truly wish to learn," he told him. He started off, the young guardsman in tow, before looking back. "Tomorrow, we'll continue," he said in a somewhat demanding tone.

Jakob could do nothing more than nod as he watched the old man walk away, dozens of questions suddenly springing to mind.

∼

Sitting in the library, Jakob's mind wandered, and he let it, watching the shadows shift through the small window, seeing the afternoon passing and realizing that he was expected back in the yard to face the old man. *The general*, he forced himself to think.

His thoughts jumped to all the things he had ever said to the man, all the things he had left unsaid. Could he have discovered his identity sooner had he asked the man's name? Had he seemed more than foolish, a simpleton seeking knowledge of something he should not?

He had hoped Braden would offer some help, at least share a laugh and make him feel better about the whole thing, but his friend had not been at the barracks last night. Jakob wasn't sure *what* he would have told Braden anyway. *Or if I would have told him anything*, he realized. How to explain his foolishness?

He remembered the first time he had seen the old man without his shirt, the sight of the ugly scar crossing his chest, the strange tattoo, and had wondered how he'd acquired such a scar and survived. The Magi, he now knew. Theirs was a healing different from that used by other healers. There were no flowers or elixirs or aromas to their healing.

Jakob could recall each scar upon the man and wondered now about them. The story of each would be worth listening. Like those about Jarren Gildeun, there had been stories of the Denraen when he was growing up, and he knew the general of the Denraen would have his share.

Other questions came to him. Why had the general been there that night at the festival? Who had he been speaking with... and why had he been asked to carry something north? Wasn't his responsibility to the Magi?

Sitting there, he hadn't heard Novan come in, nor heard him approach. A hand on his shoulder made him sit up suddenly, and as he did, the ache in his head became a steady throb. It started pounding as Novan squeezed before letting go, and the pounding quickened to nearly a buzz. He rubbed at his temple, frowning, and stood to let Novan sit.

Novan looked down at the table, considering the book that lay open, before looking up and considering Jakob. He still struggled through the thin text the historian had given him, the ancient language proving difficult to decipher, and he had not come upon anything that helped him understand his sword any better.

Jakob worked his temple, hoping to ease the pain buzzing within.

"Something is bothering you." Novan's airy voice sounded concerned.

Jakob sighed, his gaze fixed on the table in front of him, a flush coming to his cheeks. "I've been a fool without knowing, and my folly has recently been shown to me."

Novan stared at him curiously, his eyes almost a deep yellow today, the color seeming to shift each day, varying shades of gold and yellows, before shaking his head. "I'm afraid you'll have to offer me more than that."

"In the practice yard, each afternoon, I have been—"

"You work with Endric." He shrugged. "There's no folly there if he will have you."

"With the general?" Jakob asked. He should have known that Novan would know how he spent his afternoons. He was as well informed as the priests.

Novan smiled at him broadly, his teeth glittering in the soft glow of the lamps. "I have known Endric, and he teaches whom he chooses. You were willing. It was enough for him."

Jakob was sure he stared at Novan strangely before answering. "How long have you known?"

"Since the first," he answered simply.

"He must think it foolish for one like me to try and learn from him, the leader of the Denraen!" His head now ached for a different reason.

Novan stood and brought an arm around him, guiding him toward the stairs. "It's no folly teaching those who truly wish to learn," Novan informed.

The words echoed those he'd heard from the general, and he relaxed somewhat.

"Do not let it bother you," Novan said, dismissing his concern. "At least, don't let it bother you now. I need you to come with me. There's someplace we must be." He started toward the library door. Jakob had little choice but to follow.

"Where are we going?"

"I've discovered why the Magi came to the city. Today, there is going to be a choosing of a delegate. I would like to be there for this, and perhaps offer my suggestions."

They strode quickly from the library and out onto the palace grounds. The sky overhead was cloudy, and there was a smell of rain and decay in the air. It reminded Jakob of the day of the raider attack. Novan kept a brisk pace, his long legs leading them to the palace, and Jakob hurried to keep up. Their path took them toward the temple where the Magi roomed while staying in Chrysia.

Jakob looked over at the tall, circular building; it was hard to miss its tower rising into the sky. A replica of the true Tower, and a visible reminder of the nameless gods, the temple loomed over everything in the city, as it did all of Thealon. Nothing taller was allowed to be built. The palace had been set near the temple. It was oft wondered if it was for better guidance of the Council or so the priests could keep a closer watch.

Strangely, the doors to the temple were closed. Rather than inviting believers inside to share prayer and meditation, they were shuttered. Jakob wondered if they were closed because of the Magi presence, though they had been left open in the prior days. They kept walking, as if toward the palace.

Nearing the palace doors, a boom erupted from behind them.

Jakob spun in time to see an explosion rock the eastern wall of the temple. Stone shook and crumbled in a thunderous crash, dust and debris flying across the lawn as a massive fire spewed forth smoke and ash. An acrid scent hung in the air, and several smaller explosions shook the temple again.

Everyone was frozen, unmoving in shock, but slowly, the dust settled, and a gust of wind swept the smoke away. The temple doors burst open and priests streamed out, many covering their faces, and most coughing.

Father?

The thought hit him as he watched the priests come forth. He started forward, but a strong hand on his shoulder restrained him. Jakob looked back to see Novan holding him.

"It's not safe, Jakob." Concern was etched in the soft features of his face and the tight squint of his eyes.

"My father," he cried, coughing as he struggled to speak. Smoke was coming out of the temple in huge plumes now, and the palace yard was heavy with it.

"I know," Novan said. "We must wait to see him come out."

There was logic in what he said, but Jakob's mind wasn't thinking logically. He had lost his mother and his brother. Would the gods now take his father from him too?

As if in answer, another massive explosion suddenly rocked the temple, making the earth shake with its force. The top of the tower fell forward with a thunderous crack, raining down huge stones and chunks of rock as the upper floors of the temple fell in a loud groan of snapping stone. Dust billowed up from the ground before slowly settling, and by that time, smoke streamed out from the open doors and windows.

The priests nearest the doors screamed as they were thrown forward onto the lawn or crushed beneath fall rock. A wave of heat ballooned outward and forced Jakob back a step. He brought an arm to his face as a shield while his eyes watered and his nose clogged with smoke and ash. His ears rang slightly, and everything had a muffled quality to it.

He felt Novan pulling him backward, away from the temple, away from his father. Jakob struggled, but the historian was stronger than he looked and easily pulled Jakob toward the palace. He kicked, trying to break free to run to his father, but could not.

"What is this, historian?"

The voice was strange, a slight lilting quality to the words, and Jakob squinted against tears and smoke to see. A Mage stood before them, his dark robe hanging around him and his bearded face annoyed. Jakob had never seen one of the Magi before, and his watering eyes and racing heart made it difficult to appreciate him.

Novan released him, and Jakob staggered forward before catching himself. The historian turned toward the Mage. "An explosion, Haerlin," Novan said. "The temple."

The Mage looked at Novan, his slightly arched eyebrows raised in a curious expression and his dark hair fluttering in the slight breeze blowing through the yard. Mage Haerlin reached a hand up and scratched his nose before smoothing his dark robe. "An accident?"

Novan snorted. "I think not. What is there to explode in the temple?"

"You think this planned?"

Novan nodded.

"To what end?"

"Perhaps none, perhaps it was only an accident," he started. "Yet an explosion in the Urmahne temple only days after the Deshmahne priest was seen. I believe you are staying within the temple?" Novan didn't pause to see the Mage's nod in response. "I think it more than coincidental."

"The Deshmahne was not seen," Haerlin objected.

"Only sensed?" Novan asked. The Mage raised his eyebrows with the question. "This one saw him." Novan motioned toward Jakob.

"Him?" the Mage asked, eyes flashing to Jakob before returning to Novan. "The High Priest was here?"

Novan nodded.

The Mage turned his full attention to Jakob. Jakob could feel the weight of his gaze and couldn't turn away. It felt as though his mind was being rifled through, as if his soul was bared, and he blinked, suddenly dizzy. His head pounded, and there was a brief sensation of movement as he felt himself falling. A hand tried to catch him, but it was not enough, and he sank to the ground as darkness took him.

Why?

The question was screamed within his mind but went unanswered. Why would the gods do this to his family again?

A thought struck him as he passed out, a memory. It was his father's voice, and it spoke into his mind, almost mocking him. "There are always answers," he had said. "They just may not be to the questions you thought you were asking."

With that, Jakob faded into darkness.

CHAPTER SEVEN

Roelle stood in the debris from the explosion. The destruction of the temple had happened rapidly. Had she not been working with Endric and the other Denraen soldiers, she might've been within the temple as well.

"They intended for us to be caught in the explosion," Haerlin said, studying the rubble.

Dust hung suspended in the air and didn't seem as if it would settle. It created a haze, a blackish fog that drifted, mixing with a bitter sort of stink, something that she'd never smelled before, but there was a familiarity to it.

Roelle used her Mage ability, pulling on the motes of dust from the air, drawing on the power the Magi referred to as *manehlin*. Haerlin glanced over at her, his mouth pinched in a frown, but she ignored it. He should have been the one to remove the dust so the priests could better see where others had fallen.

"They wouldn't be attacking the Magi directly, would they?" Roelle asked.

"You saw what happened on the road to the city. They failed then, but they nearly succeeded this time." Haerlin's eyes seem to take in the line of priests making their way out of the remains of the temple, visible now that Roelle had settled the fog.

So many were lost. Roelle didn't count the bodies, heartbroken that so many could die so quickly. And for what? If this *was* the Deshmahne, what had they proven? The Deshmahne claimed to have power to reach the gods, but that wasn't what the Magi knew to be true. What did so much killing accomplish?

She forced herself to watch as broken and bloodied bodies were pulled free. How many people had lost those they cared about? How many faithful to the Urmahne had now fallen?

The answer came easily, as did the anger that accompanied it. Too many. "If there is any question about our purpose here, this should solve it."

Haerlin shook his head. "No. If this does anything, it makes me wonder if perhaps your uncle was right."

Haerlin had mentioned that before, but what *had* her uncle suggested? What was there that the Magi knew that might be able to defeat something like this? If the Deshmahne were willing to attack like this, what prevented them from taking such violence further? What prevented them from reaching their city?

Roelle knew the answer. Nothing prevented them. That was the plan. The Deshmahne spread fear and discord wherever they went. They claimed violence as a means to knowing and understanding the gods. And they backed that up through their actions. How many more would suffer and die because of the Deshmahne's desire for power? How many more would suffer and die because of their forced conversions along the way?

"This tells me that we must choose soon," Haerlin told her as he turned away from the fallen remains of the temple. "Then we can return to the city. We can work with these delegates, and see if there's anything that can be done."

"Why do I get the feeling you're unconvinced?" Roelle asked.

Haerlin shook his head. "When the Council first instructed us to find these delegates, I thought I saw something that would allow them to succeed. Now... Now I am no longer certain."

Roelle watched him as he started away, worry creeping through her. Hearing such thoughts from anyone else, she wouldn't feel quite so unsettled. But Haerlin was one of the minor prophets. He was the first one gifted with the ability in many years. When he saw things, it meant something.

What had Haerlin seen?

And worse... what had changed?

~

Jakob awoke with his head thundering. He recognized his room as he looked around, but a soft light filtering in through the curtain flared the pain in his head. Novan sat upon the plainly made chair near his bed, completely engrossed in a book.

Jakob cleared his throat, and the historian looked up. He wore an expression that Jakob had never seen before. "What happened?"

The historian shook his head, his pale eyes more sunken today than usual and the glimmer to them duller than usual. "I'm not sure. You fainted. Perhaps it was the explosion, or the smoke. I don't know."

Jakob frowned. He didn't think that was it, remembering a strange sensation as he had passed out and the Mage who seemed to be causing it. He didn't linger on the thought as another came to him. The explosion.

"My father?"

Novan walked to where Jakob lay on his bed and knelt beside him, gripping his arm more forcefully than necessary. He cleared his throat before he started. "Jakob," he said and sighed. "I'm sorry, but he did not make it out. Many did not."

Jakob pushed himself up as Novan kept a restraining hand upon him. "What do you mean?" Tears already began to well in his eyes. He knew what Novan meant, had somehow known as he watched the temple crumble. His head hurt with a different pain, one that constricted his throat and threatened his breathing.

The gods had taken everything from him.

"He's gone. He was helping a priest trapped beneath a fallen timber when the second explosion came."

Jakob fell back down on his bed and let the tears come. Novan tried giving him a reassuring squeeze on his arm, but it did nothing to reassure him. "Gone?" he repeated weakly.

Everyone is gone, he realized.

His mother first. Scottan to the madness. And now his father.

He was alone.

Taken. His entire family now taken from him.

"I'm truly sorry," Novan said.

Jakob didn't look up to meet the historian's eyes. He didn't think he could do it without crying, screaming, or worse. Novan remained silent, his hand still resting on Jakob. It was cool through the fabric of his shirt, and he didn't try to shrug it off.

What had he done to deserve this? Why had the gods taken everything from him?

"The priests will hold a ceremony for their fallen brethren," Novan said finally. "It is to be tomorrow."

Jakob nodded, numb and unable to say anything.

"I will not be able to attend."

Jakob looked up then, a slow stream of tears starting to roll down his face. He quickly wiped them away. Why wouldn't Novan attend the ceremony for the priests? Novan had always been friendly with the priests—it was why he was allowed as much freedom as he was—so it seemed strange that he would choose not to attend.

"Why?"

Novan let go of his arm and stood. The historian was tall, and the long robes he wore only served to make him appear taller. There was a stoop to his back today that wasn't there before, a weight upon him that Jakob only guessed at. "The Magi will leave tomorrow. After the attack, they decided to choose quickly. It was to have been a priest," he said, "but their first choice perished in the blast as well. They've chosen another and will be returning to their city. I'm going to observe for as long as I'm allowed."

Jakob nodded his head slowly, uncertain how to respond. All along, he had known Novan wouldn't stay in the city permanently. The man had warned him early that it was not his way, not the way of a historian. It had been so long that Jakob had simply forgotten.

Then he would be truly alone. "I will help with your arrangements."

Novan waved a hand. "There will be no need."

"Will you return?" Not when, but if, Jakob knew.

The tall historian pursed his thin lips and tilted his head in thought. "I may not."

He tried not to think about what *he* would do once Novan was gone. "I'll be available to you as needed," he said numbly.

"I know you will." He paused and turned to him. "Listen, Jakob. You have lost much, especially recently. You must wonder what the gods have in store for you, must wonder why you are being tested." The historian put words to Jakob's fears before pausing, looking at Jakob as the tears streamed forth again. "I have no answers," he admitted. "But I can teach you how to ask questions, how to observe, and learn from that which exists around us."

"What are you saying?" His head still throbbed and there was a slight ringing in his ears, making it difficult for his mind to work through things.

"You've demonstrated a keen eye and a quick mind," Novan said. "Even Endric says it is so," he said, almost to himself. "You may come with me, but we must leave with the Magi and would miss the ceremony. I need to accompany them if I am to understand what they intend. They may not have acted nearly as swiftly as was needed."

Jakob leaned back again, uncertain what to say, if anything. Novan offered him a familiar face if nothing else.

Is this what I want for myself?

He didn't know, had never known, not like Scottan or Braden.

If I go, will I become a historian?

Jakob didn't know what Novan had in mind for him.

And if he did go, what of Scottan? What would become of his brother?

"Know that if you go, your brother will still be cared for," Novan said, as if reading his thoughts. "The priests will see that he wants for nothing. Your father has always been a faithful servant of the Urmahne."

His father was nothing if not faithful to the Urmahne. It was not the same for him; he'd been losing his faith over the years, and his father's loss was the final blow.

Novan walked over to Jakob's door and opened it, pausing at the threshold. "You may find answers to questions you did not know you had," he said before leaving.

Jakob wrung his hands. The comment was something his father would have appreciated.

~

When Jakob had been escorted back to his father's room, he saw a dark silk shroud had been placed over the door. Only family was allowed past for the next week. He'd been surprised to learn the priests' quarters had been essentially unharmed. They were a separate building from the temple, though attached. Many thought they were one and the same, but Jakob knew differently. The explosions had destroyed much of the temple, and the priests were already busy clearing and cleaning that which could be salvaged, with many of the Ur working alongside the priests.

Jakob's crying had begun the moment he parted the shroud and stepped into his father's room. He couldn't stop them. The smell of incense still hung in the air, and a ceremonial candle stood atop his father's desk, though it was not one he recognized, too tall and thin to be a Turning candle. A robe lay on his bed, gray and not one Jakob had ever seen him wear, but it all reminded him of his father.

There were few personal items, but he would take them just the same. The ornamental jewelry belonged to the Urmahne, so he would leave that, as well as the robes and other clothing. A few books were scattered about the room, several on the desk and another under the bed, and so Jakob grabbed those. There was nothing else. Nothing that reminded him of his father, or his family. All he had to show for his loss were the sword and some books.

His father had changed little over the years, even less since his mother's death three summers prior. It was now a reminder of sadness and loss.

Looking around the room for the last time, a thick knot formed in his throat. He ran a hand across the robe lying on the bed, feeling the embroidery hidden in the folds, before finally leaving.

Outside the room, Braden stood waiting. His brow was furrowed, and a look of concern pained his face. He reached and pushed a strand of dark hair out of his face, shifting uncomfortably on his heels before speaking. "How are you"—he looked around, and seemed to struggle with what to say—"handling this?"

"Not well." He could not meet his friend's eyes and stared at the three books in his arms. They were small and light, and he wondered briefly if they belonged to his father or if they needed to be returned to the library.

Braden squeezed his arm. Jakob startled with it, and a throbbing pain shot up into his shoulder. An alarmed look crossed Braden's face before passing. "I'm sorry. Is there anything you need before the ceremony tomorrow?"

"I'm not going." He hadn't known what he would do until now but realized it was true. Regardless of what else he chose, he was not going to the ceremony. He would not taunt the gods further.

"What? You have to go. The city is preparing—"

"No. I'm leaving tomorrow. Novan leaves with the Magi and has asked me to come. I'm to be his apprentice." He paused, glancing back at the shroud on the door. "There's nothing for me here."

"What of your brother?"

"Scottan is with the healers. There's nothing more I can do for him." His brother had been nearly dead for the last year. Nothing of the Scottan he had known remained, nothing but a face Jakob barely recognized. And he didn't know how much longer he could stand to see him that way. It was too hard the last time. "I'll miss seeing you, but with the Ur keeping you busy..."

Braden leaned back against the wall and sighed. "We both leave, then. The Denraen have asked several of the Ur to join them."

Jakob felt a moment of reprieve from the sorrow of the last few days. "You're to be Denraen?"

Braden nodded, and he struggled to keep from smiling. His blue eyes sparkled. Jakob knew it was something many of the Ur dreamed of, the honor of being chosen as one of the Denraen, to guard the

Magi. It was something Scottan would have wanted, and it fit Braden.

"When?"

"The Denraen leave with the Magi," he reminded. "Listen, Jakob, I think you should reconsider. You saw the raiders, what the Ur faced. It could be worse than that if you follow Novan. The Denraen think it could be much worse."

"I've thought of that," he said, though had not, not truly. He tried not to remember what the raider attack had been like, the fear he had felt, the sounds of men dying. "I'll have my sword." He laughed weakly at the idea of him using the sword in a way that would actually protect anybody.

Braden didn't laugh. "You'll need more than basic sword skills to face the raiders, more than luck to survive."

Jakob had almost forgotten he had told Braden about his attack. Almost. "I've been practicing. I've improved." His time working with the general had grown his skills quickly.

Braden frowned but did not say anything before he grabbed Jakob's arm again. When again, a jolt of pain shot up to his shoulder and his already throbbing head pounded harder. Jakob pulled his arm away and rubbed where Braden had grabbed him.

"I'm sorry. My head still hurts from the explosion."

"It must have been horrible."

He had a flashback of the first explosion, the smoke, the acrid smell. All he could do was nod.

"I should let you mourn." He froze with a comment upon his lips that went unsaid. Instead, he shook his head. "I guess I'll see you tomorrow."

When he left, Jakob looked at his father's room one last time before walking away.

~

Jakob found Novan in an unexpected location. The historian was standing in the practice yard talking with the general. It was only the two of them, and they were deep in conversation. The tall historian had to look down at the smaller Denraen, but Endric carried himself with an air of confidence that made the height difference negligible.

Jakob stood off to the side, waiting, and didn't mean to eavesdrop, but their conversation carried to him anyway. He wasn't sure if he should turn away and give the men a little more space or if he should stay. While he debated, something caught his attention and answered the dilemma for him.

"The Conclave fears delay," Novan said.

The general sniffed. "There is no delay."

Novan tilted his head slightly and frowned. "I think she would say differently. You're still here."

"I am. As is my duty."

Novan laughed and shook his head. "You *are* stretched thin, aren't you?"

"Don't worry. I'll see the Magi safely back and turn my attention north."

"Some think our time is short and that we may already be too late."

Endric shook his head. "We're not."

"You're certain?"

The general nodded once. "As I can be. I know little more than that, little more than you."

Novan sighed. "Then that's enough. I am sorry this burden must fall to you. She had no one else to ask. If she's right, and you're meant to be—"

Endric cocked his head and flicked his eyes briefly toward Jakob, cutting off Novan. "Perhaps she didn't look very hard."

Novan saw Endric's gaze and turned toward Jakob and straightened slowly as he carefully looked around. Motioning him over, he said, "Jakob. You know Endric."

Jakob nodded as he approached. "I'm sorry. I was told I could find you here, Novan," he said as he ran a nervous hand through his hair. It was the general more than the historian who intimidated him. He had been such a fool! "I've decided," he said.

"Of course. And what did you decide?"

"There's nothing left for me here. There's Scottan," Jakob said hurriedly in explanation, "but he's with the healers and nothing more than a shell of himself."

The historian rested a hand on Jakob's arm to comfort him, and Jakob saw the general cock an eyebrow at the gesture. Novan was not one who suffered emotion, preferring logic and knowledge, so Jakob knew it was unusual for the historian. He was thankful for it nonetheless.

"I would be pleased if you come with me," Novan said, giving his arm a squeeze.

"With you?" the general interrupted. "Perhaps I may have asked the boy to join the Denraen."

Jakob was taken aback, but the general laughed, and he knew it for a joke. Novan looked at Endric seriously though and released his light grip on Jakob's arm.

"You would have him?" Novan asked, a strange look on his face.

The general snorted. "The boy is a quick study. He shows a natural ability with the sword. With time, I could make a Denraen of him." The general shrugged. "And a good one, at that."

Now Jakob was truly taken aback. A natural ability? He wondered if the general was joking again, but there had been a different tone to his voice this time, one that reminded him of how his brother had once appraised a horse.

Novan smiled strangely. "Good. Then you wouldn't mind if he continued to work with you while we travel?"

The general laughed. It was something he did easily, and it seemed out of place on a soldier. "You know I don't mind teaching those who wish to learn." He turned to Jakob. "You would wish to continue?"

Jakob nodded. The times he had spent with the general had left him feeling almost normal over the last few weeks.

"Excellent," Novan said. "I fear he may need some basic sword skills where we're to go."

"He's already beyond basic, Novan," Endric said. "But if I'm to do this, then I'll ask something of him." The general turned to Jakob. "You'll work with the Denraen, serve as one of my men, while you and Novan ride with us. There are things you cannot learn from books."

Novan shook his head. "I think you know how I feel about that."

Endric shrugged. "That's my requirement."

Novan looked at Jakob.

He'd come to the yard thinking he would only have a chance to continue working with Novan, and now he was being given an opportunity to keep studying with the general? What choice did he have?

He nodded.

"That is that, then," Novan said. "He may work with your men when I don't need him." He paused and looked at Jakob. "We'll be leaving soon. Gather whatever belongings you would like to bring and meet me in the plaza." Novan turned to Endric. "And we will speak more later."

Novan walked off leaving Jakob standing alone with Endric. *The Denraen general,* he reminded himself.

The old man stood casually, an unreadable expression on his face as he watched Novan depart. "You can learn much from that one," Endric finally said. He shook his head briefly as if to clear it. "Find me after we camp in the evening. The other men will know where I am," he finished before he, too, turned and left, leaving Jakob alone in the practice yard.

In the distance, near the ruins of the temple, a low, smoky haze clung to the ground. Jakob could smell the char and ash, and as it clogged his nostrils, the throbbing pain in his head returned. He turned from the sight as a tear welled again in his eyes, and he wiped it away angrily.

It really was time for him to leave.

CHAPTER EIGHT

They rode for a long time the first day, the Denraen pushing
them hard for reasons Jakob didn't fully understand.

Surrounded by Denraen, with two Magi further up in the proces-
sion, the departure was somewhat surreal. But Jakob did not let his
thoughts dwell on it now, knowing there would be time later. He
could not see Braden among the riders, though given the sheer
number, he was not surprised, and struggled only to keep his
borrowed horse next to Novan as they rode.

They traveled west, crossing grassy plains that gently rolled ever
onward, and quickly passed beyond the lands Jakob knew. Their path
skirted quietly around several small towns that he could barely make
out in the distance. They stuck to the road mostly but seemed unconcerned about leaving it at times to cut across country. He saw a few
people pass by as they traveled, farmers mostly, and none who
followed. They kept a good pace, not so fast that the horses fatigued,
but crossed ground quickly enough.

Novan was quiet, keeping to himself and occasionally riding ahead
for a short time before returning to ride alongside Jakob. He
suspected the historian rode up by the Magi, but he wasn't sure,
having been unable to see from his vantage among the Denraen.

There was little talk from the men around him. The Denraen were either very serious in their duties or were uncomfortable talking around him and Novan. Perhaps it was a little of both, he decided.

Over time, they veered along a northern road, and the grassy plains eventually started to merge with a smattering of trees. It was about this time that two things happened. First, the sun dipped low in the sky, low enough that long shadows of the stunted trees stretched across the road. The other was a little more unsettling. There was the feeling of a presence such that the hairs on the back of Jakob's neck stood on end. It was the feeling that something followed them, watching them. It was a strange gnawing on his senses, a tickle to his mind, yet he couldn't see anything awry.

As the day grew darker and they showed no signs of slowing, he found himself turning and staring off to each side of them, looking hard into the distance. He couldn't shake the feeling of something following them. It was almost like an itch in his mind he couldn't scratch.

Novan must have sensed his unease. "What is it?" It was the first time he'd spoken in several hours.

"I don't know. It feels as though something's following us," he answered.

Novan glanced around, staring into the growing darkness before shaking his head. "Unlikely," he said. "The Denraen have scouts all around us, so someone following would be quickly found."

Jakob shook his head. "Then it's probably nothing."

A strange frown turned on Novan's lips, and he nodded. "Or perhaps it *is* something," the historian suggested. "We pass near an old ruin, one lost so long ago following the destruction that there are no records of what it was."

Jakob followed the historian's gaze but saw nothing but clumps of rock in the distance. "That? That was a city?"

Novan snorted before looking back to Jakob. "One day, your own beloved Chrysia may know the same fate." He watched as the rock fell farther and farther into the distance. "There's a power to walking among those rocks, a sense of time, the weight of history. I would give much to know their story."

Novan's voice had taken on a faraway quality and Jakob smiled, wishing he knew a passion like the historian had for the past. Neither spoke any more about the strange sensation, but it never really faded. But Jakob managed to push it to the back of his mind.

It seemed another hour passed before the call came back for them to stop for the night. It was atop a small rise and gave a good view of the landscape around them. Defensible, he suspected, knowing little of such things but knowing a party of their size would be unable to hide. Better to see what was coming. He still felt strange eyes were watching them and was thankful for the vantage.

Jakob dismounted quickly when they came to a stop. Standing next to the horse, he felt the cold night air seep through his cloak, his shirt, his breeches, and he shivered. He held tightly onto the reins, wondering what was next. He leaned down, massaging his thighs briefly. His backside ached from the ride, bruised and stretched in ways he'd not known before. He wondered how his body would tolerate riding more tomorrow and if he'd ever grow used to days in the saddle.

"Your body will adjust."

He turned, expecting to see Novan speaking to him. The words startled him, and the strange feeling left him. The tall historian still stood nearby, but it was not he who spoke. Instead, a Denraen stood before him, his youthful face capped by long, dark hair pulled back and knotted. The man had a crossbow slung over his shoulder and a curved sword at his side. Jakob forced himself to smile, unsure if the man would even see it in the waning light.

"First day in the saddle?" the man asked. He had a slight accent, one that Jakob couldn't place, but not as thick as that of the general.

Jakob nodded. "For this long, at least," he answered hesitantly.

"Stretch before sleeping and when you wake in the morn. It will make tomorrow more tolerable," he said before turning and joining a few of the other Denraen who began to gather the horses together.

Novan chuckled as the Denraen soldier left. "He speaks the truth about the stretching. Otherwise, you'd rather walk tomorrow." He grabbed Jakob's reins, handing them to one of the Denraen, and motioned for him to follow.

Jakob followed stiffly, worrying briefly about his belongings before shrugging it off, focusing instead on how his body was slowly adjusting to the ground and his own movements again.

All around them, the Denraen were making camp. Each group had an assigned task. Several made quick work of starting a few fires, small at first but growing quickly larger, and around the fires were others setting up tents, arranged neatly and in a pattern he couldn't quite see. Every person worked quickly, efficiently, at their task, and there was little talk as they did. He wondered when the general would begin his work with the Denraen.

Novan led him past all of this to a smaller open area where another tent was set. It was larger than some of the others, and there were two Denraen standing guard who waved Jakob and Novan past, the first women he'd noticed among the Denraen. One leaned on a long staff, much like the one Novan had brought with him, and the other carried a crossbow. Both had a dangerous look to them.

Inside, a few tables were arranged, and lamps were set atop, casting a flickering light. The two Magi stood looking down at one of the tables where a map was spread. The new chosen delegate, Thomasen Comity, hovered nearby trying to listen and was ignored by the Magi. A Denraen stood alongside the table, as well, motioning to the map as he talked. The man was enormous, a bear of a man, and thick arms strained at his uniform. He was nearly a head shorter than the Magi.

"He is the Raen, the second-in-command," Novan whispered.

Jakob remembered the man from the raider attack and could easily believe him the leader of the Denraen. The general didn't strike him the same way. Endric had a casual air to him while this man seemed intense. There was strength in his posture, in his gaze, that he'd not seen in the general's. His sheer size was intimidating.

"Bothar's group is here," the Raen said, stabbing at the table with a thick finger. A long scar traced the side of his face and pulled tight as he spoke. Others could be seen around his neck, each a shiny angry line. "Perhaps another week before we meet them, maybe more." His voice was husky as if he had been yelling all day. The Raen looked up from the table and saw Novan and Jakob, nodding to each in turn.

At the motion, the Magi looked up as well. It was Haerlin. The bearded Mage stared at Novan, saying nothing, an unreadable expression to his dark eyes. The other Mage, a woman, younger by all appearances, wore an interested expression, occasionally touching the back of her neck. Haerlin turned his gaze upon Jakob, and he felt the uneasy feeling he'd had the first time the Mage had stared at him, as if he were being looked through, examined, and then discarded. Nausea swept through him, and he shuddered, trying to suppress it. He felt a moment when blackness threatened to overcome him, but it finally passed. His head pounded, thudding with each beat of his heart.

Haerlin finally turned back to the Raen, and Jakob shivered involuntarily. "And the raiders?" Haerlin asked.

"I'm not certain they're all raiders, not if we've seen Deshmahne. But they're here," he pointed to a location on the map. "Another here. There's likely a larger party as well that we haven't found. We think that's all."

"Think?" Mage Haerlin asked.

"I can't be more specific. You didn't allow a larger party."

The Mage huffed. "A larger party would have traveled too slowly." It had the sounds of a familiar argument. He waved his hand in the air dismissively. "Will our paths cross?"

The Raen shook his head. "We can ride around their known locations. The scouts will help. Otherwise..." He shrugged.

"We cannot risk too much delay," Haerlin said.

"Your safety is worth a slight delay," the Raen answered firmly.

The Mage Elder shook his head before speaking again. "Fine." The word was thick with his frustration. "Do you know who's with Bothar?"

"We do," the Raen smiled. The gesture pulled strangely on his scars such that only half his lip moved as it should. "Allay Lansington."

Novan grunted a surprised sound. Jakob looked up at him, but Novan's face quickly became unreadable. Thomasen Comity was the son of a councilman, near nobility in Chrysia. Could this Lansington be another? There must be other delegates they were meeting, all of whom chosen like Comity.

"Lansington?" Comity asked, speaking for the first time.

"That may help." Haerlin ignored Thomasen as if he weren't there. The Mage was silent for a long moment. Finally, he spoke again, "Report again tomorrow." It was a dismissal.

The Raen nodded before leaving. For a large man, he moved gracefully and with a light step. A dangerous man, Jakob knew. His departure left them with the Magi and Thomasen Comity. The other Mage had been silent through the exchange, but now she motioned Comity and led him from the tent as well, leaving them alone with Mage Haerlin.

"You agree that Lansington is an interesting choice?" Mage Haerlin asked Novan. He did not wait for a response. "The Prince may provide greater traction than this one," he said, nodding toward the tent flap. "I wonder about the others. Can this work?"

"You have not yet informed me of what it is you intend," Novan answered quietly. "Nor why you chose him when you had your sights set on one of the priests."

"Historian," Haerlin began sharply, his eyes staring icily at Novan before softening as he sighed. "I guess I cannot keep you from knowing."

"You cannot. I know enough already about your delegates."

Haerlin faced the map, his fingers tracing the lines upon its surface. "Delegates. Yes, that is what some would call them. I prefer the term ambassador. Our influence is not what it once was, and so much of the land is unsettled."

"The Deshmahne."

Mage Haerlin traced his fingers over the map. "You said that the High Priest was in Chrysia while we were there." The city name sounded strange as spoken by the Mage, foreign. "There, as he has been in other cities. Now he finally braves Thealon. He has sent others north before, but never himself. What does it mean that he now comes?" He looked up to Novan with the question, and his eyes were worried. He no longer stood arrogantly, appearing somehow smaller for it.

Novan shook his head and seemed as if he would not answer. "I do not know what it means."

"Do not know or will not say?" Haerlin asked pointedly.

"It's possible he seeks something," Novan started. "You seek to influence, yet why Comity? Why Thealon? The priests rule Thealon."

"We need solidarity, unity. Thealon has not yet felt the influence of the Deshmahne." Mage Haerlin seemed to stop himself, as if wanting to say more, but thinking better of it.

There was something larger here that Jakob did not understand, something to the Deshmahne priest. He had seen the man, sensed him and felt the fear, so he understood the concern, but it seemed a disproportionate response. He was one man. What were they not saying? What else did they know?

"You don't seek the Uniter," Novan stated.

Haerlin eyed him a moment before sighing. "You know too much," he whispered. "We chose a different tact this time. A Uniter, yes. But not to unite with the Deshmahne. We must unite all nations *against* the Deshmahne. The Denraen will assist in this, but our delegates will help lead."

"This is what you hope?" There was a hint of disdain to his tone. "And when it fails? The High Priest is the keystone to the Deshmahne. Do you really think your ambassadors can do anything against his influence? The Magi must take a stand in this, Haerlin."

"That is not the Urmahne way," Haerlin answered. "Nor the way of the Magi."

Novan raised his eyebrows and was silent for long moments. Finally, he inhaled deeply. "You don't fully understand the consequences of delay."

Mage Haerlin sniffed. "And you do?"

Novan's eyes were piercing. "More than you know."

"You doubt the wisdom of the Magi? And the Council? You who has seen more than any not Mageborn?"

Novan drew his shoulders back. There was a resigned look to his face as he answered. "I do." He let the words hang in the air for a long moment before he turned and walked from the tent. Jakob stood looking at Haerlin's surprised expression before he followed. Novan's long legs had carried him quickly away, and Jakob hurried to catch him.

Night had settled, and the air was cool. He was sweating in spite of it. He could smell the smoke of the dozen fires of their camp, could nearly taste the smoky aroma, and the hunger pang he felt made him wonder when he would eat. When he reached Novan, the man slowed and looked down at him. "You should find your swordmaster and continue your instruction." Novan glanced back to the tent and shook his head. "Arrogant. If only they knew," he started before realizing that Jakob was still watching him and waved him away.

Jakob left and wondered at first how to find the general before realizing that his ears could guide him. The crack of wood staves was loud. The men of the camp didn't make much other noise, and Jakob quickly found the general. He worked with a tall figure near a larger fire; its light just enough to make out their movements. They were moving quickly through catahs, flashing from one movement to the next, their practice staves whistling through the air. He had thought the general casual, not as dangerous or intimidating as the Raen. He shook his head with the thought.

The general moved quickly, his steps a light dance, and he darted from one catah to the next, nearly a blur. Jakob could barely keep up. There was a fluidity and efficiency to the movements that he marveled. The man was deadly.

Yet the opponent kept up. His own stave swung as quickly, its movements nearly as fluid, nearly as efficient, but there was hesitancy to him, barely noticeable, that the general didn't share. Jakob watched in amazement before becoming aware that he wasn't the only one standing and watching. A dozen or so men of the Denraen stood around watching, each man holding his breath at the performance. Long minutes stretched, the only sound the crackling flames of the fire and the *crack crack crack* of staves smacking against each other.

Finally, Endric's opponent stumbled, and Endric moved in, deadly as a viper, ripping the stave from the other's hand and swinging his own down in a deadly arc that stopped just shy of the man's head.

He tapped the stave lightly on his chest. "You're dead," he growled.

The men around Jakob whistled appreciatively, and one or two clapped, before turning back to whatever they were doing. It was the most sound Jakob had heard from the soldiers. The general helped up his opponent, and they walked over to the fire, the general speaking quietly to him before sending him on his way. When the man came toward Jakob, he realized he wasn't a man at all.

It was the younger Mage.

She stopped near Jakob and when she saw him staring, leaned over to pick up her robe that had been folded and tucked carefully away.

"I'm Roelle," the Mage said, her voice breathy. She still panted with the effort of the challenge match. "You the historian's apprentice?"

"Jakob," he answered, shock keeping him from saying much more.

Roelle must have seen it before. "I may not use my abilities against another, but that doesn't mean I can't protect myself," she said as an explanation. Her voice was calm, but there was a hint of something deeper beneath the surface.

"I'm sorry. It's just that you're so good!"

A smile twisted her lips. "At least you're not telling me I shouldn't work with him because I'm a Mage. I got that too often from these others at first. Now..." She shook her head. "It doesn't matter to Endric. Besides, I'm still not good enough. Just once, I'd like to..." She looked over Jakob's shoulder.

Jakob turned and saw the old general standing behind him. There was a smile on his face.

Endric chuckled. "One day, perhaps. It's more than your Elders can claim." He turned to Jakob. "Your turn." It was not a question, and Jakob realized the man was not even breathing hard. "This is different from in the city," the general told him as he walked him over to the wooden staves, throwing one to Jakob. "When you're ready."

Catching the practice sword, he nodded. "I'm ready to learn."

"Then I'm ready to teach," the general said.

Jakob followed the general into the clearing and stepped back into his ready stance, waiting as the general did the same. He quickly learned how it would be different from their encounters in the practice yard. There was no demonstration of the catah tonight, no chance to learn the movement before learning its defense.

The general moved suddenly into attack, sliding through the motions of a catah Jakob didn't know. He defended as best he could, struggling with the practice sword and feeling the sharp blow of the general's wooden sword hit his arm and back several times. The general stepped back before starting in again suddenly, and Jakob realized what the man did; he demonstrated a catah in full, showing all the movements before stepping back to signal its end.

After the second time through, Jakob thought he had the movements and leaped in a quick attack, his sword moving fast, but Endric's moved even more quickly in defense. He struggled to note the defense, knowing it another lesson the man taught, and struggled to keep his attack.

His legs left him, and he felt the wind knocked out of him as he landed on his back. His head ached as it hadn't for a while, but still, he stood shakily and dusted himself off, reaching to pick up the wooden practice sword. The general took him through several other catahs and their defense, and Jakob found himself on the ground many times before he knew he had to stop. He ached all over as he stood for the final time, dusting himself and leaving the wooden stave on the ground.

"You do well, boy. You must see your opponent's move before it happens. When you do, it will be as if the fight has slowed and your movement easy."

Jakob was unsure how to answer. He didn't think he could ever reach the point where it seemed the fight slowed. He struggled to keep his mind on his own motions let alone think he could know his opponent's before he—or she—moved.

"Tomorrow, you will come again."

Endric moved on to another student, and Jakob limped away so he didn't find himself in the middle. His legs and back hurt differently than they had after a day in the saddle, and he worried how tomorrow would go. He would be a mass of bruises before the week was over.

"You're too tense."

Jakob looked up. The Mage Roelle stood facing him. He hadn't noticed before, but the Mage could not be much older than he was. With her raven black hair, she was lovely.

"You're not bad for a scholar," she said.

Jakob arched an eyebrow. He had never thought of himself as a scholar. Apprenticed to a historian, what else but a scholar? "My brother was the soldier."

Roelle laughed. It was an easy sound and unexpected from the Mage. Jakob found himself liking her. "Relax through the catahs. Let them flow. Don't fight the river, move with it."

"You sound like a priest," Jakob offered, wishing immediately to take it back. Did he just insult a Mage?

Roelle smiled. "I'll take that as a compliment." She paused. "I come because I would know how men fight."

"But you're a Mage."

"You're lucky Endric is willing to teach you. It took me weeks to convince him to teach me. It's taken the others longer to accept it."

Jakob shrugged. "I didn't realize he was the general when I first started working with him."

"Who did you think he was?"

Shaking his head, Jakob answered, "An old man willing to work with me on the sword."

Roelle laughed deeply then. "In my city, there's no mistaking Endric. I should go, but I'll speak with you again, Jakob."

Jakob watched Roelle walk away, a smile stuck to his face. Sparring with the Denraen general and talking with a Mage. What would happen next? Maybe some good could come of this.

The feeling was short lived.

As he started away, he had the unsettling sensation of something watching him again. He resisted the urge to look around, but a fear began to creep through him. Had he left the city only to suffer from the madness?

CHAPTER NINE

Morning found him sore in ways he had never considered. The ache of the previous day's ride was mixed with the bruises blossoming on his arms and back from sparring the night before with Endric. The headache from the night before still throbbed faintly, a quiet pulsing behind his eyes. Finally, there was the stiffness from his first night spent sleeping on the hard ground. His blankets had provided little padding, and it was good he had been exhausted, else he may not have slept at all.

As it was, it was a restless sleep. Dreams had come to him again, as they had so often of late. Visions of a strange woman calling for help and trapped in a fog. There was something regal about her, and he sensed a helplessness to her. He felt golden eyes watching him and found a strange comfort in that. Lastly, a man with flaming eyes had startled him awake, but not before it seemed the man saw him and laughed.

Jakob had finally settled into the deepest portion of sleep when the call went through camp waking him up. He sat up slowly, his body unused to the abuse he'd inflicted upon it lately, sending sharp pains of revolt from head to toe. He looked over to Novan, but the historian was already up and out of the tent. Jakob wasn't sure the man had even slept.

Finally awake, he quickly gathered his few belongings and stuffed them in his sack before strapping the sword onto his belt and standing. It still felt awkward and strange, as if he was posing as something he was not. The feeling was one he had known most of his life.

Novan found him as he exited the tent and led him to breakfast where he kneeled and ate. A shadow crossed over him, and he looked up expectantly, a surge of anxiety pulsing through him before passing as he recognized the person. It was the Mage from last night, Roelle.

"Are you bruised?" the Mage asked.

When Jakob stood hurriedly, his sword smacked his shin, and he tried not to wince. "I am, Mage Roelle." Jakob suddenly felt stupid. He didn't even know the proper way to address a Mage.

"Roelle is fine." The serious tone she used was belied by a slight smile to her face.

When she smiled, Jakob noted again how lovely she was, much more than any Mancley sister. A flush washed through him, and he hoped Roelle couldn't sense his thoughts.

"I am bruised." She paused, looking over to where Mage Haerlin stood whispering to Thomasen Comity. "Haerlin has turned a blind eye to my lessons, but it's been many days since I last worked with Endric. I couldn't hide the body aches well this morning."

Mage Roelle chuckled to herself as she said it, finding mirth to it that Jakob didn't understand. How could he understand the humor in upsetting a Mage? "I bruised, and I've been working with the general for a few weeks," he answered without thinking, wondering if he should be so blunt with a Mage.

"Your bruises will be less if you relax more. How long have you been apprenticed to the historian?"

"Novan came to Chrysia over a year ago. It was around that time my father was trying to find something for me." He remembered it well, having argued a long time for his father to let him follow Scottan into the guard. Strangely, it had been Scottan himself who had kept him out.

"What is it that you wish to become?" Roelle asked.

He had often asked himself the same question. There was never a satisfactory answer. Would that he could be Jarren Gildeun. It was what he had wanted as a child. There was something about the idea of wandering the land, exploring places no one had been in centuries... or ever. But he'd been stuck in Chrysia until now. "I couldn't be the priest son my father wished."

Roelle looked at him curiously. "Do you not follow the Urmahne way?"

Careful, he reminded himself. He was speaking to a Mage, someone who was the voice of the gods themselves, endowed with abilities by them. "I follow Urmahne."

It was a cautious answer and not completely true. His faith had grown distant with the loss of his mother and had faltered more when Scottan fell to the madness. He was not yet sure what remained now that his father was gone.

There was a moment when Jakob feared what Roelle would say, feared what the Mage might think. He didn't know how honest he should be with her but worried she would know if he was not truthful. Yet the truth was painful. His father worshipped the nameless gods, preached the peace he believed, but how could these peaceful gods let the madness touch the world? How could his brother be taken from him by it? How could his mother suffer the way she had?

And now they had taken his father from him.

He wondered if the Deshmahne had the right view. Were power and force what the gods understood? Jakob worried these thoughts showed on his face. What would the Mage Roelle do then? What would she say?

Does she speak with the gods? he wondered.

"I've found that you must question your faith in order to have it. If you don't ask the questions, how do you know the answers?"

"My father once said something like that," Jakob said, remembering the conversation the last time he'd seen his father. He felt a surge of sorrow with the thought.

"Your father sounds like a man of wisdom," Roelle said, a faint smile pulling at her mouth.

"He was a priest."

Roelle arched an eyebrow. "Was?"

Jakob nodded. "He was killed in the temple explosion."

"Ah... I'm sorry."

Novan came up to him then, casting a curious glance at the Mage Roelle.

"Don't fear the answers," she said, looking casually at Novan before turning and walking back to join Haerlin.

Jakob let his eyes follow her, trying to ignore the way she walked, and the sway to her hips, and focus on her comment. It was strange, and he didn't know what to make of it. There was something different about Roelle, something less arrogant than Jakob expected from the Magi, something alluring.

Novan didn't give him a chance to figure out what it might be. "It's time to ride," he said.

The ache in Jakob's body made him wonder how he'd handle the saddle.

～

They rode harder than the day before. The sun was often hidden behind layers of clouds, and the day was cooler for it. The air was crisp, making it clear winter was not far off. There was a dampness in the air, a hint of rot, almost a sense of decay, though overtop this was the familiar scent of earthiness and the fragrance of flowers. He had noticed smells more often lately and began to wonder why.

Novan was silent for much of the morning. The historian rode tall in his saddle, making notes in a notebook occasionally before tucking it carefully away. "What do you see, Jakob?" Novan asked suddenly.

Jakob looked over to the tall historian, seeing the man's thin features, the wrinkled face, and tired eyes. He had been pushing himself hard lately. Was there are reason behind it? "I watch the Magi," he answered honestly.

Novan looked toward where the Magi rode, his blue-gold eyes rimmed in red today. He chuckled, and Jakob flushed. "The Magi are said to be the link to the gods. Some say the hands of the gods, some would say the voice. This is part of the Urmahne teaching. Your father would have instructed you on this, Jakob." Novan turned toward him, a question in his eyes.

"My father taught me many things about the gods. I'm not sure what's true." Novan arched an eyebrow at the critical comment but said nothing. "Why do the Magi no longer involve themselves in the Urmahne?"

"What I think is of little consequence, Jakob. I'm little more than a recorder, a reporter, of what I see. That is what historians do."

He had seen Novan acting as more than a reporter more times than he could count, including when discussing the High Priest. His opinion had been asked and given many times. "A historian is more than a reporter. There is an element of interpretation required, I think."

"Oh?" Novan asked. "What makes you say this?"

"The books you have had me read have all had an interpretation of what they recorded. I have seen you do it as well."

"I am, perhaps, not the best example. But you're right. One must place what he sees in the appropriate context. That's part of the historian's duty."

"Then what of the Magi?" Jakob asked again. Novan seemed to be avoiding the question.

The historian rode on in silence, and Jakob wondered if he would even answer. "The Magi are of the Urmahne. They await the Return. This they tell us," he began. "Some would say they *are* the Urmahne, more so than those of the priesthood, as they are the Founders of the Urmahne." Novan stared at the Magi. "I've seen the Magi do many things, great things at times. Their abilities are impressive, said given to them at the time of the Ascension, giving them powers others don't have. This would seem to make them godly."

Novan paused, seeming to be lost in thought, then continued. "Yet they seclude themselves from the rest of us while claiming that they still speak to the gods. Their abilities could be used for such good, yet these days they rarely are. Is this what the nameless gods have instructed? Is this what the Urmahne preach?" He shook his head in answer to his questions. "It was different, once. I fear it will have to different once more."

It was more of an answer than Jakob had expected. He had seen how Haerlin set himself apart from others, but Roelle seemed different. Were the Magi more like Haerlin or more like Roelle? "Do you think they speak to the gods?"

"There are others who might better answer that question." There was a long pause before he continued. "But are we certain that gods even exist?"

Jakob felt a moment of shock. He had never suspected Novan to be an atheist. "But the Tower—"

"Built by gods or by those with abilities like the Magi?" Novan offered.

Jakob shook his head, not knowing how to answer. He had felt guilty for doubting the Urmahne faith, but Novan took it a step further, doubting even the gods' existence. *What if he's right? What would it mean?*

Jakob wasn't comfortable asking those questions so near the Magi. "How can Roelle learn the sword? The Magi are said to be the epitome of the Urmahne, and peace is the core of the teaching."

Novan smiled. "That's an interesting question. The first Magi were warriors, and I wonder if there are those among the Magi who would be like their Founders. That is another thing I would like to learn in Vasha. As to Roelle, I'm not surprised she's drawn your interest."

"I..."

Novan flashed a smiled, but fell silent once again as they rode north and west, and Jakob didn't press. They moved steadily and stayed on the roads as much as was possible. As the sun peaked overhead, they stopped at a small stream to water the horses and to eat. Clumps of trees broke up the horizon and grew thicker in the distance to the east.

A growing sense of unease crept through Jakob. He had felt it all morning but thought it the effects of his conversation with Novan. This was different. Almost familiar, and he realized what it was that made him uncomfortable: the sense that they were being watched had returned.

Jakob did not know how to describe it, even to himself. It was a strange sensation, an unpleasant irritant in the back of his mind. He constantly resisted the urge to look quickly over his shoulder, yet he still found his head frequently turning, hoping to catch a glimpse of what he felt. It did not happen.

The feeling stayed with him throughout the day. The first stop was brief; it was only long enough for Jakob to stiffen again and dread the remainder of the day in the saddle. His body was not made for this, he decided, yet knew it was too late to come to this decision. The column continued in the same direction, and Novan said little more throughout the day, though he would occasionally make notes in the small book he carried.

The sun gradually drifted beyond the horizon, and stars appeared overhead. Still, the feeling of being watched was with him. Once, he had looked and thought he saw an animal stalking them, but he couldn't be sure and didn't think it was what he felt. It wasn't until they stopped and the camp was set for the evening that he felt it disappear.

Novan dismissed him, and Jakob used the opportunity to set his bags in their tent before wandering to where Endric once again practiced. Fires danced brightly, and the moon shined brightly overhead, letting him see more easily than the night before, not that it would help.

Roelle had again beaten him to the old general. They sparred a long time, the fluid dance going much the same as the previous night before the general finally ended it. The Mage came over to him, panting. "Relax," she reminded when she stopped nearby to catch her breath.

Jakob stepped forward to grab the practice stave, doing his best to relax as Roelle suggested. Endric led him through a new series of catahs, his movements almost too fast to catch, and certainly too fast to remember. Jakob defended as best as he could, moving to the offensive briefly when he realized that Endric expected him to, before struggling to defend the barrage of attacks. It lasted longer than the night before, though Jakob wondered if it was just his imagination. He had been tired, and his focus had been lax, yet because of it, he had felt a little more fluid.

Endric ended it with a flourish before waving him off. "Tomor-row," he called as Jakob was leaving.

At least he had that to look forward to. Perhaps when he was better rested, it would be different. Unlikely, but he could hope he would improve.

"Better," Roelle offered as Jakob approached. This time, it was he who was panting, trying to catch his breath. "You didn't force it as much tonight."

He started to say something but was interrupted by a strange scream that split the night.

A call went rolling through the camp, a sentry yelling and ringing the alarm. There was an odor, one he couldn't place. It was the stench of decay. The sound of steel ringing off of steel echoed through the camp and then came the sound of men shouting and screaming. Jakob started forward, but a firm hand on his shoulder held him back.

"You're unarmed," Roelle said. "Let the soldiers do their job."

Jakob turned to her and saw a strange look to the Mage's face. Concern? Frustration? He wasn't sure.

"Raiders," Roelle said. "We came across them on the way toward Chrysia, but they left us alone."

"Then why attack the camp?" Jakob asked. It didn't make sense for them to attack the Denraen unless they had enough numbers, and Novan had repeatedly said they were too unorganized for a sufficient attack. Yet they had attacked the Ur. And Deshmahne had been involved in that attack.

"Our numbers should keep them from attacking."

A man suddenly burst into the firelight, dressed in dark trousers and a loose shirt. The light flickered strangely across his features, almost as if it was drawn to him. Two Denraen chased him, but the man reached Endric where he stood talking to another soldier. Endric was unarmed, but reacted quickly, grabbing one of the practice staves to protect himself from the raider's quick thrust.

The man laughed. It was a hysterical sound, and he yelled some-thing in a language Jakob didn't understand. Endric's smile showed that *he* understood, and he unleashed a volley of blows with his sword. The raider was good, deflecting most with ease and circling around Endric, keeping the Denraen in front of him. The raider parried, slicing forward and feinting an attack on Endric before catching the other unarmed soldier and dropping him.

Endric roared and danced forward, his movements so fast Jakob couldn't follow, finally catching the man in the head and knocking him to the ground.

With that, the camp went silent. The underlying odor remained, and Jakob couldn't clear it from his nostrils. He followed Roelle over to the raider as Endric knelt by the man, binding his wrists and ankles tightly before brushing himself off and turning to the injured man.

"S'all right, general," the man said. "Just my arm." He held it up to prove it, and Jakob saw a deep, angry cut through the man's upper arm. It bled heavily.

Endric nodded to him before helping him up. "Hold pressure. And see that it gets stitched."

"He shouldn't have been able to reach this far into the camp," Roelle said to Endric.

"He should not have, yet he did." Endric squatted beside the bound man, still unconscious, and pulled up the sleeve of his shirt. Dark tattoos were etched into the skin, easily visible in the firelight.

Endric spat suddenly before reaching into his belt and grabbing a knife. He cut deeply into the tattoo, cutting out a section nearly two fingers wide, before spitting again. Dark blood oozed over the tattoos, smudging the designs. "Cover this," he commanded a nearby soldier. Two men came over quickly and picked up the raider, carrying him off to be bandaged and restrained.

Roelle had watched this silently, waiting until Endric stood again before she said anything. "What—"

"Deshmahne," Endric said, spitting the word as if he hated to even speak it. "The markings grant strength, quickness."

"You think destroying the tattoo weakens him?" Roelle asked. "I haven't heard that it was so."

"Disrupt the pattern, and you disrupt the power." His attention shifted to another Denraen who approached. "How many?"

"We counted at least twenty attackers. Ten of them are down, the rest ran."

Endric nodded. "Ours?"

"Two injured, one serious," he said.

"Search the bodies, then burn them. Look for any markings and let me know what you find," Endric said.

The soldier nodded before running off.

"What were they after?" Roelle asked.

Endric shook his head, his eyes narrowing. "A test, I think."

"Why you? Why not come after Haerlin or the ambassador?"

Endric shook his head and said nothing.

"And you think they're Deshmahne?" Roelle asked.

"Perhaps not all." The general didn't say any more, turning toward his tent.

Roelle stood silently watching the old general leave. "He knows more than he says."

"What do you suspect?" Jakob asked. He didn't expect an answer. Why would one of the Magi need to answer him?

"I don't know. There's much that's not known of the Deshmahne. Endric has seen these markings before, has some idea of what to do when he does. There's something he's not letting on." Roelle turned to Jakob. "Did you see how fast that man moved before Endric knocked him out?"

Jakob nodded. "It reminded me of you."

Roelle laughed. It seemed out of place after what they had just witnessed and carried into the night. "I'm glad Endric doesn't finish me the same way he took care of the Deshmahne."

Jakob surprised himself by laughing. "If he does, I'll keep him from tying you up," he offered.

"That would be appreciated." Her eyes tensed, and she stared at the ground where the Deshmahne had been. "I should discuss this with Haerlin. Sleep well, Jakob."

Jakob nodded as the Mage disappeared and realized that he needed to report to Novan. The historian would want to know what he had seen.

≈

Dreams had haunted him again that night.

Jakob stood on a hillside under a dark sky. A man with fiery eyes and dark tattoos upon his arms watched him from a distance, laughing. Jakob had yelled out something strange, words he had seen in his recent reading, but had not been quite sure what they meant.

He felt something else pacing farther away, something with golden eyes barely visible, that was summoned by his words. Heavy clouds moved ethereally overhead, threatening rain and bringing an earthen scent with them. The man with the fiery eyes stared up at the clouds and smirked before turning his attention back to Jakob. He felt the man as he stared at him, his gaze burning into the back of Jakob's mind, and hopelessness settled through him. A slow sharp cry pierced through it all, and he found himself dragged away from the hillside.

Jakob struggled to waken, hearing the sharp horn of the morning alarm. He opened his eyes slowly, and consciousness returned to him. Novan was not in the tent, and his bedroll did not appear used.

It wasn't until they were nearly ready to depart that Novan finally joined him. The historian pulled his horse alongside Jakob as they started out. His face was lined and tired and his eyes looked as if he had stayed up chewing rumbala root the night before. The man looked exhausted.

"You should have slept," Jakob offered.

Novan looked at him and said nothing for a long moment. "Sleep does not come well to me, though last night I didn't really try."

"The Deshmahne attack?" Jakob asked.

"You were with Endric?" When Jakob nodded, he pressed. "What did you see?"

Jakob reported on what he saw during the attack. He started with hearing the alarm, and included the fight with the general. He finished by telling how Endric had cut out the tattoo of the man who'd attacked him.

"It won't work," Novan said. "You would have to disrupt each tattoo. Endric would know that."

"It did not work."

Jakob turned to see the Roelle riding along next to them. A few of the Denraen nearby looked at her briefly before ignoring her as they had grown to ignore Jakob and Novan.

"He was killed last night without telling us anything," Roelle went on. "He awoke and killed one of the Denraen guards before he was brought down. This was while he was still tied." Roelle looked up to where Endric rode, surrounded by his Raen and a few other high-ranking Denraen, before turning to address Novan. "I'm curious, historian, what can you tell me of the Deshmahne?"

"What has Haerlin told you?" Novan asked.

"Haerlin says it's not for untrained Magi."

Novan raised an eyebrow. "Then what do you know?"

"This is the second attack upon us on this journey, historian. It is two more than was expected."

"It's been many years since the Magi faced opposition. I do not claim to be Urmahne, but it has its redeeming qualities. The Deshmahne are different. It's a twisted religion. One of force and violence, born out of their frustration with the Urmahne. The Deshmahne believe shows of strength appease the gods. There are many who see its appeal."

Jakob watched as Roelle looked around the Denraen. What little he knew of the Deshmahne would appeal to soldiers, he realized. Could any of the Denraen practice Deshmahne?

Not Endric. The general seemed to despise the Deshmahne attacker.

"I don't think Endric would allow it," Jakob said. Both Novan and Roelle looked at him. "Just the way he acted when he saw the man was a Deshmahne," he explained. "There was hatred in the way he handled the man."

Novan looked up to where Endric rode, a slight smile tugging at the corners of his tired mouth. "Hatred is mild, I think."

"You know much of Endric for someone not of the city," Roelle said.

"We've met before. He has always been kind to historians." He cast an accusatory glance at Roelle.

The young Mage laughed, her voice sweet and almost musical.

"Talk to my Elders, historian. I'm not to blame for the secrecy you despise. I'll share what I learn if you reciprocate."

Novan eyed her briefly before nodding. Roelle smiled then spurred her horse forward to rejoin Haerlin.

Novan watched her ride ahead. "She... is one for me to watch, I think." His tone was friendlier than it had been. Novan turned to Jakob. "It's an interesting point." His voice was pitched low, and Jakob suspected only he could hear what was said. "Though it should not be possible, the Deshmahne could appeal to the Denraen."

"Why should it not be possible?" Jakob asked.

Novan ignored the question. "I have an assignment for you. You will observe the Denraen, work with them. Endric has already asked for this. It will give you a better perspective, I should think. Document what you see."

"Document?"

"That *is* what a historian would do, Jakob."

Jakob flushed. "I just haven't—"

"You've reported to me, and you've given your opinion. Your comment about Endric confirms that you're ready. I'll have notebooks and ink for you each evening."

This was what he would become, wasn't it? He had agreed to apprentice a historian, but it was one thing to serve Novan while he remained in the city. It was another to actually begin his training.

As he nodded to Novan, the sense of unease settled upon him again. He turned but saw nothing. Jakob resolved to ignore it.

A thought lingered. Did someone follow them, watching as they passed, or was it something worse? Didn't Scottan start the same way? Would the madness claim him too?

Jakob shook his head, but the feeling did not leave. Neither did the queasy knot in his stomach.

CHAPTER TEN

"Name's Rit," the man offered.

His face was a crooked mess. His nose had clearly been broken more than once, and one ear appeared larger than the other. A slight smile cracked his scarred face, and one of his front teeth was missing. In spite of that, or perhaps because of it, he came across as friendly. "We have horse duty this eve," he informed, leading Jakob and his mare.

"Jakob," he told the man, trying to sound confident.

Rit led him to a small clearing where a line of horses had been set. Other men were already at work brushing down the mounts while still other men worked quickly at erecting the line. "Each night, we pull different duty. Tonight, we groom and feed the horses; tomorrow, we cook. We rotate so that each of us knows all parts of the camp."

Rit helped him tie his mare to the line and loosen the saddle. Jakob said nothing, thankful for Rit's explanation but more comfortable in the silence. It was full dark, and he brushed his mare carefully, feeling his way along. He had only limited knowledge of horse grooming and wasn't sure if what he did was right.

"Like this," Rit demonstrated, sensing his uncertainty.

He strained in the dark night to see what the man did and tried to copy. His hands followed the large, sure hands of the other man, making the same motions, until Rit finished his horse and moved down the line. Jakob followed silently and began work anew. As his hands grew practiced, he found the work went more quickly.

"You the historian?" Rit asked, breaking the silence between them.

"His apprentice."

Rit grunted but said nothing.

Jakob kept his hands busy, and they spoke no more. The work was mindless and let him reflect on the day. The ride had gone little different from the day before. The feeling he had, the unease, stayed with him longer and had not left until they were fully camped for the night. Jakob had struggled to ignore the sensation all day, but the longer he did, another sense of unease started to creep through him.

When the madness had claimed his brother, Jakob had seen it first-hand. And now he wondered if this was the beginning for him. Was this how it started for Scottan? He forced his mind away from those thoughts, but it was difficult to do. He wanted someone to talk to about his fears, but he didn't dare go to Novan, and he hadn't seen much of Braden.

Nearby, he heard the distinctive clap of wood on wood as men practiced the sword. A large fire had been built, and the crackling flames grew bright in the growing dark. The night was crisp, and the smoky aroma of the fire mingled with the stench of the horses' lather. From where they stood, Jakob could see how the old general almost lazily fought off a young guardsman. The younger man moved quickly, but Jakob saw the general's sword strike flesh more than once. He watched for a little longer before turning back to his work.

"Any can work with the general," Rit said. "Endric isn't gentle, but you can learn much."

Jakob heard a cry and looked up to see that the sparring was over, the younger soldier down. "Do you?"

Rit's wrinkles cracked the corners of his sharp eyes as he smiled. "There was a time I did. Better to practice with others I think."

The crack of wooden practice staves and an occasional cry of pain or laughter continued to break through the quiet of the camp. As they reached the end of their line, he looked up to Rit.

"Eat. Later we take watch. You probably don't have to stay up for that."

What did Novan want him to document? All parts of serving as Denraen. That meant the watch too. "I'll join."

Rit's face took on a serious expression. "After last night, we'll take it."

"How will I know when?" Jakob asked.

"I'll find you." Rit stood and stretched, cracking his back, before leaving Jakob.

He needed to eat, but he ignored his hunger, instead walking toward the general. Strangely, it was the one part of his day he enjoyed. Endric stood talking with the hulking Raen, and Jakob stood patiently to the side, knowing well enough not to interrupt. Without intending to, he heard a piece of their conversation.

"I'm torn, Pendin," Endric said, his accent thicker tonight than normal.

The muscular Raen stared at Endric before answering. "Our duty—"

Endric interrupted. "You think I do not know our duty? No. I know it as well as any, but there's another responsibility I can't ignore."

"I understand," Pendin said.

"No. You don't. But when you lead the Denraen someday—perhaps soon—you will."

The Raen cocked his head. "And this other?"

Endric shook his head. "I can't refuse the Conclave. Or her. This request may be the most important of all."

"What does it mean?"

"That you may replace me sooner than I had expected."

Pendin snorted. "Is that all?"

Endric frowned, looking carefully at Pendin before laughing. "No. But it's enough. You've learned much of the Denraen, Pendin. Soon you will be the protector of all our secrets."

"For now, I follow your command," the Raen said, and his scarred face pulled grotesquely as he smiled.

Endric sighed. "Keep vigilant. The Deshmahne will come again. They must not succeed."

The Raen nodded before turning and leaving.

Endric caught Jakob listening. Instead of a reprimand for listening where he should not be, the general surprised him. "How's Rit treating you?"

"Like his men."

The general laughed. It came easily for him, though from what Jakob had seen, so did his anger. He was a man whose emotions flashed quickly. "It's all I asked of him. Perhaps you'll become a Denraen instead of a historian."

Jakob didn't know what to even say. His brother was the soldier, not he, but there was a certain appeal to Endric's offer.

The general seemed to sense his struggle and grinned. "Come on then if you want to continue your lessons."

Jakob nodded and followed Endric to practice.

～

His head buzzed.

The last two nights working with the general he'd noticed a strange humming in his head that had stayed with him the entire practice but didn't seem to interfere with his concentration. Tonight, toward the end, as he was moving into his first attack, there was almost a pulsing within his skull. His vision had cleared, and his mind seemed to slow. If Jakob didn't know better, he would almost say it helped.

Perhaps he *was* mad.

He had never learned how it began. Voices were common. What else came with it? None knew what caused the madness, only that there was no cure. Was he next?

Other than the humming in his head, the practice had gone better tonight. He'd managed to defend himself longer and actually threatened an attack once. Actually, each night was better. He no longer felt clumsy with the sword, and he was thankful for the general for that, but he worried what would happen in a real battle facing a true enemy with his sword in hand. The memory of the Deshmahne attack remained with him, the feeling of helplessness, and the luck that had saved him.

"No practice tonight?"

Jakob turned to see Roelle strolling in the direction from which he had just come. She was dressed in pants and a loose-fitting shirt, much different from the Mage robes she wore during the day. It made her more appealing.

He tamped down those thoughts. "I already have." He rubbed his arm where the practice stave had hit him last, quickly ending the practice.

Roelle grinned, brushing back a strand of black hair and tucking it behind her ear. "Then what now?"

"Rest first, then watch."

Roelle cocked an eyebrow. "The historian has you taking watch?"

"He has me observing the Denraen. I've been assigned to one of the units—"

"A raegan," Roelle corrected.

Jakob nodded. "I've been assigned to a raegan to observe."

"The historian has you watching the Denraen then. Is this about the Deshmahne?"

Jakob said nothing, unsure how much to reveal. It was answer enough.

"Clever. Though I doubt you'll find much. True Denraen walk the path of the Urmahne."

"What of the recruits?"

Roelle frowned, crossing her arms over her chest as she surveyed the soldiers camped for the night. "That's a good question. How well are they chosen? There are nearly a dozen new recruits among us. Do all follow the Urmahne or have some slipped through?"

"Would it matter?"

The Mage shook her head. "I don't know. I can't deny there's a strange power to the Deshmahne." Roelle frowned as if considering her own words. "You mentioned something before that has troubled me."

"What?"

Roelle smiled a disarming smile. Jakob flushed, thankful for the dark.

"You mentioned a brother. What happened to him?"

Jakob swallowed. He tried not to think of Scottan, or to think about the fact that he had been left in Chrysia with no family around him. Novan claimed that he'd be taken care of, and Jakob didn't doubt it, but that didn't change that he was his brother, and he'd been left alone.

"He fell to the madness."

"You said that before," Roelle said. "What is the madness? Is it some Deshmahne attack?"

He hadn't considered that before, but if it were, wouldn't the priests have known? "I don't think so. There's something... wrong... with certain people. My brother fell to it. The healers don't know how to help. They waste away, having visions and speaking in tongues—"

"Touched by the gods," Roelle whispered.

Jakob grunted. "If that is the gods, then I don't want their touch."

Roelle looked troubled and forced a smile. "I should go before Endric leaves for the evening. Wish me luck." She paused. "And Jakob. Don't fear to reach for the gods. They have a plan for us all."

~

Roelle walked away from Jakob, glancing back every so often. He intrigued her and was not at all like she had expected when she first met him. In the time that she'd gotten to know him, she had discovered that he had suffered much. Not only the loss of his father but also that of his brother to the strange illness. He didn't speak of his mother, but she had the sense that he'd lost her as well.

How could the gods take so much from one person?

And still... Still, they had given him much as well. She watched the way he worked with Endric, noting the speed with which he improved. That clearly was a gift from the gods; it could be nothing else. Now, he had progressed to the point where he presented a challenge even for her, and there were few even among the Denraen who presented any challenge to her other than Endric and Pendin. That was the gift of her Magi heritage, the benefit of being Mageborn, giving her the ability to move and react quickly. It was a skill that her kind had been gifted from the gods. Endric had developed his over years, while she had developed hers over a period of months.

Haerlin met her in the tent. He stared intently at a notebook as he made a few notes, glancing up briefly when she entered. "Tell me again about the most recent attack."

The abruptness surprised her. "The Deshmahne?" she asked. When Haerlin nodded, she said, "He reached all the way to the general. Had Endric not been there, I'm not sure what he would have accomplished."

He'd gone for Endric, not the Magi. That bothered her. Hadn't they been led to believe the Deshmahne were after the Magi?

"Yes, the general. He knows more than what he's letting on."

"Why do you say that?"

"Him and that historian. There's something about them. I haven't discovered what it is, but when I see them together, it's like a surge of light."

Roelle considered this. Was Haerlin mentioning a prophecy, a vision of something that he saw with the historian and the general? Or was it something else, something more mundane?

"What does it mean that the attacks continue to press north?" Roelle asked.

Haerlin sighed. "It means that we must move more quickly. These delegates... If they're going to do anything for us, they must reach the city."

"How does bringing the delegates to the city change anything about the Deshmahne presence in the north?" Roelle asked.

Haerlin shook his head. "That won't be on the delegates. That will be on the Denraen. Endric will be tasked with keeping the Deshmahne from the north. The delegates will maintain the peace and, if they're successful, will reestablish the role for the Urmahne."

"Not only the Urmahne but the Magi influence as well."

Haerlin nodded. "The Magi have been too far away from influencing things for too long. It is time that we get ourselves involved again.

Roelle couldn't deny the wisdom of that. The Magi once had been the priests of the Urmahne religion. Over time, they had given up the responsibility to those who now served as priests. Eventually, the Magi had stopped exerting their influence on the religion at all.

Haerlin stood and stuffed his notebook into his pocket. "Keep your eye on the historian. Watch him and his apprentice. There is something there that I can almost see."

Haerlin left her, and Roelle stood at the opening of the tent. She didn't disagree. There was something about Jakob. It was more than his intriguing swordsmanship. He was an interesting man, and she felt a connection to him, though she didn't understand it fully. Maybe it *was* only the swordsmanship. She hoped that was it.

Roelle sighed and shook away the thought. She needed to focus on her responsibilities. They didn't involve getting tied up with a historian apprentice. She should use him for practice, nothing else.

Why then, did she find herself thinking of him so often?

CHAPTER ELEVEN

The next week passed much the same. Fatigue began to overwhelm Jakob. It was a product of taking watch with the Denraen at night and the long days in the saddle followed by documenting what he'd seen. Each night, he rotated through different tasks with Rit and the raegan, learning about caring for horses, tending the cookfire, and setting up the tents, but he heard nothing that Novan found interesting. The men were friendly enough to him, but close-mouthed just the same.

Jakob continued to struggle with the small book Novan had given him. He pulled it out in the evenings and trudged through it. What had seemed so interesting at first had become laborious and difficult. Too often, the language eluded him, the ancient words impossible for his mind to grasp and translate even though the book seemed written such that someone could learn the language as they went. So he pushed forward, knowing Novan expected it of him and hoping what he gleaned would grant him additional understanding of his sword. He'd not taken the time he needed to study it, partly because he hadn't wanted to unsheathe it while riding and hadn't had the time once stopped for the night, but partly because he felt an imposter with it compared to the Denraen.

Work wasn't the only reason he was tired. Sleep was no longer restive for him. Dreams had been coming more vividly, and when he awoke, he found that he often could not fall back asleep. Always, there was the dream of the woman. She was trapped, though Jakob could never see what held her. One night, it was as if she saw him and tried to pull him into the dream with her, but he turned and ran, afraid of what would happen. She called after him, her voice a song of sorrow, and it tore at Jakob's soul to leave her, though he didn't understand why.

Other dreams haunted him too. Occasionally, he would dream of the High Priest, seeing nothing of his face but pools of red for his eyes and a haunting laugh chasing him. Something seemed to keep the man at bay, something always at the edge of Jakob's dream vision, a specter of shadow in the haze of his dream. Each time he saw the man, he awoke sweating, his heart pounding.

Worse was that he'd barely seen Braden since their journey had begun. He could see his friend in the column each day riding next to another of the Chrysia recruits, Tolsin, but at night, between his work with the general, his responsibilities Rit, and his time with Novan, he had no time to look for Braden. Jakob had grown to know Tolsin back in Chrysia through Braden, and they had been nearly friends, yet a part of him resented Tolsin. As a soldier, he had more in common with Braden than Jakob did. Jakob hoped their friendship would make the ride less lonely, but it had not been the case so far.

The countryside and trees had given way once more to rolling hills and immense plains of late fall grass. He hadn't seen a town or hamlet since the first few days when they left the road, moving across country and tramping their own path through the thick lawn of drying reeds. Flies and huge natmins chased them, and he had begun to wonder if they were the only creatures in this grassland.

The peculiar sense of being watched stayed with him. Every day was the same; it started shortly after they left for the day and continued until well after they stopped for the evening. Occasionally, he saw an animal in the distance. One time, he was convinced it was a fox or some type of cat trailing them, but what he saw was too large to be a fox. He'd not seen it since.

Jakob asked Novan if he saw the creature, but the historian said he'd seen nothing. It didn't put his mind at ease. If this was the madness setting in, nothing could be done, so he tried to ignore it. Each day, he found it increasingly difficult to do so. One night he even convinced himself that he saw eyes in the darkness and nearly sounded an alarm.

Now, he was no longer sure if what he saw was real.

Jakob found time each evening to work with Endric. His head tingled as he practiced, and each night, it grew stronger. It had become more of a buzzing, something he could almost hear. Jakob worried it was more evidence of his growing madness, but a part of him grew thankful for it as well. It seemed that it sharpened his focus sharpened and allowed his skill to improve more quickly so that he held his own with Endric more and more each night. His mind seemed to slow the more it vibrated, allowing him to see the quick movements of the general and determine the best defense for the catahs and increasingly mount an attack. He still found new bruises after each session, but they were fewer in number each time.

Tonight, though, Endric was not where Jakob had expected him. He found Roelle instead.

"Endric won't come tonight," Roelle told him. She held a practice stave casually and flicked it a few times, stabbing the air.

Jakob still hadn't gotten past her easy way with the sword, or the friendly way she spoke to him. Neither was what he had expected of a Mage. "Why?" The overheard conversations teased his memory, and he wondered if Endric had gone north as he had promised the woman during the Turning Festival.

"There's been another attack."

"An attack? I should have heard."

"Different this time. Several scouts were captured. One was sent back with a warning."

"Which was?" Jakob asked. He'd grown more comfortable with Roelle over the last week and found it easy to ask the Mage questions. She was often free with answers, surprising for a Mage. It didn't hurt that he found her appealing.

Roelle studied him a moment before answering. "His head. I'm not sure what else. Endric was apparently quite upset."

A sudden chill worked through him that had nothing to do with the cool night air. "What does this mean?"

Roelle just shook her head. "I don't know. I don't think Endric does either. The men captured were scouting the far north." She hesitated before continuing. "There have been other stories out of the north. Has the historian shared those with you?"

"Only that he's heard rumors. There's more, though I'm not sure what it is."

The Mage sighed. "That would have been too easy. Haerlin has excluded me as well. I know there's something far worse than raiders roaming the north that has Haerlin nervous. He and Endric have spoken about it several times, and I've been excused each time."

"What could make a Mage Elder nervous? The Deshmahne?" Jakob asked.

Roelle shook her head again, her long hair bouncing with the movement. "The Deshmahne are little more than a curiosity to Haerlin, I think. The Elder feels the Urmahne need not fear them, that the gods will protect us." Roelle paused as if considering what she had just said before shaking her head and continuing. "This is something else. I will have to remain patient." She looked suddenly at the practice sword she held in her hands. "So, without Endric, what would you say to sparring with me?"

The sudden change of topic surprised Jakob, and he laughed. "I think you'll find me an easier opponent than Endric."

"I've been watching the last few nights. I think it'll be closer than you think."

Jakob doubted it, but grabbed a wooden stave and moved into his opening stance, forcing his mind to relax. He struggled with the process but knew the more relaxed he was, the easier the sword would flow. He had found that when he was tense, his reactions were too slow, like he moved through mud. Taking a deep breath, he sensed the slow vibration in his head and embraced it. It was a trick, he knew, but a trick that had started to work for him. As he did, his vision sharpened and his mind seemed to open.

Roelle gave little notice and leaped forward.

Jakob reacted quickly, bringing his sword up in defense, recognizing the catah Roelle used and knowing its defense. Slicing through the movements, Jakob could see what Roelle was doing by the slight twitches of her arms and was able to anticipate where the Mage would go next. In spite of this, he was not fast enough. He felt the sting of Roelle's sword on his arm two times in quick succession.

Jakob stepped back and moved in a slow circle around Roelle, considering how to proceed. The vibration in his head hummed, and he sank into it, feeling it spread through his body. He took a deep breath and released it, letting the vibration envelop him. Then he pulled at it, hoping to use it.

The sense of it consumed him, and he didn't resist.

Jakob couldn't explain what he did, but he was suddenly more aware, everything clearer. Time almost slowed, yet his thoughts moved more quickly.

He jumped forward, catching Roelle unprepared. Jakob whipped his sword through a quick catah, remembering it from one of his bouts with Endric. Roelle met his sword but not before Jakob caught the Mage across the shoulder and then her back.

Jakob pressed his attack, spinning and swinging, his mind forcing his body from one dance to another. Roelle was quick, her sword nearly a blur, yet Jakob saw it differently tonight than he had seen before and was able to react quickly, knowing each defense.

Jakob spun, twisting as Roelle thrust her sword down, barely avoiding it as it whistled past. The vibration rolled through him, and he danced with it. It carried his sword, moved through him, and he allowed himself to move with it.

The vibration intensified through him. His sword moved as if guided by another hand, and his mind knew where it must move. Spinning and turning, spinning and turning, and suddenly, he stopped.

Roelle's sword was across his chest. He had not seen it.

Looking down, he realized that his sword was resting across Roelle's chest. Both were breathing heavily, and he was all too aware of how close he stood to her.

Jakob suddenly felt the bruising he'd ignored before as pain pulsed through him, nearly causing him to stumble. "I guess we both lose," he laughed, trying to catch his breath.

There was a strange cast to Roelle's eyes. "That was impressive, Jakob. You moved like no other man I have faced."

"I doubt that. I've seen you with Endric. I know I can't compete with you."

"I was pushed as hard tonight as I ever am with Endric," Roelle answered, replacing her practice stave. "You're an interesting man."

Jakob didn't know how to take the praise. He wasn't even sure what he'd done. The strange vibration still rolled through him, but it had lessened and continued to fade. He let it go and noted his energy drain as it did, suddenly exhausted. What did it mean?

"Come, let us get a drink," Roelle offered.

Jakob nodded. He would ignore his worry for now.

They started out of the clearing, and both realized they'd been watched. Several Denraen stood talking and stopped as they approached.

"That was excellent. Who were you facing, Mage? Tell me he's one of ours."

Roelle shook her head and turned to Jakob. "The historian apprentice."

"Where did you learn to fight like that?" the first Denraen asked as he turned to him.

What was the answer? He'd always been an average swordsman before, knowing enough not to hurt himself but could claim little more skill than that. His days spent with Endric had begun to change that, had opened his eyes and his mind so that he now actually found himself improving.

"General Endric," he answered, unsure what more to say.

The Denraen grunted. "I've seen you with him. You and this young Mage here are the only ones foolish enough to face him each night."

One of the other men chuckled. "I'm surprised he hasn't tried to enlist you," the man said, his voice heavy with a thick northern accent.

"The historian instructed me to learn from him."

"I face Endric as little as possible," the northman said. "Too bruised."

Jakob and Roelle laughed at the comment. "I've bruised," Jakob said, still laughing.

"You can bruise more than your skin," the first man said knowingly.

"Aye, but the skin hurts more," the northman said.

"It's the other that lasts," came a rough voice behind them.

They all jumped, turning to see the general. Rit stood with him, looking at each face in turn carefully. Endric cast his gaze upon everyone, as well, lingering on Jakob.

The Denraen all stood at attention and said, "General!" in unison.

"Easy, men. You are dismissed." The general watched his men disappear before turning to face Jakob and Roelle. "Rit tells me you have been serving well."

Jakob shrugged, wiping a bead of sweat from his forehead and pushing his hair back from his eyes. "It was what Novan asked of me."

Endric smiled. "It is. The historian worries about the Deshmahne." He turned his attention to Rit, who had been quiet during the exchange, and asked, "Do you think any of my men are Deshmahne?"

Rit shook his head. "They cannot be, sir."

"Why?" Endric asked the man.

"The Choosing is an Urmahne custom, blessed by the gods to allow the Denraen to see a man's heart. No Deshmahne could pass."

Jakob noted that Rit had spoken the words as if by rote. "I've seen the Deshmahne." Jakob chose his words carefully. "They seem to have a power that rivals the Magi. How do you know they could not use it to pass the Choosing?"

"Indeed," a voice said behind him.

Jakob jumped and turned to see Novan standing behind him. The tall historian had a mischievous look on his face and his dark cloak billowed behind him in the night's breeze. A hint of lavender hung about him, as if perfumed, and it was not unpleasant.

Endric frowned, tight lines pulling his aged face into something more like a sneer, before softening. "Historian, you sneak like a thief.

But your apprentice raises a point that has me worried. Come. We must talk."

~

They sat quietly within Endric's large tent, a single lamp casting light enough to see. Haerlin sat covered in his heavy dark cloak, his head tilted forward, his eyes narrowed as he waited on Endric to begin. Rit and Pendin stood behind the table casually, looking over the general's shoulder. Novan paced, every so often pausing to look down at a canvas map that lay upon a makeshift table, different colored pins scattered along it marking troop locations.

Jakob could see how they appeared surrounded. How many were Deshmahne?

"How many raiders?" Novan asked.

Endric flicked his eyes to the map before meeting Novan's gaze. "Enough." His rough voice was subdued, and there was an edge to it that Jakob hadn't heard from him before. "Though that's not the real question, is it?"

"No. It is not."

"The Deshmahne have not been seen in great numbers even in Gomald where they've crossed over from the south," Haerlin said quietly. "This cannot be accurate."

Pendin shrugged his broad shoulders. "My scouts can count. And see." He tapped a finger toward the map for emphasis.

"This isn't how they have converted in the past," Haerlin objected. "Nor how they have attacked the Magi."

"No." Endric eyed the Mage. There was a darkness to his expression, and Jakob wondered again about the passion behind it. "They have cowed, coerced, and taken. Rarely have they spilled blood. Rarely." The last was said with particular venom, and his gaze turned to Haerlin. "This is not about conversion, though." His gaze glanced to a corner of his tent. Was that where he kept the trunk he'd agreed to transport?

"Why?" Jakob asked. "What do you think it's about?"

Surprised eyes turned and focused upon him. Haerlin's seemed the heaviest, and the unsettled feeling he had when the Mage looked at him fluttered through him briefly before fading. Jakob fought back a bit of nausea. Roelle had a small smile quirking her lips, and she feigned a yawn to cover it. Jakob almost laughed.

"They haven't needed to attack the Magi," Novan explained. "The Deshmahne is a religion that started quietly far in the south. Their numbers built slowly, the stories about the Deshmahne, mostly rumors at first, spread quickly. Before that, few knew anything about them. Secretive, they sequestered themselves away from the larger cities, supposedly building a Deshmahne fortress."

Novan paused, and Endric took over. "Then they came forth. First Coamdon. Then Lakeliis. Before long, Deshmahne were common throughout the entire south. Gaining influence. Little was done to slow it." With the last, Endric looked briefly at Haerlin before glancing down at the troop locations. "Now, they move north. They have attacked us once before"—Jakob noted that Haerlin stared at Endric, his gaze hot—"and now they press their influence through Gom Aaldia and toward the Magi in Vasha. Toward the north. They have gained power quickly."

"How so quickly?" Roelle asked.

"There are theories," Novan began.

"They are just that," Haerlin interrupted, scratching his bearded chin in irritation.

He remembered the helpless feeling that had come over him when he'd seen the High Priest, like a power pushed upon him. Cold eyes, glowing with reflected light of the night fires, had stared at him, and everything else drifted from his mind. Jakob shivered with just the memory. Could the Deshmahne affect a person's feelings, their emotions?

"I would think the Magi understand they are more than theories," Novan said. Haerlin met his gaze, and Jakob noted Roelle looked from one to the other, confusion on her face.

"There's more to it, isn't there?" Jakob asked.

Novan paced toward him, and a dark look flickered across his face before it was gone, replaced with a blank serenity.

Endric looked briefly from Haerlin to Novan before he turned his gaze upon Jakob and held him in his intense stare. "Novan claims you've seen the High Priest. There are few who can make that claim."

All the eyes in the tent fell upon Jakob. Sweat moistened his hands, and he clapped them to his side. "I saw him once. At least, I think I did." He glanced up to Novan who nodded. "In Chrysia during the Turning Festival. He passed near me wearing a dark cloak, and I felt a sense of hopelessness so vast..." He shook his head to clear it of the memory. "Remembering leaves me wondering if the Deshmahne can manipulate emotions."

Haerlin chuckled and turned away, shaking his head. "Not even the Magi can perform that feat, boy," he muttered, turning his attention back to Endric.

The general ignored the Mage, still staring at Jakob, his heavy gaze weighing him. "I have the same question," Endric admitted. "I know the Magi think it impossible, but the Deshmahne have powers unlike the Magi. None, save the Deshmahne, know the extent of their abilities. The priests endowed by their dark arts have speed, strength. Men who face them feel fear they would not otherwise know, often laying down their swords without a fight." His hard eyes bored into the Mage. "The gods only know what the High Priest can do. This would explain much."

Jakob remembered the Deshmahne attack, how quickly the man had moved, how he was nearly the equal of Endric. The Deshmahne frightened him.

He glanced toward the corner of Endric's tent, thinking of the other thing he'd seen that night at the Turning Festival. "What do they want?"

Novan stopped pacing and spoke. "The Deshmahne were once thought a cult, something to be dismissed. Little more than barbarians blaspheming the truth that is Urmahne. Yet they gained influence. With influence came credibility and something more." He paused, collecting his thoughts. The others in the room waited, and Novan held them in anticipation, letting it build. "Doubt. What if the Urmahne isn't the path to the gods? Could the Deshmahne speak the truth? These questions went unanswered."

Novan stared at Haerlin. The Mage did not meet his gaze. "Silence held its own power, and soon, the south began to wonder. Had the gods abandoned those who followed the Urmahne? Once, the Urmahne faith was strong, demonstrated by its first followers. Now, few see the Urmahne faith in action, understand what strength there is in the peace the priests preach." Novan's eyes had not left Haerlin. "The Deshmahne demonstrated their strength. This was something men could see."

Haerlin stood abruptly, his chair tipping. "Enough, historian." There was a quiet heat to his words, and the hairs on the back of Jakob's neck stood as the Mage spoke. "You will not criticize the Magi in such a manner." Haerlin motioned briefly to Roelle who stood more carefully than her Elder, pausing a moment to eye Jakob, then Novan, before following Haerlin from the tent.

Novan watched them leave, a hint of amusement tugging the corners of his mouth before it turned into a frown. The tall historian scrubbed a hand across his face and sighed deeply as if collecting himself.

"You push too hard," Endric said. He paused to whisper something to Pendin who nodded and followed the Magi from the tent. Rit stood waiting.

Novan nodded. "It was necessary."

Endric tilted his head. "I am not sure it was. It changes nothing."

"Why was it necessary?" Jakob asked. He wasn't sure what had just happened or why the Mage had become so irate, but Endric seemed to know.

Novan righted the chair Haerlin had tipped over and sat down at the table. "Haerlin needed to be reminded of his past. One the Magi forget. Their religion has been weakened."

"And there is another reason you press," Endric suggested.

Novan nodded slightly, absently twisting the dark stone ring on his finger. "You know the urgency."

Endric sniffed. "All too well, Novan. The search is not left only to us."

Novan closed his eyes. "We are too few, Endric, and you know it." He looked over the map, staring at the markings as he took a deep breath. "Yet the Deshmahne are here." There was a hint of resignation in his tone. "These numbers are for something more than I had thought. This is not only about reclamation."

He turned to Endric. The general stared at him, waiting, though his eyes narrowed suspiciously. "There can only be one purpose to this."

Endric nodded. "I fear the same."

"What purpose?" Jakob asked, feeling lost in their private conversation.

Novan shook his head, pointing at the map, at the markers indicating raider presence. And Deshmahne. "If I'm right, the High Priest has a far more dangerous plan than I had thought. And we might already be too late to stop him."

CHAPTER TWELVE

"You've come a long way," Roelle offered. The Mage ran a hand through her still damp hair before pushing it behind her ears. She studied Jakob with an appraising gaze. "Faster than most."

Jakob held the practice stave, the dancing flames giving light to the clearing. He wiped droplets of sweat from his brow as he caught his breath. "Still the same result."

Even so, he took a measure of satisfaction from the fact that he'd been improving. There was something relaxing to holding the sword, wooden or otherwise, that he had never known or felt, a relief he couldn't explain. Perhaps Scottan had understood—it was probably why his brother had pushed to have him learn the sword—or maybe Braden did.

They'd moved slowly today, scouts moving carefully to ensure safe passage, so they didn't travel nearly as fast as they had been. Jakob hadn't been certain Endric would even welcome him to practice, but once they settled in for the night, he had.

Working with him tonight had gone better. And worse. He'd lasted longer, somehow keeping up with the scarred old general longer than he had any other night. The slow throbbing that he now experienced with each practice had come quickly, sharpening his focus, and he wondered if the quickness of its onset was at all related to his experience with Roelle the time before. Yet it ended no differently than any previous encounter with the general—his body bruised and sore, only worse tonight because he'd lasted longer.

Roelle chuckled. "Best be prepared if ever you defeat him."

Jakob eyed her, frowning. "Why?"

"It's how one assumes command of the Denraen, at least a part of it. It's how Endric assumed command from his father, Dendril."

"I'm at little risk of challenging him anytime soon," Jakob said.

"You keep improving as quickly as I've seen, and it may not be long."

Jakob laughed. It was cut short by a burst of pain in his side where one of Endric's blows had struck a rib, and he reached for it as his laughter turned into a cough before dying out. Neither spoke for a time, the only sounds the smack of wooden staves behind them, the crackles of fires around the camp, and the occasional chirp of a nocturnal insect. It was Jakob who broke the silence.

"Why was Mage Haerlin so upset last evening?" He wasn't sure he'd get an answer from Roelle, but asking Novan wasn't the right approach. The historian would prefer he learned some things on his own.

Roelle sighed, tugging on her shirt. "Haerlin is an Elder. And he sits upon the Council of Elders. As such, he expects a certain level of respect. And it seems your master shared something he did not want shared. Even with me."

"Novan speaks his mind." Jakob had seen it before with the priests in Chrysia, the city council, and most recently with the Ur captain. "I don't believe he ever means offense."

The young Mage offered a half-smile. "Perhaps not. I think there's some history between them, as well, though Haerlin doesn't speak of it." Roelle paused. "Why do you and the historian travel with us?"

"He says he comes to observe the delegation." There must be more to it for Novan. The historian had many layers to everything he did.

"I think the delegates are not the reason the historian travels to the city."

"Why else would he have us come?"

"I suspect he seeks the Council." Seeing Jakob's frown, she explained, "They are select Magi among the Elders who serve as keepers of the Urmahne. They are the Magi leaders, but they also serve the traditions of the Urmahne. Few not among the Council know the extent of what they keep and protect. The historian could learn much from the Council if he was allowed access."

"More than he could learn from the priests?"

Roelle nodded. "The priests serve the Urmahne, but the Magi *are* the Urmahne."

Jakob thought about the comment for a moment. Novan had mentioned something similar about the Magi, once. The priests taught that the Magi were the voice of the gods, touched with their abilities. If Urmahne was the path to the gods, then it would make sense for the Magi to claim that they *were* the Urmahne. Something about the thought troubled him.

"Why, then, do you learn the sword?" It was a question Novan had asked but hadn't had any answers either.

Roelle considered for a while before answering. "How does one justify war with the Urmahne ideal of peace? The Magi have taken a hard line on this, stating that to the Urmahne, there are no just wars, that destruction cannot be tolerated, and that a peaceable solution must be found to every conflict." The young Mage shook her head. "There are others who follow the Urmahne who believe differently."

"The Denraen?" Jakob asked. "But they guard you."

"Not directly," Roelle started. She sighed and shook her head again. "I haven't answered your question. How is it that *I* came to learn the sword? As far as I know, there have been few among the Magi who've ever bothered to learn something as barbaric as the sword or staff. It started with boredom, I suppose. There is only so much time I can spend sitting in a classroom and studying." She flashed a smile. "I think I've already told you how difficult it was to convince Endric to allow me to work with him. But he saw that we wouldn't be dissuaded, and I've discovered that we of the Magi have a specific knack for it. Somehow our abilities have granted us a certain physical prowess, a muscle memory if you will, and that allows rapid growth in our skills. This was surprising."

"To who?" Jakob was surprised Roelle would share as much as she did.

"Myself and others. No Magi since the Founding has bothered to try. I only started it as a curiosity, a way to pass the time. Now... Now I worry it may be necessary for more than curiosity."

"The Deshmahne," Jakob said. He suppressed an urge to shiver as a brief memory of the High Priest threatened to overcome him.

"Yes, though I think there is more that I do not yet know."

"Novan worries that whatever is in the north is worse than the Deshmahne. He would not say more."

Roelle frowned, and the expression looked strange on her face. "If the historian worries about it, then there is even more than Haerlin knows or admits."

Jakob glanced across the clearing. The general was tied in conversation with several of his officers and glanced up, as if sensing their attention, and Jakob turned away quickly. "Endric may know."

"He may know, but I doubt he will share with me." The Mage sniffed, a sound of frustration. "Share what you learn?"

Jakob thought about the request a moment. Roelle had opened up to him unexpectedly, so how could he refuse?

"Until later, then," Roelle said, and turned and left the clearing.

Novan parted the tent flap and came in quickly, a slight gust of wind following him that was scented with an odor of rain and earth and fluttered the pages of the small book Jakob struggled through. The historian peered down at him before making a small sound in the back of his throat and sitting nearby. He pulled a small notebook from the pouch at his side and scribbled something inside.

"I spoke with Roelle last night," Jakob said, choosing to break the silence. Novan would have let it draw on before asking a seemingly inane question.

The historian looked up, and there was a question in his eyes. He waited.

"She thinks you seek the Council of Elders."

Novan's smile didn't spread to the rest of his face. "She's correct."

Jakob frowned, unaccustomed to Novan being so forthcoming. "I thought we traveled to observe the delegates."

The historian tilted his head before thumbing his nose. "That's one of the reasons we started the journey."

"But now?" Jakob began, but the answer came to him. "Now you worry about the High Priest and what he's after."

"Roelle explained the Council serves as keeper of Urmahne artifacts?" Seeing Jakob nod, he continued. "Some artifacts are very old, perhaps older than even the Magi know and understand. There is one, an ancient text, valued beyond all else the Council possesses. I have only managed to see it once. It was not long enough to study it, to learn and understand it." Novan shook his head as disappointment or frustration flashed across his face. Jakob could not tell which.

"Would the High Priest also look for this?"

Novan nodded carefully. "I doubt he cares much for the text, but there are other items that he failed to claim once before."

Jakob waited, wondering if Novan would share anything about the trunk, but he didn't. "What does he want?"

"Power. The artifacts are a way to power. Even the ancient text possessed a certain power within the words, within the language. Power, and something more, I suspect."

"How can there be power within words?" Jakob had read many of the books Novan had asked of him, and none seemed capable of granting power. They were historical documents, analysis at times, but little more than that.

Novan seemed to track the line of his thoughts. "There's some power to knowing what has happened, in understanding it so that it's not repeated, in learning about a time long forgotten, but this is something different. The words themselves contain a certain amount of strength." He nodded to the small book Jakob held.

Jakob stared at the book. "The ancient language?"

When Novan nodded, his eyes glittered.

"You said that when you gave me the book to read."

"I said it because it's true," Novan agreed. "There are things written in the ancient language that are more powerful than others. And this text is different from any other."

"Why?"

Novan shook his head. "It was written by those who knew the ancient language better than any know it now. There's an insight into the language that could not be gained in any other way. Yet there is more." He turned toward the entrance to the tent, as if looking out into the night. "It may be part of the reason the Deshmahne push as they do now. Endric is out of the city. The Magi's greatest defender in the open. The High Priest knows this and that the Deshmahne are finally strong enough to challenge the Magi."

"You said part of the reason. What else?"

"There's something he seeks, a reason for him to come himself rather than to send those beneath him. Something that will make him more powerful than he already is."

The trunk he'd seen. It had to be. "You think he will attack us here?" Jakob's heart started racing as he thought about getting caught in the middle of some attack. He might have gotten better with the sword, but not so much that he thought he could help in a war.

"If their numbers are as we saw in Endric's tent, then that's the only possibility I see."

~

The following few days went quickly. Jakob grew increasingly tired of riding, and his evenings were spent working with Rit before seeking out the general to practice, a new urgency driving him to improve. He fell asleep exhausted each night, dreams barely more than memories in the morning, but still haunting him as he awoke. Dark shapes danced just outside his vision, and always there was someone he couldn't see or reach calling to him.

The sense of being followed, being watched, was now with him day and night. During the day, it was barely more than a whisper at his senses, a tingle at the back of his mind that made the hairs on his neck stand up, and at night it was nothing more than dreams and visions. Jakob had not mentioned it to Novan again for fear of what it would mean. There was the constant fear that the madness had found him.

He couldn't let that thought linger. There were other concerns he struggled with. He spent each night poring over the book Novan had lent him, now most of the way through it, but still barely any better at understanding the ancient language than he had been when he started. At least he recognized the lettering, but he still didn't think he'd manage the inflection. The words felt strange to him, and his mouth struggled to pronounce them when he tried. Even the name of his sword, Neamiin, was a challenge to him. He couldn't pronounce it nearly the same way he remembered Novan speaking the word.

Novan had said it was a word full of meaning, and Jakob thought he would discover something of it by reading through the text, some reference to it—even if he didn't understand it—but had found little. Tonight was no different.

After working with Rit setting the tent line, he learned watch was later. Rit had excused him, but Jakob insisted. He was determined to act the role of Denraen while assigned to the soldier. Rit grunted before agreeing; Jakob imagined Rit wore a pleased expression as he set off, leaving Jakob to head to his tent to read until their watch began. Exhaustion hit him before he had gotten far, and he found his eyes heavy, barely able to force through the page he'd been staring at for some time.

Shaking his head to clear it, he forced himself up and stored the book in his pack before stepping from his tent. Outside, the night air was crisp and carried with it the leafy hint of fall decay mixed with the rain he'd sensed for days. His stomach grumbled, and he thought to ignore it before thinking better and turning toward the central cook-fire to find something to eat. The sound of someone hurrying toward him gave him pause, and he turned to see a Denraen jogging his way.

It was Braden.

He'd caught only glimpses of his friend since leaving Chrysia, enough to wave and nothing more. Jakob expected Braden to find him, but he also understood that his friend would be busy settling in with the Denraen as well.

"I have a night free. I thought I'd see how you've managed since we left," Braden said. There was a hint of breathlessness, and sweat beaded across his brow. He'd always been a muscular person, but he was even leaner than when they had left.

Jakob suspected he looked different, as well, but it was more a reflection of the time he had spent working with Endric. He'd always been tall like his father, but never had the muscle that he gained now. "We've both been busy."

"So I've heard. What's happened?" he asked, his gaze dropping to the sword sheathed at Jakob's side.

"You mean with Endric?"

Braden laughed. "Do I mean Endric? Of course, I do! Who else works with him as often as you do? But more than that, how'd you get so *good?*"

"I don't know," Jakob answered. "I started working with him before leaving the city. With him teaching, it just clicks."

Braden laughed. "I can't say I understand. I don't dare face him."

Jakob wasn't sure he would have dared to face him had he known who he was from the beginning.

"The men of the Denraen talk about you," Braden said. "Some call you a fool."

"Only some?" he laughed.

Braden arched an eyebrow and tilted his head before shrugging. "There are those who don't," he admitted without elaborating.

Who *wouldn't* think him foolish for working with the general? Endric never said he couldn't work with him, and Novan expected it. Between those two, there was little choice for him.

"That's not why I came looking for you, though I'm curious what you might have learned from the general. Perhaps now, you could teach me something."

"I doubt that." Braden was nearly as good a swordsman as Chrysia possessed.

Braden ran a hand through his hair, looking over his shoulder nervously as he did. "I need advice." There was a momentary flash of worry to his eyes, maybe even fear, though Jakob wasn't sure he saw it in the shadows of the night. "There's something I've seen, something I fear. I'm not sure where else to go, or to who—"

A man came up behind him, interrupting them. "Nialsen," Tolsin said. He was shorter than Braden and had a rough face, his nose wide as if broken repeatedly. He scratched at his arm absently. "Braden, you're needed," Tolsin said.

Braden frowned before nodding. "Who?"

"Iker," Tolsin said.

Braden cocked his head. "Give me a moment?"

Tolsin shook his head. He had worn his hair long before joining the Denraen, and the close-cropped blond stubble looked strange upon him, giving his scalp a pale glow in the night. "Orders were to get you without delay."

Braden snuffed before turning to Jakob and giving him a half-mouthed smile. "Orders," he said. "I will find you later, then. Maybe then I can see what the general's taught you!" He followed Tolsin, glancing back once. The expression on his face was one Jakob wasn't used to seeing from his friend: one of anxiety.

Watching Braden depart, he wondered what could have gotten his friend so anxious. There had been real concern in his eyes, a worry Jakob had never seen. There was a little stoop to his shoulders that was new, and a little of the swagger he knew was missing. Fatigue, he hoped. The gods help him if it was something more.

"Something burdens you."

Jakob spun, surprised that someone had come upon him so silently. Roelle stood behind him, a bemused expression on her face. Roelle wore her dark hair tied back with a cord. A long wooden practice sword hung loosely in her hand, and she was dressed in a light shirt and pants in spite of the cool night. There was an easy grace to her steps, a confidence, and Jakob stepped back momentarily before catching himself.

"I thought I'd find you to spar since Endric is unavailable. I need a good challenge."

"Not me then," he answered without thinking.

Roelle laughed. It was low and throaty and did not carry far into the deepening night. "You continue to underestimate yourself. If only you could see yourself as others do, you might think different."

Jakob shrugged and they walked in silence for a little while before he spoke. "Novan admits that he seeks the Council."

Roelle turned to him. "I thought as much."

"There is some text he seeks. He thinks the Deshmahne High Priest seeks it as well."

Roelle slowed a step before picking up her pace. "Has he spoken to Haerlin of this?"

Jakob shook his head. "They're not on the best of terms."

The Mage laughed. "I don't think he'll be granted access to what he seeks."

"Why?"

"The historian didn't leave by choice the last time he visited. I suspect it has something to do with this text. There are certain items within the capital that only the Elders on the Council are allowed to access."

"Novan said there was power in the text."

"There is much the Council possesses that is powerful," Roelle agreed.

Jakob paused before pressing forward. "What do you know of the ancient language?"

Roelle smiled. "I've learned a little but will learn more when I'm fully trained. It's not for an untrained Mage." There was a hint of annoyance to her words.

"Why is that? I think Novan knows some of it."

Roelle snorted. "I wouldn't doubt it." She shook her head. "You mention powerful texts. There is power in the old tongue, something innate to it, almost an energy it focuses. Few know how to properly control it." She shrugged before adding, "I know little of it myself."

They reached a small clearing near the center of the camp where the Denraen had taken to practicing. Roelle grabbed a second wooden sword and tossed it to Jakob, twirling the remaining one in her hand. "Now, let us break the silence of the night."

Jakob stepped into a low crouch to prepare when he saw someone coming toward them. As the man neared, Jakob realized it was the general. Rit was with him.

"Such an unlikely pair," Endric said.

"Not as unlikely as you would think," Roelle said.

Endric focused on Roelle for a long moment before blinking and turning to Jakob. "I'm sending a scout mission. Men are missing, and we will know what happened. Rit and his raegan are going. I told him I knew where to find you."

"You want me to go?" Jakob asked, surprised.

It was Rit who answered. "You're part of the raegan, if unofficially."

"The historian knows of the mission," Endric said. "He's asked you to observe."

Jakob felt a mix of emotion. Surprise and fear mingled together along with a nervous excitement.

"But observe only," Endric said.

"I'd like to go as well," Roelle said suddenly.

All eyes turned to her.

Roelle shrugged. "Call it curiosity. I will go if you will have me," she said to Rit.

"This is for scouting only. Not rescue. Your eyes will help." Mage eyesight was known to be a little sharper, especially at night. "We will leave soon."

~

They started off through long grasses, nothing but a sliver of moon overhead lighting the way. Rit led them at a slow jog, and Jakob glanced longingly at the line of horses.

"Quieter without," a man named Tian informed. He wore his hair long and in tight braids, a polished crossbow at his side. He was the Denraen Jakob had spoken to the first night they had camped. Other than Rit, Tian had been the most welcoming of the raegan.

The heavy plod of hooves could be heard for long distances. Their footsteps were quiet, though he felt his were much louder than the others, stomping through the thick grass tearing at his ankles. He wondered if they left a trail that could be easily followed and hazarded a look back. The knee-high grass, so lifeless and brown by daylight, was a flowing sea by the light of the moon, and the areas they had trampled just flowed back together, hiding their tracks from all but a close inspection.

They ran silently, and Jakob soon huffed with the effort. He'd need to gain conditioning if he was to survive this new lifestyle, though he'd probably gain it if he tried or not. His sword hung at his side, and he was slowly becoming accustomed to its weight. Rit and Tian ran ahead, their breaths growing only slightly louder in the silence. Another Denraen ran behind them, carrying his short bow and his quiver strapped to his hip. Roelle ran next to him; she'd said nothing since they left but had found a thin sword and had it strapped to her waist. She had left on her dark pants and shirt and blended into the night.

They had run a long time, down several valleys only to rise up the sloping hills again, when they saw light in the distance. Rit slowed them and signaled them to drop, and Jakob did so as quietly as he could manage.

They crawled, the sound of their passing lost in the blowing of the wind across the grassy plain. Jakob felt the wet of the evening dew begin to soak him, and he struggled not to shiver. The ground under his hands and knees was moist, and he occasionally thought that something crawled near him. It took all his will power not to stand.

Another feeling returned, one he dreaded. He felt a crawling in his head and looked out into the surrounding night, wondering what he sensed. Now was not the time to fall to this madness. He imagined a dark shape crouching low by a nearby tree, but when he blinked, it was gone. Jakob forced the feeling out of his mind.

Reaching the crest of the hill, they looked down on a camp. "Reckless," Rit muttered but said no more.

Several fires blazed high into the night, lighting everything for them to see easily. Tents were arranged without care or organization. Lines of horses were carelessly tied near a small stream. Men lounged near the fires, some eating, some drinking, others playing at stones. There were women that wandered the camp, some who cooked and others who sat near men with hands that wandered. A few of the women seemed willing, but most did not.

It was a large camp, and nearly four times that of the Denraen. If these men were all raiders, there was more coordination here than had been suspected. Novan would have his theories when he reported back to him. Jakob searched for evidence of the captured scouts.

His eyes were pulled to where the tents were arranged differently, more carefully, and there was a more solemn tone to the men around it. Jakob almost imagined a separation between the men in this part of the camp and the other part of the camp. Something structural, but there was something else as well. Jakob wasn't sure what he sensed.

Just then, he saw something else, something that would stay with him for a long time. Wooden posts were arranged around a small fire, and men with the Denraen gray were tied to each. As he watched, one man was kicked casually in the chest, one of his legs already hanging useless as he struggled to stay upright. Jakob wondered why the man bothered.

A raider dipped a long steel wand into the flames, the metal quickly turning red, and brought it out to place it on one of the captive's cheeks. The man screamed again.

Jakob was more fearful than ever of being caught. Forcing himself to watch, he stared at the men around the fire. Another man stood before the branded man, asking questions. With each shake of the Denraen's head, the brand touched his face. Jakob found it difficult to tear his eyes away.

His right hand crept to his side until he grasped the hilt of his sword. He felt the twinge of a headache growing, but he ignored it. Pulling on his sword, feeling the sensation in the back of his mind, he paused as another man entered the circle, followed closely by several others. The man was dressed in a dark robe, and there was a sense about him that Jakob felt even from a distance, one he recognized.

The High Priest.

The Deshmahne priest had been haunting his dreams.

Why was he here? Why torture Denraen? His heart began to pound.

A dark haze floated around him, smoke and dust starting to

shadow his view. Another scream pierced the night. The man in black moved to the nearest edge of the circle, and the smoke seemed to follow, surrounding him and blurring his features. Suddenly, he looked up and scanned the night, almost as if he sensed something near the camp, before looking right at where they should be hidden by night.

The sight of the man sucked the wind out of him, and he dropped fully to the ground, but not before seeing his eyes. They were lit unnaturally by light reflected from the fire.

Jakob's hand still gripped the hilt of his sword and the weight of his body atop it prevented him from unsheathing it. His head pounded again, vibrating with the pain, and he forced himself to relax.

Rit crawled back to him, concern evident on his face. "It's difficult for us all." Tian hadn't moved but kept watch over the raider camp. Roelle looked at him with a guarded expression.

"That's not it," Jakob whispered.

"What, then?" Roelle asked quietly.

"I've seen the man in black," Jakob whispered, his voice barely above that of the wind, and he wondered if Rit would be able to even hear him.

"What man in black?" Rit asked.

Jakob carefully looked up and looked at the camp again. The man was gone. "He was there. I've seen him before."

"Where?" Rit asked.

"Chrysia. It is the High Priest."

"Are you sure?" Roelle asked.

Jakob nodded.

Rit silently tapped Tian on his boot. They crept back, eyes alert, until they were safely back to the base of the valley. Even then, they didn't speak and moved carefully, bodies low to keep their profiles from the growing moonlight. They moved more slowly back toward their own camp, yet Jakob felt the same fatigue he had known when they'd started. He suspected it was the hyper-vigilance his body trembled with, every sound a raider creeping up on them, every gust of the wind carrying their scent.

Thoughts were startled from him as the three men appeared.

Steel glinted angrily in the thin light as the men raised their weapons. Rit quickly unsheathed and Tian pulled his crossbow up and aimed. The Denraen with the bow readied nearly as quickly as Tian. Jakob fumbled a bit with his own sword but managed to unsheathe it.

There was a *snick* of Tian's crossbow loosing a bolt. One of the men in front of them cried out and dropped into the grass as the other two men took off running. Rit and the other Denraen chased, but the men were quick and distanced themselves easily. He heard another bolt as it whistled through the air, but it missed its target and fell harmlessly away from the men.

The man Tian had dropped lived, but barely. The bolt had taken him through his left shoulder, and his shirt was dark with blood. Tian searched the body. There was nothing but his sword, which Tian collected. His clothing was plain, brown burlap, all of it, and it stank. They left him where he died. Jakob wondered briefly if it angered the gods that they didn't return him to the earth.

When Rit returned after failing to catch the raiders, he led them back with a purposeful step. They needed to report what they'd witnessed, Rit to Endric, and Jakob to Novan.

Another concern worried him almost as much. They'd been seen, and the High Priest would soon know.

CHAPTER THIRTEEN

"Report," the general demanded inside his tent. A single lantern flickered with an orange light, leaving shadows hiding the edges of the tent. Endric's voice was rough, almost as if he'd been sleeping. His eyes denied it; they were bright with awareness.

Rit spoke. "Northern raider camp, sir. Nearly three hundred, mayhap more. Women among them. About five miles north." The general nodded with each succinct statement, taking it all in as if he had been there. Jakob could almost see the man's mind working. "Three scouts," Rit continued. "Tian took out one. Two escaped." There was irritation in his voice at admitting two had escaped.

"There's more?" It was not really a question.

Rit spoke reluctantly. "We saw our men. Each was bound to a post and tortured."

The general's eyes blazed in anger. "What else?"

Rit nudged Jakob, and he found himself answering. "There was a man, dressed all in black." He hazarded a look over to Rit who urged him on with a nod. "I think it was the High Priest."

"Damn him!" Endric swore as he squeezed his eyes tight. As they opened, there was an extreme focus written upon his face. "He dares to take my men and thinks to intimidate us with their numbers?"

A man parted the tent flaps and came running in. "Raider camps are mobilizing, sir," he panted.

The general turned to him. "When?"

The man shook his head. "Soon. The north, mostly," the man hurried. "But some east and west."

"It's too soon," Rit said. "It should take longer to organize an attack."

"And now he thinks to attack? The historian might be right about this," Endric sighed. "And happening sooner than I had expected. We must get the Magi to safety." The words were spoken over their shoulders.

"We're less than a day's ride to the other camp," a voice from behind Jakob answered.

He recognized the hard tone and turned to see the Raen, his scarred face solemn. The man had stepped into the tent and was already dressed and ready, his sword strapped to his side. There was an air of intensity around him that made Jakob take a slight step back.

"If we can meet the other camp, we'd have greater numbers," the Raen continued.

"Agreed," Endric said. "We may have to delay until they reach us. Send riders ahead as warning."

"I have," the Raen said.

Endric paused. "There is the other," he said, speaking only to Pendin.

Jakob looked over to the man and saw conflicted emotions cross his face.

"I am yours to command," the Raen said.

Endric gave him a long look, considering. "That is for me," he started, then shook his head. "Was. You'll be needed. The Magi must be protected. I think the bastard anticipated my dilemma."

The Raen nodded, a flash of relief crossing his face, and turned to leave, taking all but Jakob and Rit with him. Shouted commands followed him.

As Endric turned to Rit, his eyes lingered on Jakob. "Yours is a different task. The Magi escort has been only part of our mission. There's something else we escort north, something of power the

Deshmahne must not reach. I was to have been the one to complete this mission. When this is over..."

Endric sighed. "If the High Priest was there, the Magi must have a full escort. I can't abandon them to the Deshmahne." He squeezed his eyes shut and then nodded. "You will take your raegan north," he said to Rit. Grabbing a large map rolled up behind him, he opened it. "Here," he said, pointing to a location far to the north. Around it was nothing but mountains.

Rit arched an eyebrow. "What is it we take with us?"

Endric turned again, carefully removing a small trunk before setting it on the table beside him. The trunk was plain looking. Painted a deep purple, it was almost black, and tight lettering surrounding the lid. There was something about it that seemed ancient, yet the wood was polished, and the ornately decorated clasp remained bright.

"You must take this and deliver it here," He jabbed at the map. "This is what the Deshmahne are after."

Rit frowned. "Sir?"

"This is what they were after in Chrysia. This is why the temple was destroyed. Inside is something valuable, something the Urmahne have protected for centuries. The gods only know how he learned of it." Endric studied the map intently before sighing and straightening his back. "I have known you a long time, Rit."

Rit nodded. "You have."

"Know then that this may be the most important mission I've ever asked of you. If we fail... the Deshmahne may be free to roam the north."

"This will stop them?"

"It is part of the key to stopping them."

Rit turned to look over his shoulder, toward the tent opening. Jakob could sense the man's thoughts, his concern for the Magi he had sworn to protect, the men he had sworn he would stand next to and fight, but Jakob knew the general left little room to do other than he asked. Rit turned back to face the general. "It will be as you command."

An edge of tension seemed to leave the general with the words. "I know you will. I'll return the Magi to Vasha and meet you there. Make haste, and the gods willing, I will find you soon."

Rit carefully picked up the small trunk before turning to leave.

~

Jakob found Novan only moments later. The camp was hastily being broken, and men were readying for a quick departure. Novan paced where their tent would have been, his thin frame full of nervous energy.

"You were with them then?" he asked without preamble.

Jakob nodded. "I'd gone on the scouting mission."

"And you recognized the High Priest?" Novan asked, scratching his head as he spoke.

Another nod. "I didn't feel him as I did before, but even with the smoke surrounding him, I knew it was him."

Novan stopped pacing. "Others didn't mention the smoke."

Jakob shouldn't have been surprised Novan had spoken to the other men, getting a full accounting of what was seen. "Mention it or not, it was there, almost following him."

"Are you sure it was the High Priest?"

"It was him."

Novan looked at Jakob carefully before continuing. "You were with Endric for the reporting?"

Jakob nodded.

Novan had started pacing again, fiddling with the ring upon his middle finger as he looked out at the night in deep concentration. "Who continues north?"

The question surprised him. How had Novan known this already?

"Rit," he answered. "He's taking his raegan. The general intends to meet him once he returns the Magi to the capital."

"Rit and a raegan?" Novan paused briefly, then started pacing again. "Not Endric?"

"As I said, he's escorting the Magi."

"Damn Deshmahne. *This* is what they planned? The timing is too suspect. How could they have known?" Novan's irritation reminded

Jakob of the anger Endric had when he had discovered the Deshmahne attack. "Endric is right, though. If there are even a few Deshmahne with those raiders, it will be difficult. And they might be able to divert the Deshmahne attention." He scratched his chin. "Perhaps this will work."

He looked at Jakob intently. "Endric was tasked with something of vital importance. He, like myself, is a member of an ancient society. Truly, it should be he who travels north."

"The Conclave?" Jakob asked, remembering what he had overheard.

Novan stared at Jakob, twisting the ring on his finger as he nodded. "You are observant. The Conclave needs that trunk to travel north. The priests revealed it to the Magi when there was word of the Deshmahne threat coming from the south. The Conclave decided the Magi could not be trusted with its safety."

Jakob watched Novan, who seemed to be considering the plan Endric had in mind. "Endric *should* be the one traveling with it, but perhaps he is wiser than I. For now, I'll remain with him and continue with the Magi. It's possible that we can draw them away. And there's something I need to find in their city and keep from the Deshmahne, else I would not ask this of you."

"Me?"

"I need someone I trust to go north. Since it can't be me... I need to ask something of you. For this, you might even be better prepared." He looked at Jakob a long moment, his eyes falling to the sword strapped to Jakob's side. "Endric tells me that you've become quite skilled with the sword. What I ask will put you in danger, but is important to have a witness.

"This must be documented, Jakob. Do this well, and you will be well on your way to becoming a historian, but you'll need every ounce of skill you've acquired. You and I have spoken of the attacks in the north. There are more than raiders in the north, more than Deshmahne to fear." He locked eyes with Jakob. "Know that I don't send you on this journey lightly, but you can serve in an important way, and this may actually require your special skills."

"But I have no special skills," Jakob stammered.

Novan smiled. "You're more skilled than you know. I need you to go on this mission to the north. If they're attacked, I'm of little use. I'll follow the Magi to the capital and travel with Endric when he meets up with you." He stopped, looking carefully at Jakob. "This is important, Jakob. You should know that much depends on the success of this journey."

What was he to say? Novan asked him to ride into possible danger so that he could observe and record. What would the historian say if he refused?

His life had changed dramatically in the last few weeks, and for the most part, he enjoyed it. Could he return to Chrysia and be happy? There was nothing there, nothing except a brother barely more than a body. He had no other family in Chrysia and no reason to return.

"I'll go. I'm afraid," he told Novan honestly, "but I'll go."

"I wish I could tell you there was nothing to fear but know there is danger along my path as well." He paused, looking around the camp that was nearly a memory. "I promise you'll know more when we meet up again in the north. For now, observe only. Don't interfere. Travel swiftly, travel safely, and keep your eyes open. But do everything you must to see that trunk to Avaneam."

"I will," Jakob said.

"And Jakob," Novan continued. "Stay alive."

It was a frightening warning, and with that, he left, uncertain if he would see Novan again.

Roelle caught Jakob as he was heading to find Rit. Tents were disassembled, and the line of horses was getting arranged. All around him, everyone prepared to depart. The Mage had not changed back into her robes, remaining in the pants and shirt she'd scouted in. She looked more the part of soldier than Mage.

"You're leaving," Roelle said.

"Novan asked me to go north with Rit to observe."

The Mage frowned. "Why north?"

"I... I don't really know."

Roelle seemed pensive. "There's something going on in the north, but I haven't learned what it is. I wish Haerlin had shared more with me. I fear there's more danger along your path than mine."

"Novan fears the same," Jakob said.

"Yet he sends you instead of himself? What does he seek?" she wondered, more to herself. "It's a shame we didn't have a chance to know each other better. I wish you the safety of the gods, Jakob. May you have their protection. And may we meet again."

There was little the gods would do to protect him. He'd lost their favor years ago, had seen their displeasure as they took first his mother then his brother and father from him. Still, he nodded. He wouldn't argue with a Mage.

"May you have their protection, as well, Roelle," he replied.

As they parted ways, Jakob knew a moment of sadness. It wasn't the idea of not seeing her again, though she *was* beautiful. He'd never seen a woman quite so stunning. Yet... it wasn't that. She was a Mage, a hand of the gods. In spite of that, Roelle had been becoming a friend. He would miss his friend.

CHAPTER FOURTEEN

"Endric told me that you would come." Rit spoke quickly, hurriedly checking his horse and running along the line of horses and speaking briefly to each man.

"I'll try not to be a hindrance," Jakob said.

"I've seen you with a sword. You'll be no hindrance."

"I was told to only observe," Jakob answered.

Rit nodded, and his smile twisted his crooked face. "I can't promise. Might be you're needed for more."

He said nothing more and walked down the line of the horses, finishing with the last man. Jakob looked around at the nearly dozen men who rode with him, recognizing the men of Rit's raegan, and realized others would come as well. He saw the northman and the other man from earlier in the evening. Each wore a serious look on his face and something more. Irritation? Anger?

Starting off, Rit spurred them forward at a quick clip, and they left the remnants of the camp behind. Jakob hazarded a glance back and saw the rest of the camp moving quickly to the west. Roelle rode to the rear before looking over to him and raising a slow wave, a sad smile on her face. Though he tried, he didn't see Braden and hoped his friend would be safe.

The night was not dark; the light of the moon hovered overhead, and they rode swiftly, the cold air biting through his cloak. They hadn't ridden long before Jakob felt the crawling sensation creep back into his mind. He looked around, the strange irritation making him jumpy, and thought he saw catlike eyes in the distance. When he blinked, they were gone.

"The night will do that," a voice next to him said.

Jakob looked over and saw Tian. "There are times I feel we're being watched."

Tian nodded. "Might be we are."

Jakob looked around again, wondering if Tian had seen something, but the Denraen man just grunted. Jakob looked over and saw the man staring up. "You think the gods are watching us?" he asked as realization came to him.

Tian shrugged. "I think they do. Them, or their servants." He was silent for long moments. "Or maybe it's just a wolf."

A man behind them laughed. Jakob turned and saw the northman. He was still grinning.

"His faith is like that of a priest," he said seriously, and then laughed again.

Jakob smiled before turning back around. They were moving too quickly to lose his focus. If he fell from the saddle, he wouldn't get up easily. As they rode, a faint sound drifted toward them from the way they had come. Jakob looked back, wondering what it was that he heard.

"The battle has begun," Tian said quietly.

Jakob looked over to the Denraen. "Already? Is that what I hear?"

Tian nodded slowly. There was a hint of regret in the movement. Jakob wondered what it took for these men to leave their friends behind, even ordered as they were. He knew it wasn't fear driving these men forward. Could he have stayed behind and fought? Was it better that he'd been sent north?

At least it kept him from battle, but what more might he face? What more existed in the north?

The sounds of the battle behind them grew fainter and fainter until they were merely imagined. Jakob pushed all thoughts from his head, including the strange feeling, and tried to keep his focus on the ride. He was tired; he'd not slept tonight, and dawn was not far off. The scouting mission had taken much out of him, and it wasn't until now that he was suffering the consequences. What he'd seen had kept him awake until now, but suddenly, he was finding it difficult to stay alert in the saddle.

Jakob shook his head, trying to maintain awareness. None of the Denraen seemed to struggle, but none said anything, either. All were silent; the only sound that of steady plodding of their horses over the ground. Jakob wondered if he would even hear anything if they were attacked.

At the thought, the sound of hooves raced toward them. There was a quick whistle followed by one in response, and Rit called a halt. A Denraen man rode up, his horse heaving with the effort.

It was a scout.

His clothing was tattered, his once-crisp uniform now frayed and bloodstained. Slowing, he sat high in his saddle, his back straight.

"Report," Rit ordered.

"The attack. Not far from camp, we were attacked. Large group, we were outnumbered. Most dead. Mathin's men from the south arrived. Turned the tide. Endric taking remaining men and Magi north fast," he panted.

Two words struck in Jakob's ears. Most dead. Were Novan or Braden among those lost? At least it sounded like the Magi were safe. It was small solace. "How many Deshmahne?"

The scout turned a skeptical eye to him before shaking his head. "Too many," he answered. "It was why our casualties were so high."

"How many survived?" Rit asked.

"Fifteen, maybe twenty men."

"Fifteen men of our squad left?" Rit asked incredulously.

The scout shook his head. "That's all told, includes Mathin's men from the south."

"They were nearly eighty!" Rit said.

The scout frowned. "If I hadn't seen it myself, I wouldn't believe. The raiders sent men near as good as the general at us. They tore through our lines. Endric took out a handful of them but will have another scar."

The men grunted approval. The Denraen didn't disapprove of scars.

"The young Mage even joined. Saved the historian's life as he was about to be struck down. She moves about as fast as the general."

Roelle joined the battle. How would that sit with Haerlin? How did that fit with the Magi's unwillingness to harm another person? From what Jakob had seen, Roelle had a different view of what it meant to be a Mage.

"What of us?" someone asked.

Jakob turned to see who had said it but couldn't be sure.

Rit did the same. "We continue as ordered."

The scout nodded. "That's why I'm here. General wanted you to know what happened but to ride on as planned."

"Can they handle another attack?" It was the northman who asked. These men would not disobey their orders, but they had real concern for their men, for their general. He shared it.

"I don't know. I'm to rejoin them. I was to check your safety and return. With the gods," the man finished.

"With the gods," Rit said.

The scout turned his horse and rode off, quickly disappearing.

Rit wasted little time. He turned them north again, and they rode hard. Jakob quickly lost track of time, and his legs and thighs began to throb. Rit rode them at a faster pace than they had ridden the previous week. Gradually, night faded and the hint of daylight touched the horizon.

"How will we find this place?" he overheard Tian ask Rit as they rode.

Rit took long moments to answer. "It lies along the Elasiin path, near Siirvil's Peak."

Tian sucked in his breath. "But the reports."

Rit nodded. "I know the reports as well as you." He looked over to the Denraen with a grim look on his face. "We need speed. It is the only way."

Tian said nothing. "What do you think is there?"

"Endric didn't say. Said he'd rejoin us before we reached the destination."

"Not that," Tian replied.

Jakob did not think Rit would answer, but finally, he did. "The reports are brutal. Towns empty, families slaughtered. A rotting stench overtop of everything." He heaved a heavy sigh. "Each report the same. That is not raiders."

"Then what?" Tian asked.

Rit shook his head. "I don't know. But I fear we may find out. And if what the general says is true, what we carry may be the only way to stop what's coming."

Jakob shivered at what he heard. What had he gotten himself into?

His fear deepened as they rode northward, unease mixing with the strange sensation sitting in the back of his mind. Not the madness. It couldn't be coming on him now. The air smelled of horse sweat and dust, but there was a hint of something else. Rot? He shook the thought from him and tried to push it from his mind.

If these Denraen were concerned about the north, what chance did he have? Turning around wouldn't get him anywhere. Where would he go? What could he do? He had no skills, no other training. His life was this now.

A thought came to him, and he wondered if it was the lack of sleep or delirium that brought it. Would Jarren Gildeun feel afraid?

He is nothing but a story. This is real. My life is real. This danger is real.

The scenery changed little as they rode. Small copses of trees dotted the countryside, and long grasses were brown with late fall and fell before their horses. They stayed out of the trees, heading straight north, cutting through the grass. There were occasional streams that meandered before them, and they often paused to give the horses a drink, but it was never long.

Jakob was exhausted. He had struggled to stay upright in the saddle before, now it was a force of will alone that kept him alert. The men around him were growing equally weary, and Rit seemed to sense it, leading them at a slower pace. Jakob wondered how long they would ride before resting, wondered how much longer the horses could maintain their pace. His eyes drifted closed.

Dreams of creatures and places from Novan's books taunted him with words he did not understand, though comprehension drifted just at the edge of his mind. He felt fear, could smell it, and could almost see walls surrounding him stretching up and up. There was a flash, and he suddenly saw mountains in the distance, strange hairless creatures crawling along the mountain passes, and storm clouds rolling toward him. He felt himself surrounded, though couldn't see who stood nearby. He sensed the others around him, but looking around saw nothing but fog and smoke. Jakob smelled neither. Peacefulness radiated from the smoke and fog, and he felt at ease.

Turning his head, he was now in the mountains, something pulling him forward. Pale gray rock around him stretched high into the sky, and he saw snow-covered peaks in the distance. The dark clouds were now overhead, and he could feel the oncoming storm deep within. Alone, he could not see the invisible force that pulled him forward. There was something here he needed, could feel its importance, and he knew his mission necessary. The sense of peace was gone, replaced by fear and emptiness. Jakob had known this feeling before, knew the source...

Suddenly startled, he looked around, fearful of what might have awoken him. He had been dreaming, but the dream was unlike any he had known. His dreams had been so vivid lately, a depth to them that was nearly real, and he had attributed it to his fatigue. This was different, almost a vision.

It became more and more difficult to deny what was happening to him. It had to be the madness.

Turning back to address his men, Rit said, "We will rest atop this rise—" He froze.

His hard eyes scanned behind them in the early dawn, and what they found was not to his liking.

"To the trees!" he hollered, steering the men to a nearby grove.

The horses leaped forward, slower than they had been earlier in the day yet still responsive. Jakob glanced back, wondering what Rit had seen and felt the sudden heavy weight of fear grow in his stomach.

They were followed.

The raiders who chased them were close. How long had they been following, and how they had managed to get so close without being spotted? There were at least two dozen men bearing down on them quickly. He looked ahead to where Rit led them. The small copse would not hide them, but Jakob quickly realized that was not Rit's intent. Their horses were too tired to run far or fast. The men were nearly as tired, yet Rit obviously intended to fight.

They reached the trees that were not particularly large, with trunks only a foot or so wide, but Rit intended to use them to aid their defense. Rit quickly dismounted, and several other Denraen did the same. Rit held onto the general's trunk in one hand and held his sword in another. He shouted a rough order that Jakob didn't catch, and suddenly, three Denraen still mounted on their horses, raced forward, swords out and ready. They reached the advancing raiders and tore through the first several men who had been caught unprepared, dropping them quickly from their saddles before turning hard and riding back toward the trees.

A crossbow bolt dropped one of the retreating Denraen from behind, and he yelled out as he fell. The other men hunched low on their horses as they rode.

"Dismount!" Rit yelled. Jakob hesitated, and Rit stalked over.

"The historian—"

"We are outnumbered. You will fight with us, or we all die."

Novan had told him to observe only, but Novan had also wanted him to survive.

Jakob unsheathed his sword, feeling its heavy weight as it nearly vibrated in his hand. He'd never fought with a real sword. Would he be able? The question mattered little, he knew. There was only one option.

The distraction had worked, buying them some extra time. The Denraen were arranged deep enough in the woods that the raiders would have to come at them without their mounts. Jakob wondered if that gave them an advantage. The raiders rode toward them, outnumbering them nearly two to one. Suddenly, several of them went down, and Jakob looked over to see Tian and several archers preparing another volley. They didn't have time.

The raiders were upon them.

Jakob remained toward the back, watching. The Denraen fought well, but the numbers were against them, and there were screams as several men went down. The clang of steel reverberated through him, and his head pounded with it, mixing with the cries of men injured or dying. And then there was a raider in front of him, his face splattered with blood.

The raider brought his sword around in a hard arc, and Jakob reacted, blocking the blow.

The sharp sound of metal on metal was different from the clack of the wooden practice staves, and his sword moved differently than the practice staves. It was heavier, almost awkward, and he nearly lost an arm blocking the man's second swing.

Something was familiar, though. The slow vibrating, the pulsing at the back of his head was there. It beckoned him. Another barely blocked blow came, and Jakob reached for the vibration as he had only one or two times before, and felt it course through him.

With it, his vision was crisper. His sword felt lighter, more natural, and it felt as if he was suddenly released.

Jakob let his mind go blank, and he danced with the man, stepping through a quick defensive catah before jumping in attack. A few quick strokes, and he cleaved off the man's sword arm and he went down.

Jakob faltered, and it seemed as if everything lurched forward. The sounds of the battle were chaos around him, and the air was heavy with the stink of blood. He shook that from his mind and looked at the raider.

Was this what his father would have wanted for him? Was this what he was meant to become? A killer?

The battle was going poorly for the Denraen. Only about five men still stood, and he counted nearly a dozen raiders moving among them. As he watched, three of the Denraen went down, and it was only Rit and Tian still standing, and both were severely injured. Blood from countless cuts on both men soaked their uniforms. Tian nearly collapsed before Rit pulled him up, and they used a large tree near the center of the grove for cover. The raiders were slowly circling, and it was only a matter of time before they would be taken.

Something propelled Jakob forward.

His sword whistled, one side blazing bright with light reflected off the early morning sun and the other side black as night. The vibrating in his head was nearly audible, and it sent waves washing through him, waves he welcomed.

And then he was among the raiders. He flowed through the catahs, his body and mind working seamlessly, his sword knowing where to go. It was as if he was too fast for the men, and he dropped two raiders before they knew he was there.

Jakob didn't hesitate. His sword hummed with his head, almost knowing what he wanted of it. Three men turned to face him, and he didn't hesitate.

There was a clarity to his thoughts that he'd only known while holding a sword, an awareness he couldn't explain. It allowed him to see where the men were moving. They attacked together, and Jakob stepped through a careful dance, his sword blocking the men's slower movements. He twisted, his body flowing with the waves pounding through him, and as his sword met resistance, he pushed through it to move on to the next wave.

The men facing him fell, and he turned, looking to Rit and Tian. He was too late. Tian was down, and as he watched, Rit was dropped as a sword took him in the side. There were still five raiders left, and it was only he left standing.

The raiders all turned to face him.

Two men jumped forward, and Jakob was ready. He flowed through a catah, his body nearly vibrating, and the men fell. Again, his sword had known where to go. Two more men jumped forward. He brushed through one, taking him harshly across the chest, and turned to the other man when something made him pause.

Recognition.

"Tolsin?" he whispered.

The clarity faded, and his mind seemed to suddenly slow. What was Tolsin doing with the raiders? He was Denraen, having joined them during The Choosing in Chrysia. Yet dark markings were etched along his arm, twisting their way from his wrist to his elbow.

Tolsin was Deshmahne.

The Denraen had been infiltrated.

Had Braden known? Was this why Braden had come to him?

"Jakob?" Tolsin asked. He looked back at the remaining raider. "I can't do this. He's a friend!"

The remaining raider laughed. Jakob saw that both of the man's arms were covered in thick tattoos. Several worked their way up his neck. Another Deshmahne. Jakob had seen the Deshmahne attack Endric, had seen how even the general had struggled with the Deshmahne warrior.

A chill went through him.

"Use him to show the gods your power," the man growled.

Jakob looked back as Tolsin hesitated. "Don't do this, Tolsin. You're Denraen!"

Tolsin shook his head slowly. "I was never Denraen. I've been Deshmahne for nearly a year. This was my assignment." He raised his sword, readying for attack.

"How?" Shock that filled him was slowly replaced by the low humming in his head, a vibration that warned caution.

Tolsin shook his head again. "You can't know the pain I have been through for this. Braden would understand. I offered him the chance to be more but—"

"Braden is a soldier and Urmahne. Always both." Jakob squeezed his sword, and the vibration intensified, and with it, his alertness perked. There was a flicker of motion, and Jakob spun.

The Deshmahne raider was behind him. A stench emanated from him, and Jakob jumped back, keeping Tolsin and the Deshmahne in his sight. The Deshmahne flashed forward, his long sword a blur, and Jakob reacted, swinging his blade in defense.

The Deshmahne moved quickly, his sword almost invisible as it whistled through the air, nearly taking off Jakob's head.

Without his heightened alertness, he would already be dead.

Yet, the heightened awareness was still not enough. The Deshmahne's sword sliced across his back, and he felt the blood ooze out. There was another sharp pain, this from his leg, and he staggered.

He sensed his own death. The gods would curse his entire family.

His mind began to swim and his vision blurred. Somehow, he

reached for the vibration, pulled at the source of it deep in his head, and felt as if something tore.

He cried out, his head splitting with pain. A slow worry overcame him as he wondered if his head had been struck. He was dying.

He saw the Deshmahne clearly. The pain in his head helped him ignore his injuries, and he focused on this, pulling upon it.

The sensation spread through him, down through his arms, down his body to his toes. It seemed as if time slowed.

He attacked.

The Deshmahne was still fast and defended his blows, but Jakob kept up. He didn't know how long he would manage.

He desperately pulled on the buzzing again. Time moved to a crawl.

Jakob flashed through a catah, hoping to end this before he passed out, but the man blocked him. He attacked again and again before finally catching the Deshmahne through his leg. The man stumbled.

"What are you?" the man demanded.

Jakob looked at the Deshmahne and then to where Tolsin was frozen with a look of horror on his face. Tolsin turned and ran from the grove. Jakob didn't have a chance to see where he went.

The Deshmahne had seen Tolsin leave as well. "I'll take care of him next."

Jakob heard the words distantly. His head was buzzing, and he was beginning to have a difficult time seeing. Everything seemed as if a fog surrounded it, and he felt drunk. The Deshmahne attacked again. It took all of Jakob's skill and concentration to slow him.

And then he slipped. Something on the ground caught his foot and he fell. The Deshmahne moved to stand overtop him and laughed. "The gods will see my power now," the man said, his voice harsh, menacing.

Looking into the face of the man who would take his life, Jakob's thoughts were a mix of regret and loss. He regretted that he wouldn't be able to help carry the general's box north. And he had a sense of loss that filled him, and he wondered at it. Did he mourn himself?

A terrifying roar suddenly echoed through the trees, and he snapped his eyes open briefly. A huge animal, a blur of reddish fur with a body near the size of a horse, leaped over him and grabbed the Deshmahne powerfully, tearing his head from his body. The man dropped limply to the ground.

The creature stalked over to him, staring at him with golden eyes that seemed to see through him. Then blackness overtook him.

CHAPTER FIFTEEN

The attack came quickly.

Roelle sat atop her mount, staring quietly at the stars overhead, wondering where Endric sent his Denraen and why Jakob had traveled with them. What purpose did the general have splitting his troops? Endric didn't act without planning. There was more to this mission than the general was letting on, but she couldn't figure out what it was. Something important, she suspected. The Denraen would need all the men they had if the raiders attacked.

A quick cry of warning suddenly silenced was followed by the sound of swords unsheathed by the Denraen. The horses stopped, and the Denraen on the perimeter shouted orders that were passed back. Near her, Haerlin turned his head nervously about, looking out into the dark and straining to see anything that might be hiding. Still, nothing moved.

It was the historian who saw it first. "To the north," he whispered, stretching his arm out in warning.

Roelle looked in the direction the man pointed and barely saw a blurring of darkness. The night was nearly a complete black; heavy clouds had rolled in and covered the half-moon that had been guiding them earlier in the night. The raiders had waited and chosen the perfect time for an attack. She wondered briefly how the historian could have seen it before she had but shook off the thought as a strange new cry split the night.

The shadows morphed into the clear shapes of the raiders, and they were soon upon them. One jumped straight toward Haerlin, dark tattoos twining down his arms seemed to swirl independent of the man's movements.

Roelle had her sword in hand before she knew it.

It was instinctive; the motion of grabbing her hilt and unsheathing the sword happening more quickly than she could think. There had been many times she had wondered how she would react if faced with a real battle. Would her Urmahne instincts trump her sword training? And now it was upon her and she had reacted.

The man moved quickly, and Roelle barely stopped his blade from decapitating the Mage Elder. Haerlin's face contorted in a look of shock and fear at the attack, yet the Elder said nothing.

Roelle took a quick breath, slowing her thoughts as she'd been taught, and parried the man as she leaped from her saddle.

On the ground, she stepped easily through familiar forms, blocking the Deshmahne attack. This was different from practice with Endric. The stakes were higher. She could easily die. Possibly worse, though, was that she could kill.

Her hesitation was enough for the man to flicker an attack at her, a quick feint followed by a thrust at her stomach to disembowel her. The sword sliced the fabric of her tunic as she slid to the side, and the Deshmahne smiled as he stepped back for another attack.

A sudden wave of hopelessness and fear hit her, almost a physical attack and unlike anything she'd ever experienced.

In spite of what Haerlin believed about the Deshmahne and their abilities, the rumors were true. Even knowing what they might be able to do, it was one thing to be warned about such a possibility, knowing the Deshmahne capable of a strange emotional attack, and quite another to be faced with it.

Still, when Roelle was chosen to accompany Haerlin on this journey, her uncle Alriyn had seen to it that her training had included defense against something like this. Had he known what she might face?

The Deshmahne was not attempting subtlety, else he may have had more success. It was a surge of emotion that slammed into her, relentless, and pressing upon her and *into* her. It had an oily, slick feeling, a dark current of fear, and its presence made her stomach roil with nausea. She felt despair, pain, and terror come from it, and she shivered. It was like nothing Roelle had ever felt, and she wanted it away from her.

She honed her concentration as her uncle had taught, forcing her will against that which pressed upon her and pushed. There was a long sense of resistance as the emotions tried to slip past her concentration, but Roelle focused harder and felt the emotions slide away. She staggered back as the pressure left her.

The Deshmahne cocked his head and sniffed the air a moment. "A Mage?" he hissed, frowning as he eyed the sword in Roelle's hand.

Roelle didn't answer, instead darting forward, nearly a blur, and slashing at the Deshmahne, quickly severing his head. A surprised look was frozen on the dark priest's face as he died.

She heard a gasp from Haerlin nearby. She couldn't let it slow her or others would die. Roelle wouldn't allow that to happen while she was capable of doing something. Too often, her people stood idly by, waving the Urmahne beliefs as a blanket defense of inaction while others suffered. Her parents had died because of it.

A shout of alarm cried out from behind her, and she turned to see two raiders trying to sneak up on her. They were not Deshmahne, and they fell quickly. She didn't stop or rest, turning to the sound of wood clacking and splintering nearby. The historian sat atop his horse, barely keeping another attacker at bay with a staff, protecting the delegate Comity. He spun it well and smoothly, but the attacker was Deshmahne, and the historian was not fast enough.

Roelle put herself between the dark priest and the historian. This Deshmahne was more heavily tattooed than the other, and she wondered what that meant. The tattoos crept up bare arms, onto his face and bald head. Shadows seemed to shimmer and swirl around the

Deshmahne, distinct from the overcast night. Hatred radiated from the man.

A wave of emotions oozed toward her, similar to the last attack, and she deflected it nearly instantly. It was easier this time, or perhaps she was simply better prepared. Either way, the strange attack didn't hit her quite the same way.

The Deshmahne smiled darkly, and Roelle barely saw the sword.

The Deshmahne moved unlike anyone she'd seen.

She was lucky to block the attack. It felt more like her sword got in the way rather than her placing it properly. Was she skilled enough to defeat the priest?

Another attack came, and again, she was barely fast enough. Roelle followed her training, taking slow shallow breaths to find her focus, and moved from defense to an attack. The Deshmahne blocked it easily.

I cannot defeat him like this.

The dark priest seemed to sense her thoughts and smiled again, more a sneer this time. A blanket of emotion swept toward her again, and she felt it slam into her focus, nearly unsettling her.

The Deshmahne were rumored to convert those they captured, many by force. Would she be forced to convert? What would Alriyn think? He'd been more than an uncle to her, almost a father figure, and Roelle knew he'd be devastated and disappointed by this failure. It was probably best that her parents weren't alive to see this happen to her. No family should see such failure.

Her arm sagged, and her sword drooped while fatigue settled into her and with it, an urge to surrender. She couldn't win. Best to let the Deshmahne finish her quickly.

These are not my thoughts!

Roelle shook her head as she recognized the foreign influence for what it was.

This Deshmahne was dangerous and had almost succeeded. The dark priest flashed forward in a lightning attack too quick for her to stop with a sword.

Roelle acted without thinking.

She opened herself to her Magi abilities and used the *manehlin* surrounding him to freeze the Deshmahne in place. It happened faster than thought, faster than the priest could move.

Roelle flicked her sword forward in a quick attack that left the Deshmahne bleeding heavily from two wounds, dark blood pumping from them, until Roelle released him and he fell noisily to the ground. The dark priest spasmed briefly before falling still, and even then, the tattoos on his arms and face seemed to shimmer.

Around her, other small battles raged. Roelle moved in to attack. There were no other Deshmahne, only raiders, and they fell almost too easily for her. Then there were no more attackers, and as quickly as it had started, the attack ended.

Roelle looked up into the night and saw that the moon had come back out from behind the clouds. She tried to catch her breath and slow her racing mind, though was not sure she was ready to process what had just happened. The dying sounds of battle echoed around her, and the pungent metallic odor of blood was strong in the crisp night air. There were occasional cries of pain, but on the whole, the night grew silent.

Roelle looked to see who still stood. How many raiders had attacked? How many Deshmahne?

After her confrontations with the two dark priests, she had a new respect for Endric and worried how many Denraen survived the attack. The historian sat atop his horse nearby, staring at her strangely. The delegate remained near Haerlin, an unused sword in his hand. Haerlin would not meet her gaze.

Roelle knew why.

She was Magi. And she had killed.

She wasn't sure she was ready for the consequences. There would be many. To the Magi, violence went against the core of the Urmahne tradition, and she had just violated the most central tenet of her people's faith by taking another's life. And more than one man's life.

Roelle wiped the sweat from her brow with a sigh as she looked around, taking count. She owed it to those whose lives she ended. Scattered on the ground were nearly a dozen men, raiders and Deshmahne both, lying dead or dying in awkward positions. The pale light of the moon cast strange shadows such that the night flickered around her, and she shivered before turning away. She wasn't sure she could stare upon what she'd done.

Had there been a choice? The attack had come quickly and silently. The raiders had been upon them with little notice, and if Roelle hadn't acted, Haerlin at least would have died. Likely the historian, too, though the man had managed reasonably well with his staff.

It wasn't the fact that she'd killed that bothered her, though it *did* bother her. That had been instilled within her as a child of the Urmahne. Rather, it was the unsettling ease with which she had done it. The sword had felt an extension of her arm. She had barely needed to use her Magi abilities during the battle, and then only when facing one of the dark Deshmahne.

Would I have survived otherwise?

It was difficult to admit, but she didn't know.

How many Denraen would have died had Roelle not acted? Those men had needed her skills today, however she'd come by them.

The Magi had long known they had certain physical abilities—innate reflexes, quick healing, long life—and Roelle had learned there was something more to them as she acquired skill with the sword. This was still more than she had expected. Did any of the Elders know how easily they could kill? Was this the reason Haerlin wouldn't meet her eyes?

A hand upon her shoulder startled her, and she spun quickly, flashing her sword up before her. It collided with another blade, and the clang reverberated into the growing silence of the night.

"Easy," the general said, lowering his sword.

Roelle brought hers down to her side and shook her head. What would have happened had any other than the general come up to her then? "I'm sorry."

Endric reached his hand back out and settled it on her shoulder, giving it a long squeeze before releasing. With it, a bit of the tension went out of her, and she sighed again before sheathing her sword.

"You've nothing to apologize for," the general said. A small gash oozed blood down his face. He cast his dark eyes around the ground, quickly taking count of the men Roelle had killed. "Your Elder would have died without you. The historian too. And many more of my men."

"I know." It didn't make the consequences of what she had done any easier.

Endric seemed to understand, and for that, Roelle felt another sense of relief. "The gods will not look upon you less favorably. I follow the Urmahne, and I am Denraen. They are not exclusive." The general paused, giving the words a chance to be heard. "It's a shame what the Magi apprentices fail to learn," he said quietly. "Consider this one of your lessons, one that you will someday understand all too well."

Another joined them, slinking in from the darkness, tall and darkly cloaked. The historian was slender yet carried himself with confidence. Roelle had not heard him dismount. The man moved like a thief. There was an air of mystery about him that Roelle found intriguing, not the least of which was his utter lack of fear before Haerlin. It was not often that a man would challenge a Mage Elder.

"How many?" the historian asked.

Endric shrugged. "Enough." The look in his eyes said that he had a complete count. Roelle wondered briefly why he did not share it.

Novan smiled tightly, but there was no malice to the expression, merely a barely hidden amusement. He tilted his head and scratched at one ear. "How many Denraen were lost?"

Endric narrowed his eyes, and Novan took a slight step back. "Enough."

Roelle wasn't sure if it was an answer or a warning. Probably both.

"Were they successful?" the historian asked.

Endric frowned and looked out into the night before shaking his head. "I sent the trunk north in time."

"Are you certain?"

Endric frowned. "I don't know."

"But you have an idea."

He nodded. "Possibly." He looked around then shook his head. "I hope so."

"What was this about?" Roelle asked. The loss of life that both sides had experienced was more than she had ever seen, and the general thought it all for only a warning? If so, it was a warning well received. Would she have believed the danger the Deshmahne posed if she had not seen it?

"Testing a diversion," Novan said. "But not only that."

Endric looked to him a moment before shaking his head. "No."

Roelle looked between the two men. "What?"

"The High Priest had another goal in mind, I think. This was only a feint," Endric said.

"What goal?"

Roelle turned to see Haerlin come walking up to them, Elder Bothar at his side. Those of the other camp had joined just before the battle started. It had added another element of confusion to the attack. Bothar looked from Novan to Endric to Roelle. Haerlin almost purposefully avoided her gaze, staring at Endric as if intent not to look elsewhere.

The historian seemed to take it all in and chuckled lightly. In the night air, the sound carried, and Haerlin turned to face him. "What goal?" Haerlin repeated.

"The same goal the High Priest has elsewhere, I suppose, but one he can more easily accomplish if Endric is not in the city." Novan paused, glancing to Endric. "I think he delayed us enough to get past us so that he could reach the capital first."

Haerlin arched his eyebrows and frowned. It was Bothar who spoke. "You mean—"

"The Deshmahne will do what they've done in the south, and what they have done in Gom Aaldia, and have now attempted in Thealon. There is only one way for them to take what I suspect they are after. I fear they seek to infiltrate your city."

CHAPTER SIXTEEN

Alriyn, Second Eldest on the Council of Magi, barely heard the knock at the door. It was little more than a soft tap. He stood quickly and opened it a crack. Karrin stood in the dark hallway on the other side with the shadows of the hall masking her expression. He ushered her in quickly before closing the door again.

She smiled at him slightly, tilting her head as she looked around before taking a seat on one of the hard wooden chairs that lined the walls. Little about his study was not hard. Books stacked about made it seem cluttered as well.

"You sent for me?" she asked, her voice soft.

He looked at her a moment before answering. Her dark hair hung unkempt at her shoulders, no attempt made to style it. She was not one for such frivolousness. Her gray eyes probed him, waiting for answers.

"The delegates travel to the city now," he told her.

She nodded.

He had expected she would know as much. Counted on it, really. "Nobles, all," he continued, shaking his head. The idea still worried him. Would it be enough?

"They were chosen by those on the Council, Alriyn," Karrin soothed.

He nodded in response. He knew they had. He trusted the motives of those sent, though not all agreed with him. "After what I saw, I still think we need to send the Magi—"

"We have tried. Not all are interested in leaving the city like you.'"

"With the Deshmahne moving in the south, and these rumors to the north—"

"Rumors only," Karrin said.

He cast his gaze around his small study, looking over the piles of books and fragments of texts. "You didn't see what I saw," he said, not looking at her. "You didn't see the fear in the people's eyes." He shook his head sadly. "The towns were *empty*. Mining towns, still with wealth to find."

"We don't know for sure..." Karrin began.

"Do you know that I've spent my life searching for answers? I've wanted to know what we overlooked in the *mahne*. There has to be something we've missed, something more to the prophecy." Their most precious text, what they referred to as the *mahne*, was clear in the prophecy and the need to maintain peace, but less clear on many other things—such as the process of choosing the Uniter. "With everything now taking place, I don't disagree with Jostephon that we must exert more influence, but what if this requires more?"

That had been what bothered him the most. Not the idea of the delegates. He recognized the truth in Jostephon's plan, and the need to begin reasserting their influence would take time. But he worried that they would need more than delegates. Perhaps more than the Magi. What if they needed to find the answer to the prophecy?

Karrin looked at him a long time before speaking. "Why did you ask me here today, Alriyn?"

"What if this is wrong? What if we delay—"

"The Eldest knows the *mahne* better than anyone," she said.

"Jostephon does, but he hasn't been outside the city. He hasn't *seen*." Alriyn wouldn't have gone either were it not for rumor of a specific text he could find. He hadn't found the book he'd sought, but

174 | D.K. HOLMBERG

what he'd seen had worried him even more. "Sometimes I think he forgets what happened when the Deshmahne last attacked our home."

"The Denraen stopped that attack."

Alriyn nodded. "They did. And this horror in the north? What if it is something like the ancient threat?"

"Only the gods helped us the last time," Karrin spoke.

Alriyn knew the truth in that. His people all believed their ancestors had stopped the ancient threat. It was a time when the land had been ravaged, most destroyed, though none really understood how. Or why. All they knew was that his ancestors, the Founders of the Magi, had been key to the survival. And even then, he suspected they had done little but slow the tide

But someone had helped. Someone only referenced in the *mahne* as the *nemah*, the ancient word for Uniter. They had learned little about the Uniter since the ancient threat and the Founding, most of the records lost in the destruction, but had learned he was somehow chosen to bring peace when it was needed. He knew this person had helped during the threat, *had* slowed the progression. What if they needed such a person now?

"We failed the last time we tried," Karrin said again, as if reading his thoughts.

It was true. His people had tried several times to choose a Uniter when war called for such a person. None had been successful.

He shook his head. "The *mahne* is explicit," he began. "The Uniter is the key when the balance of peace begins to fail."

"*We* have failed," Karrin said again.

"Should we let our failures keep us from trying again?" he asked.

She shook her head slowly. "What do you propose?"

He looked into her gray eyes for a long time, hoping to see something he knew he would need. He could not move forward without it. "Nothing yet," he answered. "A council only."

"But the Council has already decided..."

"Not *the* Council," he interrupted. "*A* council. Fewer." He looked away, thoughtfully, before continuing. "Myself, you, a few others. We study only, prepare for what *might* come."

Her eyes narrowed at the idea.

"Haerlin, Bothar," he stated.

"Isandra," she offered.

He nodded. He had wondered about Isandra.

"Why did you bring this to me?" Karrin asked him, her eyes almost begging for the answer.

He waited a long while before answering. "A feeling," he answered truthfully. He had never been very close to Karrin, and he knew it strange to trust her with this. He just felt he could.

A slow nod was her only response.

"We must wait until the others return with their delegates," he spoke. "It's possible Jostephon was right and that they can be used."

She nodded again, quiet. "We should trust the Eldest."

"I trust him. He knows more than any Mage alive about our past."

"Which is why we should listen to his recommendations. What do you fear?"

Alriyn sighed. Jostephon might be the most knowledgeable scholar alive, but Alriyn had studied under another Mage, one who had warned him of something like this, almost as if he had a prophecy, though Tresten didn't possess that ability. "It's not what I fear, it's what Tresten feared."

Karrin's eyes narrowed. "You know how the Eldest felt about Tresten."

"I know. Which is why I won't include him until we are certain. When we know more, we can pull Jostephon in."

"You know where this could lead, Alriyn." It was a statement. She caught on quickly.

"Yes," he answered. If he were wrong with this plan, it could lead to another Magi failure, and if that happened, would the Deshmahne use that as an opportunity to eliminate the Magi influence for good?

CHAPTER SEVENTEEN

J akob awoke slowly. As he opened his eyes, he had to squint
against light filtering through the trees overhead. His head still
pounded, but it was a different sensation. This throbbing was a
traditional headache, almost as if he'd been drinking too much. An
awareness of the pain in his chest and leg came to him, and a sudden
memory of the battle came with it.

He was alive.

How? He remembered the Deshmahne standing over him,
laughing at him. He remembered fading to blackness, aware that he
would die. Yet something had happened. Something had saved him.

The animal, his mind prompted.

He remembered the ear-splitting roar, could almost still hear it.

Had he actually seen it or was it a dream?

He was no longer sure. He thought that he had, thought that he'd
glimpsed a blur of reddish fur and a face larger than any wolf, but
wondered now if he had. Could he have imagined eyes that seemed
intelligent in a way that no animal should be?

Jakob stood and looked around. It was still daylight. Bodies
littered the ground, and he saw no movement around him. He caused
much of that, but didn't know how he'd managed to survive when

none of the Denraen around him had. His head hurt to think too much on it.

A large pool of blood led to a body with arms covered in tattoos that led up to his shoulders. This was the man he'd faced, the Deshmahne who'd nearly killed him. His neck ended, and jagged edges of flesh remained where his head had been torn from his body. He tasted a hint of bile as he struggled not to vomit.

All around the man were huge paw prints. Though Jakob had never been much of a tracker, he'd not seen anything like it. They were catlike, but each was as large as his footprint. They were scattered around where the man had fallen, and several lighter footprints peppered the ground near where he had lay, but nowhere else were they found. It was as if the creature had materialized out of thin air, then disappeared.

Jakob staggered around the grove, looking at the bodies and searching for signs of life. His leg throbbed nearly as badly as his head. The combined pain of the two enabled him to ignore the pain in his back. None of the horses remained, scattered or slaughtered.

It took all the energy he could muster to look upon the dead. Jakob finally vomited after looking at the third Denraen, recognizing the northman. His eyes were glassy in death, a huge slash in his throat.

Finally, he found what he was looking for. It had been farther than he remembered.

The tree where Rit and Tian had made their stand stood scarred and bloodied, nearly as much a participant as any of the Denraen. Tian lay facing the ground, his crossbow partially underneath him and his body propped at a strange angle. Nearby was Rit. Jakob knelt carefully next to him.

Rit had fallen on his back. One leg twisted behind him, and Jakob couldn't see his left arm, though whether it was missing or covered in debris, he wasn't certain. The man was gone.

Rit's chest moved.

A huge gash in his side oozed blood and made a sucking sound as Rit struggled to breathe. His breaths came slowly, raggedly. Gently touching Rit's right shoulder, he realized the man's left arm was missing rather than hidden.

How did he still live?

"Rit?" He didn't expect a response.

Rit's eyes flickered open briefly, and a spark of recognition flitted across them. "The historian." The words came out wetly, and Jakob heard the wound in his stomach bubble as he spoke.

Jakob nodded before catching himself. "Yes."

Rit struggled, trying to move before finding himself unable to do so. Jakob placed a gentle restraining hand on his shoulder and Rit slowly relaxed. "How many?"

Did he tell the truth? Rit could not survive. Did he not deserve peace?

His pause was too long.

"Just you?" Rit asked.

"Yes."

"The Deshmahne?" Rit whispered. His words were losing power.

"Dead."

A smile actually crossed Rit's face. "I told you... not hindrance."

Jakob laughed as tears welled up in his eyes. He blinked them back. "What now?" Fear and uncertainty overpowered him. How did he expect Rit to answer him?

"You must go..." he started before falling silent.

Jakob watched his chest slowly rise and fall with long pauses in between. Each time, he worried Rit had died.

"North... go north," he said finally. "Avaneam... trunk. Meet Endric. Key to stopping... Deshmahne. Maybe... more." He took a breath, and Jakob thought it his last, then his eyes snapped open. "May the gods protect..."

Rit fell silent again except for the slow sucking sound of his chest.

Jakob knelt back, waiting for Rit to regain consciousness, and after a while, wondered if he would. Jakob started to stand but Rit spoke again.

"We failed..." His chest rose and fell and did not rise again.

Tears streamed down Jakob's face.

Whatever else Rit might think, the gods didn't protect Jakob. He'd known their wrath his entire life and had done nothing to provoke it.

How could he do what needed to be done? He was no soldier—but what *was* he now?

He didn't know the answer. Could he still be Novan's apprentice after what he'd been forced to do? Novan asked him to observe—not intervene—but if he hadn't, he would have died.

More than that, it had felt natural for him to hold the sword. There was a rightness to it, a comfort he couldn't explain, but now he had so many questions and no one to answer them.

How had he managed to live when all the Denraen had died? What was the vibration within him when he held the sword?

A part of him was afraid of the answer. Was it real or imagined? Both frightened him. If imagined, it meant the madness came for him. If real... it meant he had some other power. Maybe something like the Deshmahne.

Jakob stood slowly, shoving the thought aside. The bodies had already started to stink. He walked back to where he had fallen and recovered his sword, his injured leg loosening up so that he limped less.

His head still pounded, and the movement mixed with the bright sunlight didn't help.

Blood covered his sword. The sight of it nearly made him retch again so he wiped it off on one of the raiders. The blood wiped off easily, almost repelled from the blade, and he sheathed the sword.

He forced himself to ignore the death around him as he struggled deciding what to do next. His gaze lingered on the trunk Rit died trying to protect. Sunlight glittered off it, making the sides almost glow. Anywhere else, it would be beautiful.

There was no easy answer, yet only one true choice.

He had to go north. No one else could do it now.

He would find Endric and return the trunk to the general. It meant traveling north alone, into dangers possibly worse than Deshmahne, facing whatever caused the strange rumors about the north.

Jakob took the trunk from where Rit protected it, hefting it and noting it not heavy, but the size made it awkward. When he stood, he wasn't able to look at Rit and Tian lying motionless any longer.

A thought came to him as he turned away. He dislodged Tian's crossbow from beneath him, once so deadly in his hands but useless in his dead grip, and strapped it to his belt so it hung opposite his sword.

Endric and Novan were members of this Conclave but what was it about the trunk that was so important? They were questions he'd have to reach Avaneam—or find the general first—to have answers. How was he to even reach Avaneam? He'd heard mention of the Elasiin Path, and Siirvil's Peak, but all he knew was that he had to go north.

The trunk was too ungainly to carry in his arms for long, and he hoped against logic that he'd find the horses. Luck struck near the edge of the trees. His own horse had become ensnared by a branch and stood grazing. His saddle and saddlebags were intact and undisturbed. At the sight, he hesitantly offered a silent prayer to the nameless gods.

It was the first time he had prayed in years.

CHAPTER EIGHTEEN

Alriyn glanced over to the Mage joining him as he strolled through the darkened hall, his gaze skimming past the teralin sculptures, the metal giving off a reassuring warmth. There had been a time when the Magi worked with it regularly, thinking it a way to reach the gods, but that had changed when the Deshmahne demonstrated the dangers of it. Now it was decorative only, and harmless.

Karrin walked quickly, her shorter legs forced to take long strides to match his gait. Something about her was determined tonight. The thrust of her jaw or the tight cast to her eyes, he couldn't decide. Either way, something was on her mind. It was best to wait for her to tell him. She wouldn't wait long.

"They're here," she spoke finally. She had waited until they rounded a corner and saw the hall empty.

He nodded. Word spread quickly through the palace these days. Almost too quickly.

She grabbed lightly at the sleeve of his brown robe. "Have you seen them?" Her voice was barely above a whisper.

He patted her hand. He knew it did little to soothe her. "Tomorrow, Karrin."

"But your niece!" she said urgently. Her voice was almost too loud for the hall, and she looked around quickly.

No one followed. He had not expected any differently. "My niece will come to me in time." Now he understood the track of her thoughts. The Deshmahne. A foul religion, a taint upon all the good the Urmahne had done, yet they had gained influence, especially in the south. Now they chose to wield it and attacked the Denraen.

What did that mean?

Nothing good. The High Priest had been pressing for decades—longer than most understood. Finally, he reached across the sea, the long arm of his influence touching Gom Aaldia. They had even attempted attacking Vasha once, seeking Urmahne relics, but that had not been a true Deshmahne attack; they had help. The Denraen were better prepared now—Endric ensured they were—and they understood the Deshmahne in ways they had not before.

It was a twisted religion, yet powerful with arcane magics he wished he understood better. It was the reason he'd left Vasha, wanting to see for himself how far the Deshmahne had pressed, yet when he'd heard the rumors out of the north, it was as if he were compelled to investigate.

"The prophecy—"

Alriyn shot her a silencing glare. "We can't speak of that openly."

"But you're the one who came to me. You said we needed to find the Uniter, not these delegates."

The peacebringer. That wasn't entirely what he'd suggested, though there was sense in it. "I said we needed to use our influence once more."

Karrin nodded. "Then we must use it on these delegates."

"I intend to, especially now with word of the Deshmahne attack upon the Magi."

Alriyn had been shocked when Princess Danvayn, one of the delegates, had made it to Vasha with word of the attack on the plains of Gom Aaldia. If not for the badly wounded Denraen standing next to the delegate when she'd arrived, Alriyn would not have believed it. Danvayn had barely survived, yet she had. What would have happened if the Coamdon princess had been killed crossing through Gomald? He shuddered to think of that.

More bloodshed, and what would that mean for the *mahne?* It was an ancient text, a fragment that their entire belief system—and the Urmahne faith—had been founded upon. It demanded peace, warned of the risks if they failed, risks that were greater than any outside the Council would—or could—understand.

More than that, it was the first prophecy. The text was incomplete, lost over time so that all the Magi possessed was but a partial version of the original, the *mahne* spoke of a time when a Uniter of Men would arise. The Magi had attempted—and failed—to choose this person in the past.

Alriyn wondered if they had the translation correct. The ancient language called this person the *nemah*, which translated to Uniter of Men, but like many things in the ancient language, it could be translated in other ways. All his studies had failed to clarify it for him.

There had been other times when the Council thought they needed to choose the *nemah*, the Uniter, but they had failed. It made them hesitant. Now that the Deshmahne gained strength quickly and forced their will and beliefs upon a continent, no longer did the south know peace; a thousand years of balance now lost. Constant violence was now the norm. Did that not demand the Uniter?

Alriyn shook his head, thinking to the delegates.

They were a step in the right direction. They would help with the Magi influence, which would keep them from needing to choose a Uniter. They had failed too often for them to choose again.

Yet, it troubled him. Danvayn was only the first arrival—other delegates still traveled toward the city. Would Roelle be safe?

She has learned the sword. She will be safe.

He had long suspected the Magi gifts extended to the physical but had not been certain. It had been centuries since his people had needed anything save their minds for protection.

Since we became Urmahne. And since then, there had been little need for any type of protection. The Urmahne taught peace and harmony. Balance. The *mahne.*

And we are Urmahne.

"Tonight will not make a difference to those we can use," he answered, finally.

"Have you called for Haerlin?" she asked.

Haerlin would be the next they approached to bring into his council. "After," he answered and her gaze flickered around the hall. She *was* nervous.

She squeezed the fabric of his sleeve. "I'm sorry, Alriyn. It's just that I've been..." Her gaze shifted around the hall again before settling on him once more. "Each day, I hear information that grows more and more worrisome."

He turned to face her and looked into her gray eyes as he spoke. "It's the same for me, Karrin. Worse, though, is what I've seen myself." The memories haunted him at night. The towns desolate. The people scared, terrified, and the entire northland somehow *wrong*. He could think of no other way to describe what he'd felt.

Too much at once to be coincidence. Deshmahne pressing from the south, strange attacks in the north, and a madness spreading through many of the cities like a plague. The priests called for action and the healers had no answers. Too much at once, too much unknown.

How could the Council let this happen, especially after they had nearly overlooked the Deshmahne before? The warnings had been there from the beginning. The *mahne* guided them, and the warning in it was even more dire. The Eldest, the keeper of their greatest secrets, knew it, just as he knew they couldn't act hastily. Alriyn had to trust his guidance, but at the same time, Alriyn didn't want to neglect the possibility that Jostephon didn't have all the information.

Karrin caught his eyes, and after a few moments, nodded. They turned and kept walking, the pale light of the hall guiding their footsteps. "What will we do?"

He thought a while before answering. His thoughts drifted again to what he had seen, the devastation he'd witnessed and the fear the people still knew. He thought about what could cause that and he knew his answer. "I don't know," he told her truthfully.

A few more moments passed before she spoke again. "Do you

think we can slow them?" Her dark eyes searched his face for answers, almost begging for something.

"It will not be about us, but about the Denraen."

In some ways, he worried more about the north than the Deshmahne. If these attacks were anything like what was described in the ancient fragments of text he'd discovered... they were unprepared. Even with their Magi abilities, there wouldn't be anything they could do to stop a threat like that.

Worse, why must both occur at once? The Deshmahne drew the Magi attention away from the north, and was that the point? If so, what was the connection?

Alriyn shook his head in irritation. He had no answers. It was not something he was accustomed to. That worried him more.

~

Brohmin looked north one last time before turning his horse south again. His shirt was soiled with a day's worth of old blood. He clutched his wounded shoulder close. His arm ached. At least the horses were unwounded. It was a blessing they weren't.

The ride north had been harsh. After the encounter with the groeliin in the forest, they had reached the lower hills without further incident. Salindra had looked at him differently, though. She had not pressed him, but he knew she had questions for him. They were questions he would not answer. Could not answer.

Once up in the mountains, they had a different experience. They hadn't climbed very high before the first attack began. At first, he fought solely with his sword but quickly grew tired. Salindra helped as much as she could. She was able to see the beasts at least. That was better than most, he knew. The extra eyes had helped him more than he thought it would. She just was not a fighter. None of her people were.

He laughed to himself about it. He could afford to now.

As they climbed higher, the attacks became more frequent. Each day, he resisted the urge to turn back. Salindra never asked. That surprised him. When his strength had gone, he was forced to rely on his other talents. The strain of that effort wore on him quickly. At the end of those days, Salindra looked at him much differently. He would still not answer her questions.

She grew weaker too. He could feel the toll the branding about her ankles was taking on her. Could feel her strength leaving her even if he could not see it. Several times, he had tried healing her even more than he had, but was unsuccessful. The brandings were beyond him.

His stomach roiled with the thought. Just the notion of the brandings scared him.

Her weakness had hurt them. Between healing her and fighting off the groeliin, he had suffered. The mission was important. He had traveled north to learn how much time they had left to report to the Conclave. The sheer number of the beasts he'd encountered told him all the answers he needed. Not much time.

They traveled south now. Though his own mission had taken him north, searching for more evidence of the groeliin, a mission of another of the Conclave brought him south again. Word had come to him in a dream from the goddess, as it often did, forcing them south. And Salindra along, hoping for more than he could offer.

He looked over to her again. She was slumped in her saddle, her dark hair falling into her face. He looked at the sharp angle of her jaw, her dirty hair covering it, and smiled. She was good company. Better than he had expected.

The horses stopped to drink at a stream. He took the chance to do the same, uncorking his water skin and taking a long drink. It was cool and tasted of copper. Much like his homeland. He smiled.

Salindra awoke as they stopped, looking over to him with sleepy eyes. "How much longer today?" she asked, her soft voice weak from sleep.

He looked up at the sun. It was dipping low in the sky. Around him, the grassy fields were slowly turning into forest. The trees were growing closer together. They provided more cover, but at the same time made it harder to check ahead. A slow-rising slope stretched before them, the darkening day casting long shadows along the still grassy ground.

Finally, he shook his head. "As far as possible. We have far to go," he answered.

She nodded. He knew she was used to long days in the saddle. There would be many more of them before their traveling was done.

"How do you feel?" he asked, nodding to her ankles.

She looked down as if being reminded. It was a good sign if she was forgetting them. Shrugging her shoulders, she answered, "Better, I think." She looked at him with her deep brown eyes. "Since you last healed me," she told him.

The unspoken question hung loud in the air. He let it hang. "Good." He looked up the hill before them. "Let us see what is beyond the horizon," he urged.

She nodded.

They rode several more hours that night. The moon was high above them by the time they stopped. The horses were tied quickly, and they laid down for their rest.

As he drifted to sleep, Salindra asked, "Do we have a destination for our travel?"

"Yes," he answered tiredly.

She snorted at his simple response. "Where?"

He looked over to her. In the pale light of the moon, he could see the Mage she had been. Powerful. Confident. He would tell her. "Rondalin," he answered.

A long moment passed before she nodded.

CHAPTER NINETEEN

R oelle sat silently in the large room, her head down, and her thoughts not on the task at hand. Words bounced from wall to wall, and the frail instructor in the front of the room tried to out yell the reverberations of his own deep voice. It was a soothing timbre, and her head was not the only one that struggled to stay erect.

"The war continued. We remained uninvolved, hesitant to act. The results, some one hundred years earlier, had not been as expected. Records indicate that the rest of the world was already set on destruction by the time we had chosen a course. Each nation battled the others. The Urmahne priests could not allow that to continue, and so finally, the Council argued that the ancient tradition must be following and they..."

Roelle had only been back a few days and already tired of the routine. She'd hoped that after what she'd been through, what she'd seen, she'd no longer require the daily lessons. It was not to be.

Even with the classes, she couldn't get the memory of the frantic battle with the Deshmahne out of her head, nor could she stop the visions of the men she'd killed that came to her as she tried to sleep. The knowledge that she'd done what was necessary didn't change her struggle with it.

She forced her attention back to the lecture, wondering how these lessons helped. She'd seen the Deshmahne raiders, knew their strength. The dark priests wouldn't be stopped with talk.

The Elders she'd traveled with had been frustratingly silent about the Deshmahne since their return. The historian and the general both felt the Deshmahne had entered the city before them, infiltrating it to influence its people as so many in the south had been influenced and affected. Novan feared they sought something the Magi protected, though Roelle didn't know what that might be. The Elders brushed it off, denying the possibility.

Roelle had gone to her uncle without success. Alriyn had not been accessible, too busy with the visiting delegates to have time for her, so Roelle had been sent back to her classes. She sighed with irritation and tried to focus on the lecture.

"The peace accorded by the early treaties was shattered when several kings and their generals were assassinated. Each nation felt the other had violated the treaty and planned an invasion. Further bloodshed was spared by the response of the Council.

"The Council announced the Uniter had acted independently, not on their orders, and proclaimed that he would be held accountable for his actions. Parties were sent for his capture, but unlike Josu d'Thealo before him, Brohmin Ulruuy evaded capture, and justice was denied. The nations..."

The Elder was interrupted by a question. "Elder, since Ulruuy was such a failure five hundred years ago, has the ancient practice been disregarded?"

Politt looked up from pacing behind the long table at the front of the room to focus on the young Mage asking the question. "That's a question best left to the Council," Politt answered, then stopped and looked at the questioner a moment longer before turning to the rest of the room.

Another Mage raised his hand, one Roelle knew well. Her friend Selton's angled jaw and muscular frame belonged on a laborer, not a Mage, but Roelle knew he had a keen mind. "I've heard many speak of Brohmin Ulruuy as a failure, but he did accomplish his mission and reestablished a broken peace," Selton commented slowly.

Politt's long face nodded thoughtfully. Quiet moments passed before the answer. "That has been suggested before," he began, his words slow. "Yet his mission was not only to stop the fighting and bloodshed. His mission was to restore peace to the land. His unorthodox actions almost destroyed the process. He certainly instilled a distrust of our role in the peace process. It is not possible to stop war through actions of war."

The Elder almost glanced in her direction with the comment. She took no offense, knowing how the Magi Elders felt about the sudden interest among the apprentices to learn conventional defense. Peace was something instilled in the Magi at an early age—part Urmahne peace and part Magi tradition. The decision to work with the Denraen had started as a diversion, curiosity, but now that she'd seen the Deshmahne in person, seen how they attacked, she wondered if there was any way to stop them short of violence.

"If no one has anything more to add, we will stop for today. Tomorrow we discuss the ramifications of the war."

A quiet restlessness crossed through the room at the prospect of finishing. Finally, a hand shot up from one of the younger students. "Elder, what of rumors Brohmin had a hand in the Slave Revolt?"

The Elder shook his head, a wry smile coming to his lips. "You should pay better attention to the dates in the lecture. The Slave Revolts were only fifty years ago. Brohmin was chosen Uniter hundreds of years before that." He turned to the rest of the audience. "If there are no serious questions, you are all dismissed for the morning."

Roelle walked from the lecture hall and paused. She hadn't spoken to Selton since her return and hoped to catch her friend. Selton came through the doorway, his muscular frame nearly filling it, and blue eyes glittered with an intelligence masked by his slow speech.

"Your question kept us longer," Roelle stated, feigning annoyance. She hadn't seen Selton much since she'd returned to the city, and then when she finally decided to return to her studies, she'd intentionally come in late, not wanting to face the questions she knew she would be asked. But she needed to talk to her closest friend about what had happened.

Selton shrugged. "It was a fair question, I think." He frowned at her, his wide brow furrowed. "I haven't seen you much since you got back," he started, concern in his voice. "The rumors say you were with Endric."

Roelle wondered how much of the attack was known. She'd said nothing, had been cautioned to say nothing, yet Politt seemed to have known. "I was," she admitted.

"Rumor says you brought down ten men." There was no hint of judgment to his tone.

It might have been more than that, but she didn't want to admit it, nodding instead. She saw their faces if she closed her eyes. She told herself there had been no other option, that others would have died had she not acted. Was not that also the way of the Urmahne?

"All our practice, and I... I was forced to kill," Roelle said.

"The others will want to know what you experienced. You're the one who convinced us to begin learning."

"Eventually," Roelle said. She wasn't ready to share with the others what she'd done. Not yet.

"Is it true?" Selton asked. "Were they Deshmahne?"

"Some were."

Selton whistled softly. "What does Endric think this means?"

How much to share? She looked to her friend, saw the worry on his face and knew the answer. "The general thinks the Deshmahne seek access to the city."

"Why?"

She shook her head. There was something else they worried about, but Endric hadn't shared. "There was a historian who traveled with us. He thinks the Deshmahne are after something the Council protects."

Selton considered the comment for a moment. "Historian? I suppose he's traveled here?" he asked and didn't wait for Roelle to nod. "We haven't seen one here since the last was kicked out of the city. My uncle was displeased with him then." Her friend paused. "Have you spoken to Alriyn yet?"

Roelle shook her head. "I haven't been able to reach him since we returned." The Second Eldest may be able to help her sort through what she had seen. Roelle didn't know where else to turn. "Perhaps today," she muttered, mostly to herself.

Selton eyed her. "And what are you doing now?" His body language and tilt of his head implied the question.

Roelle shook her head, knowing what her friend wanted, but there was no time to practice the sword today. "I really need to find Alriyn." Perhaps her uncle could provide guidance about what she had seen. And done.

"After you do, there are others who would like to hear about what you experienced if you're willing."

Roelle sighed. She had avoided the others at first, struggling with settling back into the routine of the city, hiding even from her closest friends, but seeing Selton made it clear that she couldn't remain hidden indefinitely. She *had* to rejoin the others, especially since they had followed her lead in seeking the Denraen to teach them.

"After I find Alriyn," she promised.

CHAPTER TWENTY

Jakob had been riding all day. Fatigue had all but robbed him of his focus, and sheer exhaustion nearly dropped him from the saddle. He had been pushing north for the better part of two days, stopping only for water. Hunger pangs had become one long ache, and the water could only sate it so much. At each stop, he checked the trunk, making sure the straps holding it to his saddle still held. Too much had been sacrificed to lose the trunk.

Once, he had tried the clasp, wondering what was inside, but the clasp was locked tightly, and the keyhole held the broken end of a piece of metal jammed into it. He had cut his finger trying to pull it out and gave up quickly. It was not his to open.

Stars crept out overhead as the darkness deepened. A small hill sloped in front of him, and near it was another copse of trees where he decided to camp. Cresting the small rise, Jakob noticed lights far down below him. Many lights scattered across the valley in all directions, flickering like the stars overhead but closer. He had used the star Entril to guide him north and north was through the city.

As much his tired, aching body was yearning to stop for the day, his stomach pulled him forward. The city meant food and perhaps a real bed. He had coin enough for both, thanking Tian and the pouch of gold he discovered hidden among the man's crossbow bolts.

Something behind him made him turn—instinct or luck, he didn't know. Three men moved quickly on horseback, dust kicked up and trailing them as the horses were spurred faster.

A sense of foreboding stole through him mixed with panic. Had raiders found him? Or worse—Deshmahne? He'd seen no sign of them over the last few days, but that didn't mean they'd given up. With everything they'd done to attack so far, he didn't expect them to abandon the chase easily.

His eyes blurred as he tried to gauge the distance to the city. The fatigue was overwhelming. He didn't know if he could stay awake to make it, and didn't know if his horse had enough left to carry him.

Nearing the copse of trees at the crest of the hill, his horse decided for him as he nearly tumbled from the saddle.

He came out of it awkwardly on his injured leg and quickly unsheathed his sword before untying the chest from his saddle.

He slipped his saddlebags off the horse as well and slung them over his shoulder. If his horse were to separate from him, he didn't want to lose the remainder of his belongings. Stumbling, he fell onto a dead branch and rested long enough to become uncomfortable, his eyes fighting to stay open.

The rumble of hooves nearing brought him more awake, and he moved deeper among the trees, placing the trees between him and the riders.

Jakob fashioned the straps into a net to hold the trunk and attached it behind him on his belt. He twisted, and it moved slightly yet stayed attached. It was awkward, but he hoped it would work.

Craning his neck, he peered around the tree hiding him. The grove of trees was not very thick, and he easily saw what he feared he would. The riders had reached the hilltop and slowed, now following his tracks toward the trees.

Jakob shifted the sword in his hand. His arms were tired from riding, and his head and back still ached. Dread filled him. He could not survive against three raiders, let alone Deshmahne.

The men neared the tree line and dismounted. A stench of decay came with them. Each step they took closer increased the scent until it was nearly suffocating. The riders unsheathed swords, and the sound of the metal blades echoed among the trees. His dread increased and his heart thumped wildly in his chest.

One man was larger than the other two, his size immense, and there was something else about him more fearful than his size. Tattoos crossed his face and bald head, running down his neck onto his arms. The ink nearly covered all of his exposed skin.

From this man, he felt something that made the hairs on his arms stand up. He shook his head, trying to think straight. The slow pulsing had returned. There was something else about the man, something nearly visible, almost an energy radiating from him.

He jerked his head back out of view and squeezed the hilt of his sword. He had to protect the trunk.

He felt strongly about this. It was more than just about the men who'd died protecting it, though that was part of it. Endric's concern for it had imprinted upon Jakob, and he felt the urgency the general had felt in seeing it safely to Avaneam. He owed something to the general for the time he had spent with him. Only he could protect the trunk and see it to Avaneam.

The pulsing in his head intensified, and Jakob tentatively opened himself to it. He had no control over it, but his awareness heightened with the vibrating, and he welcomed the feeling as it washed over him. His head throbbed with it, and the pulsing sent a slow tingling sensation through the rest of his body.

Carefully, he pushed his head out from behind the tree. The Deshmahne moved cautiously closer. The almost imagined energy radiating from the man was now more of a thin fog surrounding him.

Jakob recognized it; he had seen something similar. A similar fog had surrounded the High Priest. Did that mean he'd be as powerful as the High Priest?

Suddenly, the man brought his eyes around and locked on him. He made no motion as if to move. Simply stared. They knew where he was.

The Deshmahne started forward as one.

"You will come with us," the large Deshmahne said. It was not shouted, but felt loud in Jakob's ears. "The Highest summons."

A chill ran down Jakob's spine. The High Priest knew of him.

"No," Jakob croaked, shaking his head, though the word fell from his mouth meekly.

The other two Deshmahne laughed, but the larger man did not. "This is not a request." His words were felt as much as heard.

In spite of himself, Jakob felt pulled forward before he realized what he was doing and stopped.

"No." This time his voice was stronger.

He raised his sword in front of him and pulled at the vibration within him as he remembered doing during the battle, and felt an excruciating pain in his skull. It was a tearing, as if a part of his mind ripped loose. The feeling rolled through his mind, through his body, an agony unlike anything he'd felt before. Throughout the pain, the pulsing in his head grew stronger, humming loudly in his ears, shooting through his body.

He screamed.

Jakob struggled to keep his eyes open as they watered with pain. He couldn't see the Deshmahne, and turned his head side to side quickly, but felt nausea with the movement and stopped. His sword grew heavy, but he feared lowering it, else the Deshmahne would push forward and attack. Jakob smelled them as much as anything, a stench like rot coming from all directions, but could no longer see the men responsible.

He stepped forward, and as he did, his vision cleared slightly.

The large Deshmahne stood before him, almost near enough to touch. His sword was curved and he brought it up. "You will come." His sword was a taunt as he carefully swung it.

Even through Jakob's heightened awareness, the sword was a blur. He stepped to the side, his head clearing enough to see, and barely brought his sword up to block. He couldn't win against this man.

In a panic, he pulled on the vibration within him, praying for the awareness he needed to stay alive, to escape. He'd need every advantage he could manage to survive.

His mind felt ripped asunder, as painful as the last.

Jakob staggered forward, nausea rolling through him.

With the nausea came the feeling of movement and he fell to his knees, his mind spinning. He leaned over to retch, but nothing came. Through it all, he struggled to keep his eyes open, his focus upon the Deshmahne. But he could do so no longer, and collapsed.

Jakob couldn't move. The trunk was captured. He could almost hear the Deshmahne laughing, thought he felt hot breath on his neck.

What have I done?

He heaved himself forward and felt another tearing of his mind, unbearably worse than the last.

"No!"

The word echoed through his head was chased by strange thoughts: Was this real? Could this all be the madness? Hadn't his brother screamed like this?

But he had seen Tian die and had watched as Rit took his last breath. He had seen the clearing full of dead Denraen.

Hadn't he? What if that had all been in his mind?

Jakob threw himself forward again, nausea and a sense of spinning returning as he did. Pushing through it, he surged forward again. And again. And again.

Finally, he couldn't muster another surge. All the strength had left him. His head was a steady drumbeat, a pulsing pain that sent waves throughout him.

The stench of rot was gone.

Daring to open his eyes, he noticed everything was different.

His vision was hazy, as if a smoky fire obscured his view. He could still see trees, but the sky was different somehow, now gray and clouded where it had been growing dark before.

Strange.

It was the only thought that came.

Then he noticed something else seemed different as well. The ground was not flat as it had been. All around him were hills, rolling and flowing into the horizon. He knew without looking that the city in the distance was gone.

Where was he?

When he turned, two figures stood behind him.

Panicking, he dove to the ground, rolling as he landed, and felt a sharp pain as the trunk crashed into his back and his saddlebags slipped off his shoulder. He twisted noisily as he rolled, eventually coming to rest behind a large bush, ready to defend himself if needed.

He peered out around the bush. Through the haze, a man and a woman stood in a clearing. Not a woman as he knew them, he realized. Her hair was a light flaxen blonde, her skin deeply tanned from the sun. Her face was long and sloped with a slightly different shape.

She was beautiful. There was a warmth about her, friendly and reassuring.

The man was dressed in a simple woolen vest and dark breeches. A sword was sheathed across his back, a dark leather scabbard covering the weapon. Jakob could almost make out the figures adorning the hilt of the man's sword. Something about them tugged at a memory, but passed. Gray hair was cut raggedly and short gray whiskers covered his face in a beard.

These were not Deshmahne.

They were talking and didn't seem to notice his appearance or noisy roll to cover. He didn't know how they could not, but he listened and could just make out their words.

"Sharna, the split was not successful. The people hide in the south, and though no longer attached to the mainland, they reach us still," the man said.

"We have done much, Niall Tinmril. My people have suffered to save yours." Her words had an almost musical quality to them.

A pained look came to Niall's face. "The north is lost, Sharna. The south will soon be, I fear." As the man spoke, tears welled in Sharna's eyes. Her eyes were as yellow as the brightest sunflower. "They use ships now to reach us. It was bad enough when they could just cross the land bridge and reach us in the south. Your people stopped that with the split."

"And many were lost. My husband was lost."

Niall looked visibly shaken at the news, and tried to regain his composure before going on. "Yet they keep coming. And there are so many of them that the ships keep coming. Ours can only hold them off so much longer," he said.

THE THREAT OF MADNESS | 199

Sharna nodded. It was a sad gesture.

"The people expect you to save them. Some still think the gods will save them."

Sharna laughed lightly, a sweet sound. "Some still think us to be gods, Niall." She stopped for a moment, looking around. "We are what we are. And we will not be for much longer."

"I know, my lady. To some you are. To others... to others, you never will be."

"Much the better, I should think. Better to not have been and failed than to have the hope and the failure. Failure is all I can see. All many can see."

Jakob sensed an enormity to their words. They spoke of war, though he had heard nothing about a war such as they described. Would Novan hide that from him?

Jakob shook his head. Novan would have shared that news.

Observe and report.

The thought interrupted, and he focused on the two people in front of him. It was what Novan would expect.

Niall nodded. "I have heard." He seemed to hesitate. To Jakob, it looked as if he was uncertain about how to proceed. "Some still see hope. Some saw the possibility."

Sharna's words came out a whispered reply. "The fibers are twisted, that much is true. I can only untangle so far"—she demonstrated with her hands, spreading them wide—"before the tangle falls back into place. Others, they can see farther. That is why you were chosen. That is why you are the one." She paused long enough to take a deep breath. "Hope? I will not say there is none. Only that I cannot see it."

She fell silent. There was something different about the haze around her, not the fearsome fog that surrounded the Deshmahne, but similar. Softer, warmer. It was almost welcoming.

Niall seemed content with her answer. Jakob had moved slightly to the side of the bush without realizing it as he'd listened to their conversation. He noticed that he was now completely out in the open. Though he was visible, the hazy smoke still obscured him somewhat from their view. He shifted to his knees, his fingers clawing at the dark grass, and moved slowly back behind the bush.

Sharna glanced in his direction. A slight glance, more occasional than chance alone would have it. He wondered if she knew he was there.

Niall spoke again. "Have your people considered my proposal?"

"It... is risky." Niall nodded in agreement. "And many more of my people would be lost."

"Why?"

"That much change, that much energy requires that we give up our own. We have learned this from experiences in the past."

"Can you not do it slowly?" Niall offered.

She shook her head. "What you ask requires that we work quickly. Otherwise, the effort would be in vain. And speed requires strength. Some among us no longer have that strength."

The words rattled Niall and his eyes widened.

"We have considered, though. That is enough for now."

Niall nodded. "The people will be ready. I assure you of that."

"That is why you were chosen, Niall Tinmril. That is why you are the Uniter."

Uniter.

Jakob knew the term. Novan had mentioned it and had him read about the Magi practice of the Uniter.

Was this woman a Mage then? She looked nothing like the Magi he'd seen, though admittedly that was few. In many ways, she was different from any woman he had ever seen. He considered the idea that she could be a goddess.

Sharna's glances became more frequent in his direction. At the same time, he felt as if the energy he saw, what he thought of as her aura, reached toward him. It seemed to beckon him, calling to him. He didn't know how to respond but knew he needed to leave. Soon. He didn't feel threatened, but didn't want either of these people to think he'd been listening.

Finally, Jakob heard Niall ask, "What of our cousins to the east?"

Sharna paused as she thought. "We don't know. They've not come to us in some time. They're capable in their own ways, though. Doubtless, we could use their help."

After a brief silence, Niall asked, "What can I do now? How can I serve?"

Sharna shook her head, long blonde hair moving only slightly with the motion. "We must go on as we have been. We will contact you as needed. You still have the gift?" she asked, eyes seeming to examine him before looking back to his face and nodding. "Good."

"We need to stop him, you know. It could change everything."

"It may be that he cannot be stopped now. The man has grown strong over the years. We're not sure how. We don't know what it will take to stop him now." She stopped for a moment. "We should have been more careful with him."

Jakob could almost feel Sharna pull at him now. Her energy seemed to encircle him, cradle him in warmth. As he struggled to figure out how to leave, the pain in his head returned. Not as strong this time around, but still a tearing of his mind. Nausea rolled through him, and the pulsing came again. His head spun, around and around, and he felt the urge to vomit.

Something was wrong.

He struggled against the nausea and the pain again, futile. He felt things move beneath him and the ground tremble. The pain intensified in his head, ripping at his mind. Colors flashed before his eyes. He opened his mouth and his lungs burned.

He screamed until he could no longer hold breath. He panted with the pain, panting because he could do nothing else. It stretched on, seeming an eternity.

Finally, everything ceased.

The pain pulled back to a slight throb, and everything was gone except the pulsing in his mind.

He felt wetness on his cheeks.

He opened his eyes and saw himself surrounded again by trees. Trees so high they blocked out the sun and the sky. Trees so big around, he knew he would grow tired trying to circle them. All about him was strangely dark greenery. He was deep within some great forest, but didn't know where or how he'd come here.

Am I dreaming or is it the madness?

The smoky haze had followed him so that nothing was clear. No edges were really straight and everything had a slight blur to it, a fuzziness so that he squinted to see. It was much worse here than it had been in the last clearing.

He found himself walking a bit, short strides on his part seeming to take him miles at a time, and he decided that he must be dreaming. The scenery blurred even more as he walked. Pausing, he realized the smoke didn't clear as he moved. He turned his head, looking around, trying to see if he could make sense out of where he was.

The forest still surrounded him. He was lost. In spite of the anxiety, he felt a sense of serenity and peacefulness.

He took another step. Trees blurred past him and the terrain changed.

Another step and the blurring continued.

It was almost as if with every step, he jumped hundreds of miles, but he knew that couldn't be so.

He stopped again and his head still throbbed.

Jakob was in a clearing and all around it huge trees formed an almost perfect circle ringing the clearing with their monstrous branches reaching higher into the sky than any others. Dark leaves covered the ground in a thick layer, the smell of their sweet decay teasing his nostrils. Huge gray boulders formed another circle in the center of the clearing. He counted thirteen. Beyond the boulders, he saw little.

Three figures perched atop the boulders. Jakob knew he could be seen standing where he was, just inside the clearing at the edge of the trees, but something told him that he couldn't. The smoky haze still covered everything, almost in a film, and made it difficult for him to even make out features at his distance. He believed something about the haze protected him, hid him.

He shuffled closer, careful not to move too fast, pulled to the boulders as though by a magnet. He reached the nearest stone and easily climbed atop it. He watched the others as he did, and they seemed not to notice.

One of the people was familiar to him—the blonde hair, darkly tanned skin—and he knew it to be Sharna. Something about her was different, changed from the last time. It took a moment before he understood. She was younger. Her face was smoother, her features a little less severe. He wondered briefly how that could be. Around her, he could clearly see colors, an energy. Pale and vague, but he knew he saw it this time. It swirled off of her, toward the other two, occasionally touching the others and pulling back.

The others were the same as Sharna with the elegance in their form, the shape of their faces and eyes, and the slight point to their ears.

Was he looking upon a meeting of the gods?

How can it be they don't see me?

The madness. That could be the only explanation.

Both men were dressed identically, simple brown cloaks made of some fabric he'd never before seen. It looked too smooth, too soft to be anything he'd known. One of them had dark hair, black as night, and the other had reddish hair, standing wildly and the color of fire. The same colors, the energy, surrounding Sharna surrounded each of the men.

"The great cities of the north are nearly empty," Sharna said. "The mines deserted. All head south across the land bridge. The south cannot sustain that many people."

The fire-haired man—likely god—nodded. "It is as you say Sharna day-Morin." The words came flowing out, the name spoken in another tongue. He wondered how he understood what they were saying. "The north will be empty soon."

As the man spoke, a finger of his energy, his aura, stretched out and touched that of Sharna. She made no movement away.

"What drives them south?" Sharna asked.

Her energy stretched fingers out to both of the men as she spoke, touching their auras before pulling away.

Both the men shook their heads slowly. Neither answered for a while. The quiet of the forest was almost too much.

"We do not know the nature of these creatures. We do not know what they are." It was the dark-haired man that spoke now. "But

Treval sen-Pornot speaks rightly. The north will soon be empty. The remaining cities cannot hold for long."

Sharna nodded. "They cannot see what they are fighting, and we can do nothing?" The question seemed to be asking more than what it was.

"We must not interfere. Ours is a purpose much greater than that of mankind," Treval said, answering the extra question Sharna implied.

Sharna seemed upset with the answer. Her words came out slightly more agitated this time. To Jakob's eyes, the field of her aura, the pale cloud surrounding her, grew wider with her agitation. "Without mankind, what do we protect? What do we save?"

The dark-haired man answered. "You know we protect more than mankind."

Treval nodded. "Denmri sen-Kalub and I are in agreement. We cannot interfere. We must wait."

Sharna looked from man to man. Her words came quietly as she said, "You know what was foreseen. With destruction, he gains strength. With strength, he will break free. Soon we may not be enough."

The words left a chill in the air.

He looked around again. The haze still covered him, cloaked him, but he noticed something else as well. All about his arms, his waist and legs, was a field of the same energy that surrounded the other two. It was pale, cloudy, and vague, yet it was unmistakable.

The madness.

He brought his eyes up fearfully. If he could see their auras, surely they must be able to see his. So far, they hadn't seemed to notice anything. None of the three even bothered to look in his direction.

"He has gained the power to lead them," Denmri said.

Sharna shook her head. "He too has grown strong since last we knew him. A man, and yet now..."

Treval picked up for her, finishing her thought. "Now he is more than a man. It does not bode well."

Sharna looked right at Jakob. Bright yellow eyes seemed to peer right into his simple blues. His heart jumped, and he could feel it start to beat wildly. A finger of her aura came tentatively toward him, feeling its way along. The two men looked over, following her energy with their eyes, and began to send much thicker fingers his way, probes as thick as his legs.

Jakob needed to get away.

The pale energy neared him. His mind raced, frantic, and a sudden pain tore at his head again. It ripped from the front to the back of his skull, as if tearing parts of him loose as it moved along. He reached up to grab his head, to steady it, and with the motion felt the nausea return. It rolled in waves up and down his body, through his head.

He leaned over, thinking he might retch.

It was worse than it had been before. The pulsing in his head began vibrating in a scream and combined with the tearing pain into some awful twisted hybrid of feelings. He opened his mouth, needing to scream, needing to shout in his agony.

As he did it ceased.

The world stilled. The spinning stopped. The pain pulled back to a dull ache. The pulsing softened, but did not go away.

Jakob opened his eyes. The haze was thicker now, and it was much more difficult to see. As he looked down at his feet, hard rock was all he saw through the haze. He brought a hand to his face, and still saw the pale energy around him.

What did it mean?

His mind provided the answer and he feared the truth of it.

The madness.

There could be no other explanation.

He took a step and the horizon blurred. He almost felt the whistle of the wind as it whipped across his face, loud in his ears. The faint impression of ever-heightening rock ahead of him pressed upon him as he stopped. Browns and grays of more rock surrounded him as he turned his head. He was in the mountains.

Another step, more blurring.

All around him the rocky ground sloped away. He was on the peak of one of the mountains.

Below him, he saw dark spots all along the face of the mountain that he suspected were caves. His eyes struggled to see through the thick haze, and he saw shapes stream from the mouths of the caves.

No, that's not quite right.

It wasn't that he saw actual shapes but rather many small circles of energy. An energy, or aura, that was both the same and completely different from what he had seen around Sharna and the others. It was dark, almost black, and seemed thick and heavy, whereas the energy around what he believed to be the gods was wispy and light.

He sensed that it was bitter cold. He shivered from watching. There were hundreds all the same, thousands even. Straining his eyes, he felt the now ever-present pulsing grow stronger in his head and as it did, shapes of creatures formed out of the dark energy.

The creature was grotesque, even through the haze. Its skin was the color of gray stone, and the head was completely hairless. Walking on two legs, brown breeches covered the creature's lower half, while the hairy upper half was left naked. The face was a monstrosity. Ears were only holes on each side of the head. Narrow eyes were more like a rat than anything else, and he caught a glimpse of sharp teeth within the mouth. There was nothing natural about the creature. Nothing pure. It seemed a creature straight from a nightmare. Evil.

Other figures walked among the creatures. They were taller, with skin a soft pink, and he realized they were men and women walking naked, looking dazed. Some carried weapons. Others carried food or led horses.

Even from where he stood, he could tell they were slaves.

Jakob couldn't bear to look at the creatures any longer. Their shape, their coloring, and mostly the sense he felt from their aura disgusted him. They churned his stomach in an uneasy way.

Through the thick haze burned another field of energy appeared, larger than any of the thousands of others streaming from the cave. It was dark and cold much like the others, but different too. Part of the energy pulsed and twisted. Hundreds of fingers of energy shot out from this aura and touched each of the creatures. A finger would touch one creature, pull away, and move on to the next. It was almost a dance as they twisted and twined about, never tangling.

Something about the aura tugged on a memory. He had seen it

before. He stared through the haze, and his vision cleared enough for him to see a dark cloak hanging limp around a balding man, short gray hair still barely ringing his scalp. The man turned to look up the slope of the mountain where Jakob stood. Black eyes, dark as the darkest night, stared up at him. Flecks of fiery red jumped about within those eyes.

Jakob knew the man.

The Deshmahne High Priest.

He felt himself jumping back to get away and was suddenly falling.

Petrified, he didn't know what was happening, or what he could do to save himself. He kept falling. He squeezed his eyes shut, resigning himself to his fate. He knew he could do nothing to stop or slow his fall. He didn't even know how high up he had been, or how far he had to fall.

He dropped for long moments, felt the wind stinging his bare flesh. He kicked, fighting, before realizing it was useless. He would not survive this fall.

A feeling came to him then. A feeling that part of his mind opened. It was almost what he felt when the tearing pain came, though this time, it came without agony, without ripping. The pulsing came on stronger again, pushing away all thoughts, pushing away all fear. He welcomed it, pulled at it as he had learned he could and welcomed the humming in his head. It spread throughout his body, touching his heart, stomach, and moved into his legs. Strangely, it touched his fingers last. The sensation left him vibrating, and he could almost hear it in his ears. He thrilled in the feeling of the tingling, thrilled in the fall.

He cried out.

As he did, everything stopped.

The sense of falling ceased. The wind stopped howling in his ears and biting at his flesh. The pounding in his head stopped.

He opened his eyes, expecting the haze.

Instead, he lay on the edge of a forested area. A hard-packed road ran nearby, heading straight west based on the direction of the sun. Weeds that had not yet been trampled by travelers peeked through the road every so often. The haze was gone from his vision, and with it the blurring.

A dream. It was all a dream.

Or was the madness?

It seemed chillier, and he noted that the landscape was different. The sun was shifted from where it should be in the sky, and after he pondered it, he realized why. He was farther north.

How?

He propped himself up, looking around. There was no sign of anyone else around him, no sign of the Deshmahne attackers. His sword was still with him, the trunk still hung from his belt, and his saddlebags still draped over his shoulder. Relief surged through him before being replaced by despair.

His horse was gone. He would be on foot.

Jakob walked to the road, knowing what he needed to do. North. The Elasiin path toward Siirvil's Peak and Avaneam.

Looking north, there was nothing but dark forest, and he knew he wouldn't find the path through the forest.

West first. Then north.

After that, what would he do?

CHAPTER TWENTY-ONE

A knock at his door drew his attention, and Alriyn looked up. "Come," he called. His voice felt rough. He had done much talking lately. Part of him missed the traveling and the solitude of his studies.

Karrin opened the door and slipped in. She glanced quickly toward the empty chairs before sending a curious glance his way. Her pale yellow robe swished quietly around her as she moved. She smiled at him, lips only curling partly up. She wasn't happy about something.

"We'll wait for—" Another knock came at his door. "Come," he called again.

The door pushed open and Haerlin slipped in. "You summoned me, Alriyn?" His words trailed as he saw Karrin in the room. "What is this?"

"Close the door, Haerlin," Alriyn said.

Haerlin did as he was asked, then asked again, "What is this?"

"You faced Deshmahne," Alriyn began.

Haerlin shook his head. "Not I."

Alriyn laughed, knowing the truth of the statement. Endric had made mention of how Haerlin had corralled the delegate in the center of the Denraen at the onset of the attack. Roelle, on the other hand, had been something else—something he'd never dared dream to hear about—a warrior Mage.

Alriyn felt mixed emotions about that and kept the pride he felt hidden—few would understand, could understand.

"They were Deshmahne?" Karrin asked.

Haerlin nodded, and Karrin whistled quietly. That now made four confirmed attacks upon the Magi. They should all remember the attack decades ago. It had been the one that set Alriyn on his course to discover what lay beyond the borders of Vasha. That the Deshmahne continued their attacks could not be mere chance. Alriyn had sought out Endric when they returned. The man was tired, worried, but not about the Deshmahne.

"The Denraen can kill Deshmahne," Endric had said.

"Yet you worry," Alriyn had pressed.

"There are some things we cannot kill," he replied.

The comment, off-handed though it was, had carried a deeper meaning. Endric was never one to easily pass on information. He was Denraen and served to protect the *mahne*. Alriyn had learned long ago to trust what Endric said and to look for another layer. In this case, he wondered what he would find.

Never had the Denraen been as distant as they had under Endric's leadership. The Denraen had been founded nearly as long ago as the Magi and were tasked with protecting the *mahne*. Most felt they were guardians of the Magi, though they were not, not truly. The Denraen kept peace when others could not.

"The Denraen can manage the Deshmahne," Alriyn said to the two Elders.

"Manage?" Haerlin asked. "The Denraen haven't stopped the Deshmahne's influence from spreading in the south. They barely stopped the attack when the Desh—"

"Their purpose is not to start war," Alriyn reminded, "but to maintain peace. The balance." He watched Haerlin, realizing how much the attack he'd experienced had shaken the man. "And the delegates can serve us. I don't dispute the Eldest's plan."

"Then why am I here?" Haerlin asked, glancing from Karrin to Alriyn.

"The stories from the north grow stranger." The stories had become wilder since his return. He wondered which to believe, which to ignore. It didn't seem prudent to ignore any at this point.

"Rumors," Haerlin shot.

"More than rumors," Karrin said.

Alriyn nodded again. "More than rumors. You traveled with Endric. What did you learn from him?"

"He lets on only what he wants to."

"He does." The comment mirrored Alriyn's thoughts.

"There can be little truth to the tales," Haerlin pushed.

Karrin shook her head. Alriyn suspected that she would have heard similar tales. He hoped so. The far north was a growing wasteland. Winter was coming, and it would be much more difficult to do anything during the harsh northern winter. Worse, though, was the word that this menace moved south.

"The delegates will train as the Eldest directed. The situation is in hand," Haerlin said.

"The delegates were chosen to help with the Deshmahne and the disruption in the south." And, if Gom Aaldia continued down their current path with the Deshmahne, perhaps the delegates would be needed closer to home. "Unless the Deshmahne have pushed farther than we know, the delegates can do nothing about the north." He looked hard at Haerlin before turning to Karrin.

"I've seen some good from them," Haerlin said.

Alriyn cast a strong eye at the words. "A prophecy?" The man had a rare gift, though was not a true prophet. Haerlin was the first in many years to show any signs, however weakly. They had learned to trust Haerlin's visions long ago.

The other Mage shook his head. "I don't know. I look at the delegates together... and I see a mixture. Good with bad. Bright and dark. A mixed message." He paused. "When I look at each alone, I see nothing clearly. I don't know what it means."

Alriyn considered what he'd just heard. He hadn't expected that. "They will be of use, but even with the old tradition, the Uniter, we missed something." There was something to the selection that they'd been unable to learn. The *mahne* was incomplete, and Alriyn had spent his life trying to fill in the holes. A fragment he possessed, that few had seen, spoke of a test. Years of searching had taught him nothing more of this test. "How can these delegates help?"

"Some are stronger than others," Karrin suggested.

He arched an eyebrow.

"Lansington, for one," she continued. "The boy has an inner strength."

Haerlin nodded agreement. "When Bothar and his group joined us for the remainder of the journey to Vasha, I traveled with the boy. Son of the High King of Gom Aaldia."

"Any others?" Alriyn asked.

"The boy from the west, om-Elraihn. A quiet one, and strange, but there is more to him, I think."

Alriyn clasped his hands together. "I must speak with them," he declared.

"To what purpose?" Haerlin asked. "The Eldest guides their training."

He turned to Karrin. They had agreed Haerlin would be the first they spoke to. "There's something worrisome about the north, Haerlin. It is more than stories. There is an ancient threat, one I've read about in my studies—"

Haerlin looked at him carefully. "What studies?"

"Us." Alriyn said. The word hung in the air. "The Great Mother. Our Founding."

"Founded in a time of war, the Great Mother brought us together, settling the bloodshed and sealing our futures, and we became the Urmahne," Haerlin recited.

Karrin looked at Alriyn with uncertainty. Their Founding was taught to them at a young age; any Mage could recite the same line. Alriyn shook his head. "Yes, but before that."

"We know almost nothing of that time. The records are lost," Haerlin said.

Alriyn shook his head. "There is the *mahne.*" Ancient, unclear, and written in a language long-since dead, it was the only surviving recording prior to their Founding. It was written with knowledge and explained much of their purpose, their gifts from the gods. "I've seen the old texts, the fragments. There was something terrible at that time, something only our people could face. We must buy time and determine if *now* is the time the *mahne* calls for." He feared whether the others would agree with the need to call for the *nemah*, but the more he heard, the more he wondered if perhaps the delegates wouldn't be enough. "There is too much strangeness for my liking, too much that sounds like what happened then," he admitted.

Haerlin was nodding slowly now. That was good.

"There is something," Haerlin began, his voice barely more than a scratching whisper. "Something I saw of a boy."

Alriyn looked at him a moment. "A vision?"

Haerlin shook his head. "I don't know. I thought..." He shook his head. "I thought it was wrong. He traveled with us when we first set out on our journey, an apprentice historian."

Alriyn looked at him. "Novan?" Alriyn had been surprised to learn that Haerlin had allowed the historian to travel with him.

Haerlin snuffled. "Novan, indeed. A new apprentice, and one whom your niece found quite interesting, I might add. I saw it twice; the first time, I thought I imagined it. The second could not be ignored." He looked around, eyes searching for understanding. "It was nothing I had ever seen before. It seemed almost a ball, circular, and dark. As if he held everything *and* nothing in his future."

Haerlin sighed. "It was brief, but I think on it sometimes. It seemed that if I looked, I could see everything, could know any answer I needed. Or lose myself trying. I can't explain it. It was both frightening and exhilarating. I still don't understand." He paused before continuing. "I hoped to see more along our journey, but it never came."

Alriyn didn't know how to react, didn't know what it meant, but suspected. "You let him leave?"

"Not I," Haerlin replied. "Novan sent him north with the Denraen. They carried something for Endric. Novan felt it important to observe." Haerlin looked at him expectantly. "I could not find out what it was. And I did not stop him."

North again, and now Endric was involved.

What was that man up to? What did this mean?

He needed answers, and he suspected Endric would not be forth-coming. "We need you and a select council of others to study this further."

"Which others?" Haerlin asked.

"First you join," Karrin demanded.

Haerlin's gaze shifted from Alriyn to Karrin. "After what I saw, I am with you. For now."

Alriyn smiled to himself. It was enough. It had to be enough. "Councilors only. They must know and understand the *mahne*. It is too dangerous otherwise. Bothar, Isandra, though we have yet to speak to them." He looked over to Karrin. "Time is moving faster now. We must follow."

"We will have to have a compelling reason to choose the Uniter, Alriyn," Haerlin said. "My hazy visions will not be enough, and neither will rumors."

Alriyn nodded, and worried what more they might discover.

～

The next week passed slowly. Brohmin's body tired, though they hadn't pushed too hard. His shoulder still ached from his injury, but he had cleaned the blood from his shirt. At least he felt cleaner.

Salindra still rode next to him. He had wondered if she would disappear as they neared Rondalin. She surprised him when she cut her hair short and rubbed jensain root in it to darken. She looked different. Different enough that he doubted she would be recognized.

He glanced over to her with the thought. She sat tall in the saddle, her confidence returning with her strength. Somehow, his healings were helping. Each night he tried again. At the least, it helped slow what was happening. She looked more like the woman she had been. She would have to carry herself differently to pass as a common woman. She was too tall to be anything but Mage.

They came atop a hill. The sun was only partway along its path for the day and bright overhead. In the valley far below them, a huge city came into view. Massive walls encircled its entirety, and a huge fortress stood in the center of the city. Separate walls blocked the fortress from the rest of the city, higher than the outer walls. He knew it to be a strong fortress. A poor location, though. The hill he stood upon could easily hide an army.

He looked over to Salindra. She did not return his gaze. He asked much of her by returning to Rondalin. She risked much.

He spurred his horse down the hill and Salindra followed. The ride toward the city passed quickly. They were soon upon the main road leading into the city proper. The road was empty, though packed hard from use. It hadn't rained in several weeks, so it was dry as well, kicking dust up on them.

"I am afraid, Brohmin," Salindra whispered next to him.

He looked over to her. Her voice was softer than he had ever heard. He could see her shaking slightly. He had not thought a Mage could know that much fear. "I promise no further harm to you, Salindra."

She shook her head slowly. "I'm not sure you can."

With her words hanging in the air, he looked toward the city. They were approaching the main gate, and he could make out the sentries standing guard. Their presence surprised him somewhat. Rondalin had always been an open city. He looked over to her again. "Why?" he asked finally.

She did not take her eyes off the gate as she answered. "I did not think this could be done to my people," she answered. "What if the same is done to you?" she asked worried.

He laughed lightly. "I am not of your people, Salindra," he told her.

She looked at him then. Her eyes were harder than he had seen from her since their journey together began. "You must be of..." she began.

"I am not of your people," he reassured.

She stared at him a long time before turning away. He knew the question she didn't ask and laughed at what he knew she thought. He knew he was little different from the guards at the gate. She would doubt him if he told her that.

"When were guards posted?" he asked to break the silence.

She looked in the distance. "Several days after the new advisor arrived. Only a short while before I left the city."

Her words were hurt. He knew why.

They rode silently up to the gate. Reaching the sentries, he looked down at them, eyeing their uniforms with curiosity. Bronze helmets capped their heads, and polished silver breastplates covered their chests. The sun reflected brightly off the metal. The shirt and pants underneath were black and green, hugging muscular frames.

"Visiting or staying?" the guard to his left asked. The man rested a firm hand atop his sword as he asked. The way he held himself said he knew how to use it as well.

"Visiting," he lied.

"For the day or overnight?" the other guard asked.

"The day," he lied again. "Just here for supplies."

A single flick of the wrist passed them through. It was not until they were well beyond hearing that he looked over to Salindra. "What was that?" he asked.

She shook her head. "I'm not sure," she replied.

He looked around. The streets were thick with people, crowded more than he had ever seen the city. "Crowded," he mused. "All coming south for the protection of the city," he thought. And nothing was being done about it.

Salindra nodded. He thought she looked nervous. He understood. He would keep her from harm. Nothing would happen to her while in Rondalin.

"What now?" she asked.

"We wait," he answered.

CHAPTER TWENTY-TWO

The dust around Jakob no longer settled. The dirt of the road was now dry and floated about him. Each step filled his nose with it, caking his skin and turning to paste with his sweat. It had been many days since the last rain. Many days of enduring the discomfort of wandering alone, with no shelter. Many days since he'd felt clean.

It was cold, the autumn now threatening to change fully into winter. Jakob had been thankful for his cloak, but still it hadn't been enough to keep him warm. Mostly it'd been clear weather with only one day of rain. He didn't know if he should be thankful for that. Today's sky was clear again, and he could hear the sounds of the nearby forest as he walked. They were the sounds of crickets chirping, leather bugs humming, and the occasional caw of a crow overhead.

The path before him was empty, as was the path behind. He long ago gave up the hope of finding someone else along the road, companionship, or food. His belly called to him. The small roadside berries had not been satisfying, and he'd had little water to drink. He had tried hunting, but luck was not with him. It was a long way from the road to any stream. The one time he'd gone searching, it had taken him hours to make his way back.

The road had headed straight west. Jakob had followed it much of the first day, his injured back and leg not allowing much speed. Camping along the roadside, he slept soundly the first night, but awoke in a fit of panic, certain the Deshmahne had found him. The itching in his head he'd known while traveling with the Denraen had returned, but he no longer cared.

Worse, he feared for his sanity.

The strange dreams that had haunted him for the last few weeks had stopped, and there had been nothing like the strange waking dream he had experienced before ending up along this road, but he couldn't shake that last one. It had been more than a dream, something so real he could have lived it.

Jakob staggered onward. The weight of the trunk was a constant reminder of his mission, but worry rose within him that he'd be too late to find Endric. Would Novan then think him dead?

He needed to find another horse, somehow, so he could reach Avaneam and meet the Denraen.

As he walked, he decided that living the life of Jarren Gildeun might not have been as exciting as he'd hoped.

He had abandoned his saddlebags early on. His few belongings were now tucked into his heavier cloak and the rest discarded. There had been a moment of surprise, then sorrow, when he had discovered the books he had taken from his father's room. Those he tucked carefully into an inner pocket of his cloak. Novan's book of the ancient language went next to them. He had little else to call his own.

During the second day of travel, he'd taken a break and sat down, pulling out his father's books. One was smaller than the others, and something about it looked different. Leaning against a rock to read and rest, he discovered another surprise. The book was similar to the one Novan had given him, written in stretches of the ancient language. A small stone ring had tumbled out of it, dark black and without any adornment. Jakob knew it was different from the jewelry the priests wore. There was something familiar about it, but he couldn't place what.

Memories of his father and his now lost family had overwhelmed him, and tears streaked his dusty face. Finally, he had taken a deep breath and, on impulse, had put his father's ring upon his middle finger. Its weight was a pleasant reminder of him.

Jakob read the book for an hour before pressing on. At each stop, he pulled it out and read from it again. It was slow, but the words came more easily each time he opened its pages. This was more of a historical text describing Thealon over a thousand years ago. Though dry, something about it was fascinating.

On the third day, he came upon an intersecting road. It led north and south while the one he was on continued west. Jakob went north. The trunk almost pulled him forward, and he continued onward for several more days.

And now, his legs ached. He figured he'd been walking nearly a week and couldn't travel much farther without food, or water, or shelter. But the road was well worn and had about it the look and feel of something serviceable, so he prayed he'd find a city at some point. A city meant supplies and another step closer to Endric.

Another hill loomed before him, climbing high above. It had been like this for several days. Hill after hill, each one was higher than the last. He looked up, saw the sun approaching its midday peak, and knew that he'd been walking for several hours already. He had no choice but to keep on. He raised a hand to his forehead and wiped a bit of the sweat off, leaving his arm smeared with the grime that coated him.

Topping the hill, an enormous city appeared far in the distance. Jakob could make out huge walls surrounding the sprawling city, but little else from his vantage. Elation welled in him, and he considered running before deciding against it. From the size of the city, he gauged the distance still a long way off. His pace still quickened, and he found the day passing. He didn't bother to stop and rest, leaving the strange books tucked in his cloak for the first time in since he'd begun reading them. With nothing left to eat or drink, there was no other point in stopping.

Before he knew it, the sun was setting behind him, and stars blinked on in the night sky. Up ahead, around the city, other lights flickered on, candles in the night. As he neared the city, he saw that tents and makeshift houses had been built and the road led through them. People gradually joined him on the road as he walked, traveling toward the city gates.

The houses and tents all appeared hastily thrown up without any sort of order to the manner in which they were arranged. Simple wooden houses that seemed frail enough to fall over in a brisk wind had tents of all kinds surrounding them. The tents were made of all sorts of fabrics and furs, some propped up with many wooden shafts while others had a single pole at the center.

It was like this as far as he could see. Small openings between each dwelling allowed access further off the road, but the spaces were narrow, and he wouldn't want to wander blindly through there in the dark. People had used whatever they could to build themselves a shelter. Lights scattered throughout lit up the night.

Ahead, the wall to the city proper was still nearly a mile off. The makeshift houses and tents squeezed in tighter closer to the walls. Eventually, there was no room between them, many simply butting up against the next.

He couldn't imagine living this way. He noticed that between the rows of dwellings, small streets had popped up. They were a necessity this close to the walls of the city because of how tightly packed the dwellings had become. Without the streets, there would be no access to any.

He nudged around others on the road. Some stared around, while others were hawkers who had set up carts trying to sell goods. The main street was the only place this could be done as carts would not fit well on the narrow side streets. As Jakob slowly neared the walls, the road seemed busy for nighttime. Then he overheard some conversation and understood.

"I hear they've got the best ale at the Rotted Prine," one man told another in front of him. It seemed some things were not offered outside the city walls.

Finally, huge iron gates barred the way before him. On either side of the gate, standing atop the wall, stood a guard dressed in heavy armor and brandishing a crossbow. He checked through his cloak and felt Tian's crossbow and fell into the line that had formed, some fifty people deep, awaiting access to the city.

Two men in front of him still discussed drinking locales. They were thin men, unshaven, and both looked to be as covered in grime as he felt. Their shirts and breeches were stained and torn a little.

"Strange," one of the men said to the other.

"Aye," the other replied nodding. "There's not been a line like this before."

"Too many come south," the other answered.

"Maybe Thealon would be safer. At least there, the gods offer protection."

"If they ever come out of that damn Tower!" the other laughed. His friend laughed with him.

Not much farther in front of him stooped an old woman with her gray hair pulled back tightly into a bun. She wore a dark shawl wrapped around her shoulders. At her side stood a young girl who looked to Jakob barely seven or eight years old. She clung to the old woman's arm, her head down. Her cheeks were sunken, and in the lamplight, the tone of her skin was ashen.

"Keep her away from us! We don't need to catch it!"

The old woman looked around in disgust. She couldn't seem to find the person who had yelled. "I can't help it there's a line." Her voice was weak and crackly. "We go to see a healer!"

"Wait until no one else is around!" someone else shouted. "There are too many sick as it is." A stone came flying toward the woman from out in the line. It missed, but he turned his head in disgust.

"A nice sword you have there, boy."

He spun to see who spoke. It was an old man behind him in the line. His back hunched, and he leaned on a wooden cane. The naked flesh of his chest was pale and sunken, and the man stank. He wore little more than badly torn breeches; his shoes nothing more than patches of leather tied to his feet.

Jakob turned back around, hoping to avoid the stench. He had almost forgotten about his sword. He had grown used to its weight, and as he looked around, he realized no one else wore steel.

They came for protection. I come with protection.

He resisted the urge to feel for the hidden crossbow.

"Where might one such as you acquire such a sword?" The man's voice was high pitched and gravely. His breath stunk of rotten teeth. The remaining teeth were yellowed and broken.

"My family." Jakob said over his shoulder, keeping his gaze facing forward, hoping only to ignore the man.

Dark eyes peered curiously at him, taking in the dirt that coated his ragged clothes. "Oh?"

Jakob found himself crowding near to the two men in line in front of him. He moved away from the stench of the old man, to get away from his leering eyes. A gruff glance back by one of the men halted him from pushing too close.

Up ahead, the line inched forward. He heard someone mention that the guards were waiting until someone left before another was allowed in because the city was too crowded. Jakob grew impatient with his thirst and hunger.

In front of him, the men had moved on to a different conversation. He heard little of it, though, and strained to hear more. As he did, he felt the pulsing in his head increase, and the men's voices became clearer. "They say they're looking for someone. Maybe that's why the line takes so long."

The other nodded in agreement. "Wonder who they're looking for."

"We'll know soon enough," the man replied, nodding to the shortening line. "I wonder what they did."

The line continued to advance, and he was close enough to see the two guards. Both were garbed in lightweight chain mail, with simple leather helmets covering their heads and short swords sheathed at their sides. Heavy leather boots covered their feet. They stood to either side of the gate, blocking entrance to those in the line. Another man stood behind them, hidden by shadow.

Another guard? Jakob couldn't see clearly and would have to wait until he got closer. As one person left the city, the guard farthest from the line would nod to the nearer, and who would quickly look the person over before letting them into the city. For each person, it was the same.

The old woman and the sick girl made it to the head of the line. Disgust lined one of the guard's faces as he looked upon the girl. The man shook his head at the old woman. Finally, he heard the woman plead.

"I'm taking her to a healer. Please, she may not live without!"

The guard was unmoved. He shook his head and raised his arm, pointing her away. Several people in line jeered at the woman.

"Please?" the woman begged.

The sick girl reached out toward the guard, and the man shrank back from her touch. A gloved hand came up and drew back to strike. Jakob didn't want to watch but could not stop himself. The hand came down. At the last second, the man standing behind the guards caught it and waved the woman and her child through. A glare passed between the two guards, but they didn't say anything.

He moved closer and heard mumbling farther in front of him. A description. "They say he's tall and plain looking. Say he has brownish hair and deep blue eyes."

"What'd he do?" someone asked near the head of the line.

It was one of the guards who answered. "He killed a priest."

A few people sucked in a breath in surprise. Someone in the back of the line yelled out, "I killed me a man too!" followed by a burst of laughter among those who heard him.

Jakob didn't laugh. They could've been describing him.

He focused his gaze on the man standing behind the guards, staring hard as he tried to see past the shadows. The slow pulsing in his head intensified, and his vision cleared so that he could see through the darkness. The man wore a cloak with a hood covering his head, but Jakob saw the markings around his eyes and knew the man wore them on his arms as well.

A Deshmahne.

Jakob needed to get away.

The guard spoke again, ignoring the comment. "He's a thief too. Snuck away with the priest's sword. A valuable bauble."

One of the men in front of him glanced back at him again. His eyes widened as he saw first Jakob's height, then his hair, eyes, and finally the sword. The man nudged his friend who looked back curiously, and his breath caught.

Without warning, he felt a hard *whack* across his calves. The old

224 | D.K. HOLMBERG

man behind him brandished his cane and cocked an arm back for a second strike. From behind him now, one of the men yelled, "Here! The killer is here!"

Jakob panicked, trying to move, but the mass of people blocked him.

He vaguely heard someone farther back in line joke, "No, I'm back here you dolt!"

At the front of the line, he heard the sound of swords being unsheathed, followed by the terse shout, "Hold him!" and "Stay where you are!"

The old man started to bring his cane down, arcing from high overhead and swinging toward Jakob's skull. He ducked from the blow and turned. One of the men in front of him grabbed at him. He twisted and broke free of clawing fingers and ran.

At first, he ran back down the main road he had come in on. But the further out he got, the more people seemed intent on stopping him. Reaching arms forced a sudden left on a nearby street. It was narrow, almost too narrow, and he had to slow down to slink past others along the street. He was comforted knowing his pursuers would have to do the same.

Fear raced through him as he ran. The Deshmahne were in the city.

Where was he that Deshmahne would be openly in the city? But not just in the city. It appeared they controlled the city and the guards.

As he ran, the fatigue of the last week threatened to overwhelm him. He pushed through it, hoping to get far enough away that he could hide.

He noted people huddled near small fires for warmth. A few people were cooking as he ran, and his empty stomach ached and his mouth watering. It had been a long time since he had eaten.

Those he saw were dirty, unable to clean themselves. Fear in their eyes changed to relief when they saw it was not them being chased.

What could make them scared like this?

People almost cowered. The fear he saw, the suffering, their defeat almost made him give up. It reminded him of the feeling he had during the Turning Festival. If the Deshmahne were here, would they always feel hopeless?

With the question, a slow helpless feeling crept through him and settled. His steps slowed, and he nearly stopped. Jakob felt hollow and useless.

Why bother? I'll be captured eventually.

The thought came unbidden, and Jakob felt its truth. He faltered again, heard the sounds of his pursuers nearby and readied his surrender.

Avaneam, came another thought. *The general.*

Jakob felt the weight of the trunk as it hung from his belt, and his mind snapped back into focus as he remembered that too much had already been lost to lose the trunk now. So he ran.

He took corners, side streets each smaller than the last, until he was panting. His breath was loud in his ears. His empty stomach churned, crying for food. Slowing his pace, he looked around. It looked the same as any other place in this outer city, with ramshackle houses and makeshift tents that had sprung up almost haphazardly. There was no one around him and, for a moment, he thought himself safe.

Reaching an intersection of sorts, he paused to get his bearings and saw that he'd come almost half way around the city. Catching his breath, he took in the streets around him. Suddenly, he saw two men running toward him dressed in simple shirts with heavily tattooed arms exposed. Each carried a long, curved sword.

Deshmahne.

Could he face two? Jakob wasn't sure. He'd barely survived the last two times he faced the Deshmahne. Now he was exhausted and starved.

Jakob adjusted his sword and ran. The pulsing in his head hummed and became a steady throbbing. He looked across the street, then back to his left. If he went straight, the street narrowed so that it would slow him. Being slower risked being caught. If he went left, he'd be forced away from the city.

He ran left.

He pushed past people as he ran, shouting a warning as he could, but not daring to slow. At one of the intersections stood a beggar woman. She was a big woman, and a few coarse whiskers poked out along her face. A dark scarf covered her head. She pointed a crooked finger at him, and reflections of all the small fires danced about in her dark eyes. He had seen eyes like that before.

She shouted at him, cursing, and as he passed, the beggar woman somehow transformed into the shape of the High Priest.

Fear and anger emanated from him, and that sense of hopelessness pushed upon him again. Jakob's head pulsed harder, and a tingling spreading throughout his body, and the hopeless feeling dissipated. Suddenly, chaos took charge.

The houses lining either side of the street fell inward, toward the street. The High Priest cackled with laughter. A dark smoke emanated from him, and the stench of rot and filth flowed with it. Flames suddenly licked the tops of houses as they fell. People all about the street screamed and ran.

He froze. He was trapped.

Climbing out and over the mess of houses would take too long. The Deshmahne would be upon him before he made it ten feet, if he even made it that far in his weakened state. The High Priest started toward him with eyes of fire flashing anger.

He needed to do something, needed some way to stop the fall of the houses so he could get through and keep the trunk away from the High Priest.

Desperation flooded through him, and he threw his hands up in the air, frantic and scared.

With the thought and the gesture, his head split in agony. A tearing within his skull that was the same torture he remembered from his last encounter with the Deshmahne. It was blinding in its intensity, and he could think of nothing but the pain. The pulsing reverberated through his mind, his ears, and his body.

He shook with it, and he screamed, wondering what the High Priest was doing to him.

Then time seemed to stop.

Not time completely. Everything seemed to freeze as it was. Except for him.

The night went silent. Where wood and fabric had been falling toward the street, it was now frozen. Houses hung in mid-air and flames leaping from falling houses no longer danced. People all along the street were frozen as they stood, with expressions of fear upon their faces and mouths open in screams of terror. One or two lay trampled along the street where others had been careless and pushed them down in their fear. Silence enveloped everything.

The Deshmahne with swords had arms half raised as they neared him and had prepared to attack. The High Priest had his arm raised, mouth open. Darkness flowed from the man's tattoos. Jakob saw something else about him. His eyes still moved and followed his motions. The reflected fire within them still danced about almost angrily, the only other motion in the night.

He ran, holding tightly to his unsheathed sword, uncertain that he could even wield it in his tired and weakened state.

Once past the houses frozen in their fall, the pain in his head receded. Everything jumped forward again. Screams filled the night as frightened people ran. A loud clatter covered the screams as the houses finally hit the street behind him. Flames crackled, slowly consuming the falling houses. The smell of the smoke was thick in his nose. The fires would consume much this night.

Reaching the edge of the city, he hazarded a look back. What he saw struck terror in his heart. Where the houses had fallen, where the fires ate at the downed structures, a path flung itself open. The fallen wood and flames almost threw themselves to either side of the street.

The path stretched toward him, and the High Priest stepped from the mouth of the fiery path into the now cleared street. Jakob turned quickly and ran, sheathing his sword as he did.

A steep hill led up to the edge of the forest, and he grabbed at grass to give him better grip as he climbed. He slipped, dropping to one knee and stopping, and as he did, something whistled by his head. He dared not look back, and his panic urged him faster.

Jakob grabbed faster at the grass, trying to regain his speed. The grass was wet with the night's dew, and he slipped again. As he struggled to get up, something hit his leg. He screamed as pain shot up his thigh, spreading through his body. Heat came with the pain, fire burning with it, but he could not slow, and crawled forward, slowly climbing.

Shouts echoed behind him, then a few more arrows whizzed past. None missed by much.

Finally, he reached the top of the hill, gasping for breath. His lungs burned from the smoke in the air and the stench from the city.

Jakob staggered toward the trees. He didn't know if he would be safe there, if he would be able to hide, but he needed to try.

He couldn't stop. The Denraen must know of this. The general must know. The trunk must find Avaneam. It was the key to stopping the Deshmahne.

Behind him came panting as the men chasing him made it to the top of the hill. It would not be long now. The pain in his leg was nearly unbearable, and he wouldn't be able to go on much longer.

Suddenly, two arms grabbed him around the waist, constraining his arms against his body. He screamed, tried to kick, but was too weak.

"Quiet!" he heard whispered in his ear.

He looked up, and the person nodded toward his pursuers. They ran toward the tree line, but as they did, an arrow suddenly caught one man in the stomach, and he fell. Another arrow followed, catching the other man in the throat in a spray of blood.

"We're here to help." The voice was soft and high. It did little to ease his fear.

Jakob looked at the woman, suddenly worried.

Black eyes stared back at him.

He jerked back, but the hands around him held firm. Then he saw brown hair, shorn short around the tall woman's head. A Mage?

"Quiet," she said again.

He nodded. As he did, a man emerged from another part of the forest, bow in hand. *A Denraen?* Hope flared before he realized it could not be. No soldier traveled alone.

"Deshmahne," Jakob found himself saying. "Where are they?" He jerked his head around in a panic as he tried to find them.

The man crept back toward the hillside, quiet as the night. The Mage turned a questioning look toward the man, and he nodded. The

Mage looked to him again, a look of surprise to her eyes. Almost disappointment.

He wondered at their relationship. The Mage seemed to defer to the man. No Mage ever deferred except to her own.

"They do not follow. Yet." The man looked around quickly, checking out the hill where the men had fallen. "And we need to go."

CHAPTER TWENTY-THREE

The hall twisted and turned until at last coming to the wide entrance to the first of three equal towers that framed the palace. Roelle passed through and traced the steps along the familiar stairway to the eighth level. The hall opened wide on this floor, and she rushed to a door partway down the hallway. She rapped on the wood and heard a faint reply. Relief flooded through her that Alriyn was finally in his room.

"Open."

She twisted the door handle and pushed. In a corner, sitting at a table, was the lean figure of her uncle. Long, gray hair was pulled into a tight knot behind his head, and a white robe draped to the floor into a pool of silken cloth. An aged and wrinkled hand curled around the quill of a pen, the tip dark with ink, and his back hunched over a manuscript. He didn't turn around at the sound of his door opening, merely waved his free hand toward a chair in one of the other corners.

Roelle followed her uncle's instructions. She knew from experience that when Alriyn was involved with his writings, she should practice patience. The chair was all too familiar to her. She had sat upon it often during lessons—and punishments. Smooth and hardened from years of use, the original staining was worn in places, so the pale creaminess of natural wood shone through. Roelle leaned back to wait.

She looked around the room. It was a large study and the table her uncle worked upon lined the entirety of the back wall. Papers were scattered everywhere, almost haphazardly, about its surface, but she suspected Alriyn knew exactly where to find everything. A large bookshelf lined the opposite wall, and leather-bound books leaned randomly against anything from piles of papers to other books. She had often wondered at the texts her uncle read. Growing up, she'd seen more than a few written in tongues she didn't recognize.

Several chairs formed a circle in the corner opposite of where she now sat, as if her uncle had recently met with others in the room, and to her left, a doorway led to Alriyn's personal chambers. Roelle knew a huge comfortable bed took up much space within. Other strange items, carvings and sculptures among others, littered the remaining shelf space and the floor.

Finally, her uncle looked up. His face was stained with a blob of ink and wore no expression. Roelle grinned and pointed toward her own face, motioning her uncle where to wipe off ink. Alriyn's hand moved halfheartedly to his face and attempted to wipe away the stain. It only smeared further, and Roelle chuckled. Alriyn's dark eyes turned serious, and she stopped grinning.

"You returned safely?" He scratched a quick note on his pages while waiting for Roelle to answer.

"I returned," she answered.

Alriyn carefully set his pen down. "I spoke to Haerlin."

Roelle bowed her head. She had worried about this moment, afraid most of all to tell Alriyn. Her uncle had been a father to her. She'd been sent to the city as little more than a child and knew only her uncle as family. Her parents had been Teachers, representatives of the Magi, though not Mageborn. Leaving her under her great-uncle's care, they'd traveled the south, visiting rarely but writing often until one day even that stopped. It was not until much later that she learned they'd died.

Roelle took a deep breath. There was nothing she could do but face the consequences of her decision. "I violated Magi tradition. I faced the Deshmahne with force, and men died at my hand."

Alriyn met her eyes and held her gaze. A silence, thick with years of expectation and education, hung heavy in the air. "The Deshmahne attacked the Magi. I fear it will not be the last time, Roelle," he said, his tone solemn.

Roelle frowned. It wasn't the expected answer.

"We face a dangerous time, Roelle. I fear there are few among us prepared to handle the tasks placed upon us. The Deshmahne are threat enough. That they would attack the Magi, even under the guise of being raiders, is surprising, but not unprecedented," he said. "Theirs is usually an indirect attack, pushing the Urmahne into arguments, rarely open battle."

"The High Priest was among them. And Endric thinks they entered the city."

Alriyn looked at her carefully before nodding. "That is what Haerlin states as well." He paused, scratching at his face and smearing the ink further. "How is it that the High Priest was seen? He's never seen, always a hidden menace. Why show himself now?"

Roelle shook her head, not knowing the answer to the last question. "There was one among us, the historian's apprentice, who'd seen him before."

"This is what I am told."

Roelle sat back. She'd thought on Jakob occasionally since she'd returned to the capital. The man was interesting, an amazing swordsman, one who even Endric thought of highly. It said much about him that he held Endric's regard. When the Denraen had divided into separate traveling parties, Endric taking the Magi and the historian with his group, there had been little chance for farewell as she and Jakob went separate ways. For someone not Mageborn, he had a definite appeal, but they hadn't the chance to get to know each other long enough to matter.

"All we have is the word of the historian," Alriyn started.

Roelle frowned. "You dislike him?"

"None among the Council get along well with Novan," Alriyn

answered quietly. He did not elaborate. "Where did Endric send the other group?"

Roelle shook her head. "I don't know."

Alriyn stood and began pacing in front of his desk, pausing occasionally, but saying nothing. Roelle could only guess at his thoughts When he finally spoke, all he said was, "North, always the north." A long finger scratched his chin, leaving another dark streak of ink behind. He glanced down at his desk, shuffling a few pages before stopping and reading for a long moment.

"What is it, Uncle? What's in the north? There were rumors, stories, but Endric would never reveal what he knew."

Alriyn stopped and looked at Roelle. "I don't know for certain. When I traveled the north, I discovered something dark and worse than the Deshmahne. Rumors," Alriyn continued. "Stories mostly, but too frequent to be dismissed. Towns are empty. The people simply gone. Some have gone south. Others... I don't know."

"What did you see?"

"I saw nothing." Alriyn looked up him with a pained expression to his face, a decision made. "There is something ancient, something... evil," he started before turning and pointing to the books on his desk. "Something barely described in the old texts. An ancient threat. But I can find little that helps me understand. It wasn't why I traveled north, but when I saw the desertion..."

Roelle waited for more, watching her uncle seeing what she could not, but nothing more came. "What can we do?"

"We need to know more, and I think the historian and Endric might know something. You've grown closer to Endric?" When she nodded, he took a breath. "Good. Seek out Endric. Find what he knows."

If Alriyn was concerned, there was reason for worry. There was something her uncle wasn't telling her, something more. Roelle knew that it must be significant for her uncle to push this much. She was not yet sure what it meant.

Alriyn said nothing more and guided her to the door. Roelle knew better than to press. As she stepped past her uncle, he touched her shoulder. "I'm glad you returned safely, Roelle. May the gods grant it lasts."

Roelle walked back down the hall and wondered what could possibly be worse than the Deshmahne. A shiver passed through her with the thought, and she prayed Endric would have answers. Someone needed to have them.

CHAPTER TWENTY-FOUR

The meeting chamber was well lit once again, and fires along each of the walls crackled with the heat of roasting logs stacked inside. Shadows blended with the dark stone but were still visible to Alriyn's wandering eyes. They fit his mood. The other members of the Council seemed either lost in thoughts of their own or listened carefully as Daguin spoke.

Alriyn himself had long since lost track of the man's words. His eyes traced along the edge of the table before stopping on the Eldest. His gaze was brief, but he noted Jostephon concentrated as little on the meeting as he. What distracted him?

A comment caught his attention, and Alriyn focused again on the conversation around him.

"The Rondalin general took his troops north. Tales speak of his disgust at the stream of travelers coming to the city each day, bearing stories of family and children lost to this unstoppable, unseen enemy. Disgust led to what is now called his treason for taking those he did from the city to attack. His army only numbered two hundred men, but the men were all veterans of the Rondalin army, and each was a highly decorated soldier.

"Needless to say, the king was not pleased with the sudden loss of so many healthy fighting men, especially with conditions as they were in the city. Many had died throughout the city, sickness rampant within the close quarters, and the army kept control in the streets. The king ordered a squadron of men after the general—to bring him back or to aid him and speed his return, it is not known. What is known is that the king allowed his advisor to pick the men sent north. Rumor says the king wanted the general brought back to face charges. Other rumors speak of different tales. It is difficult to sort out the truth from fiction."

There was something to it all that sparked a faded memory, though Alriyn couldn't place what it might be.

"The men sent after the general were gone barely a month when they stumbled back into town. Every man returned alive, albeit wounded and barely able to go on. None were able to tell what it was that had injured them. They had not found the general or any of his men and had not even seen traces of the general once they reached the northern mountains. Almost as if a trail they followed vanished. It has been a month or so since the men returned, and there is still no sign of the general's return."

Daguin went silent. Alriyn thought he had heard all the stories from the north, but somehow the story of this general had escaped his ears. The implications of the tale were even more numbing to him.

Bothar spoke up. "If what you're saying is true, then most of the towns in the far north are empty."

Daguin nodded. "Scared and panicked people leave family homes and head south. This trend is sweeping quickly southward. Strong-holds that have stood for generations deserted and mining villages with mines still heavy with wealth have been left for the perceived safety of the south. Worse is that the cities these people run to, places such as Rondalin and Riverbranch, quickly fill beyond capacity. People have been turned away in some places."

Fear. The Deshmahne thrived on creating fear. Fear and strength were how they believed they curried favor with the gods. Could this be the Deshmahne influence as well? Rondalin was farther north than he would have expected, but what other explanation was there for this? Unless this was more of what Alriyn had witnessed.

It was moving too fast. The south was in complete upheaval, and now it was starting in the north. Gom Aaldia was only the first, and now Rondalin. How much longer until Thealon fell to it? Worse, there had been grumblings of Gom Aaldia readying an army. Given the old strain between Gom Aaldia and Thealon, what was next? Even with their prior experience, could they have underestimated the Deshmahne and their reach?

Would the Council agree to choose a Uniter? They all feared failing, but if the balance became unsettled, what did it matter if they failed?

Alriyn noticed Jostephon staring in his direction, dark eyes unreadable but somehow captivating as he casually scratched his arm. Alriyn felt his mind begin to wander, and the shadows of the room grew hazier. He concentrated, forcing his mind into focus. Feeling his thoughts lurch forward again, he knew now wasn't the time to be careless in his decisions. Any suspicions he felt must be well founded before he acted.

There was a knock on the chamber door. Before anyone could answer, Endric strolled in. He had a slow grace to his movements, and the sword at his hip hung menacingly. "Council," he greeted. His voice was hoarse, yet thundered. It was a voice of authority.

Everyone turned to look. "You were not summoned," Jostephon said.

Endric frowned. "Must I be summoned to present to the Council? The Denraen have always been granted more courtesy than that."

Jostephon waved his hand. "Of course, Endric. It's only the worrisome reports we've been hearing. Tell me that you have something better to share."

Endric eyed the Eldest then surveyed the others on the Council. His gaze settled briefly on Alriyn before returning to the Eldest. "None really. The Deshmahne are quiet. I sent nearly four hundred men, and there are no reports of Deshmahne. Raiders only."

"None?" Karrin asked.

Endric eyed her carefully before answering. "None. It's as if they've returned to the south. The north is unsettled, and men I sent to investigate were killed."

Alriyn noted a troubled expression on Endric's face.

"Deshmahne, I suspect. Raiders as well. By all accounts, it was the last of them."

"The last? There were four attacks!" Haerlin said.

"Six, by my count," Endric countered, turning his attention from the Eldest. "But the point is the same. Their attention is elsewhere. Still, my men will search." Shifting focus to get more information, he asked, "What of the north? I imagine you've heard much the same as I have."

"We gather information," the Eldest answered.

Endric eyed him warily before nodding. Something passed between them. "I fear too much delay, as you know." There was a hint of irritation, nearly imagined.

Alriyn wondered what Endric had shared with the Eldest. He would need to find out more. The stories coming out of the north were too frequent now. They must gain understanding to decide a course of action, yet the Urmahne tradition did not allow for quick action. Could that even change?

Jostephon nodded. "We proceed the same as before."

The general grunted. "The Deshmahne are not the only concern I have."

"It is what you have been tasked with," the Eldest answered.

Endric's mouth cocked in a half smile. "I decide what the Denraen are tasked with."

"You protect the Magi," Rendrem said, irritation entering his voice.

The general turned to the newest member of the Council. "We protect the *mahne*, not the Magi. As do you. You would do well to remember that." His voice was firm, and he chastised the Mage as he would a soldier under his command.

Rendrem said nothing. Silence filled the room, nearly a weight upon them, and palpable.

Finally, Alriyn chose to break it. "The *mahne* is our shared concern. Your service to it has never been questioned. We, of course, appreciate your suggestions."

The general looked at him and nodded slightly. Alriyn hoped his comment would make Endric more sympathetic at least to listen to Roelle. His knowledge and experience would be crucial.

"My suggestion remains unchanged. We need men. The Deshmahne have grown too strong in the south. The danger in the north is—"

"You said they departed," the Eldest countered.

"Departed in the numbers we'd seen, but my concern remains unchanged. I worry they've already infiltrated our city, as they have dozens of others before. Their preferred attack is not through open battle, but through subversion. Yet that is not the threat I fear the most. If they reach beneath—"

Jostephon cut him off with a shake of his head. "The city must remain safe."

Endric stared at him. "I will see that it does."

"Do what you must."

Endric turned and left, and the chamber was silent. Alriyn wondered what Endric knew. Jostephon remained focused on the Deshmahne, and on the role the delegates would play, but Alriyn feared rumors in the north.

He didn't know what they faced but knew they couldn't do nothing. If they acted too late, there might not be time to choose a Uniter.

He prayed to the nameless gods Roelle could learn what Endric knew.

Roelle stood on the second terrace of the city, and the Denraen barracks opened up around her. A massive wall surrounded them, and it was an area that few outside of the Denraen ever saw. Being built into the mountain, Vasha was set into three terraces that divided the city into distinct parts. On the third terrace, appearing to loom over everything, was the palace. As a Mage, Roelle had spent most of her life on the third terrace, looking down upon the rest of the city. Ever since coming to work with the Denraen, she had grown accustomed to seeing a different perspective. The rest of the city was confined to the third terrace, including the University of Vasha, and the only place most who visited the city ever saw.

Selton panted next to her. He leaned over his staff, shaking his head. "You got better in your time away."

Roelle laughed. It felt good to laugh. Since returning to the city, laughter had not come as easily. A part of her wondered if she deserved such mirth. She needed to find Endric as Alriyn had asked, but getting a visit with him while in the city proved difficult. She gripped the staff a little tighter; she needed answers. Not only for her uncle, but for herself.

"I didn't work with the staff at all while I was gone. Most of my time was spent working with the sword. It was pretty much all Endric was willing to show."

"Well, I'm happy to practice the sword with you."

"I wouldn't want to beat you too easily. I have to worry about that fragile confidence of yours."

Selton laughed and wiped the sweat off his brow as he nodded toward the cluster of Magi apprentices training with the Denraen nearby. Today, there were nearly a dozen. Now that Roelle was back, most would return to training in the practice yard. Before she'd left, there had been more, but fewer came to practice while she had been gone.

"You need to share with them what you saw," Selton said. "They need to understand why they're doing this."

"They're not doing this to face the Deshmahne."

"They're not."

"I wasn't doing it to face them. We started this as—"

"I know why we started this. But it's something else now. Your uncle said so himself. We do this to keep the peace."

The peace. Her uncle had shared with her more than he should have, which was why it troubled her. There were times when she was able to overlook what she'd done, and others... others when she'd struggled with what it meant that she had taken a life. What did it mean that she had found killing so easy?

The Magi had taught the importance of peace since their Founding. All Magi lived by that tenet, and now... now she was the one to violate it. She wouldn't be the reason that others followed her example.

Selton watched her, seeming to understand her struggles. He had known her a long time, nearly her entire life. "They need to understand, Roelle. There's a reason we have these abilities. It's more than what the Council ever let on. More than what any of us ever understood. We need to share that with them."

"And then what? What does that change? We become soldiers, some sort of warrior Magi. Is that what we are meant to be?"

"If that's what the gods—"

Roelle shook her head. "I'm not sure what fate the gods have in mind for us." If only Haerlin could see *that*. It might be useful.

Selton rested his hand on her shoulder. There was a warmth and a strength about him, something comforting just having her friend back with her. Had he been with her when they were outside of the city... But he hadn't. She had done what she needed to at the time. Even he didn't really understand what they faced.

"You still need to talk to them. Share with them what you saw. They need to understand what's out there. The Council keeps us isolated."

Roelle swept her gaze around the city. Snow capped mountain peaks rose in the distance. The city itself, terraced both above and below her, spread around her. "I think the city isolates us as much as anything."

"Which is why we need to share with the others. They need to understand what's happening. They need to understand why the Council is nervous. They need to understand the rumors out of the north. If there's anything to them, anything that we could do..."

Roelle nodded. She knew he was right. She didn't understand the stories coming out of the north, but Alriyn certainly did. And the historian knew something. Then there was Jakob and the fact that he had been sent north. She worried about him. He was capable, but he was one man, and the more she learned from her uncle, the more she began to fear for her friend.

Roelle looked over at the young apprentice Magi practicing. She let out a long sigh. Perhaps Selton was right. Perhaps she did need to share with the others what she experienced. They certainly had come to her often enough looking for answers. She'd put them off, telling them that she would answer questions later. So far she had not. Instead, she had chosen to work with them, using the staff rather than the sword, but it was the sword that she had killed with.

Selton watched her, a hint of a smile tugging at his face.

"Fine. I'll do as you ask. I can't promise I have anything insightful to add."

"I never said you would. I've known you too long to believe you would have any real insight."

Roelle swept her staff around and smacked Selton on the shoulder.

He winced as he laughed. "What should we do next?" Selton asked.

Roelle looked up at the palace, thinking of not only her uncle, but of the historian and the general. She had a role in this. As much as she might not want to, she had a place. All she had to do was find what that place might be. What did the gods want of her?

Her gaze drifted toward soldiers working with practice swords and she wondered: could it be the gods had given her a role as more than a simple Mage?

CHAPTER TWENTY-FIVE

The office was smaller than she expected a man of such station to occupy and filled with the musty smell of aging books and oiled leather. It was a strange mixture, and startling at first.

The room was well lit for the mid afternoon; a large window pulled open on the far wall let in plenty of light. Candles were set almost haphazardly around the room, but she suspected there was some sort of method to the chaos. None were lit. A fireplace adorned one wall, obviously not used in many years as stacks of papers filled its opening, turning it into a bookshelf of sorts. A stout desk, the stain long since worn away on its most trafficked areas, was hidden under piles of papers in front of the window. A small workable clearing had been made, though the paper from neighboring piles already threatened to invade. A large map was somehow nailed to the wall opposite the fireplace, showing what Roelle knew to be much of the known lands. Pins were stuck throughout different areas of the land.

Troop locations? Or something else?

Scattered throughout the room were books of all sorts, some propped up towering piles of papers, hard spines supporting the leaning structures, while others rested atop piles, obviously recently read. It wasn't merely the number of books that surprised her; Endric

244 | D.K. HOLMBERG

was old and had probably collected many books over the years. Rather it was the variety that surprised her the most. She saw anything from *Modern Tactics* written by the man's father Dendril so many years ago to other books on warfare, some so old they made Roelle curious. Then she saw others, books on philosophy written by Mage scholars, as well as books on history. She wondered if Endric was as educated as these books made him seem. She had never thought of him in that way.

Roelle looked back at the open door to the room. She thought she heard sounds from the hall, but perhaps it was only her anxious mind trying to convince herself she'd be seen soon. She hated this waiting. Above the door, barely noticed before, hung a strangely curved greatsword. Well-polished steel shone with reflected light. She could almost make out faded inscriptions along the pommel and the blade itself, but from her distance, the lettering was too small. She wanted a better look, but didn't think it proper to be found peering closely at the general's belongings.

Roelle turned to face the desk again, her curiosity satiated temporarily as she thought through what she would say to the general when she saw him. She couldn't quite organize her thoughts.

Suddenly, it didn't matter. A sound came from the hall again, and she turned to see Endric stride quickly into the room, staring intently at a piece of parchment held in his grizzled hands. The old general didn't even look up at her and didn't bother even a grunt of acknowledgment of her presence. He simply went to a chair on the opposite side of the desk and took a seat. All the while, never taking his eyes off the paper.

Another man followed Endric into the room. He wasn't as old as the general, but his short hair was peppered with gray, and his face had several scars along each cheek. His was not a frame that appeared heavily muscled, but he moved with a quiet grace. He seemed sure-footed in a casual way and carried himself as one who knew very well how to handle the short sword hung at his waist. Something about him seemed nearly as dangerous as the old general.

"Sir," came a voice so ragged it seemed only a whisper, "the others are waiting to meet with you." The man glanced quickly at Roelle before dismissing her and moving on. "They say they've carried out your orders and have been waiting as instructed."

Roelle was unaccustomed to being so quickly dismissed. She tilted her head as she considered the man before seeing the slight tension to his posture and the hand never far from his hilt. The soldier was like a coiled snake ready to strike. Roelle was suddenly certain the man had not completely disregarded her.

Endric nodded, and finally looked up, almost as if seeing Roelle for the first time. He glanced briefly to the other man, a nod so slight it may not have been, and the man turned and quickly left the room. Roelle wondered about the orders but forgot them as soon as the general began speaking.

"What can I do for you?"

Roelle was taken aback by the gruff tone the general used. Hadn't they practiced together for weeks while traveling? "I come to speak to you of troubling rumors, to ask advice, and possibly seek your help." She thought it a safe way to start.

Endric nodded but said nothing.

Roelle frowned, looking around. She'd not seen Endric since they'd returned to the city and had said little to the man since the attack. The general had been focused on the safety of the Magi and the delegates she'd not had time for practice since the attack. "What of your men you sent north?"

It wasn't the question she'd prepared, but she asked it anyway. She hadn't stopped worrying about Jakob since her uncle had inquired about the journey.

It was Endric's turn to frown. "The Denraen sent north were found dead." The general did not meet her gaze as he spoke. "Your friend Jakob was not found among them."

"Dead?" she asked. There had been two raegan sent north. That many Denraen should have either been able to outrun or overrun anything they came upon.

Endric nodded slowly. "All the Denraen were found dead. At least one Deshmahne found among them. Several score raiders. No historian."

"What happened?"

"I can only piece together parts of it from what I've learned," Endric answered. "And I don't know enough to answer that clearly." The general met her gaze with his steely eyes. "I only tell you this much because of your friendship with the young man, else you would've heard nothing from me."

"But your men," she interjected.

"Were sent on a mission by me." There was a finality to his tone that did not brook argument.

Roelle nodded slowly. It would not serve her purpose to upset the general. The man was obviously strained by what they'd encountered, and Roelle had seen how the man took the death of those under his command. It made him harder, more intense. And quieter. She was lucky to have found him willing to answer any questions at all.

"What's in the north?" she asked.

Endric's gaze flickered to the map on the wall back to the paper in front of him before turning his attention back to her. "You speak of the northern desertion."

"When I asked you before, you gave no answer."

"I had none I was willing to give."

"And now?" Roelle asked.

Endric looked up to the map again, seeming to stare off into nothingness before his heavy gaze fell upon Roelle, weighing her. "What do you know?"

Roelle took a deep breath, her once organized thoughts now in disarray. Endric had that effect on many; Roelle had not expected it to happen to her. "Elder Alriyn speaks of something in the north," she began, intentionally leaving out her ties to Alriyn. "He's traveled the north and seen the emptiness."

"Your great uncle traveled the north?" Endric asked, arching an eyebrow.

There were no secrets from Endric. She would stick to honesty. "He did. It was probably on one of his studies," she said. Alriyn often disappeared from the city for his studies. "He saw something there. He did not—or would not—elaborate."

Endric rested his elbows on his desk, steepling his hands together. Finally, he sighed and leaned back. "I hadn't expected that of Alriyn."

The comment was mostly for himself, and he sat in silence for a few moments. "I wonder what else he saw?"

"He said he saw nothing."

Endric snorted. "This is the Second Eldest. Surely, he saw something."

This was getting her nowhere. Roelle felt her frustration rising. "What do you know? There's something my uncle does not say. He says there is something terrible in the north, worse than the Deshmahne. What does he know?" Roelle pleaded. "What's worse than the Deshmahne?"

"He may know nothing, yet," Endric began, seeming to choose his words carefully. "It's what he suspects that interests me." The man's dark eyes stared at Roelle for another long moment. "There are stories, something few believe. Ancient rumors, mostly, and not well understood. Little has been found." Endric looked around before settling his gaze upon Roelle again. "The Antrilii know of a foul creature, like something from a nightmare, that brings death wherever it roams. Only those gifted by the gods can see it."

The Antrilii were a tribe of warriors in the far northwest. Fierce warriors, and renowned swordsmen, and it had long been rumored Endric had trained with them, had learned much of his skills from their masters. Few knew if it was true. They lived in isolation, and were rarely seen. Was this Endric's admission of his ties to them?

"What of those who could not see it?"

"They died," Endric said. "I've worried about the rumors coming from the north for a long time and have failed to find confirmation. My position makes it difficult for me to find answers myself, and so far, there is proof of nothing."

"What can we do?" Roelle asked.

Endric searched her face before answering. "What can you do?" The general shook his head. "Fight the Deshmahne with me. You fared better than most who face them in battle. They have come to Vasha before, and what you saw was not the first nor will it be the last."

The Deshmahne had been in the city before? Why would Alriyn hide that from her?

"I'm not sure that is what Alriyn had in mind for me," Roelle said carefully. Could she join the Denraen? Could one of the Magi do that? She knew she could help, knew the Deshmahne would not be defeated easily. But she was a Mage.

Endric saw the struggle on her face. "Tell me what you know of your Founders."

The abrupt change disarmed Roelle. "All Magi know the story. It's taught to us at an early age. There is the Great Mother—"

"Not your Great Mother. Earlier."

Little was known of the time before the Founders, and the Council guarded that which was known. "I know only what I've been taught."

"And that's little enough," Endric answered. "Search out your Founders. You'll find your uncle's answers there. Maybe then you'll know what you need to do."

"What do you mean?" Roelle asked.

The general turned his back on her without answering and picked up one of the nearby books on his desk.

Roelle sat waiting, hoping for more answer, but none came.

CHAPTER TWENTY-SIX

Jakob was led to a small clearing where three horses stood quietly waiting, though tromping their feet a little. The man and the Mage jumped swiftly into their saddles. He was motioned to mount the remaining horse. Jakob hesitated, uncertain whether he wanted to go with this pair.

North to Avaneam. It was almost a compulsion. Would they allow him to ride north?

"Break it off and put this in it." The man handed Jakob a powder. When Jakob hesitated, he said, "We can help."

Jakob glanced toward the city and still saw fires burning, the flames leaping brightly in the night. Turning back to the two strangers, he was still uncertain. "Who are you?"

"I'm Brohmin." His face was aged, wrinkled, but strong. "She's Salindra."

Jakob still didn't move.

"You'll be safe with us," Brohmin assured before turning his horse and starting away, tossing the powder at Jakob's feet.

Each step shot pain through his leg, and he knew he couldn't walk. He broke the arrow off carefully; the head of it was still buried in the side of his leg, and he bit back a scream. He smeared a pinch of the powder on the wound. It stank, an acrid sulfur, and burned, but the bleeding slowed. Careful to strap the trunk to the saddle, Jakob mounted. Pain stabbed his leg with each movement, but once settled in the saddle, the horse was a welcome change. His stomach grumbled, loudly.

Jakob waffled. Did he follow them or ride off on his own? How far would he make it, injured and in pain, on his own?

Yet, he knew nothing of these two.

One is a Mage.

Once, that would have been enough to convince him, but maybe his time traveling with the Magi, and seeing how Novan treated them, had changed him more than he realized.

The safety of the trunk, the mission to Avaneam, weighed on him. Continuing toward Avaneam was the only way he would find Novan or Endric again. That the trunk was crucial to stopping the Deshmahne weighed on him as well.

Pain shot through his leg again, and with it a dizzying wave of fatigue, and he knew he couldn't do it alone. He followed them.

They rode quickly. The night sky was dark, and he couldn't see much as they rode. The horses moved silently, fast sure-footed steps making little noise in the soft undergrowth and covering of leaves.

Did the Deshmahne follow?

The question worried him. Would these strangers help him travel north? Would they even believe him? Jakob glanced at the Mage woman, uncertain. Should he tell her of the attack on the Magi? Without details, it made little difference.

Jakob said nothing.

They rode quickly and generally northward. The trees blocked out the light of the moon, and it came through in flickers of pale light as it streamed through the branches overhead.

Hours stretched and still they rode on, trees growing thicker as the forest around them grew. Jakob struggled to remain awake, more sleep lost in the saddle. Pain became numbing. There was pain in his leg where the arrowhead was lodged, a trickle of blood drying on his leg, and a soreness from the saddle. The area on his back where he had been injured when he faced the Deshmahne still pained him, as well, but he was able to push that pain away. His head throbbed, a slow ache from the pulsation that never left him, and it grew increasingly difficult to ignore.

On top of it all was the itching sense that he was followed yet again.

He hadn't felt it for days—since traveling with the Denraen.

Jakob looked side to side, constantly searching the source of the feeling. He found nothing. Brohmin glanced at him occasionally, a strange look to his shadowed face, but he remained silent. As the forest grew thicker, the trees larger, the sensation increased, and he was soon looking incessantly.

Finally, Brohmin spoke. "What is it?" His voice was hoarse and reminded Jakob a little of Endric.

Shaking his head, Jakob answered. "Nothing. Paranoia, I think."

Brohmin huffed. "You have a right to it, it seems."

"It feels as if we are watched," Jakob finally said.

The woman glanced back, concerned, but Brohmin shook his head. She glared at him a moment before turning to face forward.

"May be that we are," Brohmin answered.

Jakob looked around again but saw nothing. Was Brohmin toying with him? Was *this* the start of the madness, the constant itch in his head, the feeling that he was watched? Fear of the madness was a constant concern that he fought to suppress.

"I have heard merahl in these woods," Brohmin explained. "May be they watch."

"Merahl?" Jakob asked.

"An animal, though a clever one. They prowl these woods from time to time," Brohmin said but explained little more.

They rode on in silence. Could it be all he felt was the intermittent stalking of some animal? The paw prints surrounding the Deshmahne had been real and unlike anything he had ever seen, and he *had* seen eyes in the night so many nights before while riding with the Denraen. Still, they were eyes he'd seen in his dreams as well. Jakob was no longer sure what to think.

The feeling did not leave; he'd known it for several weeks now and had almost grown accustomed to it. Merahl may be in these woods, but what had he sensed while riding with the Denraen? This seemed something else, something different.

Finally, Brohmin slowed his horse and brought them to a halt. They stopped under a huge tree, the canopy so far overhead he couldn't begin to see an outline. Brohmin quickly tied his reins around a smaller tree growing nearby. The Mage followed. There was something about her that felt wrong, though he couldn't explain what he sensed.

Following their example, he led his horse to the nearby tree and tied off. He patted it down carefully as Rit had taught him and felt a moment of sorrow sweep through him. So much lost. Jakob eyed the trunk and shook his head as he did, hoping it was worth the price the Denraen had paid.

Brohmin prepared a small pile of sticks and underbrush and then cupped his hands outward, toward the pile. A small fire erupted from the center. Jakob blinked, uncertain if his tired eyes played tricks on him while he watched the fire slowly build to consume the pile.

A cold chill shook him, and he moved to warm a little by the fire. He kneeled carefully, adjusting the sword at his side so that it didn't catch him. The move sent sharp, radiating pain throughout his leg, reminding him of the arrowhead still embedded there. He stifled a shout of pain.

Brohmin crept toward him, motioning to his leg. Jakob tore his breeches around where the arrow pierced him and groaned as he saw the bloody mess, suddenly feeling the pain of the injury anew. The jagged shaft met a brutal steel arrowhead buried deep into his leg. Jakob didn't want to consider what it would take to remove.

Jakob caught Brohmin staring at the stone ring upon his hand. Jakob had forgotten about it, the weight of his father's ring comfortably reassuring to him. Finally, Brohmin turned away and placed his hands on him, one on the arrow stump and the other on his leg. A sense of coolness worked its way through him and he shivered.

"It's done," Brohmin spoke.

He looked at the man's hands and saw that he held the remainder of the arrow. His leg still felt cold, but it didn't hurt as it had. He narrowed his eyes as he frowned at Brohmin, wondering how he'd removed the arrow painlessly.

"Not a Mage, boy," he told him as if reading his mind, "just a healer. We need to wrap that leg now and keep it clean."

After dressing and wrapping his wound, he laid back to rest. He felt complete exhaustion, and it threatened to overcome him before he found anything to eat. Jakob was unsure if he cared.

"Why were those men chasing you?"

It was the Mage woman. He hadn't even heard her approach, and he decided he needed to be more careful. The light from the fire cast strange shadows about her face, her eyes. He saw darkness to them, nearly black, and they reminded him of the High Priest. No fire danced within them, though.

There was no mistaking her height. It named her even before she spoke, a voice hard with authority. A voice used to having orders followed.

"Why were the men chasing you?" she repeated. She knelt, slowly, to look him in the eyes. It was a look that was careful in its consideration as she judged him. He would need caution in what he told her. Though Magi, she seemed more like Haerlin than Roelle.

"Deshmahne," he started.

Brohmin cast a hard gaze at him. "That was what you said earlier. Why follow you here?"

"Where are we?" Since the day he found himself along the road, missing his horse, he'd wondered how much farther he had to reach Avaneam. How much farther to reach Novan and Endric?

Salindra arched an eyebrow with the question. "That was Rondalin." There was a layer of disbelief to her voice.

Rondalin?

How was that even possible? Rondalin was north, true enough, but far to the east of where they had been heading. There should have been no way he would have reached Rondalin. More north of Thealon, it was a city isolated.

How?

"I didn't know." How to explain to them what he had been

through? "I've seen Deshmahne, fought one once, though it was nearer Chrysia than Rondalin."

"Perhaps you should tell us your tale from the beginning," Brohmin prompted.

Salindra nodded, staring at him with iron eyes.

Jakob sighed. How to begin? What would they believe?

What if they work with the Deshmahne?

The thought worried him. Tolsin had been Deshmahne.

He shook the thought from his head. No Mage would ever become Deshmahne.

"There is a reward out for you," Brohmin said.

"Me?"

"Must be you, you fit the description," Brohmin answered.

"Why?" Jakob asked, but he remembered what he had overheard at the city gates.

Brohmin laughed. "I thought you could explain. Fifty gold clips. The king's advisor wants you badly."

The king's advisor? What was this? What *had* he gotten himself into?

"Explain why we shouldn't claim the reward," Brohmin suggested, though it was spoken softly and not as a threat.

Jakob pushed himself to his feet, and felt a jolt of pain as the wound in his leg opened. He lowered his hand to the hilt of his sword carefully. Brohmin stood casually and touched the hilt of his sword as well.

"I need to go north," Jakob said. He glanced over to where the trunk had been set to the side of the fire. He couldn't move quickly enough to grab the trunk and run were it necessary, not with his leg in the shape it was.

"Tell us," Brohmin urged. There was no fear in the way he stood, no alarm that Jakob may attack. He stood ready, a cat ready to pounce.

"I... I come from Chrysia, apprenticed to the historian Novan. We left with a contingent of Magi and Denraen after they'd chosen a delegate from my city." He looked quickly to Salindra before settling his gaze on Brohmin. "We traveled north with them, toward Vasha it was presumed, when we came upon raiders."

THE THREAT OF MADNESS | 255

"The Denraen should have no trouble with raiders," Salindra said.

Jakob could sense disdain from her and knew he needed caution. She was a Mage, perhaps an Elder, and was to be respected. "They were more than simple raiders. There was an attack one night, and one man made it all the way to our general, Endric, before capture. He was Deshmahne."

"How did you know?" Brohmin asked.

"Their arms were marked. The general said it gave them strength, speed."

Brohmin merely nodded, prodding Jakob along.

"Another night, we discovered the raider camp. The High Priest was among them—"

"High Priest?" Brohmin interjected, frowning. "He rarely leaves the south."

"That may have been, but he's here now. Endric escorted the Magi and our delegate to Vasha and Novan sent me with a raegan of Denraen Endric sent north on a separate mission with a package."

Jakob paused. The retelling made it all more vivid, more real. He had become fearful that his mind created the entire story, but he remembered the sounds, the smells. This was not the madness.

But how was he to know? Certainly, there had been much strangeness around him and dreams too vivid to shake. He could still see the goddess Sharna if he closed his eyes, could remember what she said. Was not that the madness?

"What of the Denraen then?" Brohmin asked.

"They're dead. I'm the only one who survived." He felt his eyes misting. "We were chased and attacked by the raiders. There was at least one Deshmahne."

"How is it that you survived this attack?" Brohmin asked, his tone softening.

"I don't know."

"You alone out of a dozen Denraen survived?" Salindra repeated. "You must be an impressive swordsman." She crossed her arms over her chest and stared at him disbelieving.

He wouldn't let her goad him, not if they were willing to help. "Not always, but lately I've improved."

"Lately?" Brohmin repeated.

Jakob nodded and said nothing more.

Brohmin considered him before speaking again. "What of this package? What is it?"

Jakob looked between Brohmin and Salindra. This was the choice he wasn't sure he could make. Salindra was obviously a Mage, but her distrust of him was plain. Brohmin was different. He didn't strike Jakob as Deshmahne but carried himself in a way that reminded him of Endric. Still, there was something strange about him.

"I'm not Deshmahne, son," Brohmin said, reading the question in Jakob's eyes. "If you travel for the Magi, perhaps we can help." His tone was reassuring, helpful, and Jakob *wanted* to believe. Long moments stretched before Brohmin suddenly pulled off his shirt and walked to the light of the campfire. "See? No markings."

Finally, Jakob relented. He limped over to the trunk and picked it up. The weight had become familiar over the last week, and it no longer seemed as cumbersome as it once had. He carried it back to the firelight and presented it to Brohmin who took it carefully.

Brohmin stared at it silently, and his finger traced over the engravings, working around the edges before settling on the lock. He twisted at the piece of metal stuck inside but couldn't move it. Brohmin set his hand atop the box and mumbled a few words before looking back at the lock. Nothing had changed. He seemed somewhat surprised but hid it well.

"Who sent you with this package?"

"Endric."

"Endric's duty is to the Magi," Salindra said. "He wouldn't send men away if the Magi were in danger."

Jakob looked at her and saw anger flash in her eyes before it was suppressed. Had he been wrong to tell them of the trunk? "I know he agonized over it. It was something he intended to carry north himself."

"Endric intended to bring this himself?" Brohmin asked, surprised.

Jakob nodded. He didn't elaborate on what he had overheard the night of the Turning Festival, unsure if he could explain it in such a way that would make sense. Then there was the business of the

Conclave, and Jakob didn't know enough to answer questions about it.

Brohmin held the trunk in front of him. "What's in here?"

"I don't know. I'm not sure even Endric knew, only that it was important."

Brohmin took a step back to stand next to Salindra. She had been silently watching, and now her jaw was clenched tightly and her arms crossed in front of her. Brohmin settled her to the ground, almost carefully, before turning to Jakob. "We should sleep. Tomorrow we can talk on this more."

Brohmin turned from him and began to settle himself by the fire, sitting upright and staring out into the night. Jakob moved away from the fire and stretched out his cloak along the ground before lying upon it. As he settled in to sleep, the familiar itch of being watched chased him to dreams of men with fiery eyes and someone trapped behind tall walls. His sleep was fitful but at least it was sleep.

∾

Jakob woke to dawn colors streaking the sky. A faint light filtered through the treetop canopy to reach them, and he glanced around as he opened his eyes. The fire had long since died. He glanced across the pile of burned ash that had been the fire, and saw the Mage woman still asleep. The cut to her short hair seemed even more severe in the early morning light. She lay covered with a dark-colored cloak, a deep brown he could barely tell wasn't black.

Brohmin was already up, his pack already strapped alongside his horse.

Jakob stretched slowly, carefully working out his leg. There was no pain. He stretched less carefully and still no pain.

His hand wandered to where the arrow had hit. The skin was smooth and intact. Only a slight indentation the only evidence he'd had an injury.

How?

He looked to the sleeping Mage and then to Brohmin with the

question on his lips, but it went unasked as Brohmin caught his eyes and whispered, "Good, you're up. You can help."

He sat himself up and moved to where Brohmin worked, digging into the ground to bury the remains of their night, and his mind reluctantly let go of how he'd healed. He grabbed a stout stick lying nearby and began digging next to Brohmin. His short jabs at the hard packed dirt were less effective than those Brohmin made. They dug for a while, the hole growing quickly, and then shoved the ash and remains of the fire into the pit. Brohmin covered it carefully, practiced hands pushing the dirt down gently. When he was done, Jakob couldn't even tell there had been a fire.

Brohmin tossed Jakob a hunk of hard bread and a flask of water before nodding toward their horses, and Jakob understood. As he ate, he walked over to the animals, untying the one that had been his, and led it away from the others. While doing this, he watched Brohmin gently nudge Salindra awake. They talked softly for a time, and Brohmin glanced quickly to the woman's feet before helping her to stand.

She dusted herself off, wiping the dirt and leaves from the cloak she had covered herself in, and then moved quickly to her own mount. She was ready to leave only moments after she had wakened. It seemed to Jakob a practiced event.

Brohmin mounted and motioned him to follow. "We're chased. We'll ride hard today."

"How did they find us?" Jakob asked, though he had enough experience with the Deshmahne to know they could find him again.

"They have trackers who know these lands better than most," Brohmin answered.

"How will we keep ahead of them?"

Brohmin laughed, but it didn't reach his eyes. "Because I, too, know these lands. Come."

They rode as fast as they could in the ever-thickening forest, slowing considerably several times as they waded through swampy areas. Twice, they led the horses down steep embankments on foot. Brohmin seemed to be taking a direct route, wherever he was going, choosing to ride through rather than around any challenges.

The silent ride allowed Jakob a chance to consider his new companions. Brohmin was more than he seemed, and he wondered about Salindra as well. Something about the Mage was odd. Why did she travel with Brohmin? Why was she not in the Mage city?

Occasionally, faint lines of the sun shone through the tops of the trees, though it wasn't common. From the position of the sun in the sky, he guessed they were heading north and east. The strange feeling in the back of his mind was still with him, and as they rode silently, his awareness of it increased, like a slowly building fire. Glancing around, he saw nothing. Brohmin saw his movement and looked as well but remained quiet.

About midday, at least from what he could tell, they stopped as the forest opened briefly near a stream. Salindra motioned for him to stop while Brohmin dismounted and tossed his reins to her before starting off on foot into the thick of the forest.

"You do want to eat don't you?" Salindra asked. "Let the horses drink."

He walked with the three horses over to the stream and felt a slight twinge in his leg, though it was nothing like the pain he should have. The horses leaned down immediately and lapped at the cool water. He let them have their fill, then took his turn, lowering his face to the slow moving water and dipping his cupped hand in, drinking deeply. It tasted cool, and coppery. A slightly sweet taste was left in his mouth after swallowing.

He stood and turned from the stream, and watched Brohmin stride back into the small clearing carrying two dead hares. The man didn't appear to have any weapon save the sword strapped to his back, and he doubted he'd caught the hares with that. The bow he'd used the night before was still slung on his saddle. The mystery around Brohmin deepened.

The thought of hot food started churning his stomach, and Brohmin built a quick fire again. Salindra spitted the hares and began to roast what would be his first meal in weeks. Brohmin came to him as he watched the rabbits roasting.

"It'll be a while as Salindra cooks," he told him. Salindra nodded curtly. "Tell me, boy, you wear that sword well. Where did you learn the steel?"

Salindra's head cocked slightly at the question. He looked to the sword sheathed at his waist before looking up.

"First, my brother. He was one of the Ur. When he tried to teach me..." He shook his head. Brohmin didn't need to know how Jakob had never really learned from Scottan. "Recently, it was Endric, though I practiced with Mage Roelle as well."

Salindra smiled, almost to herself, and shook her head.

"The Magi do not use weapons," Brohmin said. "You'd better come up with a better story."

"I can't speak of any Mage save Roelle, and she worked with Endric nearly as often as I did. The few times I saw them spar, she was nearly Endric's equal." He flushed as he mentioned Roelle.

Salindra had stopped cooking, choosing instead to listen, her attention more direct now.

Jakob looked from Brohmin to Salindra. "I did get the impression the other Mage was not pleased about it."

Brohmin stared at Jakob, as if weighing what he said. "You say you traveled with the Magi."

Jakob nodded. "I traveled with Mage Haerlin and Roelle after they chose a delegate. We were to meet another on the way to Vasha."

"Haerlin?" Salindra said. She looked to Brohmin before turning a disbelieving eye on Jakob. "An Elder traveled outside of the city?"

"I know little of your customs, Mage Salindra, and can speak only of what I saw." He was more direct than he would have been weeks before.

Salindra laughed then. "You're quite the storyman."

Jakob smiled at the compliment. If only this had been nothing more than a story, a tale of Jarren Gildeun on one of his incredible journeys. At least Jarren survived his stories. Yet Jakob was nothing like Jarren, a man without fear, a man who traveled to impossible places. "Not a storyman. I've told you what I've seen."

Brohmin stared at Jakob with an unreadable expression before turning to Salindra.

"You know this cannot be true, Brohmin," she said. "Ask him why the Deshmahne seek him, ask why the reward. We need to know the truth."

The truth. Jakob didn't know the truth of the reward or why he was worth fifty gold clips. He now knew Rondalin was controlled by Deshmahne, though, and knew he couldn't return there.

"Too much is wrong. Haerlin leaving the city? And the Elders would never allow a Mage to learn the sword, and they would certainly not do this other."

Brohmin smiled slightly. "It rings of another practice I know."

Salindra shook her head. "Not like this. They would not change it!"

Brohmin arched an eyebrow. "I am not as certain," he told her before turning to Jakob. "There's one way I know of to find the truth."

He suddenly unsheathed his sword and swung it toward Jakob.

Jakob reacted without thought, ducking and rolling, before unsheathing his sword and facing Brohmin. Brohmin smiled as Jakob faltered with the weight of his sword. It was a smile of compassion. Jakob paused, uncertainty invading his thoughts.

These people saved my life.

Brohmin didn't want to hurt him. Instead, he offered a test.

I need to prove myself.

Their doubt must end. If he was to travel with them, it must end.

Salindra saw how he had faltered with his sword, and a smile of almost satisfaction crossed her face. She mouthed the words, "Now we shall see."

"I'll go easy on you, boy," Brohmin told him softly.

"Endric never did," Jakob answered, his words hard, almost not his own.

He turned toward Brohmin and brought his sword up. One side blazed with the light while the other seemed to suck light from around him. Jakob knew a moment of hesitation as Brohmin paused to look upon the sword, but the pause was brief. Then the man moved to attack.

He was fast, almost too fast, but Jakob caught the movement and turned his own sword around to block. A loud *clang* reverberated throughout the forest. He turned his block into a quick attack, three quick turns of his wrist. Brohmin countered each.

Brohmin stepped into a catah. It was one he knew. He moved quickly, knowing the weakness of the movement, and caught the man in mid swing. Jakob stepped into a quick attack, but Brohmin broke his in mid movement as well. The man smiled slightly.

The slight limp slowed Jakob and frustration pounded through him. He flashed through a series of catahs, flowing from one to the next, his sword a blur. But each step was blocked by Brohmin's steel. Something was different.

When he had faced the Deshmahne, his sword had seemed to lead him, and something within him always responded. Without it, he'd have no chance. Brohmin was good.

Jakob had known that from the start but soon realized the man was much better than he'd expected. Possibly as good as Endric. Brohmin was able to block every motion, stop every attack, and turn them against him. He found himself answering but realized he may not be a match for the man.

What happens if I lose?

The thought filtered through his awareness. Would they turn him in for the reward? He couldn't allow that, too much at stake and too much already lost. The trunk must continue north.

With the thought came a feeling he had known before.

The slow pulsing began in his head.

Jakob welcomed it and felt it roll through him and into his sword. He pulled through the sword, differently than he had ever tried before.

Everything seemed to shift as he did, becoming suddenly sharper, clearer. The pulsing overwhelmed him, filling him and everything slowed. He saw every movement Brohmin made in near slow motion. The man brought his sword around, blade flashing toward Jakob's face, and he brought his own sword up to block. It was an easy movement.

Jakob attacked several times quickly, almost too quickly, and thought he had Brohmin caught. Somehow, the man was able to catch his blade each time. He brought his sword around again, four quick slices, and again each was somehow blocked.

He moved harder, faster, and again felt a raw tearing of his mind.

Again everything slowed.

Two quick turns of his blade. Neither close enough to harm the man, only enough to scare him. Brohmin had no chance to block either of them. The man would have been dead if he'd not held back. Brohmin's eyes widened, and he stepped back, raising his hands and lowering his sword.

Jakob sheathed his sword and breathed deeply as the pulsing faded. His mind seemed to click, and time jerked forward again. His arm still hummed. Sweat rolled down his face, his back, and he panted, tired from the exertion. He looked at Brohmin, hoping the man would believe him now.

Brohmin shook his head slowly. His eyes were wide, surprise perhaps, before turning to Salindra. Jakob turned his own gaze to her. Her mouth hung open.

"He's worked with Endric," Brohmin said finally. Relief flowed through Jakob. "There are catahs only Endric and I know. And now you." He looked at Jakob, a question in his eyes. "I don't know how that was possible. Something else too. I've seen it only once before." He shook his head, mumbling something under his breath. He looked Jakob in the eyes. "You're a strange one, boy, but you don't lie."

Jakob was tired. What was happening to him? Why was he able to fight this way, with such skill now when he'd never had it before?

This was something other than the madness. It had to be.

He looked to Salindra who still appeared shocked. Brohmin walked over to her and whispered. Jakob heard what they said with the slow pulsing in his head.

Salindra seemed near tears, her voice trembling. "I thought... I thought you were dead."

The words were a whisper but seemed loud in his ears.

"A real fight, I might have been." Brohmin's voice had a slight tremor.

She looked up then and saw Jakob looking, and lowered her voice. It didn't matter. "How could he move so fast? His body was a blur."

"The boy is a mystery. They said he was important. There is more to him than there seems. I hope we find out soon."

They looked up, realizing he was still staring at them, and

Brohmin motioned him to join them. He walked over to them, their stares almost accusations and their eyes filled with questions.

"What do you mean 'they said he was important'?"

Brohmin surprised him by winking. "The Conclave."

Jakob stumbled. "Then... you knew?"

"Not quite. It doesn't work like that. I know Endric and Novan. I had to be sure you did too. We can talk later," Brohmin said, shooting Salindra a strange look.

Salindra watched Brohmin silently, her eyebrows furrowed and a frown upon her face. There was a question hanging from her lips, yet it went unasked.

They ate the hares silently before remounting. Jakob was exhausted from the past few days and didn't argue, yet even tired, the strange itch at the back of his mind was there. He could not suppress it as well in his exhaustion, but he didn't bother to look around. Jakob knew he would see nothing.

They rode north and east, and the trees grew taller, growing higher into the sky with each passing mile. The light of the sun was slowly blocked until it was no longer visible. Eventually, Brohmin declared it was time to stop, and they dismounted. Nearly dark, Jakob climbed down from his saddle exhausted, rolling out his cloak to lie down. Brohmin strode out into the forest again, hunting, and Salindra wandered away with the water skins, leaving him alone.

The dark night was silent. There were no real sounds from the forest, and his tired eyes struggled to stay open, so he decided to sleep, hoping Brohmin would wake him to eat. He'd learned to survive without eating every day and knew one more night would not hurt him.

As he lay down, there was a crack of broken twigs. He looked up to see someone creeping toward him and only barely saw a dark blur swinging toward his forehead. It collided with him and the darkness of night overcame him.

CHAPTER TWENTY-SEVEN

R oelle looked over at Selton, waiting for his answer. They sat in
Roelle's room on plain, sturdy chairs, away from the small desk
facing the wall covered with papers and books never read. Her friend
was silent. "What did he mean?" Roelle asked again.

Selton looked up at her, concentration broken. His hazel eyes were
thoughtful and piercing, so intelligent... and captivating. Selton had
recently taken to wearing his hair shorter and it made his face seem
more angular and broad. She'd known him as long as she'd been in the
city, and they had been friends the entire time. "The Magi were
founded by the Great Mother Isalilline Mailell. It was she who gathered the first seeds of our people and founded this city."

Roelle sat silently, considering. It was the history even the
youngest Mageborn knew of their people. The vision and forethought
of the Great Mother was taught in their earliest years and was immor-
talized in many statues. "Endric meant something different, I
am sure."

"There's nothing in the library, Roelle. I've searched."

If any were to find it, it would be Selton. He'd spent many hours
each day reading in the library. If not in the library, where could it be?
"There has to be something there."

"Sure," Selton agreed. "For Elders of the Council only. I can't access that section without severe consequences."

Selton said the words lightly, but Roelle didn't even want to consider the consequences. The Elders were fiercely protective of their section of the library and the texts contained within. Alriyn had once told her that there were secrets there not meant for younger eyes. "Alriyn won't offer access to me, and Endric doesn't give straight answers." She looked up at Selton. "Who can we ask?"

Selton drummed his fingers on his leg. "The timing is interesting. Normally, I wouldn't have any suggestions, but with Lendra having returned..."

"Who's Lendra?"

"My cousin. She's been out of the city for years, but returned to visit her parents."

"Why her?"

"Her father is the chief historian," Selton answered.

"Inilith?" Roelle asked. If they could get Inilith to help, that would give them access to more than they had otherwise. "I forgot he was your uncle."

"By marriage," Selton said. "Last I heard, Lendra had been studying in Coamdon. It's not often she returns to the city, not being Mage-born and all."

Roelle leaned back. It was more than they had. "Where can we find her?"

~

They found Lendra in the hall outside her rooms. She was not alone. A familiar figure stood nearby, covered in a long, flowing cloak and speaking quietly to her in hushed tones that didn't carry down the hall as they approached. Tall, nearly as tall as any Mage, and thin, the historian still cut an imposing figure.

Lendra, though, was something else. She was of average height and slender, though it was not her height that caught Roelle's attention. Her eyes were impossibly blue-green. A ring of yellow rimmed them, like petals on a flower. Her skin was a light brown, only a hint of a tan tickling it, bringing forth a few freckles. She was gowned in a simple white dress that glowed in the light of the afternoon.

She smiled at Selton as they approached and gave Roelle a smile nearly as wide. "Selton?" she said, and ran to him. She hugged him and laughed. The sound filled the corridor, echoing off the stone walls. "I've not seen you for..."

Selton returned her hug and her smile. "It's been too long, hasn't it?" He stepped to the side and motioned to Roelle. "This is my friend Roelle."

She turned to Roelle and grasped her hand. Hers was smooth, soft silk, and warm. "Well met, Lendra," she said. She turned to Novan. "Historian. I hope you're settling well in the palace?"

Lendra gave a quick glance to Novan. "You know Novan?"

It was Novan who answered. "Mage Roelle was one of my escorts to the city. One of the more capable ones, I might add."

Roelle smiled tightly. "The gods returned us safely."

Novan grunted in reply and said nothing more.

"So you met my replacement?" Lendra asked Roelle.

She looked at her strangely. "Did I?"

She laughed again. She seemed to do so easily, and it put Roelle at ease. "I studied with Novan in Coamdon, before he moved on," she said as she looked back at Novan. The historian smiled at her.

It was more emotion from him than Roelle had seen before. "I met the apprentice historian," Roelle said, beginning to understand. "An interesting man. And excellent swordsman. I still would like to know why he left us." She left off asking if Novan had heard about the Denraen that had been found slaughtered. That was for another, quieter time. And she tried to shield Selton from the heat that rose in her cheeks thinking of Jakob. It had to be his ability with the sword that appealed to her, didn't it?

The historian's face was unreadable. It was frustrating, but Roelle knew she would get nothing from him if he did not choose to divulge it—this was a man unafraid to bully even a Mage Elder. "I think you had a shared interest, don't you?" Novan asked.

Roelle flushed, and avoided Selton's gaze.

"Lendra," Selton said with a grin, "we'd like to speak with you when you have a few moments."

"What is it?" she asked.

Selton looked to Novan before glancing at Roelle. Roelle shrugged. The historian may be able to help them if he was willing.

"Can we step out of the hall?" Roelle asked, motioning to her room.

Lendra frowned at her. The historian gave her a strange glance, as well, but said nothing. She led them quickly into her room. It was simple and plainly appointed, a guest room and little more. There was a small bed tucked in the far corner and a sturdy desk along the back wall. Dozens of books were stacked atop the desk, several propped open, and Roelle knew they had come to the right person.

"What is it, Selton?" she asked as she closed the door.

Roelle raised a hand for a pause, stretching out her senses as she did. She heard nothing. Opening her mind, she pulled on the *manehlin* and created what little barrier she could. It was an early lesson learned from her uncle Alriyn and wouldn't stop a determined listener, but would provide some warning. Selton arched an eyebrow at her, a half-smile curling his lips.

"A precaution," Roelle answered.

"Selton?" Lendra asked again.

"What do you know of our Founders?" Selton asked.

"The Great Mother? The same as you, likely. Why?"

Roelle shook her head. "Not just the Great Mother. There's supposed to be something more to the Founding, something other than just the Great Mother."

It was Novan who finally answered, pulling a book from beneath his cloak. "The question should truly be, what do *you* know about your Founders?" The historian peered up from his book, looking over at Roelle and Selton with piercing eyes. They seemed to see into Roelle, and it made her feel unsettled, understanding how Haerlin had been intimidated.

Roelle ran a hand through her hair, struggling with how to answer. How much did she tell them? The historian had been with them through the Deshmahne attacks, so he would understand some of

Roelle's concern, but how much did she trust the historian? Then there was the matter of Selton's cousin. In any other circumstance, she wouldn't hesitate to trust her friend's family, but Lendra's ties were to the historian—she could see it in the way the woman looked at him.

"I know little enough. I've spoken to Alriyn and gotten nowhere. I've spoken with Endric and gotten little farther."

The tall man was silent. He pressed a long finger to his lips thoughtfully for a moment before speaking, choosing his words carefully. "The Second?" he mumbled to himself, considering. "Why do you seek this knowledge?"

Roelle folded her hands in front of her. "I faced the Deshmahne. An open attack upon the Magi. That has never happened before. So I know what we face with them. They're... horrible. Dangerous. In spite of that, Alriyn fears what's happening in the north as much as the Deshmahne threat."

"You ask about the north, yet you question your Founders?" Novan said.

"Endric," she explained, and Novan nodded. "It was all he would give me."

Novan smiled, but it was not meant for Roelle. "Endric," he mused. "He's a clever one." Novan motioned for Roelle and Selton to sit.

Selton looked to Roelle, shrugged, and sat atop Lendra's bed. Lendra sat next to him. Roelle stood a moment more, and Novan again waved her to sit, so finally she did. Novan took a deep breath, pulling himself upright, suddenly taller, and began pacing. The pose he struck reminded Roelle of every teacher she had known.

"To understand your Founders, is to understand the past," he said, a smile crossing his face. "Long ago, so long ago it is no longer remembered and barely recorded, there was a war. The details are few. It is clear that it was a bloody war and one that had raged for many years. Some reports suggest it was fought against strangely dressed warriors." Novan paused, considering. "Some said that men battled creatures of nightmare and fear. I don't know the truth of the reports, only that the foe was powerful and destructive.

"One thing is repeated in each of the tales. One fact alike," Novan continued. "There were certain warriors, physically gifted, that were better able to defeat these creatures. There's something, one fragment of text found, that said only these warriors could *see* the creatures. They called it their gift from the gods."

Roelle realized the similarities to the Antrilii story Endric had mentioned. "What do you think they fought?"

"There is something about the different accounts that speaks of more than mere men, something more."

"You think these creatures were real?" Selton asked.

"Were?" he asked, shaking his head. "You know the rumors about the north. What do you think caused these rumors?"

"Deshmahne, most likely," Roelle answered, but then she knew better. Alriyn had been convinced there was something else at play in the north, something other than the Deshmahne. Something fearsome enough that he was able to dismiss the Deshmahne threat.

Novan eyed her and shook his head. "You know better than that. No, there's something else there, something the world has been protected from for over a thousand years. The question is, why has that protection failed?"

"And these warriors with the gift?" Selton asked.

"You think *they* were the Founders," Roelle asked. The historian gave her a slow nod. "But how? The Great Mother gathered together those early Magi."

"And so she did," Novan agreed, scratching his ear with a long finger. "And so she did. The war was long and bloody. Men without this gift were slaughtered. Many hid. Those with the gift were more fortunate, but barely, and they were all that stood between this threat and the rest of mankind. It was a near total destruction." He stopped to consider them. "This is why, I think, that records before your Founding over one thousand years ago are scarce. A handful of these warriors, little more than a dozen, survived. Your Great Mother gathered these survivors together and came here," he said, sweeping his hand around him.

"But the Magi have always been peaceful servants of the gods and of the Urmahne!" Lendra said.

Novan looked at her softly, affection in his gaze. "They gave up their swords with the Founding and became the Urmahne, choosing to study their abilities. The Great Mother told them this was what the gods wanted."

They sat silent for a long moment before Roelle spoke. "How do you know this?"

Novan smiled again, this time with a hint of mischief. "How do you not?" He let his point sink in before continuing. "I learned it in your library."

Selton perked with the comment. "Where?"

There was a strange glitter to Novan's eyes, brief, and then it was gone. "It is there if you are persistent in your search."

Lendra purposefully turned her head away, a slight grin on her face.

Selton suddenly laughed, nudging his cousin. "If you hadn't left the city, you would have been thrown out!"

She shrugged.

Roelle stared instead intently at Novan. "So our Founders..."

"Were more like you than perhaps any other Mage in the city." Novan gave her a long look. "I have provided information for you. Now I would ask something of you. Help me see the Second."

"Why?" Roelle tried thinking through what Novan might want with her uncle, but couldn't come up with anything. From the way Haerlin reacted to Novan, she could only imagine how her uncle would react.

Novan smiled tightly. "I have something he may need, and he's been unwilling to grant me an audience."

"I can try. I make no guarantees."

"There never are," Novan said.

Roelle thought about the north, about what may be wandering there. What did her uncle know? What did he suspect of the north? Endric had sent men north, and all had been killed, though she had the sense they had died at the hand of Deshmahne.

What did it mean for Jakob? He'd been sent with them to the north. He might be a skilled swordsman, but if what Novan said was even partly true, he didn't have the necessary skills to survive.

"You sent your apprentice to the north."

Novan nodded carefully. "He was needed to observe."

Roelle eyed him a moment. "Observe. But if these creatures are real—"

"Don't worry about Jakob."

"Don't worry? How can I not after what we've learned? Have you even spoken to Endric?"

"I heard what happened."

"Jakob wasn't found."

"Your friend will be safe," Novan tried to assure her.

"Safe?" Roelle asked. "How can you be so certain?" She failed to keep the heat from her question and felt Selton's eyes on her.

Novan crossed his arms in front of his chest. "I have faith."

Roelle frowned, some of her frustration fading. "I thought you were agnostic."

"My beliefs are not so easily corralled. But that's not why I have faith. A different protection has been arranged for Jakob. He'll be safe."

"What do mean?" she asked.

"It means you need to convince your uncle to meet."

Novan flashed a tight smile and motioned to Lendra before turning and walking to the door. Lendra stood and waved to them before following the historian out the door.

Roelle looked to Selton and their eyes locked. There was little need for discussion; Roelle knew without asking what Selton would say. They needed to find out if what Novan said was true, and she could think of only one place to go.

It was time to visit her uncle again.

CHAPTER TWENTY-EIGHT

Roelle sat in front of Alriyn while Selton sat quietly to her left; her friend had never quite grown comfortable in front of the Second Eldest in spite of their years of friendship. Few among the Magi claimed much of a relationship with those on the Council, and it created a distinction between the Councilors and the rest of the Magi. For Roelle, Alriyn had always been her uncle first and foremost.

Roelle waited for Alriyn to turn and face them. He sat quietly at his desk, writing quickly, the pen scratching at the surface of the parchment with such a grating quality that Roelle shifted in her seat. There were other chairs placed around hers, enough that Roelle suspected her uncle had been holding a meeting not long before she arrived. Again. What could he have been discussing? It was not like her uncle to hold private counsel, and now this appeared to be at least the second time he had.

Finally, Alriyn turned and leveled his gaze on the two of them in turn. Selton was first, and her muscular friend shrank from the stern eyes of the Second. Roelle didn't shrink from the gaze, though the warmth it had carried in her childhood was gone from it, and his face bore the serious expression of his office. Alriyn then looked to the door and paused. She knew he sealed their conversation.

Roelle and Selton looked at each other with that realization. Something was amiss.

"You spoke with Endric," Alriyn said.

Roelle nodded. "It was little help. That man is purposefully vague," she said, letting her frustration seep into her voice.

"How so?" Alriyn asked, turning briefly to the parchment in front of him and scribbling again. One ear was cocked to listen, though, so Roelle didn't wait.

"He tells me of nightmares and suggests I learn of the Founders," Roelle answered.

Alriyn stopped writing and looked up. "Whose?"

"Ours."

Alriyn set his pen down. He sighed, and it seemed a weight pressed down on him, his proud shoulders sagging briefly before he caught himself. Roelle had seen it though. Alriyn had a great burden upon him.

"Endric suggested you learn of the Founders?"

Roelle nodded.

"And have you?" Alriyn asked.

"I thought I knew of our Founding. We're taught about the Great Mother and her role in our Founding, nothing more. Endric dismissed that, instructing me to search out the Founders."

"There is more. Few know it."

Roelle and Selton glanced at each other. They hadn't been sure if they should believe the historian. His version seemed too fantastical. But now would Alriyn confirm it?

Alriyn stood and pulled himself to his full height. "There were thirteen, all told," he began, his tone implying a lesson. "The Great Mother but one of them. She gathered them together, the few remaining who shared a gift, the ability given to them by the gods, and they founded the city."

"I know the story, uncle."

"You know what the Council has taught."

"Then who were they?" Roelle asked.

"Theirs was a time of war—the time of the destruction—and they were warriors, special somehow, gifted in ways others were not."

Alriyn paused. "Truth be told, we know little of them. Many have tried. I have spent much of my working life studying the Founding and know little more than what is taught."

Alriyn looked around the contents of his room before fixing his gaze upon Roelle. "We know that they alone fought a war that others could not. A countless many were sent forth to save mankind, and those thirteen were all that survived."

"What did they fight?" Roelle asked.

"There are no surviving descriptions. Fragments and less all that remain. A nightmare is perhaps as good an explanation as any." He paused again, looking briefly to the stacks of paper on his desk. "Years of searching has yielded little more than these barest remnants. What I have found refers to a darkness and an attack so foul that men cannot stand before them. The attack came in such numbers, as if in waves, never seen before and never seen since. And our ancestors..."

"How did they defeat such a thing?" Selton asked, surprise at Alriyn's answer etched in his hard features.

"I'm not sure they did. From what I can tell, hundreds, perhaps thousands, were sent forth to fight. Only thirteen survived to forge this city. To these thirteen, we owe our existence."

"Then how was it stopped?" Roelle asked. "Novan claims we've been protected from this for a thousand years. What has changed?"

"I don't know. Perhaps the Founders saved us, perhaps something else. So little is known of that time." Alriyn looked over to them again, seeming to consider them. "What I am about to tell you, few know. There is one thing that survived from that time. A document known only to the council. I have read and reread it so many times that I could recite it in my sleep."

"What does it say?" Roelle asked, intrigued.

Alriyn smiled tightly. "A prophecy. And perhaps the first."

Roelle sat back, stunned. She was well aware that prophecy was a rare gift among the Magi, with Haerlin the only one to have shown even the slightest ability in hundreds of years. Most among the Magi could count the Mage prophets on their hands, could name them as easily as they named their families. The first prophet, Lureen, lived two hundred years after the Founding. There had been four great prophets since Lureen and seven minor prophets, including Haerlin.

Roelle leaned forward. "What does it say?"

Alriyn closed his eyes. "The prophecy is complex, but translated, it says 'I have seen that there will come a time when we must rise again, seek the *nemah*, and restore the balance. One will come to lead the way. I fear we will grow complacent so heed this warning: they will come again. This I have seen.'"

"Who was the prophet?" Roelle asked.

Alriyn rubbed his chin. "There was no name attached."

"How old is it?" Selton asked.

Alriyn tapped his head. "That truly is the question, isn't it?"

"Why?" Roelle asked, looking from her uncle to Selton.

"To answer that, we must first establish who the prophets were," Alriyn said.

"Lureen, Davrum, Isan, Penalia, Stuvin were the great prophets," Roelle began, naming them as she had once been taught. The first lessons had come right here in her uncle's office. "Then there are the seven minor prophets—."

Alriyn waved her away. "The true prophets are all that concern me. Their visions, few though they were, the only reliable ones we have."

The minor prophets didn't have visions the same way the great prophets did, and some referred to the great prophets as true prophets. Roelle hadn't known her uncle to be one of them. Little was understood about prophecy, even those with it could not explain it well. It manifested differently than the other Magi abilities, and typically in Magi with weaker abilities.

"Lureen, the first, came two hundred years after the Great Mother and the Founding," Alriyn said. "This prophecy was written in a language that predated Lureen."

Roelle finally understood. A sixth great prophet and a prophecy written in the ancient language. Alriyn had taught her that there was a power to the ancient language and she had learned some of it from him over the years. She knew that a prophecy written in the ancient language would likely hold a different meaning from one in today's common tongue.

"How do you know this is prophecy?" Selton asked.

Alriyn frowned, his forehead wrinkling as he did. "Because it has been studied for centuries. It is a part of a greater work, one that guides the Council." Alriyn scratched his head before shaking the thought away.

"And you think this comes from a great prophet?" Selton asked.

Alriyn nodded. The implications were less if it came from a minor prophet. Their visions were cloudy, typically uncertain, and as oft as not did not come true. They saw possibilities. What the great prophets saw always came to pass.

"This is why you don't fear the Deshmahne," Roelle said.

"For all their skill, the Deshmahne can still be seen. They can be stopped. It's what has not been seen that strikes fear through me. And I fear the balance has been lost." Alriyn sat back, frowning as he pulled at the collar of his robe in irritation. "What I've shared with you has not been shared with any outside the Council. The prophecy—and much more—is found in an ancient text that forms the basis of the Urmahne, given to us by the Founders."

He paused as his gaze settled heavily upon them both and seemed to take measure of them. Roelle rarely felt awed by the Second Eldest —she'd known him too long and too intimately for that—but she felt it now.

"What I've shared with you must not leave this room." Alriyn waited until they both nodded. He sighed deeply, and closed his eyes. "This text is called the *mahne*."

Of all the words in the ancient language, Roelle knew that one had many translations. Her mind raced, but she forced it to slow, and listen to her uncle.

"This ancient text has guided our people for one thousand years. Written in words of power, it has allowed these lands to know peace unlike any other time in its history. It's the reason we practice peace. Of the many things learned from the *mahne*, there is one tenet central to it and consistent throughout. It has become the core of the Urmahne, and rightfully so." Alriyn let the words sink in before continuing. "There is a critical balance we must maintain through peace. The *mahne* is clear on this, not only through the prophecy."

"Is this what Novan and Endric think the High Priest seeks?" Roelle asked. Roelle wasn't surprised Endric would know of such a text, but how would Novan?

Alriyn eyed her a moment before agreeing with the barest of nods. "It is possible. There are other artifacts, but they would not be nearly as valuable."

"What will he gain by accessing it?"

"Its guidance has helped secure peace for a thousand years. The Deshmahne seek destruction. He must not acquire it."

"Why keep this to the Council?" Roelle asked.

"There are some things found within the *mahne* that should only be known by those prepared for them—the Council." He looked from Roelle to Selton. "I don't disagree with this practice. Neither of you is prepared for everything within the *mahne*."

"Then why tell us?" Roelle asked.

"You must know the balance is at stake. I fear a convergence, too much disruption all at one time. I worry what this might mean."

"What can be done?" Selton asked.

Roelle stared at her uncle as understanding swept through her. "You think we're the only ones capable of doing anything. That's why Endric told me to understand the Founders." Alriyn didn't say anything. "And now you're sharing this because you want us to learn what our Founders accomplished, what they faced because we must fight. But what has kept us safe from it for the last thousand years?"

Selton sat back and didn't say anything. The Urmahne training ran deep. Lessons of peace and harmony were at the core of who they were as a people.

Alriyn sighed. "I don't know. I think we'll soon learn what has been lost for centuries. Magi training has always focused on the mental aspects of our abilities. We have long ignored the physical. I fear it is too late to change. We may not be strong enough to face the foe our Founders faced, but you *can* be strong enough to stop the Deshmahne." Alriyn stared at Roelle. "We must stop them before they reach the *mahne*."

"You want us to fight the Deshmahne?" Roelle asked.

Alriyn sighed. "I know there are many who have followed your lead. I fear the Denraen will not be enough, not if the rumors we've heard of the Deshmahne are true. This will require the Magi to take a greater role."

Roelle frowned, unable to believe that her uncle asked this of her, but knowing that he was right. The Deshmahne had nearly over-whelmed the Denraen. Without the Magi intervening, would there be any sort of peace to restore?

CHAPTER TWENTY-NINE

Jakob's eyes were gummed closed. He ached all over from his throbbing head to his legs, bruises he didn't remember earning. He tried to reach up and rub his eyes, but his arms were locked behind him, and it was long moments before he realized they were bound. Thick rope ate into the flesh of his wrists, and he felt the same around his ankles.

He was captured.

Slowly, he blinked his eyes open. His vision was blurry, but he made out the small fire crackling nearby. He smelled his captors before he saw them, a light stench of sweat and rot mixed together familiarly. It came to him before long that he knew where he had smelled it before.

Deshmahne.

With the thought, he was fully awake. He counted five men but didn't know if they were all Deshmahne or only one. It didn't matter —he could do nothing in his current state.

Conversation drifted to him, and he strained to hear it. His throbbing head made it difficult, different from the slow vibration he'd lately had when using his sword. Jakob vaguely remembered the blow that had caused it.

"He wasn't alone," one of the men said.

"It does not matter," a deep voice replied. There was something to the voice, something familiar. "It matters only that he is ours. The Highest will be pleased."

Jakob had the chilling certainty that tattoos would cover the man's arms, face, and head. He'd seen the Deshmahne before and somehow escaped.

Not this time though.

"Where is the object?" the Deshmahne asked.

"There was nothing with him other than his sword."

"There should have been a case," the Deshmahne said. "He had it strapped to him when he escaped me. That is what the Highest seeks."

Jakob heard shuffling and sensed someone drawing near, so he feigned sleep. The man reached out and ran a hand along Jakob's back and arms, before standing and kicking at his legs and walking away.

He stifled a grunt and a struggled not to cry out.

"He has nothing," the man said.

"The Highest will not be pleased." There was a note of concern in his deep voice as he said it. "You will go back for it."

"As you command," a different voice spoke.

He struggled against his bindings again, hoping to loosen them enough to free his hands. With his hands free, he could find out if his sword was still strapped to his side or not. Likely the men would have removed it when they first captured him. The bindings held, and the more he struggled, the tighter they seemed. Finally, he gave up.

Jakob held back a sigh and felt a wave of fear pass through him. What would they do with the trunk if they retrieved it? Did they know what it held? Probably, just as they probably knew why the trunk was key to stopping the Deshmahne.

"What of him?" a man asked. "What of the reward?"

A dark laugh erupted from the Deshmahne, and Jakob could almost feel something radiate from him. Power. Strength. Darkness.

"I claim the reward," the Deshmahne said.

"But the gold clips," one of the men said.

"You may keep them. I seek a different reward." He sniffed the air abruptly. "He's awake."

How long had the Deshmahne known he was awake? A rough hand grabbed him and sat him up. Three men sat around the fire. One was the Deshmahne he'd heard. He stared at Jakob, dark eyes unreadable, the light from the fire flickering strangely around him, illuminating the tattoos that covered his face and arms.

Jakob shivered, unable to suppress it.

The man who had grabbed him was dressed in simple brown pants and shirt, dirtied, but more raider than Deshmahne. Jakob glanced to the man's uncovered arms and saw no tattoos. The man saw his flicker of eye movement and laughed.

"Not yet, boy, but my time is coming," he said harshly as he knelt near Jakob's feet. He remained kneeling there, waiting.

The other man, dressed similarly in brown pants, remained at the fire. Silent. His face was filthy and contorted strangely. Jakob suspected it anxiety.

"What are you?" the Deshmahne asked.

Jakob shook his head at the bizarre question. "I'm nobody." His voice was thick, and he coughed as he said the words.

The Deshmahne smiled, revealing pale, white teeth that contrasted with his dark, red lips. "Perhaps," he said and slowly stood. His long, dark robe barely brushed the ground and did not move as he walked over toward Jakob. "Perhaps not."

The Deshmahne stared again, looking deeply into Jakob's eyes.

Jakob found it difficult to look away. Hopelessness began to seep into him.

I'm nothing. Nothing compared to this man. He is powerful before the gods while I am weak.

Waves of despair rolled through him, and he sank, unable to support himself upright any longer.

I disappoint the gods with my weakness. The Deshmahne honor them with their strength.

Slowly, Jakob shook his head. This last thought was not his, and he knew it.

The Deshmahne do not honor the gods.

This thought was his own. With it, he felt his mind clearing. Despair still rolled through him, but he was able to pull himself up and sit with his back straight, briefly struggling with the binding around his wrists as he did.

The Deshmahne frowned before his tattooed face flattened. "Do you know me?"

Jakob shook his head.

"But you know my master," the Deshmahne stated.

"The High Priest."

The Deshmahne smiled. "The Highest, yes. You are the one he seeks. You will go to him."

"If I don't?" Jakob struggled to summon defiance, but he didn't intend to go easily.

The Deshmahne flashed his pale smile again. "That is not an option."

Too late, he heard a whistling sound and felt a sharp blow to his head as he was knocked unconscious again.

∼

The horse's steady steps slowly roused Jakob, and he blinked to open his eyes. He was tied to a saddle, his arms bound now in front of him and hands tied to the pommel of the saddle. It was dark, and they moved swiftly without any light to see. He smelled the Deshmahne leading them, his sweat mixed with the undercurrent of rot. Jakob wondered where he was being taken, but his aching mind slowly reminded him that he already knew.

The High Priest.

"What happened to the others?"

The question was whispered nearby, and he could vaguely see the dark shape of one of the raiders riding alongside him.

"They haven't returned," the other said.

"Why didn't we wait?"

"I don't ask."

The other man chuckled. "You think he would tell us?"

"No."

"Quiet," the Deshmahne commanded.

The men fell silent, and they rode on. Jakob felt the rope around his wrist cut deeply and was beginning to lose sensation in his fingers, but still, he struggled at it. The alternative was to give up. He was not yet prepared for that.

Would it be so bad?

The question drifted from a distant part of his mind, and he wondered, briefly, if it mattered, if he mattered. He struggled to push the thought away.

At the sound of pounding hooves approaching, the men looked back. Jakob craned his neck but was unable to see anything other than the dark. His head hurt too badly for much more. Two riders approached and quickly rode up alongside the Deshmahne.

"Just them," one of the raiders said.

"Think they got it?" the other whispered.

"Hope so. Otherwise, he'll be angry."

They fell silent as the riders fell into line. The scent of sweat and rot intensified.

Jakob suspected these new men were Deshmahne, as well. It was a smell he had come to know and detest, and it filled his nostrils so that he breathed through his mouth, though it was little better.

"Do you have it?" the Deshmahne asked of the newcomers. His large build loomed over the other two.

"We do." The man's voice resembled the coarse sound of wood splintering.

All the effort that had gone toward protecting the trunk, all that had been lost, and still the Deshmahne had it. A sense of helplessness sagged him in the saddle. They had failed the Denraen. He had failed Endric. The key to stopping the Deshmahne was lost.

"The others with him?" the large Deshmahne asked.

"There was a woman. We left her."

"You left her?" His dissatisfaction was evident in the tone of his voice.

"There was a pursuit," the other said. His voice was a deep rumble. "The case was our priority."

"Yes. It is." He paused, filling the night with silence. Finally, "Did you see who followed?"

"It was him. The Hunter."

"The Highest will not be pleased to know that he still lives," the Deshmahne said before falling silent once more. The others did not disturb the silence.

They rode onward through the darkness of the night. Their pace slowed as the trees thickened, and Jakob could occasionally make out the moon overhead. As he was beginning to think they would ride the remainder of the night, the large Deshmahne led them to a small clearing and a stop.

The raiders went to work quickly setting up a brief camp. Pulling Jakob roughly from the saddle, they left his hands bound and pushed him out of the way while they started a small fire in the center of the clearing. The three Deshmahne stood off to the side of the clearing, examining something intently. The trunk?

After long moments, they appeared to give up, and the three returned to the center of the camp. One of the other Deshmahne grabbed Jakob and pushed him to sit by the fire where the large Deshmahne came and placed the dark trunk in front of him. The fire-light reflected from the closed clasp, flickering as if alive, and he was thankful that it was not yet open.

One of the raiders came over to him and pushed a strip of hard bread into his mouth. It was bitter tasting and dry, and he quickly spit it out. The man drew back to strike him, but the Deshmahne who'd just pushed Jakob to the ground intervened. He grabbed the raider's wrist before he could hit him and tossed the man away from the fire.

The large Deshmahne approached. "What's your name?" he asked, his voice commanding.

He radiated nearly the same sensation of power as Jakob had felt from the High Priest. "I'm nobody." His mouth was dry, more so now that he had spit out the bread, and his head pounded, making it diffi-cult to think clearly.

"What is your name?" the Deshmahne demanded again.

His deep voice echoed *into* Jakob, and he could not help himself as he looked up at the large man looming over him and answered, "Jakob Nialsen."

The Deshmahne paused, staring deeply into Jakob's eyes before nodding. "Good. How have you come by the case?"

The words commanded Jakob to answer. He struggled to fight, but with his pounding head, there was little fight left in him. "General Endric sent it with the Denraen." It was difficult to limit his answer, but somehow, he managed.

"Denraen? How did you come to join the Denraen?"

"They were in Chrysia," Jakob said, unable to help himself.

"Chrysia? Isn't that where you destroyed the temple?" asked one of the raiders.

Jakob glared at the Deshmahne as he walked over to stand near the other two Deshmahne.

"It is," one of the lesser Deshmahne answered, turning his dark eyes on Jakob.

The sense of bleak hopelessness returned. "You destroyed the temple?" he managed to ask, glaring at the large Deshmahne, his voice stronger than he thought it could be.

"The only path to the gods is through the Deshmahne." The man spoke with a deep voice and said the word Deshmahne with a slight accent that was almost familiar.

The Deshmahne destroyed the temple?

The question sat with him for a moment, the hopeless feeling slowing his thoughts as he struggled to make sense of what they had just told him. Slowly, the truth settled into him.

The Deshmahne killed my father.

The hopelessness faded and was replaced by a flash of anger.

"My father was in the temple," Jakob said, seething. He fingered the dark ring, the last memento from him, and a sudden pain returned to his head. It was a slow pounding that pressed upon his temples, and he ignored it.

One of the raiders laughed. "D' you hear that? You killed his father!" The other raider joined him, and they both laughed. The Deshmahne did not stop them.

"What of your ma?" the other raider asked. "Was she in the temple too?"

His rage almost blinding him, he glared at them and shook his head, frustrated that his answers were compelled so.

The raiders laughed anew until the large Deshmahne turned and fixed a stare on them, and they quieted quickly. Turning his attention back to Jakob, he said, "The gods have abandoned you because you are weak. You could have been strong. Now..."

The words mirrored a thought Jakob had known but had never spoken aloud. His mother had been taken from him years before, her death little more than an accident, a terrible fall down the steps of the temple and a broken neck. Quick, at the least, and he had always been thankful of that. His father had never been the same after his mother's death. The Urmahne had always been a source of comfort to their family, their faith a blanket, but since her death, his father had used his faith and the Urmahne as a shield.

And then the madness had claimed Scottan. It was random, the healers all agreed, but when it claimed someone, it took them quickly and entirely. None were ever the same, and few had lasted more than a year; it had been two since Scottan had succumbed. There was no explanation for the madness, no reason.

His father had been all Jakob had left. He and his father had disagreed on many things, Jakob's faith most of all, yet he was still his father. When he had died, Jakob felt that loss the hardest. And Scottan, the empty shell of his brother, was now just a horrible reminder of the family he'd lost.

The gods had abandoned him.

The Deshmahne had helped.

He lifted his head and met the large Deshmahne's gaze and said nothing. One of the other two carried a long metal rod with a flat piece on one end. He walked over to the fire and stuck the flat end into the flames, leaving it there until it became red hot, before returning to stand near the others.

It brought back memories of what he had seen scouting with the Denraen. He knew some of what the Deshmahne were capable of and shivered uncontrollably.

"Convert," the Deshmahne said.

Jakob could not be sure which man had spoken. The three standing side by side overpowered him with strange emotions, and he felt himself being washed aside, a sense of despair filling him. Yet not for one moment did he consider conversion. He felt a pressure, a presence, radiating from the dark tattoos covering each of the men, almost a cloud pressing on him, and he knew a sense of weakness compared to these men.

Still, he shook his head, slowly, defiantly.

The Deshmahne with the rod, now glowing brightly, approached. Jakob felt the heat of it as he neared. Strange characters smoldered on the flat piece, and he knew he didn't want it to touch him. The Deshmahne swirled it in the air threateningly, and it was suddenly pressed toward him; he scrambled back and away from the rod.

The large Deshmahne stood over him and looked down. Out of the corner of his eyes, Jakob could see the rod nearby, waving in the dark night. There was something to the rod, something *wrong,* and he cowered away from it.

"You will convert. The Highest will see to that." His dark eyes tore through Jakob. "When he opens the case, you will see the strength of the Deshmahne and will ask for conversion."

The man touched a thick finger to Jakob's forehead and pushed him down. Jakob felt it throb in response and fell backward into sudden sleep.

Jakob awoke to thin light streaming through the trees and realized he was once again tied to the saddle. It was daylight, and the trees were taller and grew closer together than the day before. The Deshmahne still led them steadily, sitting tall atop their horses, their dark cloaks barely moving as they rode.

He had a headache, though it was different and yet similar to other headaches he had been having. There was an ache where he had been hit, a swelling pulsing in his forehead, and a strange tingling where the Deshmahne had touched him. Overtop it all was the slow pulsing deep within his head—that familiar vibration—and the clarity that always accompanied it.

Staring at the large Deshmahne, there was a pattern to the tattoos on the man's bare head and neck. A slight haziness floated around them. Jakob sniffed and could smell the rot he'd come to associate with the Deshmahne. It came stronger from the large Deshmahne, but some of the odor came from the other two as well. He wasn't sure how he knew but was certain of it just the same.

The raiders rode behind him. He didn't need to look back to know. He could hear their steady movements and could smell their sweat. Occasionally, one of the men would grunt or say something to the other, but it was rare. It was a quiet ride, and the forest had fallen silent around them.

With his head beginning to clear, Jakob had time to think about his situation. He suspected they were riding to Rondalin and the High Priest. The Deshmahne had the trunk, and Endric did not yet know this. Would he still travel to Avaneam? Would Novan go looking for Jakob when he did not appear?

With the trunk in their possession, why did the Deshmahne need him? He knew little of use to them, little that would explain more than he had said already. Endric had been given the trunk and a mission to take it north to Avaneam.

I've told them of Endric but not of the woman and not of Avaneam.

They would not learn it from him.

Jakob looked around, hoping to see something he might recognize from his first ride through the forest, and thought he saw familiar trees. A slow itch at the back of his mind built as they moved steadily onward, and he struggled to keep his gaze straight ahead of him as the feeling of being watched built. Brohmin had said there were merahl in the woods, though he had not said what merahl were. Could this be all he felt? Maybe he *wasn't* going mad.

That thought gave him little solace.

"Something's not right," one of the raiders muttered as the light through the trees started to fade.

"What is it?" the other asked.

"Don't know, just... something."

The large Deshmahne looked back. The tattoos on his face deepened with the growing darkness, and the shadows were prominent. He said nothing, but there was an expression of curiosity and irritation to his dark eyes and the slight squint to them.

As the light faded to near darkness, Jakob's sensation of being watched was still there, a gnawing sensation and quiet irritation in the back of his mind. Still, his head throbbed and pulsed.

Their pace had slowed considerably as the day had progressed, working their way carefully through and around the trees, forging a path through the underbrush. It was tedious work, and Jakob sensed frustration from the Deshmahne in their quiet conversation and the harsh glares they passed around.

Finally, they halted. The raiders hastily made camp, their conversation terse and hushed as they started a small fire and tied off the horses. One of the men pulled Jakob from his horse and threw him down away from the fire—and its warmth—where he landed face down, tasting leaves and dirt while they rebound his feet. As he spit out the debris from his mouth, his head was jerked back.

"What is this?" an angry voice asked.

It was one of the lesser Deshmahne. He had come to identify them that way in his head, unwilling to ask what they should be called. The man's face was touched by thin tattoos, though his arms were covered in dark ink that spread up his neck. Jakob could almost see a pattern but lost it as his eyes watered when the Deshmahne pulled again at his hair, whipping his neck back.

The large Deshmahne knelt in front of him. Jakob had not even heard his movements, but now he felt him as much as he saw him. "What are you?" the Deshmahne asked.

"I'm Jakob," he answered quickly.

This was not a man to speak carelessly around, but he didn't know what else to say. *I'm nothing. Barely a historian and soon to be dead.*

"Circles!" the lesser Deshmahne grabbing his hair said. "We've been traveling in circles. And now we're deeper in the forest than ever before."

The large Deshmahne nodded once, and the other released him, allowing Jakob to roll onto his back. He looked up at the large Deshmahne and felt the hopelessness wailing against him as he struggled to ignore it.

"There is little that surprises me, but you have done that," he said. His voice was slow and heavy, and echoed in the dense woods. "Only one with much power could lead us as you have." He reached out and tapped Jakob on the forehead before smiling tightly. It pulled the lines of his dark tattoos, distorting them. "You will bring me much favor with the Highest."

The Deshmahne moved in sync around the fire, their steps precise. The large Deshmahne loomed over the flames, and the smoke and shadows reflected from him in uncomfortable flickers of movement. The raiders had disappeared, cowering near the horses, and were silent. Fear and awe crossed their faces in alternating waves. The lesser Deshmahne began chanting, stepping quietly around the fire, seeming to snap from one position to the next. The large Deshmahne stood still, only his head swaying front and back.

Jakob sensed movement around him but saw nothing. The lesser Deshmahne continued their strange dance, a slow unintelligible chant murmuring into the night, gradually rising and falling, mirroring their movements. The large Deshmahne raised his arms slowly and let his dark robe fall from him. He wore only breeches, and his naked chest and back were covered completely in dark markings that started to crawl and circle as he swayed. One hand held the large metal rod from the night before, held carefully outward and bobbing up and down with him in rhythmic movements.

The fire stretched up and up, fed by nothing but air and yet climbed anyway until it reached the iron rod. The flames licked at the flat end piece, heating it until it glowed white-hot and hissed quietly, the sound joining with the chanting of the Deshmahne and the slow crackling of the fire. The large Deshmahne held it as the flames heated it, the rod itself becoming red with heat, yet he didn't flinch.

The large Deshmahne slowly turned until he faced Jakob where he sat away from the fire. The man's eyes still reflected the flames, a flickering dance that reminded him of the High Priest, and he couldn't look away. His lips moved, though no sound came from them. There was only the chanting and crackle of the fire. A step, deliberate, timed with the jerking movements of the lesser Deshmahne and their strange chanting, and he moved closer. His arms raised higher, the hot piece of metal still swaying up and down but now also moving in slow arcs, tracing a pattern in the darkness that Jakob could not follow.

Arms raised higher still, revealing the dark tattoos under his arms, down his sides, leaving no flesh untouched. The markings seemed alive now, swirling and twisting in time with the chanting, a haze gradually obscuring them. The rod circled wider still in slow revolutions in a pattern only known by the Deshmahne. The large Deshmahne's mouth still moved, and now audible words came forth, joining with the chanting behind him, the language strange and foreign.

Jakob couldn't make out what they said, but felt the effects. Despair and hopelessness pounded against him, and the slow pulsing in his head pushed back in answer, a throbbing that beat out of time with the chanting, almost as if working against it. Something pulled at him, and his bound arms rose up with a life of their own, and as much as he pushed against it, he could not lower them back down. The bindings of his wrists fell away, leaving red burn markings as a reminder, and his freed arms flew out and up.

The rod swung down, quickly, the heat of it whistling in the night, hissing in unison with the chanting and the dancing of the lesser Deshmahne. Their voice rose up, higher and higher, reaching crescendo in a piercing cry, as the metal rod stopped, inches from the exposed flesh of Jakob's arm. His head hummed, the pulsing intensifying to nearly a vibration, and he suppressed a scream. He saw the effort the large Deshmahne put forth in trying to force the branding onto him, saw how the man's face tightened in deep lines of concentration, his muscles taut with the strain, yet still something pushed back.

And suddenly there was a cry. The raiders yelled out quickly in alarm before being silenced.

Jakob looked over, finally able to turn his gaze from the Deshmahne. A figure stalked toward him with a sword exposed. He moved smoothly, quietly, and almost faded into the darkness of the night, outlined only by the pale light of the fire.

Brohmin.

He strode over to Jakob and sliced the rope tying his hands, then forced something into his hands. It took a long moment before he realized what it was.

His sword.

The smooth worn texture of the wrappings was familiar, and he quickly pulled it from its scabbard, slicing himself free of the ropes that bound his feet, before standing.

Jakob shook his head, clearing the strange chanting that had fallen silent and trying to make sense of what was suddenly happening around him. Brohmin circled the large Deshmahne in a dangerous dance as the Deshmahne held him off with nothing other than the metal branding rod. Brohmin twisted and thrust, spinning through quick movements, yet the Deshmahne was quicker, holding him off easily. A smile had come to his face.

He saw movement and realized that the two lesser Deshmahne had stopped their dancing and were grabbing their weapons, moving to flank the large Deshmahne.

Jakob hesitated long enough to sense the pulsing in his head, to wrap himself in it, and welcome the strange vibration throughout his entire body and the way time seemed to slow. His sword hummed, and he felt it vibrating in sync with this mind.

As he started toward the two lesser Deshmahne, they turned to face him. Each man remained covered by his dark robe, and each quickly let it fall away. Both were covered with tattoos, but not nearly as fully as the large Deshmahne. They moved quickly, taking up position on either side of him. Jakob spun his sword in a slow circle, getting a feel for it again and welcoming the weight. The bright edge reflected the fading firelight brightly, and both Deshmahne paused. It was the opening Jakob needed.

He darted forward and pulled on the pulsing within him at the same time, feeling as everything seemed to slow. His sword moved quickly, flashing through catahs Jakob knew, blazing his own pattern in the night. The Deshmahne's pause had been brief but enough. One of the men went down, a slash across his chest opening a bloody line in the tattoos. A second parry from Jakob took him across the neck in a spray of blood. He fell noisily to the ground.

Jakob spun, meeting the blade of the other Deshmahne and saw a brief look of concern cross the man's face. He moved in quick, efficient movements, holding Jakob in front of him as his sword flashed.

Jakob struggled to keep up, feeling the blade as it whistled past his ear, only barely missing him.

This was the Deshmahne who admitted to destroying the temple in New Chrysia.

This was the Deshmahne who had killed his father.

Jakob's anger rose, and the throbbing in his head became something more.

He heard a grunt behind him and a deep laugh. Brohmin was in trouble.

Jakob pulled upon the pulsing again, letting it fill him, running through his arms and down to his feet. Time slowed again, and in a quick movement, he spun, taking the lesser Deshmahne's head off as he did. A look of surprise was frozen on his severed head.

Jakob ran to Brohmin. He and the Deshmahne moved in a furious parry of attacks, nearly too fast to make sense of where the sword stopped, and the metal rod started.

The Deshmahne flicked a quick glance to Jakob, and his mouth moved into a tight line. Suddenly, the rod moved faster still, and Jakob sensed rather than saw how the man would move and brought his sword up to block a blow that would otherwise have taken Brohmin in the head.

There was another flicker of eye movement toward Jakob, almost too quick to catch, and then a loud snap filled the night. Smoke and dust rose up from the ground in a dark cloud, and the Deshmahne was gone.

Jakob looked around. There was no movement, and the flames of the fire quickly died, leaving everything in near shadows.

"Is he gone?" Jakob asked, panting.

Brohmin nodded. "He is."

"Where? How?"

Brohmin shook his head. "I don't know."

"You hurt?" Jakob finally lowered his sword and felt the pains of the last few days nearly overwhelm him. His head hurt most of all, but his arms and legs were no better. Where the ropes had bound him, he felt a raw throbbing.

Brohmin looked himself over before shaking his head. "Not enough to matter." He glanced toward the fallen Deshmahne. "How?"

"How what?"

"How did you stop that last blow?"

Jakob thought about it for a moment. Everything seemed fuzzy, cloudy. He'd sensed where the Deshmahne was going to move next and had moved to block. "Lucky, I guess."

Brohmin frowned before shaking his head. "Thanks. I owe you."

"No more than I owe you. How did you find me?"

"I've been following you since you were captured. The Deshmahne leave little trail, but the raiders I could track. We were lucky in that, else you may have been lost." He paused to catch his breath. "What did they want of you?"

Jakob shook his head. "Nothing of me," he answered though wondered if that was true. What was the strange ritual they had started? "They wanted the trunk."

Brohmin arched his brow at him and asked, "Where is it?"

A sudden worry filled him. Had the large Deshmahne grabbed it before disappearing? He ran over to the horses and saw the two dead raiders. Ignoring them, he searched the animal but found nothing.

Without the trunk, Endric's mission was lost.

"It's lost," he said. The weight of the words hit him with despair different from what the Deshmahne inflicted upon him.

Brohmin kneeled by the fire, near where the lesser Deshmahne had been dancing before Jakob had killed them. "They don't have it." He dug in the dirt near the fire, then turned toward Jakob, holding up the trunk. "I think the ritual you were a part of was meant to open it," Brohmin said as he brought it over, brushing off a layer of dust and dirt from the top of it. The clasp still gleamed as if freshly polished.

Brohmin grasped his shoulder. "I know much has been lost for this trunk. That the Deshmahne would send *him*," he nodded toward where the large Deshmahne had disappeared, "is proof of its importance. This must see its destination."

Jakob sheathed his sword, strapping it to his waist. They affixed the trunk to the saddle of one of the horses, and he and Brohmin mounted and rode quickly into the night. They rode a long time, quietly moving through the dark night until a dim light came into view. As they neared the light, they could see it was a small fire burning near a pile of rocks, with Salindra tending it.

Brohmin led Jakob to an enormous clearing where a ring of trees formed a circle, the darkening sky once again visible. The change from the brown of the forest floor, covered in dead and dying leaves, to an open field of grass caught his eye. He was shocked at the suddenness of the change. Shocked by something else too.

Around the clearing, immense trees held back the rest of the forest from entering. Within the clearing were scattered huge gray stones, some as tall as a man, the same color as his father's stone ring he had found. Something about the area sparked a memory in him.

He'd been to the area before.

A dream. Only a dream.

But the rocks had formed a circle then. Something about the arrangement had seemed important. It was where Sharna had been, and the two like her.

Brohmin tore him from his thoughts. "We'll rest here for the night. It is a safe place, hidden. Guarded." He paused, looking over to Jakob. "It is a place with much history. We can rest peacefully tonight." Salindra eyed Brohmin strangely from where she sat near the small fire, but he ignored her.

Jakob looked around the clearing again. Exhaustion overwhelmed him, and he made a quick camp, falling into sleep. A thought came to him at the edge of sleep.

Was his dream of this place a part of the madness?

He'd thought himself safe, but maybe he wasn't.

Could I have read of this place?

The answer didn't come as he fell into sleep.

CHAPTER THIRTY

Jakob opened his eyes slowly. He didn't think he'd been asleep long. The slow pulsing, almost buzzing, had returned to his head. He wasn't sure when it had left him, sometime during the ride back with Brohmin, but it had been gone before he had fallen asleep. With its return came another sensation, a soft pulling within his mind.

He shook his throbbing head, but it didn't clear.

Somehow, he'd been moved while resting and now lay atop one of the rocks at the center of the clearing. Looking up at the sky, the colors shifted from orange to pink to black as the sun dropped lower. A few wispy clouds floated overhead, barely moving.

Jakob propped himself up and looked about the clearing.

Rocks that had been scattered haphazardly before he had lain down were now arranged in a circle. Each rock was different from the next; each had a shape he suspected had some meaning, and strangely, a part of him knew the meaning. Staring at the stones, he saw slightly different patterns about them, which if he thought long enough, he could understand.

The tree line appeared different from what he remembered. They didn't seem as tall as they had when they'd arrived, though he wondered if it was just the lighting. He watched the sky for a while longer, noticing stars as they blinked into existence, before turning and looking at the forest. Something was different there as well. The trees weren't as close as he remembered, their huge trunks seeming lessened in the night.

Was that the light too?

A shape made its way toward him, dark at first, and hard for him to make out. Tall and slender, he thought it to be Salindra until he saw the approaching person had very close-cropped hair. Something about the person tugged at a memory.

He blinked, and suddenly, the world seemed to lighten. Everything around him became brighter, as if he were looking at it in daylight. It was an abrupt change, almost as if clicking over. He blinked several times to make sure he was seeing correctly, and there was no change.

The figure was garbed more strangely than anyone he had ever seen. Breeches and shirt were swirling greens, and as Jakob continued to stare, it seemed the shapes of leaves and grasses came and went. They were clothes that would blend into the forest backdrop. Swirling energy surrounded the man, and he was reminded of the dream he had of the gods.

He noted a hazy film he could nearly feel. Pale, nearly translucent, but it was there. He glanced down at himself and noted the same colored garb as the other wore and realized the same pale energy also surrounded him.

Jakob looked up at the person, and he noticed something familiar. He'd seen the shape of the softly angular jaw before. Eyes were widely set, and there was a slight point to the ears. The features were natural yet different from any person he had ever known. The man had the beginnings of a beard, dark and closely shorn. He was younger, much younger than when he had seen him in his dreams.

"Denmri sen-Kaleb." Jakob didn't know what prompted him to speak and didn't know how he knew the other's name. His voice was musical, enchanting, and fluid. "I hope the young night finds you well."

The words were not his own. He felt himself saying them, knew he spoke, but he didn't choose the words. There was something else about his voice that was different. Something he couldn't quite grasp. His speech felt strange on his tongue, almost foreign.

The energy around him stretched out, touching Denmri before pulling back.

Denmri nodded. "The night is young, but you grow old, my friend!"

He laughed, knew the comment amusing, but was unsure why. The other man laughed with him. "Soon, Denmri, you, too, will feel the pull of years. Someday, you will sit where I do and lament over an age gone by, laughing while others call you old." They laughed again.

The words were more fluid, more musical, and more natural. Earthy somehow. How had he learned enough from Novan's book to speak it?

He spoke again. "Old I may be, but it is not yet your time."

Denmri flashed a quick smile. "May it not be for a long time, my friend."

Insects hummed all about, singing, and an occasional owl called in its attack. He could pick out the individual call from each creature if he tried. Strange scents filled the air; a heavy floral scent mixed with the sweetness of the damp earth. The smell was strong, yet not unpleasant nor completely unfamiliar.

"Shoren, it is time to choose. We have found one to end the struggles, as you instructed."

Jakob didn't know what the man spoke about, didn't think he knew why Denmri called him Shoren. Strangely, a part of him did. Part of him knew what needed to be said. "I must see him."

Denmri nodded. "He is here. Chon om'Salii Jonah guided him to us." Denmri paused a moment.

It would be much easier if Chon could have been chosen, but that was not in the fibers. Denmri headed back toward the forest, blending with the trees as he reached them. He stared a long time at the night sky as he waited for the man's return. Though Jakob's sight made it seem daylight, he could still see stars.

A part of him could recall nights long ago. Nights sitting in the same spot and staring into the sky. A sky not obstructed by the trees. A time before the forest was tall.

How can I remember that?

Another part of him knew the memories were there because he'd lived them. There was a certain sadness in knowing his best days were behind him.

The sky was spotted with thousands of stars; he had known nights when there had been fewer stars. Though Jakob wondered how there could ever have been fewer stars, he somehow remembered those nights. That part of him knew he was old, could feel it in his bones and his joints, but his mind was still fresh. It was his mind that mattered now.

Two figures came into view through the trees, followed by Denmri. The two others were shorter than Denmri, several hands shorter but more like people Jakob had known his whole life.

Or is it Denmri who looks like those I've known my whole life?

It was getting hard to remember.

"Shoren sen-Alliss," one of the men began. "The fibers have brought us together again."

A part of him understood what the man meant while another remained confused. Which part was really him?

"Chon om'Salii Jonah. Your company has been missed. There are few of your kind we can truly speak openly with." Again, the words he spoke felt true to him, but he didn't know why he spoke them.

"You honor me. Another time may we be allowed to speak more." The man's words rang with sincerity. "For now, I bring to you Aalleyn om'Lai Tompen. It is he who Marli day-Ohmsan chose."

Jakob looked to the other man, Aalleyn. Dark hair was styled long in the back, shorn close on top. The custom in his country, he knew. The man looked at him with a face of awe. His eyes almost glowed with emotion. He looked ready to drop at any moment to bow.

The man's reaction was somehow not unexpected.

"Tell me Aalleyn Tompen," he began, choosing to use the less formal of the man's names. Jakob was unsure how he knew to do that, or how he knew it was less formal. "Tell me what you have seen."

The man looked to Chon uncomfortably, brown eyes searching for help. Chon offered none, as Jakob somehow knew he would not. The man needed to pass this step on his own.

"Most High?" the man questioned. "I have seen much. What of it would you like me to share?"

He knew it best not to correct the man for the title just yet, knew it best to leave his expectations and beliefs where they were. It would make things easier. "What have you seen of the war? It is a violent thing, this war. We have learned this lesson painfully."

He said the words knowingly, yet Jakob didn't truly know what he spoke about.

But... he did know. The memories were there, faint but growing stronger. It was he they fought over, he remembered. He and his people. A sad price was paid.

The man turned his head, looking to Chon again before turning back to Jakob.

Or is it Shoren?

Who am I?

Both names seemed to fit. He could remember times as both. Could remember years with Novan as Jakob, remembered the journey from the city as Jakob, and remembered the repeated attacks by the Deshmahne.

Who am I?

He remembered his first meeting with Chon's kind as Shoren, remembered the bloody war he helped stop as Shoren, and remembered deciding to choose one of Chon's kind to stop the fighting as Shoren.

Who am I?

"The war?" Aalleyn asked. "I was in Rehne when they attacked. I was in command of the city when they moved out of the west and broke our walls. We had no reports of their troops in the west. We had no reports of any of their troops in any of the north. We still do not know how they became so strong." The words were soft, spoken sadly.

A battle lost, Shoren knew.

I am Jakob!

It was good that the man knew pain, good that the man knew the cost. It would help in his training.

What training?

"We've disappointed you," Aalleyn said.

Shoren knew the man's fears, knew where they came from, but knew there was no truth to them.

What fears? Jakob wondered.

Who am I?

I am both.

The thought drifted from the back of his mind but rang true.

"The Unbelievers took one city from us. I know you've brought me here in your anger. I accept your punishment." Aalleyn hung his head in shame. Thick hair curled around his neck. "I deserve whatever you decide."

Denmri smirked briefly. Chon joined him. Both were quick to hide their amusement. A smile didn't come to Jakob's face, though. The war was fought over him and his kind—a war of clashing beliefs, faiths. Useless destruction. It must stop.

Too much had been lost. It was time to stop it.

He chose his words carefully. The subject was a delicate one. "The situation is not as you think it to be. We are not what you believe us to be." He spoke softly, a movement of his hands including Denmri in the statement.

Aalleyn's eyes widened. "You are the gods! You are *everything* I believe you to be."

Shoren shook his head. "Not gods, my friend," he said soothingly. "We are an extension of the Maker, serving and protecting that which was made." An arm stretched out, pointing around him. "We are nothing more."

What he told Aalleyn went against everything the poor man believed.

What do I believe? Jakob was no longer sure.

"Then, why am I here?" Aalleyn asked quietly, his voice quavered.

"This war is fought because of your beliefs. Because of your faith." Shoren stared sternly at Aalleyn, and the man shrank away. "War destroys that which was made, weakening the Maker." He paused, knowing his explanation was lacking but not having time to fill in the gaps. "It weakens my kind."

Aalleyn stared at him, a blank expression painted to his face.

Does he understand?

Do I?

"This war, and all wars, grant strength to that which would tear apart what was made." The words hung heavy in the night air. "Is this something you understand, Aalleyn?"

The man nodded carefully, but repeated, "Why am I here?"

Shoren stared for long moments. "You are here because you have a special path set before you. This path carries with it the end of the war." He waited, giving Aalleyn time to digest the words. It was a difficult dish to swallow. "You have been chosen because you can bring an end to this struggle, this bloodshed. You have been chosen because you can unite the people."

Aalleyn's face was blank. Shoren knew that he would be shocked, knew he should be. Much was being asked of him. Much was expected of him.

"This is not a path that we can force upon you. You must choose to accept this path on your own." He stopped again, catching Aalleyn's eyes. "Will you accept this challenge?"

Aalleyn looked at the others around him, his gaze catching Chon first then looking to Denmri and finally settling on Shoren. "Why me? Why not someone else? Him?" He nodded to Chon.

Shoren smiled. It was a good question. "We all have separate paths we are set upon. He does not have that path before him."

Aalleyn nodded again. "My path." The words spoken mostly to himself. He stood in thoughtful silence before finally looking up. Shoren knew it was a difficult decision. "If it is my path, then I must take it. What will I do?"

A small wave of relief flowed through Shoren. He had seen that the man might choose otherwise. It had taken a long time to find him. It would have taken even longer to find another.

How do I know that? Jakob wondered.

Who am I?

Shoren, he decided. Jakob was a faint memory to him, distant, at the back of his mind.

He raised his hand, motioning slightly toward the tree line. He had known that Marli was listening, but couldn't remember why she chose not to show herself.

Ah, I remember. She is afraid of them. Afraid of their violence. Does she not fear our own?

She came into the clearing slowly. He had always thought her beautiful.

I have?

If not for Aimeilen.

Aimeilen?

Ah, but Aimeilen was beautiful too. How he loved her long, dark hair, the slight pout to her chin. The tiny rim of gold to her blue eyes. Yes, Marli was no Aimeilen. Still beautiful, though.

Shoren motioned toward Marli. "You will go with her. She will show you how to begin." He watched Aalleyn walk toward the edge of the clearing with Marli. Watched as their hope left and wished there was an easier way.

It would be worse if we got involved, he reminded himself. He knew what cost that would have, knew this method to be safest.

"He has just seen his gods," Chon spoke, his words soft, careful not to disturb much of the night. "He will take some time to realize that everything was not as he believed."

Shoren nodded.

I am Shoren. Who was Jakob? He could barely remember.

"He will learn. He will come to understand."

Chon nodded. "You were careful with what you told him."

"I was."

A playful smile came to Chon's mouth. "You are much more than only an extension of the Maker," he laughed. "Yours and your kind defend much more than creation." The words were light, the subtle edge of respect tempered by the comfort of their friendship.

"It would have been too much for him," Shoren admitted. "I worry it was already too much for him."

Chon shook his head. "I think he will do well, Shoren. It was seen."

Yes, he knew it was seen. Had seen it himself.

I have?

The question came from a tiny part at the back of his mind.

I have.

"You must go with them now, Chon om'Salii Jonah. You must help him learn, help him to understand," Denmri said. His words soft, a whisper that became a part of the night instead of disturbing it.

Chon nodded. "Until the fibers bring us together again."

Shoren still saw things clearly. It no longer seemed strange.

When did it ever seem strange? He could no longer remember.

He watched as Chon made his way to the edge of the clearing, following the path Marli and Aalleyn had taken.

"It is good that he chose this path," Denmri said.

He nodded. None knew what it would have taken to find another.

"Our cousins watched from among the trees and found him to be pure," Denmri said.

Shoren found himself nodding again. "They were wise not to meet him yet. The shock might have scared him from what he must do."

"He will meet them in time."

Shoren smiled. Time. There was not enough of it. "Yes, he will need to. The requirements have been met. We must make him ready."

"He will be ready. Chon will be sure of it."

Shoren laughed at the idea of Chon working with Aalleyn. After all the years Chon had spent around Shoren's kind, the man did not see them as gods any longer. Would he be able to convince Aalleyn of the same?

Denmri's laughter joined in. Their voices floated out and joined the night.

Finally, Shoren sighed. "If only it could have been he."

Denmri laughed again. "Had it been so, my friend, would the colors along the path look so beautiful?"

"No, Denmri, they would have been plain, but sometimes the brightness of the colors can be distracting. We don't have time for distractions."

They sat for a while, and the night grew long around them. After a while, he saw Marli make her way back into the clearing. She moved slowly, gracefully even for one of their kind.

She is beautiful, he thought again.

"Shoren," he heard her begin as she neared. "Shoren..."

～

"Jakob!"

The word dragged lost memories forward, and he struggled to remember who he was.

Jakob. I'm Jakob!

He looked around the clearing. The stones were back the way they had been, scattered about the clearing. The night sky was dark, except for the bright fire blazing nearby.

It was dying when he fell asleep. Or was it?

He wasn't sure. Moments before he was sure he had been Shoren.

The dream had felt so real!

So real, he hadn't even thought it a dream.

Brohmin kneeled nearby and reached for him. Grabbing him by the shoulders, he shook him. "Wake up, boy!"

Jakob pushed him away. "I *am* awake!" He looked around again and noticed Salindra sitting not far from Brohmin, her eyes wide as she stared at him. "What is it?"

The two others look at him for a long time, silent. Finally, Brohmin spoke, "You were talking in your sleep."

The dream was fading from his memory, but remained vivid enough. "What was I saying?"

Brohmin shook his head and looked to Salindra. Her face had gone white. "I don't know. You were speaking in a tongue that I don't recognize."

Speaking in tongues. Like Scottan.

He felt the blood drain from his face. The madness.

But it was the ancient language. Wasn't it?

He could remember the way the words came off his tongue. He could almost speak them now if he put his mind to it. He could remember the way his mouth felt as it formed the words. What kind of dream does that?

No dream, he knew. The madness. He had dreamed himself a god. Would his fate be the same as Scottan's?

He could only hope to have enough time to bring the trunk to Endric before it struck him in full.

Salindra just stared at him.

Brohmin looked at him with a more measured expression. "What were you dreaming about?"

He shook his head. He was afraid they would call him mad and afraid they might be right. "I don't remember."

Brohmin smiled. It was a warm smile. Comforting. "Jakob, you can't wake up from a dream where you are speaking a strange language and tell us that you don't remember what it was about. Trust us a little."

Jakob looked at Brohmin, then back to Salindra.

If I'm mad, best they know.

"It was this clearing. Only different. The rocks there were in a circle, and I sat upon one of them." He looked out over to the rocks. It had seemed so real. *And I had been Shoren.* "It was night, or growing close to being night. A god came into the clearing."

"A god?" Brohmin asked.

"I think it was a god. They were unlike anyone else I have ever seen."

Brohmin nodded as though he simply accepted.

"Stranger still was that *I* was one of them. After a while, two men came into the clearing. One I knew. The other was unfamiliar to me, but I told him he had a special purpose, a special path we'd seen. Somehow, I knew all about this man. I told him he was going to bring about the end of some war." Jakob paused. "I told him he had been chosen."

Brohmin looked at him strangely. It made him feel odd about what he'd told them. He looked to Salindra whose face was nearly ashen now.

She must recognize the madness.

Brohmin looked back to the fire. It had begun to die again. "It's growing late. We have much to travel tomorrow."

Salindra nodded though she never took her eyes off him.

Brohmin helped the Mage woman unsteadily to her feet. They ambled over to where they were to make their camp. He helped her lie down, and then they spoke together in hushed whispers. The slow pulsing in Jakob's head had started again, and he knew he could strain and hear them, but did not. He didn't think he wanted to hear, anyway.

Jakob laid himself back down.

It was just a dream, he told himself. *Just a dream.*

Why did he fear it was something else?

CHAPTER THIRTY-ONE

W hen Novan opened his door, Alriyn eyed the historian carefully. The last time he had seen Novan, the man had been escorted from the city. Little had changed about him—he still had the same arrogant posture, the same pursed lips, the same too-knowing eyes. "You requested a meeting?" Alriyn asked.

Roelle had left a message in her uncle's quarters. He'd been avoiding the historian but worried about what would happen if he continued to ignore the man's request. What would he get Roelle into? He'd not known and chose to seek out the historian to ensure his niece's safety, especially with the task he'd set her on.

What would the Council think of the Magi patrolling the city with the Denraen?

Did they have other options?

No. None that were good. The *mahne* and the city must be protected. Roelle had proven capable, and he worried that it would not be the last time.

Novan nodded, his thin lips pursed in a tight line, neither smile nor frown. His hands played with a dark ring upon his finger as he answered. "I did." He stepped back from the door to allow Alriyn to enter, an annoying smirk on his face.

Alriyn felt his frustration grow. This man was nearly as difficult as Endric and half as useful. He would have ignored the historian if not for the knowledge he held. So far, he had kept his word—keeping the knowledge to himself. "What did you need?"

Novan tipped his head and raised his eyebrows, blinking his bright eyes slowly. "It is for what you need I summoned you."

"And what is that?"

Novan smiled. "I met Roelle."

"You traveled with her from Chrysia. She tells me you have a new apprentice."

"I do. An interesting boy with a quick mind."

"So I hear," Alriyn said.

Novan arched an eyebrow with the comment.

"Haerlin mentioned him," Alriyn offered. What would he do with that comment?

"Haerlin? And what did your minor prophet say?"

Alriyn struggled to contain his surprise. How could he know? "And where is he now?" Alriyn asked, changing course, wondering if Novan would answer truthfully.

Novan waved his hands. "North. He went to observe the Denraen."

"Observe what?"

"On that, you must ask Endric."

No clear answers would come from him, and Endric would be no different. "What do you need, historian?" Alriyn asked with more irritation than he intended coming through.

Novan chuckled. "Roelle spoke with me after she returned as well. She was seeking your Founders."

"What you shared has been kept to the Council for generations."

"Yes, but knowledge like that should be shared, not hidden," the historian stated. "The Magi should know the truth. Your Council hides the truth of the Founding from the Magi and in doing so, you remain unprepared."

Alriyn motioned to the two chairs in Novan's room. "The truth?" Alriyn asked him as they sat. "There are few who claim to understand the past and none who know the truth."

Novan raised a hand in objection. "I've read your texts. And others.

There was war then, a battle unlike any other. Something so terrible that only those with certain abilities were able to face it. There can be little doubt that the first Magi were soldiers, yet there have been no Magi soldiers since." He paused. "Until now."

Alriyn ignored Novan's last comment. "I know you've seen the texts." *But not the mahne.* Alriyn was certain the historian had not seen that sacred text. "And if you have read the texts then you know the rest."

"You became Urmahne."

"And laid down our swords," Alriyn agreed.

Novan grinned. "Did you never wonder what it was your ancestors faced?"

"Wonder?" Since his days as an apprentice, it had consumed him. "It is all I study. It was why I allowed Roelle to study with Endric in the first place."

"Ah," Novan said, mostly to himself, as if a question had been answered. "And what have you learned?"

"You've seen our records. They're vague. Some imply a war of men." He could speak of these things, knowing they were written elsewhere. "Others are stranger. The ancient threat. They talk of evil and destruction. And then stranger still there are those that mention a 'great beast,' a threat unlike no other man had faced. It was something few faced and survived."

Novan nodded. "Yet you have no description of this beast, no other accounts."

Alriyn shook his head. "And which is it—the mundane or the mystical?"

Novan smiled at the comment. "The mundane, I think, with hints of the mystical." He stood and paced, placing a long finger on his lips as he gathered his thoughts. "There is one record I have seen, one that stands out above the others, an old Antrilii writing..."

"The Antrilii do not leave records."

"All people leave records."

"They are nomads, wanderers," Alriyn said. *Antrilii* literally meant 'those who wander' in the ancient language. Would Novan know that?

"And watchers. Perhaps more. Regardless, there is a record, a document, describing creatures of the north, creatures unlike any others. They call them *groeliin*."

"Groeliin?" Alriyn knew the old language and knew the meaning. The word had rolled easily from Novan's tongue, and Alriyn wondered how much of the ancient language the historian knew. Few claimed more than a passing knowledge.

If he had found the *mahne*, could he have read it?

Alriyn suddenly considered the historian differently.

"The unseen," Novan translated. "Creatures of smoke and darkness, creatures of nightmare. Only men gifted by the gods could face them and live."

"And now they have returned."

Novan shook his head. Alriyn eyed him curiously, waiting for explanation.

"How do you know that they were ever gone?" Novan asked.

The historian was well traveled and knew much—perhaps more than Alriyn had given him credit for. "What do you know?"

Novan shook his head. "You traveled the north."

Alriyn hadn't realized that Novan discovered that he'd gone into the north. It didn't surprise him that he would learn. "When rumors began spreading..."

Novan smiled. "You had to see for yourself?" When Alriyn nodded, he said, "Why? There have always been stories about the north. Always the far north. Stories of people who have seen nothing, yet their loved ones go missing. That of towns deserted long before these recent attacks."

"These were different."

"Yes, different. And you went looking for answers."

Alriyn fixed him with a hard gaze. "What does this have to do with the Antrilii?"

They were a secretive tribe, warriors without a war, nomads about whom the Magi knew very little because they had very little contact. Some said Endric had lived with them once, but none could ever confirm that. Even the Denraen avoided the north, choosing to refrain from conflict with the Antrilii.

"I will keep the rest of their secrets, other than to say the *groeliin* did not disappear a thousand years ago."

Could Novan actually know what he'd sought for years? The historian he'd exiled from the city all those years ago? "What are they?" A lifetime of study on this topic, and the historian casually taunted him with his knowledge.

"There are some things you can only understand by experiencing firsthand. I fear the *groeliin* fall into this category. Evil. Darkness. The unseen. From what I've witnessed of the north, I don't know that any description does them justice."

"And you think this is what my Founders faced?"

Novan nodded.

"Why now?" he asked.

Novan considered the question for a long moment. "This danger has been kept in check for centuries. I do not yet know what has changed." He scratched his chin. "What did Roelle tell you of the Deshmahne?"

"That you've seen the High Priest," he answered, confused about the abrupt transition. What did the historian know? What was he keeping from him?

"Have seen? I've seen him before, but I didn't see him on this journey."

"But your apprentice—"

"Ah, well that is different. Jakob did see the High Priest. First in Chrysia and then again among the raiders."

"Why was he there?" Alriyn asked.

"They attacked the Urmahne temple, though I am not fully certain why."

Alriyn noted a troubled expression on Novan's face. "How do you know it was he?"

"Jakob felt him." Alriyn eyed him carefully and Novan grinned. "I see you understand."

"How did he feel him?" Alriyn asked. He knew what the historian meant; most among the Magi did, but would not have expected the historian to know of it.

There was a slight glimmer to Novan's eyes. "That, too, I don't know, though his father was a priest. There is no mistaking what he felt. 'I felt fear, hopelessness,' he said to me."

"That's one of their dark powers. Could the High Priest not simply have been radiating it intentionally?"

Novan shook his head. "No one else was affected."

That was surprising. The Deshmahne were suspected of using emotional attacks, pressing dark emotions upon others, but it was indiscriminate, affecting everyone around them. That anyone other than an Urmahne priest or a Magi sensed the Deshmahne without an attack was a surprise. They trained to be attuned to it.

"It is strange," Novan went on. "That the High Priest would be sensed once is surprising enough, but letting himself be sensed a second time is much more so. I still don't know why he was in the raider camp."

"Why do you say that?"

"It's said that he's not been seen outside the Deshmahne temple in over ten years," Novan answered. "And now twice by the same man."

"Their influence pushes north," Alriyn said. "We've fought to keep the Deshmahne from Thealon and Gom Aaldia."

A slight smile played at the corners of Novan's mouth. "An interesting choice of words."

"Do not mock me, historian. We do what we can. We protect the Urmahne."

"The priests protect the Urmahne. The Denraen protect the Urmahne."

"And we guide the priests," Alriyn argued.

"There was a time when you could claim that to be true." He looked at Alriyn with hard eyes. "If you still led the Urmahne, would there be a need for the Deshmahne? Had you not retreated from the world, would they have gained power?"

It was a question others had asked. The Deshmahne had first appeared over a hundred years ago, claiming the Urmahne was weak, that the gods demanded a new religion. They preached a different message from the *mahne*, where the gods looked favorably upon those with power, with strength. It was nothing like the peace the Urmahne preached, the balance the *mahne* required.

The Deshmahne had quickly demonstrated their strength in the south, pushing the Urmahne out of Coamdon and Lakeliis before the Ur could react. The Deshmahne priests had been the difference then, their strange speed and strength overmatching the common soldiers. The Urmahne priests and the Ur called upon the Magi for help, but the Council had chosen to observe, to let men handle their own affairs, as they had ever since their last failure.

Endric had guided the Denraen how he had felt fit, but by the time the Denraen had become involved, it was too late. They had been able to keep the Deshmahne to the south until now. The Deshmahne had been known to attack Urmahne priests but had never attacked the Magi before now. Something was changing.

"Why now?" Alriyn asked.

"That... is an excellent question. I have yet to find an answer."

"The timing of this and the happenings in the north has me uncomfortable," Alriyn admitted.

"As it should."

"Is there a connection?"

"I don't know," the historian answered.

Alriyn heard the hesitation in the historian's voice. "You suspect one, don't you?"

Novan nodded. "As should you."

CHAPTER THIRTY-TWO

A lriyn stepped along the corridor, replaying the conversation with the historian in his head. It had not gone as he had expected. What more does he know?

For so long, he'd believed Endric could manage the Deshmahne if it came to that. After what he'd seen in the north, he had to wonder if the Denraen could survive an attack by the Deshmahne. They'd lost countless men in the small skirmishes just returning the Magi to the city, which was why he'd encourage Roelle to use her knew skills to protect Vasha. If the Deshmahne turned this into a full-blown war...

Could the Urmahne survive a full-scale attack? They had been pushed to near irrelevance in the south, Coamdon and Liispal among the first to go, and now Gom Aaldia was weakening. Thealon would remain, but the Urmahne would be forever changed. What would that mean for the land? Certainly not the peace they'd known for the last thousand years.

The balance would be gone.

Alriyn knew what the *mahne* said about that and worried.

Would they return to what it had been like before? Information was limited. Most records of that time had been destroyed, all but fragments now lost to them. All records agree that violence and bloodshed had been more common then. True peace was brought by the Urmahne, by the discovery of the *mahne.* The Deshmahne would change all that.

Still, he couldn't ignore the north. Not if what they suspected was true. What he needed was to understand more, but where could he get more information? The historian had mentioned rumors, stories. And the Antrilii.

Alriyn shook his head, smiling. The Antrilii could not be the answer. They were simple nomads, warriors without a war.

But Novan seemed to know something more about them.

I need to find Endric.

He walked quickly through the palace and soon found himself outside. The day was overcast, the familiar low-lying clouds that surrounded the city shrouding everything in a light mist. Alriyn took a deep breath, savoring the distinct flavor of the air, before starting off. He took a circuitous route, choosing not to walk through the heart of the city on his way to the general, taking a roundabout way to the second terrace within the city. It would lead to fewer questions if he were not so easily seen seeking Endric.

His path toward the barracks led past the practice yard, and he paused. The clacking sound of wooden staves echoed dully to his ears, and he turned to look, wondering if Roelle was practicing. Scanning the yard, he saw several Denraen working together, and he looked past them, settling on the small group of taller Magi working together. They were clustered tightly in pairs, facing against each other, and Alriyn smiled at the sight.

There was a fluidity to their movements, a gracefulness different from even the Denraen, and he knew he'd been right to encourage Roelle. No longer could he doubt their physical abilities, no longer would he wonder. Were that he was younger and could stand among them, but it was not to be. Roelle must serve instead.

Alriyn had known his niece since she was barely months old and wondered if he would be able to let her do what needed to be done. Could he really think to let her face the Deshmahne in the city?

If I could do it...

Yet, he too must serve as the Urmahne intended.

The thought stayed with him as he passed the practice yard and neared the barracks where Endric's office was located. Alriyn found Endric standing outside the barracks, and the general gave him a wry look before nodding and leading him to his office, saying nothing until the thick door closed behind them.

"Second Eldest," he said finally, motioning to a seat.

Alriyn preferred to stand for now. "What have you heard of the Deshmahne?"

Endric looked up at Alriyn casually. "I presented what I knew to the Council."

Alriyn shot him a hard stare. "You presented little more than you had to," he countered. "You rarely do." Alriyn thought for a moment before he continued. "The Council is unsettled with these attacks. Most are afraid to act."

"So I have observed," Endric replied.

He should have expected Endric to know already. "Some see the Deshmahne as the only threat we face, others worry about other rumors."

Endric motioned to the chair in front of his desk and waited until Alriyn sat. "The Deshmahne have not fallen completely silent. Were that it was so simple. It appears they regroup in Gom Aaldia, gathering their strength, spreading their message."

"Adding followers," Alriyn mused.

Endric nodded. "They gain strength. Word is that Richard will convert."

Alriyn pondered that comment. If the High King converted, the Deshmahne would hold great strength in Gom Aaldia, perhaps to the point of forcing the conversion of the other kings. "With what I heard out of Rondalin, that leaves Thealon isolated," Alriyn said.

"It does," Endric agreed.

"The Ur will protect Thealon."

Endric shook his head. "The Ur will protect the Tower. The Ur defend the Urmahne and her priests."

"The priests are Thealon," Alriyn said.

"And you are the Urmahne."

Alriyn sighed. The argument felt circular, but Endric was right.

For too long, the priests had been left alone. There had been a time when the Magi guided the priests, teaching the *mahne*, shaping the Urmahne. That was when the Magi didn't merely hide in the city. The change had been gradual, but they no longer served as they once had. If they did, would the Deshmahne have grown so powerful?

"What will happen to Thealon if the Deshmahne come. Will you send Denraen for support?"

"The Deshmahne haven't moved against Thealon. It's almost as if they're waiting."

"Why?"

"I don't know. I have my suspicions, but I do not know." Endric looked at Alriyn, considering a moment. "You know they infiltrated the Denraen."

Alriyn returned the look, gray eyes weighing the general. "That should not be possible." He did not need to say that the Magi should have sensed a Deshmahne presence.

"Should not, but a recruit from Chrysia slipped through."

"You know this with certainty?"

Endric nodded.

"And where is he now?"

"Deserted. Left with the attacks."

"Is that why you suffered such a loss?" The other attacks had lost Denraen, but the one on Endric, the attack Roelle survived, had been the bloodiest.

Endric shook his head. "I think it the twenty Deshmahne we faced."

Twenty? Alriyn had not known it had been so many. "Was the High Priest among them?"

Endric shook his head again. "I think not."

"Did you see him?"

"No. The historian's apprentice was the only one who can make that claim."

"You would take his word?" Alriyn wished he could have met this apprentice and could have questioned him.

"I would take his word."

"Novan tells me he went north on your orders."

"Not my orders," Endric said. "But he went north."

"Why?"

"That's not mine for the telling," Endric said.

They fell silent, and Alriyn glanced around the office, taking in the stacks of books, the strange carvings set throughout the room, almost purposefully placed, and a large map of the known lands with pins marking various locations. There were pins marking the city, some for Thealon, others for other cities, yet why the markings to the northwest?

"Tell me of the Antrilii," Alriyn said suddenly. Stories said that Endric, once exiled by his father, had lived among the Antrilii. It was said that he mastered the sword while living amongst them.

"That, too, is not mine for the telling," Endric answered again.

Alriyn's eyes darted to the chart. "What do you know of the groeli-in?" Did Novan speak the truth? Could such creatures exist?

Endric placed his hands upon his desk and eyed Alriyn carefully. Alriyn resisted the urge to look away. "You *have* spoken with Novan."

Alriyn nodded.

"Then know that the historian doesn't lie. The threat is real, and if word reaches this far south, then it is greater than it has been in many generations."

"They are real?"

"You don't really doubt this. You visited the north yourself." The general smiled at him with a tight-lipped expression. "But there are those among your Council afraid to see this for themselves."

Alriyn no longer doubted, but the confirmation was what he wanted, what he needed. And more. Were these really the creatures his ancestors had faced?

If so, what did that mean of their teachings?

"What do the Antrilii know?"

"As I said, that's not mine for the telling. Nor Novan's." He stared at Alriyn for a long moment. "Other than to know that the groeliin should not have pressed as far south as they have." He sighed. "Regardless, I hope to learn more soon."

"How?"

Endric shrugged.

THE THREAT OF MADNESS | 321

"I have asked Roelle to aid with the Deshmahne in the city," Alriyn said.

"I have heard."

"She and the others could be of help to the Denraen."

"They could. As could the Council," Endric said before standing.

It was a dismissal. Alriyn was unaccustomed to such actions, yet he didn't think of protesting—it would serve no purpose. No, he had other concerns.

Why so secretive about the Antrilii? What else did they know?

Perhaps there was more to the north than these creatures.

CHAPTER THIRTY-THREE

The wind felt cool against Jakob's face. He stared ahead, eyes locked on the colors of the forest as they rode, ignoring the irritation at the back of his head. There remained much green to these trees for this time of year, the leaves not yet turning. The trees grew shorter the longer they rode, and he suspected they had camped the night before in the heart of the Great Forest. They rode north and east now.

"How far from the Elasiin path are we?" he asked.

"Not far. If that's the way you intend to take us, you should know the Elasiin is dangerous," Brohmin said.

Salindra's mouth curled in a worried frown.

Novan and Rit had said the same. Jakob had heard enough stories about the north that he wasn't sure whether he really wanted to follow the path. Would there be more Deshmahne there?

How else to Avaneam?

He didn't know. Without following the path, he might not meet Novan or Endric. The trunk had to be delivered, and he wasn't sure he could do it without them.

"It's the only way I know to find Endric or Novan," Jakob said.

Brohmin nodded. "We may need your sword."

If they followed the Elasiin path toward Siirvil's Peak, he would find Avaneam. That was enough. He hoped he'd find Endric and Novan before it mattered, before they came upon any danger, but how long would they wait for him? Could Brohmin pass on word to the Conclave that he'd been captured? Jakob was unclear how the Conclave operated, but somehow, Novan had arranged for Brohmin's help. Did that mean Novan and Endric were no longer coming?

The sun overhead didn't generate much warmth as the day stretched on, and Jakob was thankful for his cloak. There was an earthy scent to the air, the smell of rotting leaves mixing with the crispness to the air that hung in his nose. He had noticed it more strongly this morning when they had camped at the heart of the forest, but it continued. There was something comforting about it, though he couldn't say what.

Brohmin rode off occasionally, disappearing several times during the day only to return, looking more harried each time. "They gain on us," he overheard Brohmin tell Salindra once.

"How many?" she asked.

"They come from the west and the south, almost too many to keep track. They're riding hard."

"What do you see?" Jakob asked.

Brohmin leveled his gray eyes on Jakob, sharp and piercing. "There are several Deshmahne."

Jakob felt a sudden sickness in the pit of his stomach. "How many?" Could they even survive another Deshmahne attack?

"I counted thirteen. It worries me."

Thirteen. He and Brohmin wouldn't stand a chance against so many. "Is the priest with them?"

Brohmin nodded once.

Jakob felt his heart sink. He didn't think he could face the large Deshmahne again.

"Why does that number worry you?" Salindra asked.

"Little is known about how the Deshmahne are organized," Brohmin started. "They're secretive. None have become Deshmahne and left, yet this number strikes me as intentional. Unlucky. There were three with you when you were captured?" Brohmin asked Jakob.

He nodded.

Brohmin considered a moment before speaking. "How many the other times?"

Jakob thought about the attack on the camp but didn't know how many men were Deshmahne and how many simple raiders. The attack on Rit's party was at least one Deshmahne, perhaps two if he counted Tolsin. Most recently, the three Deshmahne had first chased him and then captured him. "At least one the first time, three the next," he said. "I don't know how many were in Rondalin when I ran from there."

"One then three," Brohmin repeated. "And now thirteen." He fell silent before letting out a frustrated sigh. "I don't know what it means." His dark eyes fell on Salindra, but she didn't meet them, keeping her own eyes locked forward. "We should ride faster."

"What of the north?" Salindra asked, her usually stern voice tight.

"We'll face that as it comes."

Brohmin spurred the horses forward. They rode hard through the late morning and into the afternoon. Jakob found his thoughts returning to the slow itch at the back of his mind, the gentle vibration that would not leave him, and the strange dream from the night before.

As he did, he couldn't shake the memory of how the madness had started with Scottan. First had been strange voices. Then there were things only he could see. And now... now he was more mad than sane.

There was no use denying it any more. This was how the madness would take him. The only question he had remaining was whether he would have enough time to get the trunk to Avaneam safely—or at least to Endric.

After a while, Brohmin slowed his horse. "You're troubled. You've been quiet."

Jakob swallowed, wondering how much to share. Didn't Brohmin deserve some trust? "The dream last night. It's... it's enough to make me think I'm going mad." Let them know about his fears. "I've seen it happen before. My brother suffered from it."

"You aren't mad, Jakob. Everyone dreams."

He looked over to Brohmin. The man's gray hair and gray-black eyes attempted comfort. He shook his head in response. "Not dreams like those. Not dreams where you speak the ancient language."

Brohmin eyed him a moment. "True enough. But we were in a place of power. Many people have strange experiences there."

His was no mere strange experience. "I dreamed I was a god, Brohmin!" His voice rose a little as he spoke. Salindra looked back briefly, cocking an eyebrow before turning her attention back to the path.

Brohmin chuckled again. "And no ordinary god, either. A god among gods. You spoke the name *Shoren*."

The word flowed from Brohmin's lips, as if familiar. He wondered what else of the ancient language Brohmin understood.

Shoren.

That had been his name. The memories Shoren possessed had been *his* memories, if only during the dream. He could still remember what Shoren knew, what he wanted, if only he closed his eyes and let his mind go back to that night.

"When you spoke the name *Shoren*..." Brohmin looked at him carefully. He felt the weight of the gaze. "It's a name I recognized. Not many would, but I did."

Jakob would soon know the extent of his madness. That was what Brohmin was about to share with him.

"You're from Chrysia?" Brohmin's voice suddenly took on a different tone, one that reminded Jakob of Novan when he lectured.

He nodded.

"Chrysia is in Thealon. In the capital city of Thealon is the Tower. The Urmahne speak of the Tower of the Gods as the house of the gods. And quite possibly, they're right. Who's to know for certain?"

They rode in silence for a bit before Brohmin finally continued. "Thealon was once known by another name. It's a name long forgotten, one from before the destruction. Little is known about the time before then. Most of the histories have been lost, only fragments found. Some remain. A city mentioned many times was the city *Shoren Aimeilen*." Again, the words flowed comfortably from his tongue. "A city ancient texts refer to as a powerful city. Powerful with the strength and proximity of the gods."

Jakob startled when he heard the name. A thought floated through his mind, something he remembered.

Aimeilen was beautiful too.

He shook it off, hoping Brohmin didn't notice.

How do I know this?

The madness. It was the only explanation.

"It can be none other than Thealon of today. Of what was destroyed during the destruction, no damage ever came to the Tower. A powerful place." The statement seemed almost to himself. Brohmin stared off as his tone had become almost one of reverence near the end.

They rode on for a time before he continued. The trees were spaced less closely together here, and it was easier for the horses to move more quickly.

"Some fragments speak of a powerful being living in the city of *Shoren Aimeilen*. One known only as *Shoren*." The words were quiet, and Jakob suspected Brohmin did not share this knowledge with many. "It is said he lived *in* the Tower."

"But the gods had no names!"

"Do you believe that, or do you think we just don't know them?"

Jakob sat quietly for a while. "But if he was known as Shoren, that could only mean..."

Brohmin nodded.

"Was he more powerful than the other gods?" Jakob asked.

A shake of the head was Brohmin's first reply. "We know little of the time before the destruction or of the gods. That which remains is kept by the Magi," Brohmin said. The stiffness of Salindra's spine let on that she listened. "It's often difficult to read these fragments that remain. The language is mostly lost."

Salindra looked back at him then. "How is it you know of this?"

Brohmin smiled broadly, yet there was an undercurrent of irritation in his expression. "How is it that you do not?"

She shook her head. "There are sections of the library restricted to the Council."

"And they have used what they've learned so wisely."

His last words hung in the air as they continued in silence, the sound of the horses' hooves along the forest floor the only noise breaking the quiet. After a while, a thought came to Jakob.

"For Shoren to have the city named after him?" he asked, his voice sounding loud as he broke the silence.

"A god among gods," came Brohmin's reply.

A god among gods?

What did this mean for him?

If Shoren was real, did that mean the rest of the dream was real? How is it he had dreamed of him? No answers came, only more questions and one worried him more than the others.

Had his other dreams been real?

~

The rest of the day went slowly for Jakob. Brohmin rode off several more times, and each time, he returned to spur them on more quickly. The sun seemed to take forever to reach its midday peak, and then even longer as it made its way back down behind them. The three rode in silence much of the time, a few terse words spoken as they stopped for lunch.

The stop was brief. Brohmin seemed more and more concerned as they rode. How close were the Deshmahne now? Brohmin didn't offer, but his terseness provided enough of an answer.

As the day grew longer, Brohmin slowed his horse to ride next to Jakob. It was a welcome distraction from the steadiness of the green and brown that surrounded them, the underlying buzz in the forest, of the birds singing and the insects chirping.

"We should reach the town of Fristin tonight," Brohmin said. "Those who follow are now several hours back." His voice was a hushed whisper, and the ever-waning afternoon light cast strange shadows about his face. It made his eyes even more hollow and aged. "We may find rest indoors tonight, but it will likely be the last for a while."

Jakob nodded and let the silence return.

Brohmin continued to ride by his side. "Tell me about your blade," Brohmin said, catching him off guard.

"It was my great-father's," he started, opting to share the truth. "It's been passed through my family for years; my father only gave it to me a few weeks before I started this whole journey."

"Surely you held steel before then."

"My brother was one of the Ur. He used to teach me before..."

"Before what?" Brohmin urged.

Best to tell them now if he was showing signs. "The madness took him."

Brohmin frowned. "You spoke of madness before. Explain."

"I thought you knew."

"Knew what?"

How could he explain the madness? Did he tell him what happened to Scottan? Should he explain what was happening to him?

Salindra saved him from having to answer. "The madness has little explanation. I've seen it myself, seen how it strikes, taking men and women in their prime, rendering them shells of themselves. It's like an illness, taking vitality, strength, and sanity. We've not discovered much more of it."

"I haven't heard of this. How long has this plague been spreading?" he asked.

"I first saw it years ago," Salindra answered, "but it's said to have always been around."

Brohmin frowned again but said nothing at first. Finally, he turned back to Jakob. "You learned the sword from your brother?" Jakob nodded. "And then you met Endric?"

"When the Magi came to the city with the Denraen, I met Endric in the practice yard one afternoon. I didn't know he was the Denraen general, only that he'd work with me."

"I'm not surprised that he did." He gave Jakob a thoughtful, yet perplexed look. "You've learned from your brother and from Endric, but how can it be that you wield a sword better than any man I have seen in years?"

"I... I can't explain it." He'd never been skilled with the sword before working with Endric. "Endric always had something new to show me, and so I was always learning new catahs, understanding how to move, how to think."

"I'm sure. Even he must have commented on your quick mastery."

Jakob was uncertain what to say.

"Tell me about you blade," Brohmin asked again. "I have never seen its like."

"I don't know much about it, only that it' s an old sword. There are letters scrawled upon it, letters I think Novan could read." He decided not to describe the shapes upon the hilt. He was not even sure if he could describe them.

Brohmin stared at him, probably waiting for an invitation to look at it. Finally, he said, "May I see it?"

As Jakob pulled it from the scabbard, his arm tingled, racing up into his skull and the slow ever-present pulsing hummed louder. With it, the colors around him were brighter, and the sounds of the forest were louder. He held on to the pulsing as he passed the sword to Brohmin. The edge that seemed to pull light away from the sky made it seem incredibly dark. The other side blazed brilliantly in contrast. Did the others see what he saw?

Brohmin's eyes slid carefully up and down the length of the blade, scanning one side and then the other, before moving up along the hilt and pommel. He looked intently at the pommel for long moments before looking up. "*Neamiin.*" He spoke the word fluidly, familiarly.

How much does Brohmin know?

How much did he understand from Jakob's dream?

"A fitting name." He looked at the sword again. "There is more here, but I suppose you have already learned of that," he said, looking up at Jakob.

He hadn't, but he nodded just the same.

"And something else," he started, looking back down and squeezing the leather wrappings of the hilt with one hand. "Shapes of some kind beneath." He handed the sword back to Jakob, catching his eye.

Jakob took it gently and sheathed it, holding on to the tingling as he did so.

"There's more to you than I thought." Then, almost to himself, Brohmin said, "More than I had been told." The words were barely audible, so Jakob was not even sure he heard him correctly.

Brohmin fell silent, and after a while, moved his horse forward again to ride with Salindra. Jakob didn't listen, choosing instead to watch the forest move around him. He became aware of the constant itch in the back of his mind and let his eyes dart around, but it was a half-hearted effort. Jakob had never seen anything. If it *was* the madness, there was nothing he could do about it now.

The green and brown of the forest began to blur past them, the forest thinning as they rode north and the trees grew more stunted. Small bushes now dotted the landscape as a path opened up before them. Jakob watched the sun fall behind the horizon, taking the rest of the daylight as it did. As the sky darkened, the sounds of the forest changed. Once, he heard the low howl of an animal far in the distance. He didn't recognize the sound.

Was that a merahl?

Brohmin had been quiet, pushing them hard. The sky overhead was nearly dark when he called back to Jakob. "Another hour ride or so."

The horses seemed to sense their urgency; their tired bodies pushed their limits and ran even faster. With the faded light, Jakob found himself entrusting more and more to the vision of his horse and the direction of Brohmin. He could only just make out the two ahead of him, and that was with the slow pulsing in his head. Would he see anything without it?

There was a thin sliver of moon tonight, and stars occasionally peeked through the cloudy sky, but otherwise, it was dark. There was a moistness to the air, thick with the scent of fall and the threat of a coming storm. The constant feeling of being watched grew worse, and Jakob slowly became tenser. His horse must have felt it as well; he jumped every so often as a strange sound in the woods startled him. Jakob struggled to stay steady in the saddle.

Unexpectedly, he began to make out the shapes of houses and other small buildings as they approached a wall circling a town. Low, about waist-high, he suspected the wall was more for peace of mind than for defense.

Fristin. But why were there no lights in the windows?

With the thought, he heard Brohmin call out, "Hold!"

It was a rough whisper, not loud enough to be heard in the small village. He moved his horse nearer to Salindra as Brohmin rode ahead. They sat quietly, waiting, staring off into the darkness of the village. The sounds of the night stretched on, unaware of their presence. Jakob resisted the urge compelling him to look around, knowing he'd see nothing. Salindra's hands trembled slightly as they clutched the reins, and a small bead of perspiration glimmered in the pale light of the moon upon her face.

Why would a Mage be nervous?

He glanced around, wondering how far back the Deshmahne were now. The small wall was not imposing and would not slow them. Would they continue their pursuit into the night? Through the night?

A shape rode toward them, and Jakob's hand drifted to the hilt of his sword until he could see Brohmin as he signaled them to follow. Jakob kicked his horse forward. Salindra paused a few moments before falling in behind.

They circled around the low wall until reaching a hard-packed path on the northwest edge leading into the town. They rode through the entrance and moved quickly along the road, not stopping until they reached the center of town. A large, single-story building blocked passage further along the road.

"We will stay in town tonight," Brohmin said in a hushed whisper.

"Here?" Salindra asked.

Brohmin nodded a reply and climbed down from his saddle. Jakob followed, grabbing the trunk from the back of the saddle. As he did, he tried to keep his movements quiet. Something about Brohmin's mood called for caution.

"In the hall?" Salindra questioned further.

Another nod from Brohmin. He looked up at her and said, "The town is empty. The entirety of the town." Salindra's eyes widened slightly. "Some didn't bother to take anything with them."

Salindra shook her head. "This far south, Brohmin? That can't be!" Her tone was anxious, and her voice struggled to remain quiet.

What would make the Mage nervous? Worse, what would make Brohmin nervous?

The Elasiin path is dangerous, he remembered.

"Perhaps they will slow the Deshmahne," Brohmin said. His tone made it clear he didn't think it likely.

"What is this? Why is this town empty?" Jakob whispered.

Salindra looked expectantly to Brohmin who shook his head. "Go inside." Brohmin took hold of the reins of Jakob's horse and motioned him inside the building. "We won't light a fire, but wait for me in the main hall in front of the fireplace. I'll stable the horses."

Salindra nodded and grabbed Jakob's elbow, guiding him toward the door. Heavy oaken doors opened softly, and they stepped carefully into the hall. Salindra pulled the doors mostly closed behind them, leaving one cracked. Light from the moon filtered in, barely enough to see by, and they stood just inside the doorway as their eyes adjusted.

After a time, Jakob could make out a few features of the room. They stood in a large chamber that seemed to take up most of the building. Maybe a meeting chamber for the town. He could make out some dark doorways along the walls, made all the darker with the contrast of the night. In the back of the main room was the fireplace Brohmin mentioned, and Jakob started to make his way toward it. Salindra lit a candle, providing a small amount of light. It was not much, but more than enough to make his steps a little more surefooted.

He reached the fireplace, a light lining of soot covering everything within except for the few well-placed logs that had not been lit. A light layer of dust covered them. Jakob stared into it, part of him longing to light the heavy logs, welcoming the heat they would bring.

"What is this, Salindra?" Jakob whispered.

She shook her head. "I hope you don't come to know."

Jakob stared through the darkness, trying and failing to make out her expression. "What happened here?"

There was a long pause before she answered. "They left. To Rondalin and safety."

Rondalin. Jakob had seen the makeshift buildings outside the city walls, more people than he could imagine cramped together. That was safety? He'd run through the crowded streets, but what could send a whole town away?

Another thought interrupted the last: How many towns were there like this?

He couldn't imagine. What would do this? What would cause these people to leave their homes for some strange city? What was along the Elasiin path?

Brohmin came in not much later. He stepped lightly through the room until he reached them, puffing out the candle as he did. "No light." His face was stern, almost angry as he crossed the room.

Salindra nodded and didn't argue.

Jakob stood still, his muscles stiff with tension, unsure what was around him, until Brohmin tapped him lightly on the shoulder. "Get some sleep. This is a safer place than the woods," the man whispered in his ear. It was barely audible.

He nodded and opened his mouth to say something, but felt a hand cup over his face.

"Safer than the woods," he heard barely whispered again.

Lying down, pangs of worry and fear began to eat at him. Dust from the floor plumed up as he lay down, tickling his nose and making him think he might sneeze. What was Brohmin keeping from him? This was more than the Deshmahne. He wasn't sure how he was going to sleep this night, though his muscles ached, and he was exhausted from it.

Slowly, a heavy presence came over him. His nerves, he supposed. He was tense but couldn't exactly pinpoint the source. Jakob tried taking deep breaths to relax, but couldn't. His breathing was hard, loud in the quiet of the night. So loud, it would keep him awake if he couldn't calm his breathing. It would be a long, tense night if he couldn't sleep.

Sleep did come, albeit fitful. Strange and vivid dreams floated just at the edge of his consciousness. Once, he awoke to strange sounds outside the hall, close enough to have been from within the town. At first, he had thought them only his dream, just another part of the strange hallucinations he'd been having at night, but realized he was awake. The heavy feeling was worse this time, almost a squeezing tightness in his chest. Jakob struggled to breathe and relax. It was not easy.

He drifted off again, more slowly this time. He awoke later to the strange noises, closer this time, and he wasn't sure how long he'd been sleeping since last he had heard the sounds. The smells of old rot drifted at the edge of his awareness, hidden by the thick dust covering everything in the room. The feeling of the weight upon his chest was gone.

Jakob saw the door crack open slightly. Brohmin slipped out into the dark night, closing the door behind him. As he lay there staring at the door, he thought he'd see the man slip back in shortly after, but so much time passed by that he drifted back to sleep.

He woke again to a different sound. A light shuffle, as if something dragged across the floor, was barely audible. It sounded close, within the hall, and he stared intently into the darkness trying to make out a shape. He couldn't see anything in the blackness.

The sound neared, and his heart raced.

It took every ounce of his will to keep from bolting toward the door, toward the light of the moon so he could see this assailant.

Still, it came closer. The hairs on his arms rose as the sound neared, and he could hear his heart loud in his ears. Likely, whoever or whatever was there could hear his heart nearly as easily as he could.

Finally, the sound stopped.

He lay still, listening. After a while, his heart still racing and thundering in his ears, he heard a new sound. He heard whispering. Brohmin and Salindra.

He couldn't make out what they were saying, and for a moment struggled to hear. Brohmin whispered something about his shoulder, then Salindra muttered something about wrappings.

"You should have taken the boy and his sword. The two of you would have been a more even match." The words were spoken so quietly, he wasn't even sure he'd heard them right.

But he did hear Brohmin's reply. He was sure of it. "He wouldn't even be able to see them. Besides, it was a small band, and I was more than a match for them."

"Barely," Salindra replied.

What was out there?

Was this Deshmahne... or something else?

What would cause entire towns to desert?

The conversation troubled him as he lay there, his pounding heart gradually slowing and the tightness in his muscles easing. The whispering either stopped or became so quiet he couldn't hear it anymore, and after a while, he felt himself drifting toward sleep again. He welcomed it in his exhaustion.

If he dreamed, he did not remember it.

CHAPTER THIRTY-FOUR

The long hall was nearly silent. Even the echoes from their footsteps seemed muted as they walked quickly along the stone corridor. As they passed each intersecting hall, Alriyn darted his eyes suspiciously down the length of the hall before turning them ahead once again. To his left, Crayn did the same. They saw nothing.

Alriyn didn't need to look closely at Crayn to see that the man was nervous. He'd been at this long enough that it no longer affected him in the same way. A small bead of sweat worked at the corner of the man's right eye. Creases worked across his forehead, and Alriyn would occasionally catch the man working his hand along his black robe, clenching fingers into a white-knuckled fist before releasing.

Crayn's eyes seemed too deeply set, almost hollowed out of his face, yet more so today than usual. It was a distinctive feature Alriyn had always associated with him. A face he could always recognize. He was average height for one Mageborn, and his hair was a well-aged gray. Much the same color as his own. He was of slight build, seemingly willow thin, but the man's real strength was his mind. It was a strength they would need now more than ever.

Crayn had always been someone whose opinion Alriyn trusted. It seemed strange that it had taken them this long to bring the man into the private council, though he had done what he'd thought best. When they moved their cause forward, everyone would be forced to make a choice. That choice would come to define their people, especially if they failed.

After speaking with Endric, he felt even more strongly they needed to choose the Uniter. Doing so meant convincing enough of the Council, but would he have enough numbers? Could they convince Jostephon as well? If they didn't their cause would fail.

Lost in thought, their steps had carried them quickly to the door of his private chambers. Pausing, he glanced up the hall again, his dark eyes squinting carefully into the shadows. Had he seen movement? The hall was empty and silent. Crayn gave him a curious look, and Alriyn nodded slightly before pulling the door open.

His room was arranged the same as it had been for the last few months. Two small candles seemed to be burning, though appeared to have been lit on air. Neither wick burning nor wax melting could be seen from these candles. A crackling fire burned in the corner of the room, its warmth comforting. The dim light was enough for him to glance quickly at the four faces around the table. Karrin and Bothar sat against the far wall, silent, while Haerlin sat with his back to them. Isandra sat next to him and leaned across the table to Karrin, whispering something quietly to her. They all turned toward the door as Alriyn entered.

"Before we talk about the reason we're all here, I would like to know what you've seen of the delegates." In some ways, convincing the rest of the Council to make this choice would be easier if the delegates failed, but Alriyn didn't *want* them to fail. If the delegates could begin the process of regaining trust in the Magi, then they would be useful.

Haerlin sat upright, tapping his finger on his chin. "I have seen some darkness among them."

Bothar blinked. "You have observed or *seen*?"

Haerlin frowned. "Partly, it is observation. I traveled with Comity —not our first choice of delegate. The priest we intended to choose was killed in the temple explosion. What I have observed of him is disinterest. Those in the south worry me more. They have already experienced the Deshmahne and think nothing of them."

Karrin nodded. "That is the way of the south these days. Many have converted."

"Have you seen anything?" Alriyn asked Haerlin.

He took a deep breath. "There's nothing clear. Occasionally, when I stare long enough, there's an aura around them. Some more strongly than others." He shook his head and smoothed his robes. "I don't know what it means other than that we need to continue to watch them."

"If the delegates won't serve as we intend, what else do we know?" Karrin asked.

"I hear rumors out of the university. Teachers have returned from the south, fearing how unsettled it has become," Bothar said.

"And they already move north," Karrin said. "I received word that Gom Aaldia prepares for war. Rumor has it they will soon ride on Thealon."

Alriyn frowned. Endric had mentioned the same. "They gain strength in Gom Aaldia," Alriyn agreed. Faces turned to look at him. "I spoke to Endric," he explained. "It's often less difficult to argue with a Mage than it is to talk with that man. He's vague, knowing there's trouble with the Deshmahe, but won't commit to his plan. He shared with me what he knows of the north. It's enough that we must convince the others on the Council to—"

The door to the room pushed open, and two figures slipped in, hastily closing the door behind them.

Alriyn stared at the shapes by the door, unable to see who was there, and excited the *manehlin* so that the wall glowed brightly.

"Endric. Novan." How had they known he was here? And why had they come?

The general smiled, unaffected by what would have scared any other man to soil himself. "Second Eldest," he replied, before looking to the others. "Councilors," he nodded to each. "Is the Council divided?"

"Not divided, Endric. Discussing what you shared."

"You intend to choose again, don't you?" Novan asked.

Alriyn glared at him. Damn the historian! "How did you come to this room, General?" Alriyn asked.

"I walked, Second. I suspect you all do the same? In fact, I have observed a few among you walking today, spending time with the delegates when you should be searching the city for Deshmahne."

"I have asked Roelle to help with the Deshmahne," Alriyn said.

He felt the others look to him. He hadn't shared that yet. He might have been too impetuous, but with her Magi skill and newfound skill with the sword, she was best suited.

"Alriyn?" Karrin asked.

"Is that why you allow the apprentices to train?" Haerlin asked.

Endric raised his hand, silencing them. "Roelle has the heart of a leader. She would make a fine Denraen."

Strangely, the comment gave Alriyn a flash of pride. "She is an excellent Mage," Alriyn agreed.

"There would be other ways you could use her," Endric suggested. "She could be of use in the north—"

Alriyn shook his head vigorously. "No! I have seen what happened in the north. If what you've said about the north is real, then there is nothing the Magi could do."

"I think you do a disservice to your people—and to Roelle—in saying that," Endric said.

"She and the others will search the city for Deshmahne. That is how they will serve. Besides, what would she find in the north but these creatures and the Antrilii?"

Karrin whispered the word "Antrilii" but Alriyn ignored her.

"Answers," Novan said.

"Who's?" Alriyn asked.

"Everyone's."

Alriyn sat back, considering. If Roelle left the city—and these creatures were real—she would be faced with a nightmare. No. Better that they unify the Council, find the Uniter—the *nemah*—who could bring peace.

"We will deal with Deshmahne first," Alriyn said. "And the Council will make other decisions."

Endric stared a moment before nodding. "Do what you must and know that I will do what I feel is necessary."

With that, Endric turned and left. Novan lingered, his gaze skimming over the collected Councilors before he turned and followed Endric from the room.

Alriyn sighed, and turned back to the others. "It seems we will be forced to make a decision sooner than I expected," he said.

"What decision?" Crayn asked.

"Whether to choose the Uniter. Endric is right about that threat. The Council needs to act. If we don't, the peace required of the *mahne* might fail."

"And if we do, *we* might fail," Haerlin said.

Alriyn looked at the others, holding their gaze. "With the growing threat of the Deshmahne, isn't that a risk we have to take?"

~

Roelle sat in Endric's office again, having actually been summoned by Endric after one of her practice sessions with the Denraen. Sweat dripped from her brow, and she wiped it away, scanning the room. The stacks of paper were as unorganized as before. He even risked a candle, as if unmindful of the danger to his pages. The map behind him seemed changed, the pins having moved. She waited for him to speak, growing impatient.

"I hear your uncle has a plan for you," Endric said.

"A plan, yes," she began. What would Endric think of the plan? "He —and I—think my Magi can be useful to you here with the Deshmahne."

Endric stared at her, his hard-eyed gaze intense. "I don't need you for the Deshmahne."

"I saw how hard they were to defeat, general. You need the Magi." Alriyn had *asked* for her help with them. Why would the general deny her this?

"Really? How many do you think you have?"

Roelle looked at the old general. His shrewd eyes saw through her, and Roelle forced herself to hold the gaze. "We have at least one hundred."

Endric leaned back in his chair, arms crossed over his chest, and nodded slowly. "One hundred. I have thousands of Denraen, Roelle. No. You aren't needed here."

Roelle sat back in the chair, feeling defeated. She'd thought that Endric would welcome her help—why else summon her here?—but if he wasn't interested, then what would she do? She couldn't sit back and remain in her classes, not after what she'd seen.

"Did you learn of your Founders?" he asked.

She blinked at the sudden change in topic. "I learned they fought something terrible, and that Novan thinks it still exists. My uncle isn't certain."

Endric offered a half-smile. "You don't believe?"

"The rumors from the north are probably Deshmahne."

"Is that what you really think?"

She didn't know *what* she believed. Novan seemed to think there was something else, but the record he would have referenced would have to be centuries old. They couldn't be accurate.

"Leave the Deshmahne to the Denraen. There is something else that you can do."

"What?"

"Take your Magi and visit the north. Learn for yourselves what is there."

"I don't think Alriyn will allow us to leave the city, not with the attacks taking place."

"Trust me when I tell you that this is something you should consider. Besides, you're better prepared than the Second would be. Your Magi training may help, but it's the *other* training that will matter."

Roelle sat, twisting her hands together. "Why do you ask this of me?"

"Your Founders survived something most don't even understand. There are times I wish we could have their guidance, but we do not." Endric sighed quietly before straightening himself. "But you are better prepared than they had been in so many ways."

"How do you figure?" she asked. Would Endric offer a straight answer?

Endric grunted. "Different training. They were soldiers first. You are Magi first."

"Does that matter?"

Endric shrugged. "I don't know. I have asked the Second, but he worries more about the Deshmahne."

"And you don't?"

"The Deshmahne are the Denraen's responsibility. What is taking place in the north… that is for the Magi. You need to prove it to the Council. You might be the only one who can."

Could they do this? There were nearly one hundred young Magi who had learned sword and staff over the last year. All had followed Roelle and Selton, thinking, as Roelle had at first, a fun game to play at soldier. The battle with the Deshmahne had changed that.

Now there was something more at stake, and they were the only Magi prepared to face it. Even were they to remain in the city as Alriyn wanted, she didn't know if the young Magi understood fully what they were getting themselves into. Would they fight if attacked?

That was the question. Most had regularly been practicing, and all had grown quite skilled. Their Magi abilities granted them a certain physical prowess. But skill with a weapon and skill in actual combat were very different. Roelle had nearly frozen in her first encounter. How many others would face the same?

But going north might be even worse. Or nothing.

"You have heard the stories of the north?" Endric asked.

She nodded. "Alriyn tells me of the north, the desolation, the fear, the crowds of people moving south for safety, and I wonder what happens if there is no safety."

"The rumors are true, Roelle. There are few who can face the threat of the north."

"Why us?"

Endric glanced over his shoulder at the wall. "Consider it scouting only. Bring information back for your council. It will force the Magi to act."

"If we do this—"

"Your Council will think it the rash action of youth. Much like when you first came, looking to learn the sword and staff." The general tilted his head and considered her for a moment before flashing his teeth. "Not much surprises me, Mage, but you have managed."

"We're only apprentices," Roelle said. Could she really be considering his suggestion?

Could they really afford for her not to?

"Apprentices who are more like your Founders than any Mage in generations. You would have my guidance, as much as could be, and"—he handed Roelle a thin leather-bound book—"the wisdom of those who came before you can help you along your way."

Roelle stared at the cover. *Tactics and Strategy*, written by none other than Endric's father, Dendril. It was a prized possession, and only two copies were known to exist. One was in her hands now. The other was hidden in the Mage library where only the Elders had access.

"It's a quick read, but a lifetime study," Endric said.

Roelle had no answer. Endric offered her the wisdom of his father. "I don't know what to say."

"Say you'll make your Founders proud. Say you'll travel as the gods guide you. Say you'll honor what you have just said to me," Endric replied. "It will be enough."

How could she refuse?

What would she say to Alriyn?

There could be nothing she could say that would explain her reasoning. Besides, if he had seen the north, he would already understand.

Roelle nodded in agreement.

"Good. There are other ways I can help. First, you'll work with me daily until you leave," Endric decided.

Roelle frowned and felt a moment of surprise. Training with Endric had been a given along the road—it was a tradition the Denraen honored—but within the city, he had many pulls upon his time. It was a generous offer, and she doubted it was lightly made.

"Choose a handful you trust. They will work with my Raen, learn to lead others. And I will send guides."

"Guides?" Roelle asked, letting the other offer slide past with merely a nod of acceptance.

"How much have you traveled outside your city?"

"If the rumors are true, they'll be of little help," she told Endric.

"They could help more than you know. And you must seek the Antrilii first."

"Why the Antrilii?"

"Because you will find your answers there."

Roelle smiled, leaning forward. "You could *tell* me the answers."

"There are things you must witness to understand, Roelle. It is much the same for your Council. If you do this, you will see what I mean. You will gain more insight than you could have ever expected."

She waited for him to say more, but he didn't. "And what of you? You're not going to return north as you said you would? You're not going after Jakob?"

Endric eyed her. "That was my intent. The historian presses me to leave soon, but there's something here I must take care of first. If you reach Jakob first..."

She nodded. "He can come with us."

Endric shook his head. "No. He has another purpose. Send my encouragement instead. I hope one day I will have a chance to know him better."

"Me too," she whispered, a flush working through her cheeks.

They were silent for a time, and Roelle prepared to leave. "There are rumors you worked with the Antrilii."

Endric nodded.

"What are they like?"

He laughed softly. "You fear them?" She nodded. "There are many misunderstandings about the Antrilii. If you find them, you will see that you have more in common than you think. Now. Make your preparations, and I will make mine."

As she stood, she wondered if she had made a mistake in agreeing to go north, but she had the sense that were she to remain in Vasha, Endric wouldn't have allowed her to fight. At least this way, she and the other Magi could be useful, and that was all she really wanted.

CHAPTER THIRTY-FIVE

The sound of quiet conversation stirred Jakob from sleep. The doors to the hall were thrown open, and the light of the early morning trickled in, casting a small amount of light throughout the hall. A single stout table was the only furnishing in the room. Brohmin and Salindra leaned against the far edge of the fireplace, locked in quiet conversation.

He stood and stretched, knots in his back aching and a slight headache coming with the slow pulsing within his skull. Jakob tried to ignore both but found he couldn't ignore the pain in his back. Brohmin noticed him and stood slowly, somewhat haltingly, and limped toward him. There was something wrong with his left leg; it moved stiffly, dragging slightly across the floor as he walked, and his face looked haggard. Lines crossed his already wrinkled face, and his eyes were duller than they'd ever seemed before. He looked very old this morning.

"Are you all right, Brohmin?" What had he missed last night?

Brohmin stared at him dazedly for a long moment before finally replying, "Yes." It was all the answer he would give. "We ride soon. Gather your things." Brohmin hobbled toward the door, disappearing into the early morning light.

Salindra prepared to leave. She didn't have any more than he did, and was soon out the door, following Brohmin. Jakob gathered his belongings, the trunk and a cloak, and followed. Brohmin was already atop his horse, and Salindra climbed lithely into her own saddle. They both spurred their horses back along the town road toward the low wall before Jakob had even made it atop his horse.

He followed down the road. The heat from the early sun warmed his neck. He rearranged his cloak so the sun could warm his back, preferring the warmth of the sun to the warmth of the scratchy wool along his neck. The days grew colder as they traveled farther north, and they would get colder still before long. They were well past the Turning now, and winter fast approached. He didn't have the clothes with him for a long northern journey.

How far back were the Deshmahne? Brohmin was in no shape to fight today, and Jakob worried what would happen if they were attacked. Had the man fought them alone while Jakob and Salindra slept? Jakob watched Brohmin's slumped shoulders as they rode, worry creeping through him.

They rode quickly through the town, passing the houses and shops he'd seen the night before. A window was open at a blacksmith shop, but no sound emerged. The doorway of a bakery was thrown open, the painted sign of a loaf of bread and basket fading. Nothing inside moved, and nothing smelled the way it should. The silence was eerie. Farther from the small town's center were the few houses they'd passed on the way in. No one stirred.

The town was dead. He shivered with the thought. It was a shiver even the warmest sun would not suppress.

As he passed through the northwest gate again and turned north, a sigh of relief escaped him. Brohmin and Salindra both looked back. A smile touched the corners of Salindra's mouth. She must have felt the same thing.

They rode a long time and harder than he would have thought Brohmin capable. Brohmin and Salindra rode ahead of him, occasional chatter between them. Their course led them more or less north until they came upon a simple dirt road.

"This is the Elasiin path," Brohmin said as they turned onto the road. "I don't know all that we may find along it, so be prepared." He said nothing more as he spurred his horse onto the dirt road.

Salindra nodded and followed. Jakob needed little prompting. This is what he'd been looking for, the only hope he had of finding Novan and Endric and turning over the trunk. Rumors about the Elasiin path had frightened even the Denraen, and then there was the emptiness of Fristin. With a sigh, he knew their only choice was to either confront the rumors or the Deshmahne chasing them. He preferred the rumors.

As they rode ever onward, the sun bright in his face as it rose, he noted that Brohmin didn't ride back as he had on previous days to check on their pursuers. They had no idea how far back the Deshmahne were, though Jakob felt a certainty they still followed. He wasn't sure what Brohmin had faced last night but doubted it had been the thirteen Deshmahne.

At about midday, they stopped to eat. After a near silent meal, the only words a quick prayer of thanks to the gods offered by Salindra, they began north again. The forest had given way to a rolling grassy plain by early evening, and by the time they camped for the night, it was little more than a dark blur in the background.

Brohmin didn't allow a fire. Jakob shivered and tried to cover himself. With the coming of the night, a chill had settled over the land and ate through his clothes. From this point on, they would rarely know warmth, and he worried that he didn't have the clothing to face winter.

Brohmin didn't search for wild game, so they ate what meager provisions they carried in their packs, after which the man moved to sit across from Jakob. At one point, Salindra came over to check on something on Brohmin's shoulder. Jakob watched, but Brohmin didn't meet his gaze, so Jakob didn't ask. The man had faded as the day had gone on, becoming more and more withdrawn.

Brohmin's injury had an effect on Salindra as well. She was quieter, and her eyes constantly darted side to side, looking for signs of attack. She stood frequently and paced around the campsite. Her nervousness was contagious, and Jakob found himself looking around nervously as well.

It was late when he finally fell asleep that night. For the first night in many, he had a dreamless sleep. It was a heavy sleep, a welcome change, and he woke the next morning feeling more refreshed than he had in many days. Salindra seemed more at ease too. Brohmin was still asleep when both he and Salindra woke, and they decided to let him sleep. Jakob tended to the horses, brushing them lightly. They, too, seemed more relaxed.

Brohmin woke not long after, though the sun was already beginning to climb at that time. He moved more quickly and stepped more lightly than the day before. In many ways, he seemed revitalized, younger than the haggard man Jakob had seen the morning before.

They rode that day across grassy plains. Brohmin began riding off again throughout the day, leaving Jakob and Salindra alone. They didn't talk.

"The Deshmahne are still behind us," Brohmin offered once upon his return.

"How far?" Salindra asked.

"Several hours at least. They're not moving as quickly as before."

"How many?" Jakob asked.

"Their number remains the same," Brohmin answered.

Pausing around midday to eat, lunch, which was two fresh gray squirrels Brohmin somehow managed to gather, passed in silence. They ate the remainder that night when they stopped for the evening.

The next day was cloudy. Brohmin continued to ride off and return. They stopped again at midday, though it was more difficult to tell with the sun obscured. Brohmin left again to catch something, and when he did, Salindra walked over to Jakob, surprising him. She hadn't spoken to him directly in many days.

"Tell me about the Magi you rode with," she said.

What was there to tell? "There was Mage Haerlin, an Elder." Salindra nodded. "You remind me of him."

Salindra smiled at the comment and Jakob relaxed. "I should. He's my uncle."

Jakob could see the resemblance. There was a certain demeanor both carried, a confidence, though that could be simply the Magi. "With Haerlin was Roelle. She was"—he searched for the right word, but how would he describe Roelle?—"kind to me."

Salindra stared at Jakob a long while, her dark eyes softening for the first time. "You say she worked with Endric?" There was little of the suspicion from before in her tone.

Jakob nodded. "I sensed this wasn't pleasing to Haerlin."

Salindra chuckled lightly. "It wouldn't be. Haerlin is a traditional mind. This would upset him. Yet permission must have been granted if Endric participated." She shook her head. "I don't know what to think. I've been gone from our city a long time. I find it hard to believe this much has changed."

Brohmin returned as she spoke. "Much is changing, Salindra. You've seen it."

"The Deshmahne alone are change enough to worry."

Brohmin looked at her sharply, and she didn't continue. Jakob wondered what it was they were not saying, but neither elaborated, choosing silence before their meal. It was rabbit again this time. Jakob didn't mind. It was better than not eating.

❧

That night, they camped in a thicket of trees. Not far in the distance, the lower edge of the mountains stretched wide to either side. White peaks were mere specks from this distance, one of which would be Siirvil's Peak. They had been following a thin dirt path for the last few days.

The Elasiin path. And then Avaneam.

There was still no sign of Endric or Novan.

What was he to do once they reached Avaneam if Endric didn't appear? He didn't know, nor did he think Rit had known. They had expected Endric to meet them. What would he do if he didn't?

There was little else in the north. Mining towns, and those few enough, and he knew the Great Valley must be somewhere near here, something he never would have thought to see.

The night was cold, and he didn't sleep well. Strange visions danced just at the edge of his mind, hazy smoke keeping him from seeing clearly. He knew nervousness, but couldn't understand why. He awoke many times, his breathing labored, and he wondered if the air was thinner.

The next day, Brohmin roused them early and announced that they would be reaching the lower hills sometime in the early afternoon. "We need to ride hard today. We're followed closely now."

Salindra visibly tightened at the comment.

Jakob looked back, as if the Deshmahne would be seen riding down on them at that moment. Behind him were the grassy hills they'd ridden over the last day and nothing more. Nothing else moved in the cool morning air. He still felt the strange itch in the back of his head telling him he was watched, yet on the open grassy plains, there was no place to hide.

The morning ride was chilly. A cold wind whipped across the plains and tore through his light cloak. He gripped it tightly and bent low to his horse for extra warmth. It helped little. They rode more quickly, and progressed closer and closer to the foothills of the mountains.

They reached the rocky lower hills just before midday, stopping only briefly this time to eat a meager helping of leftover hare. Brohmin seemed in a hurry to get them moving, not letting them dally.

Jakob looked back, south, the way they had come. They were higher up here, the rocky hills giving some vantage to see from. In the far distance, he could just make out movement. He looked over to Brohmin, who nodded.

"They're not far off. Did Endric tell you where he was to take this trunk?"

"Avaneam. I don't know how much farther it is down the path."

Brohmin stared up the mountain face. "Avaneam?" The word flowed from his tongue, spoken familiarly. "Why?"

"I don't really know. Endric was to take it there."

"Endric wouldn't have wanted that burden," he said softly.

"I don't think he did," Jakob answered, remembering his comments from the Turning Festival.

"Yet he entrusted you with this."

Jakob shook his head. "Not me. Rit and his raegan."

"It's possible Endric intended this task for you. He's nothing if not sly."

Jakob remembered Novan telling him that Endric had requested he travel with Rit, and now wondered if this was Endric's intent. "What is this trunk?"

Brohmin sighed. "The one who meets us in Avaneam can tell you when we reach it."

"Endric?"

"Not him. Not in Avaneam."

"What is Avaneam?" Salindra finally asked. "I've not heard of it."

Brohmin's mouth pulled in a frown. "No one has." He looked at Jakob with eyes rimmed with a new emotion.

Concern? Uncertainty? Fear?

Brohmin stared silently toward the north. The white peaks of the mountains stretched high above them. "We have farther to go than I realized," he said finally.

Trudging along the foothills, they occasionally needed to dismount and lead their horses around steep obstacles. By early evening, they finally reached the lower slopes of the mountains. Huge white-capped peaks stretched as far as he could see, up into the clouds, and higher than he could fathom. He wondered how much farther they had.

They rode as much as they could, searching easy valleys to pass through and trying to keep to the lower areas. They rode that way for several hours, first climbing up and then switch-backing down, staying mostly within valleys. After a while, it no longer worked, and they were forced to climb higher.

"We'll need to dismount," Brohmin announced in the early evening. The sun hung low in the western horizon, bright in his eyes.

Jakob climbed down and noticed that Salindra followed suit with a resigned look on her face. He grabbed the reins of his horse and followed the path Brohmin took. Jakob began to feel a chill creep through him. It was dark, almost a presence, and he walked on, trying to ignore the feeling, but it would not go away.

It pressed on him, and as it did, something about it tickled a memory, something he should know. He had felt this before, but when? His chest tightened as he walked, his throat closing. Jakob strained to get a full breath, struggled against the pressure, but it didn't stop, instead growing worse as they moved onward.

Are we getting too high?

When did the air begin to thin? It didn't seem as if they had climbed high enough to make it this difficult to breathe. Breaths whistled as he strained to keep climbing.

They reached a small peak and began a slow descent into the next valley. The loose rock made the footing treacherous, and his labored breathing distracted him even more. He was wheezing loudly now, each breath a struggle, as if someone sat upon his chest.

At the lower edge of the valley, he was forced to stop. His breathing was too difficult, and he couldn't get enough air to keep moving. Brohmin looked back, eyes concerned, but Jakob couldn't focus on the man. Forced to lean over, he rested his hands on his thighs as he tried to take slow breaths. A bead of sweat rolled down his face, catching in his mouth, and he spat it out.

What was happening?

"What's wrong?" Brohmin asked.

Salindra hadn't moved. A look of fear was plain upon her face.

Jakob shook his head, opening his mouth to try and speak. "I... don't... know." The words were hoarse, a near whisper, and took more energy than he had to spare. He took another ragged breath and his lungs burned with the effort.

Brohmin reached for him, and Jakob shook him off. A look of surprise flashed across Brohmin's face briefly before worry returned. "At least hand me your reins."

Jakob tossed them at Brohmin, not bothering to see if they even reached the man, and resumed his bent position, panting. Supporting his weight with his arms again, his left hand slipped off his thigh, and he fell forward. He landed on his belly, his sword beneath him. Rolling himself over, he moved his sword out of the way, and a humming flared in the blade before coursing through him. A strange tingling sensation raced through his arms. It roared through him, and he cried out, the last of his breath leaving him.

The pulsing overwhelmed him, the same strange sense he had

when using the sword, and as the vibration filled him, the weight on his chest lessened.

His breaths came more easily, and he managed to crawl to his knees. Brohmin leaned him back so that his face looked toward the sky. "I'm better," he managed, taking a slow breath, filling his chest with the sweet air.

"What was it?"

He shook his head. "I don't know. I couldn't breathe. Maybe we've climbed too high too fast for me."

Brohmin frowned. "Maybe. Rest a moment." He wiped a finger along Jakob's brow, feeling the moisture. "You look like you need it."

Sitting there, he breathed slowly and deeply. The pulsing remained, and he held on to it. He had not realized it until now, but it'd been many days since he'd known it. Taking deep breaths, the air was cool in his lungs, and he savored it.

As he did, he noted dark tendrils of fog stretch around the rocks of the valley, and nearly inky black. He'd seen something like this before but couldn't remember where.

The fog shifted, thickening, and seemed to quest almost as if alive.

"What are you staring at?" Salindra asked.

He turned his head quickly to her, and she started to repeat the question. Out of the corner of one eye, he saw a finger of the fog moving toward them, as if it had heard her question. Raising a finger to his lips, he shushed her. She frowned at him sternly and turned to Brohmin.

There was something sinister about the black fog.

Brohmin stared at him, a puzzled expression to his eyes.

"We need to move," he urged Brohmin. His words were quiet, barely even a whisper. He hoped the man could read his lips. He turned to look at the tendrils of fog; several of the fingers probed around the boulders.

"Why?" Brohmin copied his whispered tone.

Jakob nodded toward the northern edge of the valley, where the fog was thickest. It oozed down the mountain face, slowly rolling toward them. Jakob didn't know how they'd avoid it as it filled the space around them.

Brohmin looked in the direction Jakob indicated, but shook his head. He couldn't see it.

It was then that Jakob remembered where he had seen the dark fog before.

It had been a dream.

It was darker then, and as he remembered, he saw the tendrils of the fog thicken. They grew darker. There were creatures in the dream, and if the fog was real, then the creatures couldn't be far behind.

He remembered the creatures, and though he had seen them only from a distance, the evil to them was apparent. Hairless heads and eyes like a rat's. He didn't want to see one. Fear surged through him. Jakob gripped the hilt of his sword reflexively.

Is this the danger of the Elasiin path, what Brohmin faced the night in Fristin?

Or was this even real? Had the madness claimed him fully?

With the thought, a hairless head popped over the top of the northern ridge. The dark eyes were as he remembered them, black and soulless. The creature saw him as he saw it. A mouth full of sharp teeth opened up, and a hideous sound echoed across the valley.

He leaped to his feet. "We need to go!"

Salindra followed his gaze up the valley slope, and her jaw dropped. Brohmin followed her gaze before turning back to Jakob, a look of surprise in his eyes, before calmly unsheathing his sword.

"If you can see them, you can defeat them," Brohmin said.

Jakob shook his head. Fear froze him, more paralyzing than any he had known facing the Deshmahne.

"I've seen you with that sword, Jakob. Unsheathe it and join me!" The words were a roar.

Turning again to face the black auras, he watched the creatures as they wound their way down the edge of the valley. They moved quickly toward them, surefooted on the loose rock. He watched Brohmin ready himself to face them.

I must be strong. I can face this.

He counted a dozen or more of the creatures. Too many for the three of them. *Two*, he corrected himself. Salindra couldn't fight and had no weapon save Brohmin's bow.

Slowly, he unsheathed his sword, and the pounding in his head suddenly threatened to shake his body. He shifted the sword in his hand as he surveyed the ground, looking for the best place to make a stand. There were too many of them, and he'd need to hold off and defeat as many as he could.

Panic set in. In the past, the sword seemed to almost vibrate in sync with what he felt within his head. Would it respond now?

He remembered feeling the same panic when chased by the three Deshmahne, the same feeling he had known when running through Rondalin. His heart roared in his chest, pounding with the beating in his head. Waves of nervous nausea filled him. His horse anxiously tramped its feet with the trunk still strapped to his saddle.

How much farther to Avaneam? They were close now, but there was still no sign of Endric or Novan. What would happen in the trunk was lost?

That cannot happen!

He felt a sudden *shifting* in his head followed by a spinning as he had in his dream. He pulled on it, the way he had in his dream.

Waves of nausea slammed through him, and he closed his eyes to slow it.

When he opened his eyes, it was darker. The moon was up and bright, and the wind whistled through the mountains. It howled against his cloak.

He looked around wondering how it got dark so suddenly. And cold.

Though it was dark, he could see easily. To his eyes, it was almost light, yet he knew it was not. He didn't have time to wonder as a sudden stream of black auras moved lithely down the mountain face. He knew the shape, knew the source.

There must be more than thirty! he realized. *I'd only counted a dozen. How can we stop thirty?*

He reached to his side grabbing for his sword, but it was missing.

The shapes had seen him and moved toward him quickly, almost too fast to see. He ducked, hiding behind a large rock filling the path in front of him. This was no place for a confrontation. And he had no weapon. He couldn't face thirty of these creatures.

356 | D.K. HOLMBERG

I've faced many more than thirty!

The thought came from the back of his mind, unbidden.

Jakob had never faced one of these creatures, let alone thirty.

Groeliin, the thought came. *And I've fought thirty at one time. You can too.*

He was talking to himself. It *was* the madness.

No, came an answer. *If you are to use me, then use me!* It was a shout, a command.

What? he asked himself.

Was he going crazy? Looking down, he was dressed in the same strange garb as he had been in the dream that night in the forest.

What's happening to me?

The shapes neared. He looked and saw a flat plateau nearby and decided that it was a better place to make a stand.

Yes, agreed the voice from the distant part of his mind.

The dark auras moving toward him were closer now. They would reach him soon.

He ran toward the plateau, crouching as much as he could while he climbed. The shapes followed, climbing much faster than he had.

Groeliin, the thought came again.

He turned toward the approaching creatures, knowing he would have to make some sort of stand, but didn't know what he could do. He wouldn't die without trying.

Wait, bid the voice from the back of his mind.

I have no weapon!

You do! the voice answered.

He waited. Quickly, too quickly, the creatures—*groeliin*—moved toward him, surrounding him. They came up at him all at once. He turned his head frantically, eyes darting, not knowing what to do.

I don't want to die!

Then do something, the voice shouted.

I don't know what!

He opened his mouth to scream and felt another shifting of his mind.

There was a slight tug within his consciousness, and the ground began to rumble beneath his feet.

A crack opened, circling the plateau on which he stood. The crack grew wider as it opened, and the shaking of the earth tossed the *groeliin* around, tossed them down into the growing chasm. A loud hiss echoed from some as they fell, sharp teeth glimmered in the pale light of the moon.

Jakob felt a sharp pain in his right shoulder and looked down to see a small spear hanging there. He pulled on it, but it wouldn't move.

Break it off, came the thought.

He did as instructed. Pain filled his shoulder as he did, and he screamed. His voice echoed along the mountain walls.

You could have stopped that too, the voice told him.

How?

You will learn. Now leave me! the voice screamed.

Leave you?

There was no answer.

Jakob looked around again. The plateau was now circled by a huge chasm that reached deep into the earth. He stepped up to the edge and looked down. He saw nothing below.

Jump. It was a whisper in his mind.

Feeling compelled, Jakob ran and jumped, closing his eyes as he did, and felt the shifting in not only his mind, but his body, again. Waves of nausea rolled through him, and he struggled not to vomit. The sense of movement and the nausea slowly subsided. Opening his eyes, Jakob saw daylight again. Brohmin stood as he had only moments before, with sword raised, and Salindra cowered with the horses. A bow was in her hand, but there was hesitation on her face.

His right shoulder ached, and he looked down to find a broken off chunk of spear lodged in his flesh. He looked back toward the valley and saw the creatures streaming toward them. Confused, he tried to raise his sword and ready himself, but pain shot up his arm, filling him with agony. He couldn't fight, not with his shoulder as it was.

The creatures were nightmarish, and he saw them more clearly this time. Gray of skin and clad in only breeches, their upper bodies were a mass of hair. The heads were hairless, though, and the baldness allowed him to see their misshapen ears and small dark eyes more easily. The sight sickened him.

He watched Brohmin move toward the groeliin, readying to fight. Jakob struggled with the pain in his shoulder, trying to stay upright. Brohmin could not do this all on his own.

I will deliver the trunk to Avaneam!

Opening his mouth to scream, his mind shifted again.

A loud roar escaped his mouth as he shouted, "No!"

There was a tug in his consciousness. It was the same pulling he'd felt when the thirty groeliin circled him. What it was, he didn't know.

Boulders along the wall began to fall; the northern mountain face tumbled, crushing the groeliin beneath. The earth shook under his feet, and he slipped, hitting his head as he fell.

We need to get the trunk to Avaneam before the Deshmahne reach us.

As he looked up, he saw a haze around everything. Brohmin stared at him, frowning. Another shape floated into the valley. It was a tall figure, slender, and dark hair cascaded around her shoulders.

A goddess. Am I dreaming or dying?

He tried to look around, tried to look at Salindra, but could not move his head, and felt himself begin to black out. The haze before his eyes grew thicker. Spots crossed his vision. As he passed out, one last thought came to him.

Avaneam.

He had failed. After everything else, he hadn't succeeded in bringing Endric's trunk to the north. How would they stop the Deshmahne now? And what of the groeliin?

As much as he wanted them, answers didn't come.

Then the world was black.

CHAPTER THIRTY-SIX

B rohmin looked to Jakob. He'd passed out. It was best. That way, he wouldn't have to rest the way Salindra did. He looked over at the woman, her brown hair pulled back from her head leaving her sharply elegant jaw outlined in the setting sun. She was a lovely woman.

Glancing at Jakob, he wondered when the boy had been speared. He saw the blood, had seen the stump of spear, but had not seen it thrown. The thought troubled him.

Brohmin turned his attention back to the figure in front of him. The woman was tall, as tall as all her kind, though she was the last. Her black hair seemed untouched by the gentle breeze stirring across the now broken valley. Her pale skin glowed in the late sunlight. He would call her beautiful, but she was something more than beautiful.

"Must she be that way?" he asked, nodding toward Salindra. She was frozen as she crouched on the ground near the horses, a look of fear caught on her face. It looked funny to him now.

Alyta nodded. "She does not need to see me. It serves no purpose." Her voice was musical and sweet. Magical, though he knew it not.

He shook his head. He knew it would serve no purpose, but it would have allowed the woman some dignity to have caught her in a better expression. No matter, he supposed. He had seen it before, and each time, the person ended up looking the same. It was human nature, he reasoned.

"You healed me," he stated, remembering his exhaustion after Fristin.

She nodded. "It was necessary. You were weakened after fighting the *groeliin*. You all were."

Brohmin didn't know how close he came to dying that night, but suspected. Had he known Jakob could see the *groeliin* he would have taken him along. "The boy saw you," he replied. "I saw it in his eyes before he passed out. Did he recognize you?" A puzzled look crossed her face and was gone again quickly. Brohmin wasn't sure he had even seen it.

"He's seen me before," Alyta replied vaguely. "I've been watching him for a long time."

"That explains what he's been sensing."

"Perhaps," she said.

Brohmin laughed softly. There were never easy answers when it came to Alyta. "He saw them too." He nodded to the broken rock.

She nodded. "I know." The music of her voice seemed concerned.

Brohmin turned his attention to Jakob before returning to look at her. He caught her dark eyes with his own. "He saw them before I did." He spoke the words slowly. They weighed heavy in the air.

"I know."

It wasn't the expected reply. He hadn't known what she would say but didn't think she had known that. He supposed he shouldn't be caught off guard, not with this one, but still was.

"You should have warned me about him," he began. "Is he a Mage?" The question was partly to himself. "I've seen things from him that I've known from some of the Mageborn." He gave her a long look. "I've seen other things from him as well. Things I've never seen from one Mageborn."

"A Mage?" she questioned, almost evading answering.

A gleam to her eye that may not have been spoke of something she did not tell him. If only he could read her better. As long as he had known her, he never fully understood her. Brohmin knew he never would; it was not for his mind to understand one like hers.

"He had a dream the other night," he continued. "And thinks he's going mad."

"Yes. Many suffer because of the disruption to the fibers."

"You know of it." Brohmin shouldn't have been surprised that she did.

"I have tried to prevent it, but you know that he is powerful."

Brohmin did. He called himself the High Priest of the Deshmahne now, but they knew him by another name. "The madness Jakob describes is his fault?"

"Partly."

Brohmin waited for her to say more, but she did not.

He shook his head. "I don't think Jakob's experiences are due to this madness. Too much truth in them."

"Even the mad see some truth," Alyta offered.

"This is different. In the heart of the Great Forest, he dreamed." Brohmin paused, looking over to Jakob again. The boy was still, though he thought he had seen movement. That wasn't possible. Not with what she had done. "I've known others to dream in that spot. It is a powerful place."

"Very powerful," she agreed.

"But this was a dream I hadn't expected." He saw her looking at him, waiting. "He dreamed that he was Shoren."

She was quiet for a time. A long time. And then she nodded, almost to herself. "You mean he dreamed he *saw* Shoren? That is common in the heart."

He shook his head. "No. He dreamed he *was* Shoren."

Alyta considered those words longer than she had any others, though he wasn't sure what they meant. She seemed to know something, though. As she turned her own gaze upon Jakob, he saw a knowing look. If only he could know the thoughts of this woman!

They stood silently for a while. "What's in there?" he asked, eyeing the trunk.

Alyta looked over to the horses, to where the trunk was strapped.

"That had been tasked to Endric," she started. "Perhaps he is wiser than all of us."

"It's been held in Vasha for so long…" Brohmin commented.

Alyta sighed. "Sometimes, I forget how much you know," she said in answer. She shook her head, looking earnestly into his eyes. "It must return to the east. As to what's inside it… there are answers."

"What kind of answers?"

"We must convince the others to join, or Raime will succeed."

"And the trunk?"

"Possesses a message of sorts. Our cousins will know how to open it."

"Getting there will be difficult. There are Deshmahne behind us."

"They cannot cross the valley."

"I cannot either, not with two others with me."

"Brohmin Ulruuy, I would never task you with more than you can manage. That is why you have been sent to Avaneam."

"We haven't reached it yet."

"No?"

Brohmin looked around, and realized the landscape had changed. The mountains had flattened slightly, leaving a small clearing around them. The wind still gusted cold out of the north, but not as it had. The remains of a city, once a powerful place, were scattered around them, nothing more than fallen stone now. How had she managed this without him realizing?

"I haven't been here in… years," he said.

"A place of power even now. It was why I had sent Endric here. Impressive that Jakob managed to make it this far, don't you think?"

"In spite of everything he faced, Jakob managed to do what was tasked to him and deliver the trunk to Avaneam."

"It is impressive." She smiled, and peace radiated from her.

"Only impressive, not unexpected?" She didn't answer, and he shook his head. "You will take us from here?" He was no longer certain whether she could. She was still powerful, but grew weaker.

"I will take you. This is something that must be done," Alyta said. "Do you have any concerns about the crossing?"

He shook his head. He would get few answers from her. "Some, I suppose. This task... You say it was to be for Endric?" When she nodded, he sighed. The general was often the best at negotiation. He had seen much in his years, and had served the Conclave well. Now, the task would fall to him. And Jakob. Watching Alyta, he wondered if that hadn't been her intent. Or Endric's. If the Denraen general were to be sent to the east, it could be for only one reason.

He looked up at the sky, noticing it getting dark, and wondered if they would have to camp here for the night. He would prefer not to rest near the *groeliin*. "The Deshmahne still follow."

Alyta nodded. "As I said, they cannot follow us across the valley."

He nodded. "I worry about Salindra's response to the crossing."

Alyta smiled. He knew she would. The woman was frustrating at times.

"It cannot be avoided now. We must get him to the other side quickly." She looked at Brohmin a long time before continuing. "I fear time is running short." She spoke the words sadly.

He was startled by those words. "Whose?" he asked, fearing the answer.

Alyta looked pensively into his eyes. "Mine."

The word settled in his chest uneasily. She was the last. Without her, all that remained of the ancient barrier was that which the Magi guarded. And that could not be enough.

"It won't hold without you." He had known her time would come but had never put much thought to it. She had seemed invincible for so long.

She shook her head. "You know as well as I do that it must. The cycle must go on." She saw his hesitation. "We have discussed this all before. The west has the Magi. It will be enough. It must be." She looked at Salindra just then, considering. "Besides, we still have that which is in the east."

He stood stunned. He hadn't expected this conversation. "Without you, it is weakened. We do not know if it will stand."

She smiled at him then. It was a sad smile, the saddest he had ever known. Then she reached out and touched his shoulder. A wave of peace flooded through him, relaxing him. "It must stand, just as we must finally stop *him*."

"Without you, there will be none who can stop him," Brohmin said.

"I fear even I am not strong enough to stop him any longer. If he has his way, he will steal what I protect."

Brohmin glanced to Salindra's ankles and the branding there. Could the same be done to Alyta? "You are strong enough to prevent that much at least."

She closed her eyes. "With what I've seen, I'm not certain. Which is why you must succeed with this, my Hunter."

He looked over to where Jakob lay. *Was he lying that way the last time I looked?* He couldn't remember.

"There is more to the boy than I'd first thought," Alyta told him, bringing him out of his wonder. "More to him than I knew."

"I know. That sword of his. I've never seen anything like it." He wanted to say something else, ask the question she had begged him not to ask, but he did not. He would respect her in that.

"Yes," she agreed. "That was unexpected. Fortunate, though." She looked to the east, her eyes seeming to search. "You must take him, guide him. He must succeed. I begin to suspect that the young man is the key."

"To what?"

Alyta looked to Jakob, watching him for a moment. "To a possibility along the fibers I didn't know existed."

EPILOGUE

T he sky was nearly black overhead. The only light Roelle saw was that from the moon, a thin sliver barely visible through the clouds. Over a hundred others surrounded her, most she couldn't see. She shivered from the chill in the night.

"Roelle!" she heard whispered to her left.

Lendra motioned nearby. "They're ready." Her words the only sound other than the chirping of crickets in the night. All those surrounding her were utterly silent.

Endric had warned them to silence until they left the city so that they didn't tip off the Council. Roelle would travel north, scouting. By the time they returned, with whatever proof she could find, Endric planned to have removed the Deshmahne threat. He had committed to that much with her.

Finally, she nodded.

With that, three small whistles were blown. Quietly, so that she could not even swear she heard them. They had the desired effect.

Horses trod almost noiselessly from the practice field as they began the progression toward the city walls. Each was led by someone Roelle trusted, and each knew where to go. All knew what to do if

366 | D.K. HOLMBERG

they encountered problems. They expected none. They had the cooperation of the guard, and a letter from Endric if needed.

A horse approached silently, its rider leading it on foot. It was Selton. He flashed her a quick smile before climbing atop the animal. As he did, six others approached. The guides and Lendra, she suspected.

She patted the sides of her pack, reassuring herself that the sword Endric had gifted her was still attached. Losing anything else worried her less. The weapons may be needed most on this journey.

She waved her arm in a circle above her head. The commands tonight needed to be as silent as possible. Selton nodded, and Lendra urged her horse forward so that she rode next to Roelle.

The ride through the first terrace of the city was quiet. They stuck to side streets, streets that were only dirt with no hard stone for the horses' hooves to echo upon, and made their way quickly to the outer gate. Normally, it would be closed tight at this hour. Endric had seen to it that it would be open. The guards above nodded to her grimly and motioned them through. Once through, she heard the huge gates to the outer wall swing shut. She glanced back at the city longingly, wondering when they would return.

With that thought in mind, she kicked her heels into the flanks of her horse, speeding her to a slow gallop. She didn't have to look back to know the others had done the same. They rode quickly down the mountain. There wasn't much time—they were to meet at the base at noon. There was much riding to be done, tonight and in the days ahead.

~

Book 2 of The Lost Prophecy, The Warrior Mage

Roelle leads the Magi north to discover the secrets of the northern warriors known as the Antrilii. What she discovers forces her to question the role the Magi play in the world as she begins to realize how far the Magi have drifted from their Founders. Rumors out of the north are much worse than she could ever imagine and her Mage Warriors might be key to stopping a threat the world hasn't seen in a thousand years.

Jakob has reached Avaneam with the mysterious trunk only to learn that his journey has just begun. What he discovers in the Unknown Lands will be the key to the upcoming battle, if only he can survive it. His visions continue and Jakob learns there is more to them —and him—than he had known. Can he understand his growing abilities in time?

The world prepares for war. Creatures out a nightmare press south. And only a few will be able to stop it.

Book 3, Tower of the Gods, is also out now.

Want to read more about Endric? Soldier Son, Book 1 of The Teralin Sword. Set decades before events in The Lost Prophecy.

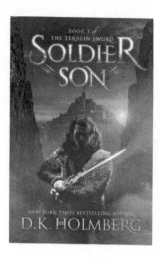

As the second son of the general of the Denraen, Endric wants only to fight, not the commission his father demands of him. When a strange attack in the south leads to the loss of someone close to him, only Endric seems concerned about what happened.

All signs point to an attack on the city, and betrayal by someone deep within the Denraen, but his father no longer trusts his judgment. This forces Endric to make another impulsive decision, one that leads him far from the city on a journey where he discovers how little he knew, and how much more he has to understand. If he can prove himself in time, and with the help of his new allies, he might be able to stop a greater disaster.

ABOUT THE AUTHOR

DK Holmberg currently lives in rural Minnesota where the winter cold and the summer mosquitoes keep him inside and writing. He has two active children who inspire him to keep telling new stories.

Word-of-mouth is crucial for any author to succeed and how books are discovered. If you enjoyed the book, please consider leaving a review at Amazon, even if it's only a line or two; it would make all the difference and would be very much appreciated.

Subscribe to my newsletter for a few free books as well as to be the first to hear about new releases and the occasional giveaway.

For more information:
www.dkholmberg.com

ALSO BY D.K. HOLMBERG

The Lost Prophecy
The Threat of Madness
The Warrior Mage
Tower of the Gods
Twist of the Fibers

The Teralin Sword
Soldier Son
Soldier Sword

The Cloud Warrior Saga
Chased by Fire
Bound by Fire
Changed by Fire
Fortress of Fire
Forged in Fire
Serpent of Fire
Servant of Fire
Born of Fire
Broken of Fire
Light of Fire
Cycle of Fire

The Endless War

Journey of Fire and Night

Darkness Rising

Endless Night

Summoner's Bond

Seal of Light

The Shadow Accords

Shadow Blessed

Shadow Cursed

Shadow Born

Shadow Lost

Shadow Cross

The Dark Ability

The Dark Ability

The Heartstone Blade

The Tower of Venass

Blood of the Watcher

The Shadowsteel Forge

The Guild Secret

Rise of the Elder

The Sighted Assassin

The Binders Game

The Forgotten

Assassin's End

CPSIA information can be obtained
at www.ICGtesting.com
Printed in the USA
LVHW011204160620
658144LV00006B/1056